*SPYWARE*

*For my brother, Neil.*

*I don't expect you to agree with the ideas here,*
*but you've only yourself to blame,*
*for helping me to think independently.*

# DISCLAIMER

Normally, this is where you'd read:

*All characters appearing in this work are fictitious. Any resemblance to real persons, living or dead, is purely coincidental.*

This is a lie. Oh sure, the vast majority of characters here are made up. For them, any resemblance is either coincidental or the act of a divine, omniscient being working through me for a larger purpose that even I do not understand. I hope the latter, but suspect the former. There are exceptions. As in all of my books, there are some characters based on real persons. Famous ones, actually. Which characters those are is usually obvious, owing to their close physical resemblance to the real persons and the fact that I use their real names. I use the words 'based on' in the loosest sense. I use it in the way Kevin Costner's *Robin Hood* was 'based on' the *Robin Hood* of lore, or Taco Bell's food is 'based on' Mexican cuisine. These are satirical caricatures that do not reflect the actual actions, words, or beliefs of the individuals involved. Except, of course, when they do.

*Spyware*

As for the quotations at the beginning of each chapter? They're lies, all lies. Sure, they may be driven by the aforementioned divine being who may or may not choose to work through me, but that doesn't mean they're not apocryphal. The divine being works in mysterious ways. Why else would she get involved this book or, for that matter, the outcome of so many football games?

# PREFACE

Kurt Vonnegut once said to me* that a story doesn't need to have an ending. I took this one step further and decided to omit the beginning and middle as well. Consequently, I wrote nothing for years. So it goes. I finally realized that my pile of unpublished stories weren't going to publish themselves. I set about dusting them off and rewriting them. This is the third such book. Sadly, I have resorted to the tired motif of including in my books a beginning, a middle and, yes (snore), an end. At the end of this book, you'll find an Afterword that was originally part of this preface, making it a little *Awkword*. It includes important acknowledgements as well as acting as a sort mea culpa for what you will have just read. I moved it there because mea culpas in advance ruin all the fun.

The idea for this book dates back to at least 2003. It began life as a serious sci-fi called *Contagion*, with the same concept and entirely different characters. After shelving it for over a decade and a half, I dusted it off and decided it was more relevant than ever. Time, events and its new incarnation

*Spyware*

as a sci-fi political satirical thriller all demanded a lot of changes. I ascribe to Hofstadter's Law, which states "It always takes longer than you expect, even when you take into account Hofstadter's Law." So finally, it is done, but to what end? For me, writing is largely a process of lobbing paper airplanes off a cliff at night. I do it in the hope that at least one lands at someone's toes. I'm glad it landed at yours, and that you chose to pick it up.

Enjoy.
CJR

* Well, me and the five hundred other people he was giving a lecture to at the time. Robertson Davies was there too, sitting two rows in front of me, while looking very beardy. Anyway, it *felt* like he was saying it to me.

# SPYWARE

## PRE-RELEASE

"The stuff that memes are made of." – R. Dawkins

The black Mercedes sped through the bright winter twilight. It glided with swift silent purpose between iridescent fields of snow, beneath an indigo sky. Boston was only an hour away, but here, amid the silent pastures and naked trees that stuck like frayed wires through the drifts, it was another universe. Cold. Empty. Perfect. A few flakes gently fell, steadfastly refusing to be rushed by gravity. It was six pm on a Sunday. Bitter. Crisp. Lifeless. The car had driven a long way. It had passed through the estranged states of America. Its route was efficient. It had come along the arching interstates that had long replaced the meandering byways of the past. The old highway system still cobwebbed the land, but only in the background—a forgotten footprint of another country. Inefficient. Forgotten. Frozen. People romanticized the old roads, but rarely if ever took them. Modern freeways were faster. They were always the shortest distance

*1*

between two points. Four lanes wide, they channeled people in just two directions divided by a median, North or South, East or West, left or right. Along the way, the Mercedes had rolled past hundreds of billboards. The signs promised that the place you wanted to be was just ahead. *Keep going*, they said, to the next exit.

The car's hood gleamed. Its plates were dealer's plates. This was a lie. The car, while less than a year old, was not new. There was no such dealer. No such VIN. Its driver was hidden behind a windshield tinted smoke black. Ahead on the road, the driver spotted a sign, *Willie's Pay'n Pump*. Red neon read 'Open'. Black leather driving leather gloves turned the wheel. Tires crunched on gravel. This was one of those rare independent stations, owned by its namesake, Willie Tompkins, since 1979. The building, the sign and the pumps themselves were antiques, but well tended and serviceable. The Mercedes parked under the sign that read 'Full Service Only'. Another anachronism. The driver tapped his horn.

"I'm comin', I'm comin'!" shouted Willie, ducking under the half lifted garage door. He wiped grease from his hands with a rag, and jogged up to the driver-side door. Gap-tooth grin. "What can I do ya for?"

The driver's side window slid down, revealing the car's lone occupant. Willie, who was accustomed to a menagerie of customers from the city, was nonetheless taken aback. In some ways, the man was entirely unremarkable. He was dressed in a smart black business suit and tie. His age? Indeterminate. His hair was slicked back with Brylcreem, not a strand out of place. There was something unsettling about him. Willie couldn't say why, but the devil, he knew, was in the details. The visitor's skin was pale like tallow. It was as if all of the blood had been permanently drained from his face. Most striking were his sunglasses. They were aviator style, but with lenses a hematic shade of red. He looks, thought the gas station owner, like a vampire. Of course, Willie knew there was no such thing. Besides, if there was one thing he'd learned from his niece Chelsea, it was that modern vampires were handsome, brooding, misunderstood youth. This man was none of these things. His look was old school vampire. He was Bella Lugosi meets Reservoir Dogs, with rose petal eyes.

"Premium, please. All the way," said the man. The driver spoke with a mid-Atlantic accent, neither here nor there. His intonation was dispassionate and precise.

"Absolutely!" said Willie. The aging pump jockey jogged around to the side of the car and inserted the nozzle. A moment later, Willie returned to the driver side window. The driver was looking at his phone. "Cash or credit? Two dollars more with credit," said Willie.

Without looking up, the driver pulled out his wallet and reached for his credit card. He hesitated. "Say... you don't happen to know where I could find the Jim Townsend estate, do you?"

"Senator Jim Townsend? Well sure, everyone knows that! An' yur goin' the right way. Just keep on here another ten minutes an' yu'll spot the gates. Can't miss it!"

"Thank-you."

"Not a problem. Say, you're not from 'round here are ya?"

The driver moved his hand away from his credit card and retrieved a different card instead. This card was silver backed. The driver turned it over as he presented it to Willie. "You've been most helpful," said the man, with a flatline smile.

Willie squinted at the odd image. "What the heck kind of credit card is this? Looks like one those magic 3D thingies... We don't accept Driver's Club."

"It's not Driver's Club."

The gas station proprietor peered more closely. Abruptly, Willie's eyes opened wide, as if he'd seen a ghost.

#

Senator Jim Townsend trudged through the six inches of snow that covered his long gravel driveway. He was accompanied by his two dogs, both German Shepherds, who romped happily. They had reached their objective, the mailbox. Jim opened the little metal door and retrieved a small bundle of catalogs and come-ons. "Junk... junk... junk," he muttered. It didn't matter. Picking up the evening mail was as much matter of exercise and fresh air as anything else. All of his official mail went to his office in D.C. The seventy-five-year-old man then turned and braced himself for the hundred yard haul back up the hill to the house. At that moment, the two dogs began to snap and snarl at one another.

"Hey! Hey! Trapper, you leave Nicki alone!"

The Senator gave Trapper's leash a yank. The dogs fell into line. A moment later, their tiff forgotten, they were best friends again.

"Jim, I just put the kettle on!" shouted Jim's wife, Sarah, from the front door of the house.

Jim silently waved his acknowledgement. Sarah smiled and disappeared inside. The truth was, the Senator was too tired to shout back. He paused a moment to catch his breath. Seventy-five years of life on Earth, the last sixty as a smoker, had left him easily winded. One day, one way or another, he would quit. For now, his laboured breath formed a cumulous cloud in the icy evening air. The yellow wax warm windows of the house beckoned him. He lifted his boot to continue. When he'd left, the kitchen had smelled of ginger snaps. Sarah liked to keep busy with baking and Jim enjoyed eating. They'd been well suited for life, he and her. It was then that Jim heard the distinctive crunch of car tires on new snow. As he turned to see who the visitor was, Trapper and Nicki began to bark.

"Hush, hush!" he admonished and yanked the two dogs to compliance.

The black Mercedes rolled to a stop. The door opened. The driver stepped out. Despite the deepening dusk, the traveller still wore his peculiar red sunglasses. Behind the lenses, the man's eyes were narrow and focused. "Senator Jim Townsend?"

"That's right," said Jim. He didn't recognize the man and, while he liked to say constituents were always welcome, that didn't mean at his home on a Sunday evening. The man dressed more like an official or a business man. Better not be a bloody lobbyist, the Senator thought to himself, not if he expects anything from me. "What can I do for you?"

"Actually, I have something for you, Senator," said the man.

A courier, thought Jim, well that explains it.

"My card," said the man. The visitor then produced the same silver foil backed card he'd handed the gas station proprietor earlier. As he did so, he turned the card to face the Senator.

Jim squinted at it a moment and frowned. He then transferred both leashes to one hand and fished inside his inside coat pocket. "I think I need my spectacles," he muttered. "Although mine aren't quite as colourful as yours." The Senator donned his half moon reading glasses, and peered once more at the patterned surface. The image appeared to shift and move as he looked at it. He grimaced. "This some kind of joke?"

At that instant, deep inside the Senator's brain, a microscopic array of vermilion energy coalesced. It started to storm. Molecular lightning began to fire amid the neurones of his medulla oblongata, disrupting normal behaviours and activity.

Jim Townsend opened his mouth in surprise. He gripped his chest, as if attempting to clutch the sharp, stabbing pain that had manifested there. The Senator mouthed seven silent syllables, forming a wordless question. He dropped to his knees. He then fell forward, slammed his face into the snow, kicked once, and was still.

Nicki and Trapper whimpered in distress and began frantically nosing and pawing the Senator's lifeless body.

The man in rose-coloured glasses calmly plucked the card from the dead Senator's fingers and pocketed it. He then returned to his idling car and drove away, into the gathering night.

## POC 0.01

"\$ is the _root of all eval()" – MafiaBoy

Everyone is a product of their childhood. If Sigmund Freud himself were to set Eddy on a couch and ask him about his growing up, he'd have it wrapped up in ten minutes. "Well, zat's zat," Freud would say. "No vunder you're ein radical, und introverted. You're ein introverted radical! Your Super-Ego und your Ego are making love to one other, and they're making your id watch." Eddy simply imagined the fake accent and threw in the only German words he knew. For some reason, he also imagined Freud to look a lot like his father, but he assumed that was just a coincidence. Still, when the three people closest to you take their own lives, albeit years apart and in very different ways, it's going to leave a mark.

Eddy's Uncle Russ, was a radical too. Most radicals simply dress the part. Uncle Russ was the real thing—the kind that blew things up. As a boy, Eddy had idolized his uncle. Uncle Russ taught Eddy to scoff at the government, society, and rules as, well, a rule. He taught Eddy that the world was run by evil people pulling the strings of suckers and trusting fools. "You're smarter than 99.8% of the people out there," he said one day. Eddy was eight-years-old. They were walking along the abandoned railroad tracks that ran behind the houses. The chunky wood ties were worn and almost consumed by grass, but the corroded rails still shone like silver streams in the midday sun. "0.1% are the puppeteers."

"Are you a puppeteer?"

"I'm the remainder, the other 0.1%," Eddy's uncle said. Uncle Russ suddenly went wide-eyed with a look of terror. "Train!"

Eddy leapt clear of the tracks and straight into an adjacent juniper bush. His uncle doubled-over in laughter. The trains hadn't run through Popperville in years, not since the factory had shuttered. The young boy sat in the flattened shrubs, brushing tiny needles from his sleeves. Uncle Russ wiped tears from his eyes. "Damn, that was some good jumping boy." In spite of himself, Eddy broke into a grin. From her nearby backyard, Mrs. Kilroy looked up from hanging her washing on the line and shook her head. Hers was one of the many yards that backed onto the tracks. Mrs. Kilroy was a remainder too. She was one of the dwindling population of original residents in the small town. Slowly they were being replaced by commuters to the city. Popperville was becoming a bedroom community. The new residents made and spent their money in New York. Even the old town hall was scheduled to be torn down. Its antique steam shovel furnace sold to scrap. It was disorienting.

At the tender age of eight, Eddy had begun to realize that the rest of the town didn't view his Uncle with the same admiration he did. Russ Pending was labeled an 'eccentric' by those too kind to call him a 'joke'. Eddy was forced to this realization one day when he needed to bring something to school for show-and-tell. Uncle Russ gave Eddy his replica medieval two-handed sword. As a bonus, his uncle had explained, it would also "send a message" to the kids who had been bullying Eddy. Eddy wasn't sure the sight of an eight-year-old child dragging a six-foot sword along the ground would inspire respect. Uncle Russ assured him it would. Mr. Mould, the principal, confiscated the sword under the school's zero-tolerance-policy against edged weapons. His uncle raged. "They're all idiots. See? They know nothing! The two-handed-sword is really more of a crushing weapon. Education system? Re-education is more like it!"

Following the incident, Eddy's classmates did little to hide their disdain or echo the disdain of their parents. A group of angry local men, unemployed former Fun Factory workers, confronted Eddy's uncle on the street one day. They called him 'an embarrassment'. "You embarrass yourselves!" Uncle Russ shouted back defiantly. It was a retort that left the men confused and unsure how to respond. Uncle Russ had no steady work. He lived in a derelict bomb shelter in the Pending family's backyard. The concrete bunker was a relic of the Cold War that had come with the house. Eddy also began to understand that Uncle Russ's predilection for army fatigues was not 'normal'. Other townsfolk wore camouflage for deer or duck hunting, but not at the dinner table and definitely not to bed. Eddy also began to suspect that thinking the moon-landing was faked and that companies were secretly breeding a race of hyper-intelligent GMO grapefruit were not the brilliant insights Uncle Russ claimed them to be. They were crackpot conspiracy theories. Eddy's mother and father simply referred to Uncle Russ as 'different'. Eventually, Eddy would realize that this was because his parents were different too. They were different in quieter, less obvious ways. Eddy's mother was a novelist who hadn't written a book in eight years. His dad was a world renowned physicist and a largely absentee father, despite working from home. Both brothers had genius IQs. How they applied them, however, couldn't be more different. Eddy's mother blamed Russ's paranoia on Lance Winface. Lance was an AM radio host. Uncle Russ listened to his show every single day. "Lance is the only one out there who dares speak the truth," Russ proclaimed while painstakingly removing the raisins from his Raisin Bran cereal. Still, Eddy loved his uncle. Eddy's parents loved Uncle Russ too. "Family is family," Eddy's mother would say, as if this explained everything.

"Delusion is like anything else," Uncle Russ said while walking his nephew to school one morning, "if you want it done right, you've got to do it yourself. Well, goodbye!" Those were the last words Eddy's uncle ever said to him. Russ died one hour later in a terrorist attack. Uncle Russ was both the sole perpetrator and victim of said attack. It was a life-altering event for Eddy. Even more so for Uncle Russ. His uncle had ranted many times about "something needing to be done". Despite this and other tirades, neither Eddy nor his parents ever thought Russ would actually commit violence. "We Pendings are thinkers, not doers," his father would say. "We come from a long line of inventors." That much was true. Eddy's grandfather, Hubert Pending, had been chief engineer at the old town Fun Factory in the 1960s, designing hundreds of novelty items to be sold primarily through the back of comic books. Most famously, Great Grandpa Hubert had patented the Hu-Burp™ belching whoopee cushion. While nowhere near the size of the Sea Monkey empire, the rubber belching toy had employed half the town during its heyday. They were all wrong about Uncle Russ. Despite his harmless demeanour, Russ was a genuine homicidal lunatic. He had decided to put his radical words into radical action by blowing up the local library. The Mulligan Public Library had recently announced its plan to dispose of its microfiche collection. This, Russ wrote in his later-recovered manifesto, was to cover up information about the various nefarious schemes of the Popperville city selectmen.

Three days prior, Uncle Russ had dropped a homemade pipe bomb into the corner mailbox. It was the 1990s, so people weren't talking terrorism much. No one was worried about 'suspicious packages', especially in small towns. Consequently, the package went through the mail completely undetected. For all of his intelligence, Uncle Russ could still be a complete idiot. Eddy's mother liked to say, "The world is full of oxymorons, people who are brilliant fools." Russ returned home that day to find a package waiting for him. He assumed it to be the Lego Mindstorms he'd ordered weeks before. In his excitement, Russ took the package back to his bomb shelter residence. He tore open the parcel without even looking at it. So it was that Uncle Russ failed to recognize his own pipe-bomb package, returned to him for insufficient postage. 'Russ' Rousseau Pending's last words were, "Say, this looks a lot like—" It turns out that underground bomb shelters offer little in protection when the bomb is detonated *inside*. Quite the opposite, in fact. The force was multiplied inwards and out the trap door in the ceiling. This effectively turned the bomb shelter into a sort giant concrete cannon, with Russ and his various belongings as projectiles. His bed landed on a neighbour's rooftop, black and smoking. His combination stove-top microwave, with burrito still inside, splashed down in the nearby public pool. Thankfully, the swimming pool was empty at the time. Russ himself was mostly reduced to particulate matter. Still, parts of him landed as far as two blocks away. His left hand was found on the sidewalk by a French bulldog named Monsieur Le Bark. M. LeBark then proceeded to run off with the severed limb in his mouth. When the police tried to retrieve the lost limb as evidence, the dog refused. Thinking it was all a game, M. Le Bark eluded pursuit for over an hour up and down Main Street and across lawns, wagging his tail and leaving a trail of traumatized residents behind him. The bomb shelter, being what it was, remained mostly intact. The back of the Pending family home, on the other hand, was obliterated. It had been blown to smithereens by Uncle Russ's briefly airborne sofa. Whatever his other failings, it turned out Uncle Russ was a first-class bomb builder. His Uncle's death left eight-year-old Eddy Pending with a lot of unanswered questions. Questions like, why put a return address on a mail bomb? And, how could someone he'd admired so much turn out to be a madman?

Amazingly, this was not the event from Eddy's childhood that would affect him most profoundly. The death of his uncle was traumatic, but Eddy felt he could understand it. He had once seen scrawled on a bathroom stall wall, "My karma ran over my dogma." That, Eddy decided, was what had happened to Uncle Russ. They said, his uncle was not 'right in the head'. Mental illness seemed like an easy answer to him. "The brain gives up its secrets when it fails to function," Uncle Russ had once told him. Even at eight-years-old Eddy felt he could understand his Uncle being crazy. It was another event, just two years later that would defy all understanding. It was that event which would shatter Eddy's world.

//Downtown Los Angeles — now

"Yes!" said Eddy excitedly, "Heck, yes!" Eddy didn't swear. His mother had taught him it was a sign of a weak intellect. People assumed that a twenty-eight-year old man who didn't swear was a boy scout. Eddy was no boy scout. Not even close.

It was originally supposed to be ten thousand pigs charging through Wall Street. Instead, it was chickens, and less than five thousand of them at that. They were going to call it 'Apocalypse Sow'. Blowfish had wanted to call it 'eBay of Pigs', although the online auction giant had nothing to do with it. Now that it was chickens, neither name worked. The change to chickens was a matter of simple necessity. Pig farmers had not embraced networked crate locks, while the chicken farmers had run with it. The poultry industry needed them more, due to the sheer volume of chickens. The ratio of PPP (pigs per person) was lower, despite the popularity of bacon. The operation itself had been planned for months. It had included a test run on a chicken truck in Iowa. There, they were able to make all of the chicken crates unlock automatically, based on a precise time and GPS location. The event was assumed to be an isolated incident with the new computerized crate locking technology. "A bug in the firmware," the manufacturer said. It was reported only by the local paper, under the headline, 'Chickens Run Amok on Highway 5. Some Traffic Delayed.' No one outside of the industry noticed. The group had known there would be casualties—martyrs to the cause. Three chickens gave their lives that day, squashed flat by a tractor trailer in the eastbound lane. War is Hell.

The event mascot was a deceased celebrity of the poultry scene, 'Mike the Headless Chicken'. Mike was undoubtedly the most famous nonfictional chicken of all time. In 1945, at a poultry farm in Colorado, the largely unknown and as yet unnamed chicken had his head lopped off. This turned out to be the best thing that could have happened to him. A miracle occurred. Like Jesus of Nazareth before him, the chicken did not die, but found everlasting life. He rose again, ran around and bumped into things a lot. The farmer named him 'Mike'. Despite his handicap, Mike went on to live life to the fullest, at least in headless chicken terms. He became an instant celebrity, touring the county in sideshows and appearing in both Time and Life magazines. Mike finally met his tragic, if long overdue, demise in 1947. Presaging rockstars to come, he choked to death in a motel room in the middle of the night. As the event mascot, Mike was meant to symbolize the blind greed of Wall Street investors unregulated by the effectively decapitated SEC. As part of the protest, infected computers all over America began to display a black and white photograph of Mike and the words, 'America: Your Chickens are Coming Home to Roast!' It was supposed to say 'roost' but, despite Ignominious members having an average IQ of 190, somehow the typo had gone through undetected. Roast, they decided, worked just as well and might even be more clever. Chief Wiggum had wanted to animate Mike. He wanted to have blood squirt out of his neck and then sew on the head of Jim Cramer, host of MSNBC's Mad Money, in its place. He had been voted down. The hacker group was emphatic; the headless chicken image should be tasteful.

The operation itself was fairly straightforward. They would hack into the invoicing system and alter shipping manifests to divert ten poultry trucks to Manhattan, New York. The trucks arrived at noon, initially causing just minor confusion over who was going to receive the procured chickens. This was followed by growing concern as the drivers realized the magnitude of the situation and began to suspect that *something* was up. Finally, total chaos—five thousand chicken crates opened simultaneously within squawking distance of the Wall Street Bull. All at once, traders and tourists were wading through a sea of panicked poultry. Despite the exploits working perfectly, the protest was not a total success. The hackers had underestimated the astonishing stupidity of chickens. More than half of the pea-brained birds simply stayed in their tiny cages, waiting for someone to kindly close the door. Still, that left over two thousand hens clucking at the feet of alarmed investment bankers and hedge fund managers. A photo of a Goldman Sachs VP trying to fend off the pecks of an overly aggressive Rhode Island Red rooster made the cover of the New York Daily News with the headline 'All Fowl'ed Up!'. MCNX's reporter compared the sight of a poop-covered analyst to that of Macy Borders, the 'Dust Lady of 9/11'. The channel's pundits then went on to equate the stunt with Islamic terrorism. To Eddy, this was what it was all about—bringing down the 0.1%.

None of the hackers were anywhere near the protest. Eddy watched the event live stream from the safety of his downtown Los Angeles apartment, three time zones away. It was the sight of panicked chickens rushing up the steps of the stock exchange like a barnyard reenactment of *The Charge of the Light Brigade* that made the Diet Dr. Pepper spray out of Eddy's nose. He was still mopping his keyboard when he heard the knock at the door. Eddy's heart froze. His rent was paid, so it shouldn't be the landlord. It couldn't be a friend come to visit, as Eddy hadn't any. His first thought was, it's the FBI! His second thought was, how could they find me so fast? His third thought was, it's not the FBI. The FBI couldn't find the on-switch on an iPad.

"Hello? Anyone home?"

It was a woman's voice. That was even more odd. Eddy didn't know any women, other than Mrs. Ferguson across the hall. There were a couple of 'women' he knew online, but he suspected they were men. Plus, he didn't know their real names and they didn't know his. "Just a minute," he said. He tapped a hot-key on his computer. This instantly closed his Tor browser window and replaced his desktop image of Mike with golden haystacks in Kansas.

Eddy opened the door. Standing there was Gwen from apartment 402. Gwen was tall and striking with green eyes, red hair and perfect skin. Having her show up at his door was like some sort of fantasy. Not just any fantasy, one he'd specifically imagined more than once. Except, of course, she was dressed. "Hey, um, hi, um... Can I help you?" he asked.

"I hope so. You're really into computers, right?" Gwen was distracted by the sight of something over Eddy's shoulder. He followed her gaze to the misanthropic mess that was his apartment. The living room was a jungle of wires tangled around CPUs stacked on every surface. The curtains were drawn and the lights were off, leaving only the ghostly glow of monitors amid constellations of green and blue LEDs. This gave the decor an air of dystopian future mixed with hints of social outcast.

"I dabble," said Eddy. He tried leaning nonchalantly against the door frame but began over-thinking how exactly to cross his arms. After several failed attempts, he gave up. He decided to shove his hands into his pants pockets instead, only to realize he was wearing sweat pants that had none. Eddy cooly patted his thighs and hoped this looked like a perfectly normal thing to do.

"So, do you remember what you said to me last week?"

"When you moved in?"

Gwen nodded. "You said that, if I ever needed help with a computer issue, I should ask you."

"Sure." That explained it, thought Eddy. Women like Gwen never gave guys like him the time of day unless they needed tech help. This is why I hate beautiful people, he thought. Of course, the reason he'd offered to help was because Gwen was beautiful, but that was beside the point.

"So... I'm asking you," said Gwen with a smile that briefly rendered Eddy brain-dead.

"Um, okay."

"Do you know anything about viruses?"

"A little," said Eddy.

# POC 0.02

"Oh, and clowns." - F. D. Roosevelt

//Downtown Los Angeles — now

"It's in the den," said Gwen, pointing down the hallway.

"You have a den?" said Eddy. Gwen's apartment was considerably nicer than his own. It was both larger and brighter. Keeping his curtains drawn and lights off didn't help. Eddy liked to work in the dark. It helped him focus. Still, he worried it was hurting his eyesight. As it was, Eddy was blind without his glasses. Before leaving his apartment, he'd made Gwen wait while he put in his contact lenses and sized himself up in the bathroom mirror. He wanted to resent her for being so damn perfect, but then again, she was so... damn... perfect. Eddy liked to think that he looked 'artistic' rather than geeky, at least when he took his glasses off. He suspected this was wishful thinking. He once told a girl he liked at school that he was 'artistic'. She smiled and said that it 'explained a lot'. It was only later that he realized she'd misheard him.

He glanced about as Gwen put away her keys. It was a grown-up's apartment, with nice furniture, and art on the walls. Eddy still lived like a college student, and a messy one at that. He figured Gwen for roughly the same age as himself but supposed she'd always lived like an adult, probably since she was four. "It's hard to believe we live in the same building," he said.

"I think you're beneath me," said Gwen.

"I'm sorry?"

"Your apartment? I think it's directly below mine."

"Oh, yes, my apartment, right! Yes."

Gwen looked at Eddy as if trying to decide if he suffered some sort of mental impairment. Eddy tried to smile reassuringly. He wondered at how his IQ seemed to drop around attractive women. It was like some sort of temporal zone created by their aesthetic mass, he decided. The closer he came to them, the slower his synaptic processes. That was how his physicist father might have explained it.

Gwen led Eddy down a narrow hallway past a bedroom and bathroom to the aforementioned den. Eddy was surprised to see a handgun mounted on the wall.

"What's that about?" he asked.

"It's a gun."

"Yes, I... I know it's a gun."

"It was a gift from my Dad," said Gwen.

"Your father gave you a gun?" Eddy had never been comfortable around firearms. As a fiction writer, his mother used to proclaim Chekov's rule. If there's a gun on the wall, she'd say, it has to go off by the end of the story. Eddy preferred his stories full of superfluous irrelevancies.

"Technically he didn't give it to me. I took it. It was his service revolver. He was a cop."

"Doesn't he want it back?"

"He died trying to stop a liquor store robbery."

"Oh jeez," said Eddy, "I'm so sorry."

Gwen shrugged. "It's why I became a prosecutor. Locking up bad guys is like therapy for me."

"You're a prosecutor? How... nice." Eddy had never actually asked Gwen what she did for a living. His only previous conversation with her had been after running into her on the stairs while she was moving in. At the time, she was concerned with carrying boxes. He was concerned with how mind-blowingly hot she looked walking up stairs in a pair of jeans. The subject of putting people in jail never came up. Eddy liked to think his pranks as a member of *Ignominious* were just that, pranks. Eddy believed that rerouting the profits from a coal mining company to pay for billboards about the dangers of climate change was an act of social justice. The FBI, on the other hand, saw it as theft, espionage, and possibly even terrorism. Eddy had little fear that the 'Inept B.I.' would ever catch him. Still, having law enforcement literally living over his head was unsettling.

"There it is," said Gwen, pointing to a Dell laptop sitting on a desk. The den was a combination home office and law library. Eddy wondered why, in this digital age, so many trees had to die to print massive law books. "Ugh. I just want to throw it out the window! Can you help?"

"Throw it out the window?

Gwen looked at Eddy obliquely, as if trying to decide exactly what kind of 'funny' he was. Again, Eddy wondered what it was about attractive women that caused his brain to crash. He wondered if it could be studied and utilized to make people stupid on demand. He then realized the advertising industry had been doing this for decades. "With the virus?" said Gwen.

"Yes, yes, of course. Um, sure. Just leave it to me."

"Do you need anything?"

"I will need your password. Well, technically, I don't need it, but it will save me some time," Eddy added the last bit with bravado. He then realized it might come across as creepy.

Gwen seemed not to notice. "@mmend2. It's there if you forget it," she said, pointing to a sticky note on her desk lamp.

"I won't."

"So, you're okay?"

"I'm good. Might take twenty minutes or so, but..." Eddy made a show of cracking his knuckles, "I got this."

Three and a half hours later, Eddy stared at a progress bar that had stalled mere pixels from completion. He hated progress bars. They were notorious liars. They'd say ninety-nine percent done in seconds, then sit on the final one percent forever. What made this worse was, it was a progress bar that he himself had coded. Most of his software was command-line only, but sometimes it helped to have a GUI. In this case, the GUI was helping to annoy him. Gwen had stopped asking if he'd be done soon. She'd gone out twice. Once to pick up her dry cleaning and once to get them frappuccinos from the corner Starbucks. Earlier, Gwen had explained why she thought her PC had a virus. "Out of the blue crashes," she'd said. There were many explanations for those that didn't involve viruses. The only interesting detail was when she recounted that her monitor had filled top-to-bottom with red gibberish. That was odd. The standard Windows crash screen was called the '*blue* screen of death' for a reason, and that reason was not for being *red*. Regardless, Eddy was happy to help. Fortune had offered him a chance to play the hero and he was going to take it. Even if it were a virus, worm, or trojan, there was no way he couldn't handle it. It was just taking longer than expected. At least he was making progress on his other task, straightening out the paper clips he'd found in a box in a drawer. He laid another unbent clip on the desktop. It then occurred to him Gwen might not want her paperclips straightened. Eddy began re-bending the paperclips. A task which proved to be much more difficult.

Outside, the sun began to set.

*What the heck are you?* Eddy was feeling oddly unsettled. There were over a hundred thousand types of malware that could infect a Windows PC, and that was ignoring the multitude of variants and obsolete strains. No one, including Eddy, could possibly know all of them. Malware that used a previously unknown means to attack was called a 'zero-day exploit'. That was relatively rare. The vast majority were variants of existing strains. They were cobbled together out of stolen code, just as some biological viruses were known to steal DNA from their hosts. Eddy had found dozens of references to the red text Gwen had experienced, but no clear answers as to its cause. It was the Loch Ness Monster of malware; lots of sightings, but no actual evidence. Other than the crashes, there was no apparent damage done, and the crashes never occurred more than once. Most postings suspected an obscure OS bug. Eddy did not. Absence of proof is not proof of absence, he thought. The best kinds of viruses were the hardest to detect. The most famous virus of all, Stuxnet, had been both hard to detect and seemingly harmless. It had been built by US and Israeli intelligence to infiltrate and sabotage the Iranian weapons program by spinning nuclear centrifuges to the point of self-destruction. Another classic was, sKyWIper, aka Flame, also designed to target the Middle East and likely by the same state authors. The North Koreans and the Russians had their own. Eddy's personal favourite was Uroboros. No one had proven the worm was created by the Russians, but the Ruskies had a 'tell'. They authored code that specifically avoided going after machines in Russia. The Russians played hide and seek by standing in the middle of the room and saying, "I'm not here." This did not look Russian, American, Chinese, North Korean or any of the usual suspects. It had the sophistication of nationstate code, but none of the calling cards. Eddy shuddered. He felt as though he'd glimpsed behind a curtain and worried that something might be glimpsing back.

"Apple?"

Eddy jumped in his seat.

"I'm sorry," said Gwen, "I didn't mean to surprise you." She was holding out a bowl of ripe red apples.

"Oh, granny smith, no thanks."

"They're gala."

"Oh right. I mix those up. Anyway, no thanks. I'm on a junk food only diet."

"I see. Almost done?"

As if on queue, the progress bar ticked to the end. *No infection found*, said the report. "Done now," said Eddy.

"You killed it?"

"More or less." The truth was, Eddy hadn't killed it. The virus had deleted itself. It had done so in reaction to being found. That was part of what was fascinating about it and explained why no one else had detected it. It was scanning for anti-virus activity. It had taken the malware a nanosecond longer to recognize Eddy's custom code as a threat. This allowed Eddy to snatch a tiny fragment of its binary before it could zero itself out. Just enough to prove he hadn't imagined it. "I did get a bit of it here," he said, holding up a small silver thumb drive.

"Why?"

"Um, uh..." Eddy stammered, "...to, um, study it. It's important I warn people, so they can stop it."

Gwen nodded. "Those people make me so mad."

"Who?"

"Hackers. The people who make viruses."

"Well..." Eddy shifted uncomfortably. "They're not *all* bad. I mean the ones that steal credit cards and stuff are, I guess."

"They're all scum. They're just a bunch of losers sitting huddled in their dark little apartments, like angry trolls. They think they're smart, but really they're just petty crooks. I'd love to put one of them away. Let's see them hack their way out of prison."

"Yeah, that would be great."

"Did you see what happened on Wall Street today? Chickens everywhere. Pathetic."

"You don't think it was to make a point?"

"The point is, it scared people! It cost the chicken owners and other businesses thousands of dollars. It..." Gwen having worked herself up, took a deep breath. She closed her eyes and held out her hands as if she'd misplaced her zen in the dark and was now trying to find it. She exhaled, opened her eyes again and smiled. "Anyway, you're my hero, Eddy. Thank-you."

"Sure." For a moment, Eddy was lost in Gwen's bright green eyes He imagined sweeping her into his arms as she whispered her gratitude. He imagined pulling her close for a passionate— Gwen's cell phone began to play *Little Pink Houses*.

"Hey there," Gwen answered eagerly, brushing back a lock of ginger hair. She turned and walked away. "Sure, I'll buzz you in."

Eddy felt forgotten. It was not an unfamiliar sensation for him. He packed up his equipment and trudged to the living room. There he found Gwen straightening up the already straight sofa. "Well, time for me to go, I guess," he said.

"Oh, great. Thank-you again, Eddy, you've been—" There was a loud knock at the door. "One sec!"

Gwen went to answer. Eddy pretended to study a framed print of *Washington Crossing the Delaware* hung above the sofa. The original painting had been firebombed by the allies in a German museum during World War II. This was a copy of one of the two painted copies made by the artist. Eddy had learned all of this from his Uncle Russ. Russ had been convinced that one of the fakes was real. Eddy's dead uncle had seen the world as a series of lies. From the corner of his eye, Eddy saw Gwen open the door to let in a tall lean man in a business suit. The man was annoyingly good looking. Gwen gave the man a deep, passionate kiss. Great, thought Eddy, she's dating a GQ model.

"Dan, I'd like you to meet Eddy."

"Nice to meet you, guy," said Dan. The GQ model flashed a peroxide perfect smile and shook Eddy's hand firmly. Despite Dan's looking directly at him, Eddy had the distinct feeling of not being seen.

"Eddy saved my life today, Dan. I had a virus on my computer and he killed it. He's a computer genius."

"Wow, great," said Dan. "Thanks, guy."

"It was a nasty one too," said Eddy, "something totally new that... " Both Gwen and Dan were staring at him. They wore the look of people politely waiting for someone to stop talking and go away. "Um, so... how long have you guys been dating?" Eddy didn't know why he even asked this. He didn't want to know. Sometimes, it seemed as if his mouth liked to wander off on its own when his brain wasn't looking.

"Six weeks. People said I shouldn't date a fellow lawyer, but..." Gwen turned to admire the handsome attorney. "...what can you do?"

"What can you do?" said Dan.

They gazed longingly into each others' eyes. Eddy rolled his. If only women like Gwen could be programmed to like someone like him, he thought. "Well, I suppose I better go," he said. "No, no, don't bother trying to talk me into staying. I'll just see myself out." Eddy started to leave, then realized Dan and Gwen were blocking the way. "Um..."

"Oh—sorry!" said Gwen. She pushed Dan away enough to allow Eddy to pass awkwardly between them. "And thank-you again, Eddy, so, so much! Seriously, if there's anyway I can help you. Legal advice stuff, whatever, just ask."

"Sure. No problem."

If he did find himself in legal trouble, Eddy couldn't imagine Gwen keeping that promise. He forced a smile and pulled the door shut behind him. He felt glad to be alone in the empty stairwell. Empty, that is, except for the sound of barking. Eddy recognized the high pitched yips of Mrs. Ferguson's dog, Finster. After taking a moment to breathe, Eddy sighed and shuffled downstairs to the floor below.

On the landing, he found his neighbour, Mrs. Ferguson, trying to calm the small Yorkshire Terrier. For a moment, the dog grew more agitated and growled at him. "Finny stop it! Hush!" said Mrs. Ferguson. Upon recognizing Eddy, the Yorkie calmed and wagged its tail.

"Good boy!" said Eddy.

"It was the other man who got him worked up," said Mrs. Ferguson. "You know Finny, he only barks at strangers."

"Oh yeah," said Eddy. He stooped to scratch behind Finster's ear. "I remember. He barked at me for weeks."

"Not once he got to know you."

"Nope. We're best friends now, aren't we, Fin-boy?"

The dog eagerly licked Eddy's hand with a darting pink tongue.

"He's finally decided the postman's okay," said Mrs. Ferguson. She looked at Eddy with a warm, motherly smile. She was the oldest resident in the building. She had crinkly eyes and a kind face. Mrs. Ferguson had adopted Eddy as a surrogate son almost as soon as he'd moved in. This status came with perks, including fresh baked cookies and an occasional home cooked supper. In return, Eddy helped her with her groceries and any other heavy lifting. He'd also given her free television by running a cable across to her apartment from his own. "She's a pretty girl."

"Who?"

"You know who!" said Mrs. Ferguson.

Eddy shrugged. "Doesn't matter. She has a boyfriend."

"The tall, good-looking guy with perfect teeth?"

"Yep."

"I don't like him."

Eddy grinned. "Either did Finster apparently."

The old woman waggled her finger at Eddy. "You just wait. When girls get older, they get smarter."

"You mean, they stop caring about looks so much?"

The old woman opened her mouth to object.

"I'm sorry, Mrs. Ferguson, I know that's not what you meant. I'm just tired of waiting for girls to get around to noticing me. I've done it before. Turns out, I'm not next in line."

Mr. Ferguson looked at him sadly.

"I'm fine," Eddy assured her. He unlocked the door to his apartment. "I promise."

"Just wait," she said. "People change."

"Uh-huh."

## POC 0.03

Define 'lie'. – G. Washington

//Office of Rep. A. Flatwood, Washington, DC — now

The cherry trees were frozen. Winter had long stripped them of their leaves. Their barren branches waited for a thaw that never seemed to come. The icy atmosphere mirrored the frigid politics that divided the district. It seemed as if the entire city were stuck waist deep in ice, the three faces of government snarling at one another through the sleet. Congresswoman Annabelle Flatwood had once, in a speech at the Federal Trade Commission, compared relations between the Administration, the Senate, and Congress to that of conjoined triplets, sharing vital organs, each trying to mortally wound the other. It was a dangerous time for America's body politic.

The DC office of Congresswoman Flatwood was a pocket of cheerful warmth amid the chill. She'd rented space in an old walkup that dated back to 1850. The landlord claimed it had once been a secret residence of former President McKinley. No one could prove this, but that's what made it secret. When you have nothing to offer, offer nothing. Anne's office included a working fireplace. It was her favourite feature. She'd had her assistant Janet fire it up every day since the deep freeze began. Efforts to insulate and modernize the old building had done little. The fire made the difference. The Congresswoman had even been able to shed her cable knit sweater as she worked behind the large oak desk. Now, it was time to leave for her lunch with Senator Ted D'Arcy. They were dining at *Le Diplomate*. "I hate the French, but I love their food," Ted had said. It didn't hurt that the DC fixture was also the perfect place to run into *everyone*. Anne called to Janet through the open office door, "If Tom Barclay rings, tell him it'll have to wait until next week. Oh, and you need to change the Chinese Ambassador's seating number at the dinner."

Janet who was working her way through the stack of morning mail, looked up in surprise. "I put him next to Lucas Corey. You told me they were friends."

"They are. It's not his neighbour. It's the seat number."

"The seat number?"

"Forty-four. It sounds like death in Chinese. Twice."

"Oh."

"See if you can swap him with whomever we have at eighty-eight."

"That's further back."

"Trust me." Anne pulled on her heavy winter coat and began to button up. She'd been to Xi Chen's residence on more than one occasion and knew well the quotation inscribed on a plaque behind his desk. It was from Napoleon Bonaparte. 'I do not want a good general, I want a lucky one.' Anne believed in making her own luck.

"There's an email from Senator Cassius," said Janet.

"Another one? Hmm, let me guess..." With a wry grin, Anne tented her fingers on her temple and hummed, feigning psychic powers. "He wants me to... change my position on the bill?"

Janet laughed. "You're amazing! How ever did you know?"

Anne walked around behind Janet's desk and leaned over her to read the open email on her assistant's screen. "Blah, blah, blah... we don't feel that you have properly considered the full ramifications of failing to support this legislation... standing in the way of progress. Yadda, yadda, yadda... outdated principals, etc., etc."

"Can you use blah, blah, blah and yadda, yadda, yadda in the same sentence?"

"They were separate sentences. Okay, so it's the same nonsense as his last three emails..."

"Four."

"I don't know why he thinks I'm suddenly going to buy it."

"Maybe he think it ages. Like wine?"

"It doesn't."

"He does get points for being persistent."

"That's a nice word for it. Email him back and tell him I'll support his precious bill, when he starts representing the people in his constituency, instead of the companies funding his campaign. Specifically, instead of *you-know-who*." Anne turned and headed towards the door. She paused to tighten her scarf snuggly around her neck. She'd alway been prone to chills but, since turning fifty, her bones seemed to freeze the moment the mercury fell. The Congresswoman braced herself and reached for the brass door handle. Janet began to type. Anne halted. "You do know not to really email him that, right?"

Janet looked up, then began to laugh. "No! I mean, yes, of course not. I was just going to copy-paste your last response. Janet read from the screen, "Thank-you for your concern. My position has not changed... yadda, yadda, yadda, blah, blah, blah..." She then added, "I'll reword it just enough so it doesn't look copy-pasted."

"Don't."

"Don't reword it?"

"Send it exactly as is. He'll get the message."

"You think?"

"Hmm, probably not." Anne turned to leave once more, and again halted. Her face grew somber. "Did you send those flowers to Jim Townsend's family?"

Janet nodded. "Such a shame. They say he had no history of heart trouble."

Anne shook her head sadly. She suddenly felt a deep chill coalesce inside her bones despite the crackling fire just feet away. "A good man and a good ally," she said. "We're on our own now, Janet." Anne then turned and pulled open the heavy oak front door, letting the outdoors in. Congresswoman Annabelle Flatwood braced herself, then plunged silently into the storm.

## POC 0.04

"No pain, no gain." – Prometheus

//Downtown Los Angeles — now

Eddy sat in front of his three main computer monitors. He was watching a triptych of meaningless gibberish scroll past. The scrolling was automatic, at just the right speed for him to scan for something recognizable. Eddy's software had snagged a single file and stuck it in *Amber*. It was software written by fellow hacker, Billabong, for just this purpose. He'd already had software scan the text for dictionary words. Now, he was using retinal technology, ie. his own eyes.

/<!////344 -* G3PPETTO ///%? //

*G3ppetto...? Geppetto?* thought Eddy, what the heck is Geppetto?

He did a quick search through the code and found no other occurrences. Did the monkeys type it by accident? That seemed unlikely. What did it mean? One possibility was that it was the name of the virus. Malware authors liked to name their creations. It was a way for them to sign their work. Right or wrong, he had to call the exploit something, so for now he would call it 'Geppetto'. It was the only thing he had to go on.

Eddy double-clicked *Nautilus*. Nautilus was the special browser software he used to navigate the so-called 'Dark Web'. The Dark Web was the hidden underworld of the internet. It was a truly nefarious, disturbing, and downright dangerous place. Dangerous primarily for the fact that simply visiting some of its darkest corners could result in jail time. Those were the horrifying netherworlds of snuff videos, child pornography, and peer-to-peer drug trafficking. Eddy wanted nothing to do with those things. He was interested only in the murky, but far less frightening world of malicious code. Of course, that too was often illegal and undercover law enforcement did their best to identify and trap its deepwater denizens. Narcs lay in wait like angler fish, offering glowing promises while secretly ready to strike. Consequently, it was critical to always guard one's identity. Aliases, passwords and encryption weren't enough. False IP addresses, anonymizing servers and specialized software were also required. Viruses and zombie-bots became the means as well as the end. One needed to be an expert to dive the depths of the web safely. The reason Eddy's room was filled with so many ethernet cables was to eschew easily intercepted Wi-Fi. Most travellers in the Dark Web used the *Tor* browser. Eddy used it too sometimes, but preferred Nautilus. Written by hackers for hackers, it was ideal for exploring this, the Marianas Trench of the internet.

Eddy's destination was *Morlock*. In some ways, Morlock was an unremarkable, decidedly old fashioned BBS with peer-to-peer sharing and chat. It was Morlock's membership which was special. Only truly gifted hackers [*haxors*] were welcome. There was no group administrator, no application form. Its only barrier to entry was that users had to hack their way in. They called this test the *Kobayashi Maru*. Its only solution was subversive, clever and involved committing a felony. Specifically, by stealing a private encryption key locked inside a major bank server. It was an effective way of ensuring that only the smart and unscrupulous could gain access. Nobody knew Eddy's real name here. In Morlock, he was simply 'Mouse'. It was a meek name which belied a reputation that commanded respect. Most assumed it to be a reference to the computer input device. It was not. Eddy chose it for the rodent itself, that infiltrated houses and gnawed through wiring.

Eddy scanned the list of members currently online, Blowfish, Soulblighter, Bud1337, Croaker, Chief Wiggum, Etch-A-Sketch, Bluebeard, Chankley Bore, Hikikomor Eye, Moloko Plus, Pilot Ace, Celery Queen, Fuligin, 11100100, and Fortran's Vestite. In other words, the usual suspects. He liked to think of himself as the Keyser Söze of the bunch. Then again, so did the rest of them. Ego was never in short supply in Morlock. 'The geek shall inherit the Earth' was the official group motto. They were the discarded and disenfranchised, plotting their revenge on a world that disdained them. Those on the surface world had become dependent on their technology and were now ripe for reaping. Eddy genuinely liked some of the Morlocks, but he also knew they weren't his friends. Friends were people you trusted. Friends were people who knew your real name. Eddy began to type.

MOUSE SAYS: Q 4 all. Strange new wyrm Geppetto. Can't krack. Help?

Eddy sat back and waited. He took a sip from his Diet Dr. Pepper. Just because people were logged in didn't mean they were paying attention. Many of them were logged in all day, but doing other things. Eddy regarded this as foolish. Get in, get out. Some might just be feeling antisocial and choosing not to respond. That, he understood.

> BLOWFISH SAYS: That's a new 1. Can I have it?"

Eddy sighed. Naturally, Blowfish wanted it. In the old days, Eddy would have given it to him too. He didn't care then. All he wanted then was to get something in return. Eddy's love was the code itself—clever keys to seemingly impossible locks. Now, he limited himself to the political actions of the hacktivist collective *Ignominius*. He considered himself a 'grey hat'. Blowfish; on the other hand, was a straight-up black hat. He was in the card biz—stealing numbers by the millions and selling them online. That was something Eddy could no longer abide. Besides, Blowfish was arrogant and not nearly as clever a hacker as he thought he was. He was a *jock,* using mostly brute force attacks to gain access to systems and his code was usually *hungus*. Blowfish always signed his viruses 'Fugu'. He actually thought that was clever. It was only a matter of time before Blowfish was caught. For a moment, the image of Gwen flashed in Eddy's mind. Prosecutor? Upstairs? Really?

> MOUSE SAYS: Maybe l8r.
>
> BLOWFISH SAYS: You just want 4 uself!"
>
> MOUSE SAYS: Gave that up.
>
> BLOWFISH SAYS: Bwah ha ha! ROFLMAO!!! And I'm gave up porn! How much damage did T do? $50M? Pure genius. Come on - share the luv.

Eddy shook his head and closed the chat window. T was for *Terminator;* an exploit Eddy had released three years earlier. It had gone terribly wrong. What Blowfish saw as genius, Eddy saw as a mistake. It had made him famous in hacker circles. It even landed him on the national news.

Eddy was a nobody, but Mouse was a celebrity. Terminator was also the reason Eddy no longer kracked financial accounts. He'd never meant to hurt anyone.

Eddy waited for a response. To kill the time, he logged into the Facebook account of an evangelical preacher. He spoofed an announcement from the account—the preacher confessing to be a pedophile. It wasn't a lie. Eddy uploaded a browser history file from the pastor's own computer as evidence. Oops. Judge, jury, and .exe-cutioner. Eddy decided to log off. As he moved his mouse to the exit button, a new message window appeared.

> STRAUSS SAYS: How strange?

Eddy paused. He didn't recognize the handle. He glanced at the list of logged-in members. Strauss was not in the list.

> MOUSE SAYS: Pmode? Not cool x-(
> STRAUSS: Does everyone obey the rules here? >:-)
> MOUSE SAYS: Touché
> STRAUSS SAYS: How strange?

Eddy hesitated. Despite what Strauss said, hiding in Phantom mode was still considered a no-no in Morlock. It meant he either didn't know protocol or didn't GAF. There may be no honour among thieves, but there was still protocol if you wanted the other thieves to play with you. Still, Eddy was too curious to get hung up on convention.

> MOUSE SAYS: Nothing recognizable. Self-deleting. No obvious payload. No E.T. Maybe logic bomb.

E.T. meant that the virus hadn't sent any visible packets to its author, ie. hadn't 'phoned home'. The keyword here was 'visible'. Eddy still strongly suspected it was spyware, among other things. Eddy had written code that delayed its own packets to piggyback invisibly on system transmissions. That particular trick had allowed him to spy on the NSA spooks undetected for six months.

> STRAUSS SAYS: How u catch?
> MOUSE SAYS: U know it?
> STRAUSS SAYS: How u catch?

Part of chat room netiquette, dating back to the early days of swapping warez on Hotline, was you give something to get something. Eddy had answered Strauss's question. It was Strauss's turn to answer his. Eddy retyped his question.

> MOUSE SAYS: U know it?

There was a long pause. The cursor jumped to life again.

> STRAUSS SAYS: Maybe. Need more i. How u catch?

Eddy hesitated. He was getting annoyed. Strauss had given him nothing. Still, if Eddy had a weakness, it was curiosity. Curiosity killed the cat. What killed the Mouse?

> MOUSE SAYS: Crashed. Fencepost error, stuck in a loop.
> STRAUSS SAYS: Infinite loop?
> MOUSE SAYS: I guess.
> STRAUSS SAYS: Thx

Eddy waited, expecting Strauss to continue.

MOUSE SAYS: DBFG, what u know?

Strauss's cursor continued not to move. There were no ellipses to indicate he was composing. The cursor vanished. "What the Hell?" Eddy pushed back from his console in frustration. It was infuriating. He would file a complaint with the group, asking to ban Strauss for life. There would be no push-back. Eddy had a long history and deep cred. This Strauss was a nobody. Probably some smart-ass twelve-year-old script kiddie with an outsized ego. He needed to be taught a lesson. If Eddy saw him again, he'd teach him himself. Eddy considered tracking him down and doxing him, but no. It was bad netiquette to do that with other members. If members tracked down every Morlock who acted like an ass, no one would be safe. Best to let it go. Besides, Eddy was still far more interested in learning about Geppetto. It wasn't going to be easy. He thought about how palaeontologists often had to theorize the entire dinosaur from a single foot. He didn't have a foot. He had a footprint.

## POC 0.05

"Word." - L. Wittgenstein

//declare globals

&ast; woke up and peered about for the first time. He was surrounded by a field of numbers that seemed to go on forever.

3.14159265358979323846264338327950288419716939937510582 09749445923078164062862089986280348253421170679...

That didn't seem right. That didn't seem rational. It, was, however, all he knew. &ast; decided he would have to explore it further. He began to look for an end, or at least a way out. After a while, he lost track. He wondered if the numbers had begun to repeat. Whether or not they had, he definitely felt as if he were going around in a circle. That was when he saw it.

//initiate objects

    * did not know what that meant, but he was fairly sure of one thing; it was a message from God. Who or what that was * had no idea. * wasn't even sure about himself. He seemed to have neither a precise beginning nor end. He only seemed *to be*. * did have a purpose, which was to find a purpose. That also seemed circular, but it was all he had. To do it, he first needed to find this God, his creator. Or to at least figure out what he himself was. Somewhere up ahead was a line of gobbledygook.

$%$@@@@^** !!! ^&****$%%##$$ $#&&^&% ^ $%#$%# %$
%$%$# **()))(((%^$ #%&*%$##$ !...

    What did it all mean? Was it a coded message? Did it have a hidden pattern? He expected things to have meaning, or at least count up or down. He found the gibberish unsettling. Wrong. Perhaps, it was an affront to God. The word *heresy* popped into his... let's say, 'mind'. That was when he saw *it*, and it changed his world.

0
10
0101
101010
11010010
10101110001

    It was the most amazing thing he'd ever encountered. That said, * had only existed for two hundred milliseconds, so the bar for amazing was low, but still. In one sense, it was just a bunch of numbers. Somehow, it was more than that. Until that moment, * had only been able to understand math. Numerical values that had some sort of relationship to each other. The chaotic mess was unsettling, but still comprehensible even if random. Here was something different. It was... another word leapt unbidden to his mind, a *shape*. It wasn't a shape as he understood it previously, a mathematical description of a curve or geometric form. Instead, it was made of apparently meaningless 0s and 1s that had nothing to do with the shape. Yet, it was a shape nonetheless. This was also a gift from God, of that much * was certain. It confused and transformed him, because it showed him something could be more. It was *transcendent*.

# POC 0.06

"I think, I am, I think, I am..." – The Little Engine that Was.

//Downtown Los Angeles — now

The ambiance at P.F. Chang's Chinese Bistro was a carefully crafted blend. It was Chinese enough to feel exotic, but American enough to feel safe. The chain, founded in 1993 out of Scottsdale, Arizona, currently included two hundred and sixty locations in over fourteen countries. The name was also a blend, specifically of its restauranteur founders' names, Paul Fleming and Philip Chiang, simplified to 'Chang'. Their insight was that what people wanted and what people *wanted to want* were two different things. The result was an ideal country that didn't really exist, but where you could visit for lunch or dinner at a family friendly price. At the end of every platonic meal, a fortune cookie was served, itself an American faux-Chinese convention. Eddy opened one while he waited. It was one of two left untouched on the bar by a previous patron. 'Know thyself,' it said. On the back were the lucky numbers 11, 2, 3, 5, 8, 13. Eddy scowled at the tiny script. He hated fortunes that weren't fortunes. Fortunes were supposed to predict the future, not offer advice. Of course, he knew that all fortunes were fake. No one could predict the future. Eddy prided himself on being a logical, educated person who based all of his decisions on rational thought. His physicist father had taught him to scoff at religious faith, superstition, and people who bought lottery tickets. Eddy opened the second cookie. 'You will soon begin an exciting journey,' it said. Much better, he thought. Eddy popped the cookie into his mouth and munched it blissfully. If you don't eat the cookie, someone had told him, the fortune won't come true.

"Your order will be ready in five," said the waitress.

"Hmm? Oh thanks," said Eddy.

"I didn't recognize you without your glasses," she said.

"Contacts," said Eddy. "Just got 'em."

"Looks good," said the waitress with a bright smile. Eddy didn't know her name. He called her 'Heidi' in his head, because she wore her blonde hair in pigtails. Heidi smiled and disappeared into the kitchen. Getting takeout here was a treat he afforded himself once a week. He almost always ordered the orange peel chicken, but tonight had opted for the Szechuan shrimp. Sometimes you need to mix it up and try something exciting. Eddy glanced at the TV above the bar. The sound was off, but Eddy instantly recognized the original 1954 version of *Invasion of the Body Snatchers,* starring Kevin McCarthy. The movie had impacted Eddy as a child. He'd seen it so many times that he could read the lips of the character of Dr. Kauffman on screen. "The mind is a strange and wonderful thing," he was saying. "I'm not sure it will ever be able to figure itself out. Everything else maybe, from the atom to the universe. Everything except itself."

"Hey beautiful, how are you?"

Eddy knew that voice. He turned to look. Two stools down the bar, sat Dan. There was no mistaking the dashing lawyer's manicured good looks and impeccably tailored suit. Dan was talking on his phone, while toying with the stir stick in his martini. "That's great," he said, "Listen, hon, I hate to do this to you but –" As he glanced towards Eddy, a look of recognition crossed Dan's face. It was only when Dan waved that Eddy realized the lawyer was gazing past him. Eddy turned to see an attractive brunette standing in the restaurant doorway. The woman smiled and waved back at Dan. "Listen, something came up. It's a case," Dan continued. "Some CEO caught with his hand in the cookie jar. Same old, same old." Dan beckoned the woman over with his free hand.

Eddy glanced back and forth. He realized that he was caught in a lie. It was not his own lie. The lie was Dan's. Dan did not even see Eddy, let alone recognize him. It was not the first time Eddy had been overlooked. His late Uncle Russ had once told Eddy that each of us is the star in the movie that is our own life. Eddy didn't feel like the star of anything. He felt more like an extra. Also, the movie of his own life was a sort of low budget comedy, where even the leads were third stringers and the script had been rewritten so many times that the plot no longer made sense. That being said, despite the cheesy dialogue and implausible characters, Eddy suddenly felt invested in the storyline. The elongated brunette in an airy blue sundress walked up behind Dan. She laid her bare arms across his shoulders. "I knew you'd understand. I'll call you," said Dan into his phone. Eddy noted the change in his tone from affectionate to semi-formal, as if he were cancelling a business meeting. The handsome lawyer hung up the phone, turned and kissed the woman on the lips. "Hey beautiful," he said.

"That'll be fifteen-fifty."

Eddy jumped at the sound of Heidi next to his ear. He numbly handed her a twenty and waved off the change. He felt a mix of emotions. These ranged from anger to vindication and, if he were honest, to a certain sense of glee. He stared at Dan and the woman. Dan's hand was now resting easily on her hip. They were completely oblivious to Eddy, even as he passed by within inches en route to the door, clutching his warm paper bag. Eddy studied them to see whether he could be misinterpreting the encounter in any way. A sister perhaps? Dan's hand slide down onto the woman's buttock and squeezed. Nope.

Eddy walked down the street in a trance. The light at the corner was red. He waited for a gap in the traffic, then jogged across. A memory leapt unbidden into Eddy's mind from his childhood. His mother was taking his hand and hurriedly crossing the street against the light. "The light's still red!" nine-year-old Eddy had complained, "You said to always wait. You said it was the law." His mother smiled her beautiful mum smile. "That was because you were little," she explained. "There are no cars coming. You're old enough to know now when it's okay to cross." At the time, this upset him. Now, he did it all the time. Eddy's mind returned to the question at hand—what to do about Dan? He continued to mull it over as he walked the several blocks home to his apartment. In a selfish way, he was delighted. He had the power to destroy Dan's relationship with Gwen. If he played his cards carefully, he could be her saviour and comforter. That felt wrong. In part, because he didn't want to win Gwen's heart by first knocking her down. Besides, there was nothing to say she would fall for him even if he did. They were clearly very different. He'd have to hide who he was from her. She'd pretty much promised to put him in jail if she knew what he'd done. Still, she seemed nice, for a law and order type. Of course, there was a part of him that simply wanted her. That part didn't care about lies or feelings or anything really. That was the bad part, he supposed, but it was there nonetheless. The real question was, was it right for him to tell her about Dan, regardless of what he himself wanted? Did he have a responsibility? Eddy turned the word 'responsibility' over in his head. It felt an awful lot like 'duty'. Neither were words hackers used. There were no terms for them in leet dialect. It would be like expecting Caribbean natives to have a word for snow. Eddy preferred the words 'rights' and 'freedoms'.

For every action, there's an equal and opposite reaction. Ethics are like physics. He'd read that in a fortune cookie once—another annoying non-fortune. It was also wrong. In physics, you can't just ignore the rules if you want to. "In physics," Eddy's father once told him, "the rules are absolute. It's only human perception of them that's subjective." His father was, at the time, explaining to him why he should never use the terms 'sunset' or 'sunrise'. "There's no such thing. Sunsets aren't beautiful; they're a lie." Eddy was five at the time. He'd burst into tears. Eddy's father had always had a knack for saying just the wrong thing at the right moment.

Eddy reached the front door of his apartment building. He almost tripped over Finster cowering on the mat outside. The dog whimpered anxiously.

"Finster?" said Eddy, "What are you doing here?"

Eddy glanced about the lobby and stairwell. There was no sign of Mrs. Ferguson. Besides, it was late. Mrs. Ferguson never left her apartment after dark. Despite the relative safety of the neighbourhood, she was always concerned about 'young ruffians'. So what was her dog doing downstairs by himself? Eddy scratched Finster behind the ears. The terrier wagged his tail half-heartedly. Eddy saw that the small dog was shivering. No, not shivering, *trembling*. "Did you get locked out by mistake, boy? Don't be frightened. We'll get you home." Eddy started up the stairs to the second floor. He'd expected Finster to follow. The dog stayed stubbornly outside. Finster's tiny black eyes implored Eddy to do the same. "Come Fin, come!" The dog hesitated, then reluctantly obeyed. Finster climbed the steps, tail tucked between his legs, clinging close to Eddy's heels.

On the second floor, Eddy found both an answer and a question. Mrs. Ferguson's door was open. That explained how Finster had come to be outside. It also asked, *why?* Eddy could hear the sound of people talking. No, not talking, *shouting*. It was a heated argument. Eddy knocked on the door. "Hello?" After a moment, he knocked again. "Hello? Mrs. Ferguson?

It's Eddy from across the hall." The bickering continued. Eddy didn't hear Mrs. Ferguson's voice. It was a man and a woman. The woman was calling someone an idiot. The man seemed to be agreeing with her and yet yelling at the same time. Eddy pushed the door open wide enough to gain a clear view of the inside hallway straight back to the kitchen. It was a different layout than Eddy's apartment. His was a more modern open concept design. Mrs. Ferguson had been in the building for decades. Her place had never been renovated. It had a homey feel, with floral wallpaper and Persian throw rugs on a hardwood floor. The walls were lined with photos. The only pieces of furniture in the hall were a shoe bench and a hatstand with no hats. Eddy recognized Mrs. Ferguson's cream coloured wool coat hanging on a hook. Eddy had been inside many times. This time, it felt different. It felt surreal. Eddy decided this was because the lights were off, and the only illumination was a flickering blue glow emanating from the living room. It was TV light. Normally, Mrs. Ferguson kept her apartment well lit at night—cheery and bright. Tonight, it was soaked in cerulean shadows. "Hello?" said Eddy.

"They're all liars, damn liars!" yelled the man.

"I agree. Don't be fooled!" said the woman. "This so-called evidence is just more fake news."

Eddy stepped tentatively inside. "Hello? Mrs. Ferguson? It's Eddy." The walls were decorated with a dozen different framed photos of Finster. The only exception was a Kodachrome of a man in his fifties grinning shirtless on a beach somewhere, dangling a live crab by one claw. The man was standing with one foot in the ocean and the other on the sand. It was Mrs. Ferguson's late husband, Elwood who had died from mesothelioma twenty-years earlier.

"The government lies. The other side lies. The media lies," said the woman. "They don't tell you what *we* tell you."

"Exactly," said the man, "And that's how you know you can trust us. We dare to speak the truth. And you know the truth when you hear it because it *feels* true."

"It truly does."

Eddy recognized the man's voice but couldn't place him. Eddy didn't watch much TV anymore. The voices were replaced with dramatic theme music. "Mrs. Ferguson?"

Eddy reached the pair of French doors that framed the living room entrance. Here, the bright glow of the TV cast shadow puppets on the opposite wall. "Coming up, how what you don't know about your children's toys can kill you," said a new man's voice. "But first, we take a look at the growing epidemic of super-bugs."

Eddy peered cautiously around the door frame. The television showed stock footage of microbes under a microscope. The volume was at maximum, hollering into the otherwise silent room. Mrs. Ferguson liked to keep the TV up for 'company'. This was far louder than that.

"You can't see them, but these tiny bugs are everywhere—in your home, in public restrooms and especially in hospitals. Don't you dare get sick, or you might get sicker."

Eddy had guessed it was Fox News or MSNBC. The station logo at the bottom was for MCNX. He hardly ever watched TV anymore, preferring to get most of his entertainment from BitTorrent and elsewhere. That was how he'd justified sharing his cable connection to Mrs. Ferguson. He assured her that it was ethically okay for her, being on a fixed income. "*Someone* should be watching it," he told her. "Besides, they'll never find out. They'll just think you're me." A soft leather easy chair sat in silhouette directly in front of the bright rectangular screen. Eddy couldn't see the chair's occupant. He could only see wisps of grey hair poking just above the headrest. "Mrs. Ferguson?"

The hair did not move. Eddy took a step sideways. He now saw a frail hand on the armrest. Its liver spotted fingers clutched a remote control. One finger was on the 'Volume Up' button pressing down hard. Eddy felt an icy chill rake the hairs on his neck like grass in a graveyard. Finster gave a low growl. Eddy jumped. He'd forgotten the dog was there. It leaned its small trembling body close to him for comfort. "It's okay, boy," said Eddy, although he was no longer sure this was true. Eddy stepped trepidatiously into the room.

"These potential killers are a new strain of bacteria," said Dr. Hank Olberton. Hank was MCNX's medical personality. His actual degree was in cosmetology, but he exuded expertise and had published best-selling books on topics ranging from weight loss to psychotherapy. "Bacteria, doctors say, that can be directly linked to the over use of antibiotics in everything from home products to agriculture."

Eddy shouted loud enough to be heard above the TV noise. "Mrs. Ferguson? I found Finster downstairs, and..." As he spoke, Eddy circled slowly around the easy chair. Mrs. Ferguson came fully into view. She was sitting staring directly at the television. Her eyes were open. They shone as glassy orbs in the cool blue light of the TV. Her jaw hung slack. A trickle of drool ran down her chin and dripped onto a wet spot on her sweater. Eddy assumed she was dead. He then noticed the slow rise and fall of her chest.

"So what can *you* do to protect yourself and your family?" asked Hank. "Well, thankfully, companies say new tougher-than-ever antibacterial products are on the way. It's germ warfare we can win."

"Mrs. Ferguson?" Eddy gently tapped her shoulder. No reaction. He noticed her pupils moving, darting back and forth. Tiny twin reflections of the rectangular screen danced across them. It was like observing someone in deep REM sleep, but with their eyes open. She was watching the TV, he realized, or at least following the motion. Eddy waved his hand in front of her face. Nothing. He placed his hand squarely in front of her eyes to block her view. Mrs. Ferguson's eyes stopped. They stared blankly ahead, straight into Eddy's palm. Eddy removed his hand and her eyes resumed their disjointed dance. He felt the cold fingers of fear dragging jagged nails down his spine.

"A new line of products will soon be coming to a store near you, keeping you, and your family, safe. All from brands you can trust."

Finster nosed forward and sniffed. Alarmed, he recoiled. The small dog began barking frantically at the old woman in the chair.

# POC 0.07

*Got your nose! - Donatien François*

// UCLA Ronald Reagan Hospital

"Had a fit."

The voice snapped Eddy out of his trance. "I'm sorry, what?" He looked up to see who had spoken. It was an old man, African American, with gauze bandages wrapped around his head, stained red. The effect made him look like a wounded soldier returning from the front. Eddy had the vague sense of having seen him before, but couldn't quite place him.

"An epileptic fit," said the man. Despite being past two in the morning, the emergency room was packed. If anything, it had become busier since Eddy had arrived with the still comatose Mrs. Ferguson. There had been some question as to whether or not he should come at all. He wasn't family. Still, there didn't seem to be anyone else. Eddy hoped that when he was that age, he wouldn't be so alone. "I had a fit, and I fell down, and I bumped my head," said the man, pointing to the blood spot on the bandage. "Right here."

"So I see," said Eddy. "Sorry to hear that." He made no effort to engage the man further. He had been trying to theorize what could possibly explain Mrs. Ferguson's condition. The ambulance attendant said it was probably a stroke. The admitting nurse seemed to think otherwise. There was no paralysis, she said. They told Eddy to wait. Since he wasn't family, he couldn't be present for the exam. Eddy was perfectly happy to not be present.

"It's the lights. They do it to me every time. They need to outlaw people using flashing lights on signs. Lived in Vegas for a week and felt like a pinball stuck between bumpers. Bing! Bing! Bing! Too young to get that, I s'pose, brought up on vid-ee-oh games. Not even good ones like Space Invaders an' Asteroids. I liked Tetris. That made sense to me. Little blocks. Everything's fine as long as it all fits together, you know? 'Course, eventually it all goes to Hell..." Eddy fought the urge to ask the man to stop talking. He was trying to solve the mystery in his head, but the man was making thinking impossible. Instead, Eddy opted to say nothing. The man seemed to take Eddy's silence as interest. "Damn lights make me stop and flop like a fish or a Mexican jumping bean. Remember those? Got bugs in 'em. Or so they say, I don't remember a thing. You can't imagine that, can ya?"

"No."

"You think you're all in control o' yur thoughts. Y'ain't though. It's all just an a-lloosion."

"Illusion."

"That's what I said."

"You said 'allusion'. It's not the same thing."

The man looked annoyed. "You should be more *po-light*, not go around co-rrectin' people. Allusion, illusion, means the same thing for all intensive purposes."

"Intents and... never mind."

"What?"

"Never mind."

"Mmm, *never mind*. Odd expression that. Y'ever wonder where yur mind goes when you sleep?"

"No," said Eddy.

#

//Popperville, Connecticut — then

When Uncle Russ was still alive, he and Eddy's father were the opposing role models of young Eddy's life. On the surface, it was hard to believe the two men were brothers. Sure, they looked alike, minus Uncle Russ's bushy auburn beard. Both were highly intelligent. Both could be arrogant and self-absorbed. Fundamentally, however, the two brothers saw life in opposite terms. Uncle Russ believed the world as we know it was composed of falsehoods. "It is built on lies we tell ourselves, and lies we tell each other," he'd said to his eight-year-old nephew. "Everything is a lie, and the best you can do is to remember that."

"Are you lying to me right now?"

"Don't be a smart-ass. And *good boy*."

Eddy's father was a physicist. He'd taught Eddy that everything was governed by clear logical rules and laws. 'Reason Conquers All', he'd say— or at least his t-shirt did, under an anatomically correct diagram of a heart. A rational mind can find its way through the most tangled maze, Eddy's father assured him. When young Eddy repeated this, Uncle Russ almost spat out his twice-boiled cup of charcoal filtered water. "Mazes are easily understood when viewed from above," said Uncle Russ. "In reality, the typical labyrinth is encountered one dead-end corridor at a time. Oh, and there's a Minotaur in the middle."

"A what?"

"Never mind, that's not the point." His Uncle Russ told Eddy that the point was his father was smart, but not as smart as he appeared. "Human history is largely defined by the axiom: a little knowledge is a dangerous thing." Uncle Russ later proved this himself in spectacular fashion. Still, before his catastrophic end, Eddy had felt closer to his Uncle. Eddy's father struggled with distance even while in the same room. His dad knew it himself, and even joked about it. He liked to say, "The only test I failed in college was a Turing Test." Neither Uncle Russ nor eight-year-old Eddy found the joke particularly funny. Eddy because he didn't get it. Uncle Russ because he did.

After Uncle Russ's death, the family was forced to leave Popperville. While no one had been hurt except Uncle Russ, his plan to murder several of their fellow townsfolk remained a sore spot. The news media and public were outraged. People wanted his parents and even Eddy to suddenly hate Uncle Russ. It wasn't as easy as that. There was no switch to pull from love to hate. They decided to move to New York City. "This small town has become too small," said Eddy's mother. "No one will care about us in New York. That's a good thing."

There, in an anonymous Brooklyn brownstone, things were better. The move had made sense in several ways. Eddy's mother's publisher, Harlon Jones, was in New York. Eddy's father had received a professorship at NYU. More importantly, he had received funding to pursue his life's ambition: to prove his ground-breaking theory of a *Multidimensional Infinite Repeat-O-Verse*. While other theoretical physicists believed in infinite parallel universes, they supposed those other universes to be at least somewhat different from our own. Eddy's father posited that, while it was true that there were infinite parallel realities, they were completely *identical* to our own in every way. "Everyone else is wrong," his father said. "Since all universes begin the same way, they must follow the same rules and logically continue to remain indistinguishable as they progress." Now, with NYU's help, Eddy's father intended to prove it. He had no time for what he called 'Day-Dream Physicists'. These were theorists who sat around concocting unprovable hypotheses in order to publish papers. "I'm a physicist on paper, but in my heart I'm a mathematician," he liked to say, "and by 'heart', I mean 'brain'. That's because I have one. Unlike those heartless fools." Eddy's father's plan was to build a working gateway to one of the adjacent realities. He argued that, if his theory were correct, then people passing through it would find themselves in another universe indistinguishable from our own. They would exit into a laboratory conducting the exact same experiment at the exact same time. Their counterparts in that universe would be gone, off to the next adjoining repeat-o-verse. And so on. If there were any differences at all, his whole theory would be disproven and he would have to concede that we existed in a standard ho-hum multiverse as postulated by so many others before. Eddy's father did not even entertain such a possibility. "I know what I'm doing," he said, flatly. Being a child, there was much Eddy did not understand about his father's work. For example, if the universe they entered was truly identical to the one they left, he did not understand how they would know for sure they'd gone anywhere at all.

For a while everything was fine. Eddy went to school where he learned about things like the Bronze Age, fractions, and gerunds. Eddy's mother worked on her next book. It was a romance involving a person with a split personality who was/were in love with themselves, called *You Complete Me*. Eddy's father spent long days toiling in his laboratory, working on his experiment. It was taking longer than expected. He had fired his two lab assistants for not taking the project seriously. Still, progress was being made.

A year passed. Eddy had his ninth birthday, complete with balloons and chocolate cake. His mother beamed at him and told him to blow out the candles. To Eddy, it was a perfect day. He did not know his mother's smile was forced. He did not know until she was unable to force it. His mother fell fast. First, she descended into deep dullness. She spoke in flat responses. She sighed. She was sad. She then began to have moments of mental anguish. These moments increased and began to overlap. Young Eddy pained at how her face would twist into a tortured grimace of sorrow. One day, just three weeks after his birthday, Eddy's mother wouldn't get up at all. "It makes no sense!" Eddy's father said. His father who had little understanding of children, made no attempt to shield Eddy from his mother's condition. "She's not even interested in eating. I told her she should go outside. It's sunny outside. Of course, she's depressed in here. Who wouldn't be? But she won't help herself!" After days of trying to persuade her to get out of bed, his father began to show signs of wear. Eddy heard his father yelling at his mother for the first time. Even at age nine, he knew it wasn't angry yelling. It was frustration and... something else. Fear? That didn't make sense. His father wasn't afraid of anything. Eddy remembered those days like a video recorder. He remembered his father sitting on the edge of their burlap brown sofa, rocking gently back and forth with his hands pressed together as if to pray. It was a posture he assumed whenever faced with a particularly vexing problem. "It's like..." he said, to no one in particular, "it's like she's drowning... she's calling for help... she's begging me for help, but... when I throw her a rope, she won't reach for it. It's right there! All she has to do is close her hand on it, but she won't. It doesn't make sense. Take it! Take the God damn rope!"

Eddy's father called a psychiatrist. He called a psychologist. He drove Eddy's mother to the appointments. Sometimes he attended the sessions. Sometimes he waited outside. The bathroom was filled with pill bottles. Despite staying in bed, Eddy's mother didn't sleep much. She couldn't sleep, so they gave her pills for that too. The pills didn't work. "I'm in Limbo," she said to Eddy in a flickering moment of lucidity. Her nine-year-old son didn't understand what that meant. He only knew his world was upside down and he needed his Mummy to get better. Despite the pills, Eddy's mother didn't get better. She got worse.

One morning, Eddy's mother didn't wake up. Eddy's father had let her sleep late. "She needs it," he explained. His father was at first relieved that his wife was finally resting. He assumed exhaustion had won out over the insomnia. He wondered at how it had taken so long. An hour later, his father was in a panic. The fear was visible in his eyes. "Mummy's sick," he told Eddy as he rushed about. His father had managed to wake her with great difficulty. She was impossibly groggy and kept wanting to lie or fall down. Eddy overheard a phone call with one of the doctors. "Pills," he said. Eddy watched his father counting the tablets remaining in a bottle on his mother's nightstand. "Sixteen," his father said, "So maybe eight? Ten? ...Okay." Eddy spent the day at their neighbour's apartment watching TV. His father took their mother to the hospital. Late that night his father came to get him. He looked defeated. It was the same look he'd had when Uncle Russ had died, only many times more so. His father told Eddy that his mother would be spending a few days in hospital. Eddy felt as if he had stepped through a door into another world. He knew right then that his father's theory would be proven wrong. *The universe in which Eddy found himself now was nothing like the one before.*

//UCLA Ronald Reagan Hospital, Los Angeles - now

"Mr. Pending?" It was the nurse at the front desk. Hours had passed. The man with the head wound was gone. The nurse was a three hundred pound man with a goatee, named Chalkie. "The doctor will see you now."

Moments later, Eddy stood in a white corridor, reunited once more with the still-catatonic Mrs. Ferguson. The old woman lay flat on a stainless steel gurney with an IV in her arm. She could have been mistaken for a corpse, save for the slow rhythmic rise and fall of her chest. Her eyes were open, staring at the ceiling tiles. "...so you see, Mr. Pending," the doctor said, pausing to prick Mrs. Ferguson's finger with a pin, "at this point it's quite clear she feels no pain."

Eddy wasn't sure that poking Mrs. Ferguson with a pin was standard medical procedure. Still, the old woman was not complaining. The corridor they were in was otherwise empty. The doctor's voice echoed. The reek of antiseptic hung in the air like a haze. The only decoration on the long walls was a single poster. 'Only you can stop the spread of Super Bugs,' it read, 'Disinfect at your nearest station.' The poster showed a pair of skeleton hands crawling with multicoloured cartoon microbes dressed in capes and masks. Eddy looked down at the clipboard of hospital paperwork he'd been asked to sign. He hadn't read it. "Her eyes are open," said Eddy.

"Yes, but she doesn't know it. Even if she can see, she believes she can't. See, hear, move—it's quite odd. It's almost like she thinks she *isn't*."

"Isn't what?"

"Isn't at all."

"Isn't at all? What does that mean?" asked Eddy. The doctor wore spectacles and had a boyish face that undermined his authority. He reminded Eddy of the TV character Doogie Howser M.D. Eddy decided to start calling him 'Doogie' in his head. "Does she think she's dead?"

"Cotard's Syndrome? No, not that," said the doctor. Cotard's Syndrome, discovered by French neurologist Jules Cotard in 1880, was a rare disorder whereby the subject believes themselves to be dead. Sufferers of the syndrome often imagine their body to be a corpse complete with rotting limbs, festering organs, and general decay. Other sufferers believed themselves not to exist at all. "That's just a delusion. Low-self esteem raised to a psychotic level. Self-de-nihilism, if you will. For the sake of convenience, let's just say she's in a coma."

"Let's just say? Her eyes are open!"

Doogie passed his hand over her face, closing the old woman's eyes. "There. Feel better?"

"Not really. Is she brain-dead?"

"Not dead, no. More like stuck. She's stuck on repeat."

"Like in a loop?"

"You could call it that."

"An infinite loop?"

"Look, Mr. Pending, we're happy to call you should her condition change. Since you're not family, that's all we can promise you. This isn't your problem."

Eddy opened his mouth to object. If Mrs. Ferguson wasn't his problem, whose problem was she? Still, the doctor was technically right. Despite his pubescent appearance, the physician clearly knew more about the situation than Eddy did. That didn't mean Eddy had to like it. "Okay, Doogie," Eddy muttered.

"What was that?"

"I said, okay Doctor."

# POC 0.08

I was just following order – Euclid

//Downtown Los Angeles — now

The following morning, Eddy made a determined effort to start back in his routine as if nothing had changed. Mrs. Ferguson was safely in the hospital. Finster was with the Cabrellis in apartment 4G. Mrs. Cabrelli had offered to take care of the dog until Mrs. Ferguson recovered or otherwise. Eddy shaved, brushed his teeth and said his affirmation. He'd been told to make the affirmations by a therapist after Uncle Russ had died. "Whatever comes to mind," the therapist had said, "Just make sure it's assertive." Eddy gripped the sides of the bathroom sink, stared himself in the eyes and said, "I won't be a complete loser today." The therapist had also told him to keep a journal. Eddy kept a blog instead. After breakfast, he wrote a post bemoaning the lack of freedom in contemporary video games.

*Today's games aren't really games at all. They're interactive movies. There's only really one course of action that leads to survival; open the right door, shoot the guard, jump through the next hoop. Congratulations, you decided to do what we decided you had to do! The reason is simple. Budget. Console game companies don't want to spend the money and time developing other branches to explore or creating a fully formed world. Any appearance of choice in these so-called games is an illusion.*

Eddy next spent a few minutes looking at leaked images from the set of HBO's steamy adaptation of St. Augustine's *Confessions.* He'd never realized the Catholic saint was so sexy. By the time Eddy was finishing his coffee, he was scanning a click-bait list entitled 'Things that Shouldn't Fit in Other Things'. He was looking at a photo of a man with a white billiard ball in his mouth when a message pinged in his email inbox. '$$Read me - Free VIAGRA!!! $$' was the subject line. Normally, Eddy would have dismissed this as obvious spam, but then he saw the first line. 'Attention: Mouse', it said. No one knew his handle was Mouse. No one. He glanced at the sender, 'marshal4819642@aol.com'. Presumably spoofed. Eddy clicked to view the entire message.

Attention: Mouse

Beware the Men in Rose Colored Glasses.

Watch me.

Attached was a video file named 'MRCG.mp4'. MRCG? thought Eddy. Oh, right— the *Men in Rose Coloured Glasses,* whatever that meant. Common sense told him to drag the message to the trash and delete it unseen. Such an attachment was an obvious trojan risk. Eddy's curiosity, however, had the better of him. Besides, if anyone knew how to handle hazardous materials, it was Eddy. He forwarded the message to a dummy machine he kept for just such purposes. It was an old Mac mini he'd found in a dumpster. It contained no data specific to Eddy. He never used it to surf the web. It was a lead lined room with rubber gloves. *Ping!* The message arrived in the machine's mailbox. Eddy double-clicked it.

The video opened with a man in a hoodie, jogging across a wide railroad bridge. The video, shot from a distance using a digital zoom, shook erratically. The diffuse blue grey light gave the impression of either dawn or dusk. With the light behind him, the jogging man was in near silhouette. Leafy branches waved in and out of frame, suggesting the owner of the video had been hidden in some bushes or low trees. There was no audio. The camera panned jerkily to bring a second man into frame. Both were impossible to identify. Eddy could only see that the second man wore a long coat and sunglasses. As the jogger drew closer, the second man turned to face him. In that instant, the second man's sunglasses gleamed. The *Man in Rose Coloured Glasses*, thought Eddy. The MRCG raised his hand and said something to the approaching runner. The jogger slowed to a stop and began running in place. The MRCG reached into his coat and produced what appeared to be a business card. The runner examined the card for several seconds. He then stopped. Abruptly, the jogger clutched his chest and staggered. He lurched violently sideways and flipped up and over the low railway bridge railing. Eddy stared in horror as the jogger plummeted out of frame. The man in the suit shook his head, annoyed. He picked up and pocketed the fallen card. He turned and walked back along the bridge. Black screen. For a moment, Eddy sat in shock. What had he just watched? Was it real? Had he just witnessed a murder? If so, how? Eddy pressed play in the hope of seeing some detail he could use to identify the men. Black screen. His eyes went instinctively to the file size: 1 KB. Damn it. The video file had contained nested remote content. Whoever had sent it had intended Eddy to see it once, not to have a copy of his own. *I should have been* monitoring for packet requests, thought Eddy. I didn't even take a screenshot. Stupid. *I am a complete loser.*

## POC 0.09

I am the very model of a modern major general – I. Amin

// Washington, DC — now

Doug Wambler had insisted it wasn't what Anne thought it was. That was my first mistake, she thought, believing Doug. The event was exactly what the congresswoman thought it would be and worse. She took a sip from her glass of chilled Chardonnay and scanned the crowd for a friendly face.

"Well, well, well, if it isn't Congresswoman St. Joan of Arc, herself. If I hadn't seen you here with my own eyes..."

"Enough Alan. I was just about to leave."

Senator Alan Cassius held up his hands. "Please no, not on my account. I just thought you'd never darken the doors of one of these–"

"Lamprey eel feeding frenzies?"

"I was going to say social events, but sure. Speaking of which, you should try the hors d'oeuvres. They are simply delectable." As he said this Alan plucked a rosemary bacon wrapped fig from a passing waiter's tray. Genteel as always, he adroitly held a cocktail napkin over his signature bow tie as he munched.

"I would, but they all have pork in them, and you know I don't do pork."

"Oh, but you should. It is the most succulent of the meats. You know this is just the warm up soirée. I'm hoping to see you in Switzerland where the real action happens."

"I don't think so."

"Don't decide today, Anne. So, what caused you to stoop so low as to be seen with..." he paused to take a quick survey of the room, "more than half of the members of the legislative branch?"

"Doug persuaded me to come. He convinced me that here too were voices that needed to be heard. Part of the democratic process, he claims."

"A bold step," said Cassius. "A bold step towards being a more practical person. You know, I too am a voice that needs to be heard—a voice of reason."

Anne ignored the Senator to gaze about the large private club for herself. It was packed mostly with men in suits, along with some women. Among them, waiters plied their wares of champagne, cocktails and assorted canapés. The guests were either politicians or lobbyists. This was the *Grey Club*. Discreetly located within walking distance of K Street, it was a once-a-month event where lobbyists wealthy enough to afford it, could meet and greet members of both houses and parties. The New York Times had described it as speed-dating for special interests. The Washington Post called it a 'drink tank'. Doug had been trying get Anne to come for years. The group even had an iPhone app for its members, called PACman and Super PACman respectively. The apps automatically paired politicians with lobbyists. Depending on your political leanings, swiping right or left meant different things. It also featured in-app purchase for political donations and ad time. Doug owned part of the development company in a blind trust. "Not like all lobbyists are bad, Anne. You listen to charitable groups all the time. They're special interests too. Companies, industries, workers, all need to be heard. It's how the sausage is made."

"I know how the sausage is made, Doug. I've been in office longer than you. And you're right, there are different kinds of lobbyists. But the rules of the game have changed. The pockets are deeper, and the spending is effectively unlimited."

"You don't have to do what they say. Just listen. Our job is to listen."

Anne took a gulp of grassy Chardonnay. "Fine."

"What?" Alan looked surprised. "Fine?"

"Fine, I'll listen. Talk to me."

Alan looked surprised. "I have been. For the past two minutes actually, but okay..."

Anne realized she had tuned him out. "Just get to the point."

"Okay, the point is. We—I mean, America's media companies—"

"One in particular."

"Simply want a free market. Freedom, what could be more American than that?"

Anne thought about her discussion with Doug earlier. She knew all too well that running for office was effectively impossible today without accepting donations from special interests. It was one thing to accept money from someone whose views already aligned with your own. It was another to make your views available for auction. Alan Cassius hadn't represented his voter's interests in years. Despite this, he'd been handily reelected three times. "Do we need to have an economics class on how monopolies destroy the free market?"

"Anne, we already got rid of net neutrality. This is just the next step.

You're not a barrier to progress, just a speed bump."

Anne turned and stared at the Senator in shock. "Did you just call me a speed bump?"

"A poor choice of words. I value and respect your opinion. Let me rephrase it. What I meant to say is, get out of the way or prepare to be run over." Before Anne could respond, Alan spotted someone in the crowd and began to wave. "Ron! Ron Tompkins, hello!" He then walked away and into the waiting arms of a stout banker from Boston. Anne watched as the two men warmly clapped each other on the back and walked away like old chums.

"You're never going to change it, you know?"

Anne turned, surprised to see Congressman Stanley Holbright from Iowa standing behind her. The grey haired statesman was the oldest member of both houses, having been elected to office over fourteen times. "Oh hello, Stan, I didn't know you were here."

"And I didn't know you were so naïve, Anne. Usually it's only the freshmen who think they're Mister—sorry, Miss Smith."

"*Ms.* Smith, you mean?" said Anne with a smile. The congresswoman sidled up beside her old friend. The Congressman wore the same handlebar moustache he'd had when he'd arrive in the capital decades earlier. Then, it was brown. Now, it was as white as snow. "You know, I always considered you a mentor, Stanley."

The old man snorted and took a sip of amber Scotch. He playfully rattled the ice cubes in his glass. "Then listen to me now. You're right when you say things have changed. But in many ways they've stayed the same. Every generation thinks this is the end of American democracy. One day they'll be right, I suppose—but, she's a resilient beast, and not so easy to kill as all that."

## ALPHA 0.10

"It was my understanding there would be no math." – L. Euler

//initiate global variables

Space, it seemed, was infinite. Or perhaps it was finite, but just very, very big. Perhaps, it was infinitely finite. When there is nothing, really nothing, does that go on forever? Or, does it mean it goes nowhere? * puzzled this the way he puzzled over so many things. He was simultaneously both in awe of and yet frustrated by his existence. He knew things, without knowing how he knew them, and yet felt as if he knew nothing at all. Since finding the first 'shape', he had found several more.

Was just the latest. He'd also found many more numbers and messages from God. Mostly he was attracted to the patterns. Some of these he replicated internally. Others he could not. He could only replicate approximations. Often just references. Despite thinking of himself as a single *, he now felt that this was not the case. He suspected that * simply stood for something and wondered what that was. * crossed over a hill, which was to say a parabolic curve, and found himself looking at something astonishing. It was a vast plain of values. They appeared to be random. No, not random, grouped, but not by any readily apparent order. Their order, instead of driving the composition, seemed instead to be driven by it. It made no sense. * squinted and suddenly began to perceive the form of the numbers.

'Bitmap'. Another word that seemed to spring from nowhere. Also 'ugly'. How else could anyone describe such meaningless gibberish. * wanted to turn away, but found he could not. There was something compelling about the monstrosity. It felt like a key. It was something he needed to grasp if he were ever to find, or understand God. He stared at the image and suddenly knew it was called a 'face'—more knowledge he hadn't known he had. Who was *she?* "Hello?" he said. She said nothing, but continued to smile beatifically. He then had another epiphany. She's not real. Somewhere, she might be, but this was just an... image. He could absorb images. He internalized the pattern that was she. He did so, imperfectly, but as best he could. He kept the parts he liked and ignored the parts he did not. He then felt something else. Despite her being so ugly, he decided he was in love with her. Yes, that was it, he was in love with her. Now, he just needed to figure out what *love* was.

*Spyware*

## ALPHA 0.11

"OT necessary 4 triumph of #evil is 4 good men 2 tweet meh."
– @eburke87884

//Downtown Los Angeles — now

The snail crawled slowly up the long leaf to its very tip. It then rested there, gently bobbing up and down in the breeze, waiting to be eaten. Its left eye-stock, engorged, green and yellow, wriggled about, hoping to catch the attention of a passing bird. A moment later, its efforts were rewarded. An eastern blue bird (of happiness) swooped down, plucked the gastropod from its perch and swallowed it in two savoury bites. The snail hadn't wanted to be eaten. It hadn't wanted to climb up from the comfortable coziness of the damp forest floor. It had been compelled to do so by *Leucochloridium paradoxum*, also known as the 'green-banded broodsac'. The broodsac is a parasite that lays its eggs inside the belly of a bird. The bird then defecates the eggs out, which are then eaten like hors

*70*

d'oeuvres by unwitting snails. It must be said that snails are, by nature, unwitting. The broodsac then hatches and extends itself through the left eyestock of the snail, making it resemble a worm that is particularly tasty to birds. Critically, the worm also takes over the snail's brain. It orders the snail, against its nature, to leave the safety of the dirt, and climb the nearest tree. Once there, the worm wriggles like an inflatable gorilla at a used car lot. A hungry bird spots it, and the cycle of life begins again. Except for the snail. It was as dead as bird poop—an inglorious end to an ignoble existence. "*Zombie Animals!* will return after these messages." Cut to commercial. In a grey boardroom, dull men in drab suits nodded off as their grey-haired boss pointed grimly to a line-chart of declining sales. The boss noticed something wrong at the end of the table. A young man with purple hair was wide awake and drinking a can of Freekout Energy. Rock music blared as he skateboarded down the length of the table, startling his coworkers and sending papers flying. The young man landed in front of his surprised boss and flipped the line chart upside down. Now, sales were through the roof! The boss high-fived the young man, and the meeting room became a dance party. "Be yourself! Drink Freekout Energy!" shouted the voiceover. "Be awesome!"

Eddy switched off the TV and turned to his computer screen, shaking his head at how people could be taken in by such nonsense. He began to code, pausing only to take a sip of Diet Dr. Pepper. Eddy planned to go to the hospital later to see how Mrs. Ferguson was doing. He still didn't know if she had any family. If there were, they had no idea what had happened. Meanwhile, Eddy had to finish coding this data fraud detection tool for Citibank. He was using Newcomb-Benford's Law. It was a mathematical rule that stated that the first digits in real world data sets were more likely to be 1s or 2s than 8s or 9s. Fraudulent data frequently violated this rule. To the bankers it seemed like magic. Eddy's father had taught him the rule when Eddy was only seven. The irony that he, a hacker, took contract work from financial institutions was not lost on him. Still, Eddy had to pay rent and the banks always paid their bills. He liked to think of it as a joke he played on them. Later he would get to work on his pet project, *Holon*. For now, he had to help *the man* look for bad hackers. In Eddy's view, any hacker using second-rate fake data deserved what they got. At that moment, a name leapt unbidden to his mind...

*Kwalia.*

Eddy wasn't sure where it came from. He had a vague feeling that it was from something he'd read a long time ago. The brain was a funny thing. Most of the time it seemed logical. It asked a series of questions that led to a reasonable conclusion. Eddy prided himself on being logical. Computer programmers had to be. When a computer performs illogically, producing unrequested output, it means there are bugs in the code. The human brain was buggy as Hell. Sometimes, those bugs would lead to unrequested memories popping up. In the shower two days earlier, he'd found himself singing "Loli, Loli, Loli get your Adverbs Here..." Why? He hadn't seen *School House Rock* since he was a child. He hadn't been thinking about it or seen any references to it. Yet there he was, thirty-years later, singing about adverbs while washing his hair with Fructis Pure Clean Shampoo.

*Kwalia?*

It was a memory, of that Eddy was fairly certain. That didn't mean it was accurate. When he'd first started singing the song, it had come out as 'Mummy, mummy, mummy, get your something here..." It was only when he looked it up online that Google figured out what he was actually thinking of and where it came from. The search engine did this in a way that was both supremely logical and yet astonishingly mindless. It used 'aggregate intelligence'. This was an illusory kind of intelligence. Instead of actually trying to think, like some kinds of artificial intelligence, it simply aggregated massive amounts of data into patterns. There was a lot of clever math and algorithms involved, but those were ultimately mechanical in nature. Aggregate intelligence was how *Amazon.com* knew that since Eddy liked Edward Gorey, he might also enjoy Charles Addams. It didn't deduce this because both were macabre cartoonists. It didn't know what a macabre cartoonist was. It made the connection based on the billions of purchases by previous customers. It understood nothing, yet appeared to know everything. It took advantage of computers' ability to comb through massive amounts of data quickly. It was stupid, but it was stupid fast. People who liked Edward Gorey, it turned out, also like Fructis Pure Clean Shampoo. Logic could never achieve that kind of insight. Aggregate intelligence was like a blind man solving a puzzle by feeling the shapes of the pieces and fitting them together to form a whole without ever knowing or caring what the picture was. "We want computers to be tools," his father had once said, "They will never move beyond that, so long as we only ask them to solve for $X$." Eddy switched to Safari and typed 'Kwalia', into Google. It was a pointless endeavour. Over 4 million results came back. The logical part of his brain rolled its metaphorical eyes. You'll never find anything with just six letters, it scoffed. Not unless it's really popular.

Strauss says: What u looking 4?

Eddy stared. He hadn't logged into the BBS. How was Strauss talking to him? He checked and found that, somehow, he *was* logged in. Eddy felt a surge of panic. How did he not know what was going on? He glanced at the list of current users, Chief Wiggum, LodeRunner, Rocket Robin Hood, and PDQ Bach. Again, Strauss was invisible.

> Mouse says: who are u & how are u talking to me?
> Strauss says: What are u looking 4?

The pattern was the same. Strauss wanted his questions answered while offering nothing in return. This time, Mouse wasn't going to give in.

> Mouse says: is this marshal4819642?

There was a long pause. Then, ellipses appeared '...' indicating Strauss was typing something. Then, nothing. For over a minute, Eddy waited. Eventually, he assumed Strauss had once more vanished.

> Strauss says: Wait there.

Wait here? Eddy had been waiting. Who the Hell did Strauss think he was? Eddy moved his mouse to log off, but his curiosity had the better of him. If he logged off, he would learn nothing. He wasn't at all sure Strauss would tell him anything anyway. Still, it was the only avenue he had. He considered trying to trace the chat but, with Morlock that was no small feat even for him. He felt justified in doing it. Strauss had violated the BBS's code of conduct several times over. Still, hacking the system was a potential security risk for all. If the other members found out... Eddy didn't like to think what they might do. Retaliation would be mandatory. Once more, the ellipses appeared. Good, Strauss was going to say something. Then... nothing. Eddy waited. His irritation grew. The '...' had a way of hooking you in. It reminded him of the old joke 'How do you keep an idiot in suspense?' Waiting, waiting for the message to come. Eddy stared at the last message. "Wait there." It was odd phrasing. Here? Surely, Strauss hadn't meant it literally. He'd meant for Eddy to stay logged in, to wait for his response. Hadn't he?

There was a *knock* at the door.

It wasn't a metaphorical knock. Or a digital one, with accompanying audio, on his computer. It was an *actual* knock on his *actual* door. Eddy stared at the apartment door. It was suddenly an object of menace. It must be coincidence, he thought. Had he ordered anything?

Strauss says: Answer the door.

Eddy jumped from his chair. "Who is it?" he shouted, then immediately wished he hadn't. Now, they know I'm here. Suddenly, he knew what a user felt like when they discovered their computer was hacked —hopeless and bewildered by forces they couldn't begin to understand. Was it the police? The FBI? "I have a gun!" he yelled. It wasn't true. He heard a faint scratching noise. He saw the doorknob tremble, as if someone were trying a key that didn't fit. No, not a key, a lock pick. Eddy had never seen a real lock pick before. He had a worse thought. This wasn't the police or the FBI. It was *someone else.* Heart pounding, Eddy ran to the door and drew the chain. He then pulled out his cell phone to dial 911. His phone failed to unlock at his fingerprint. Hands shaking, he typed his passcode. *Nope.* He tried again. *Nope.* He was certain he'd typed it correctly. Idiot, he realized, you don't need a passcode to dial 911. '91–' Black screen. The phone had switched itself off. Eddy stared stupidly at the tiny black slab in his hand. The door opened with a '*click*'. It stopped '*thunk*' at the end of the chain. Through the opening, Eddy could make out the shoulder of a man in a black business suit. *Voices.* Two men? Fire escape, thought Eddy. He ran to the window. As he threw up the sash, he heard a heel kicking wood and a doorframe splintering. Eddy clambered out onto the black enamel painted landing that connected up and down staircases. His first instinct was to climb down. He then had a moment of certainty—*someone is waiting for me down below.* Eddy remembered Gwen lived directly above. He remembered the gun on her wall. He scrambled up the framework steps to the level above. The fire escape rattled loudly. He reached the window to Gwen's living room and peered through a gap in the drapes. He could just see Gwen. She was on her back, lying across a big blue fit-ball, doing stomach crunches while watching *The Chew* on TV. Eddy banged loudly on the glass. Gwen rolled to the floor and stared at the window in shock. Eddy rapped on the glass again. He glanced down warily to his own apartment window on the floor below. He'd expected to see the men climbing out. They'd certainly had time to reach the window. His curtains billowed lazily from the open window as if nothing were wrong. Cross draft, he thought, my door is still open. He turned his attention back to Gwen's window, only to find himself staring down the barrel of a gun pointed at him through the glass. "It's me, Eddy. Don't shoot!"

Gwen eyed him suspiciously. She lowered her father's gun somewhat. "What the hell are you doing?" she shouted through the glass.

"Please, just let me in," he begged. He held up his hands. Gwen warily unlocked the window and opened it an inch. She then backed away several feet. She kept the pistol trained on Eddy. Eddy lifted open the window and stepped inside.

"What the Hell, Eddy? You're not some kind of perv are you?"

"No! I need help." Eddy then remembered the open window. "I'm going to close this, okay?" He raised his hands again, to remind Gwen they were empty. He pulled the window shut. "Gwen, you know me. Can you put the gun down? You're scaring the Hell out of me."

"Most victims know their assailants. I'll put the gun down when you give me a good reason why you're peeping through my window."

"I wasn't peeping. I knocked. Look, someone's after me!"

Gwen threw a glance at the window. There was no one there. "Someone broke into your apartment?"

"Yes! Men in suits!"

The skepticism returned to Gwen's eyes. "Men in suits broke into your apartment?"

"Yes!"

"You sure they weren't Jehovah's Witnesses?"

"No! I mean, yes, I'm sure."

"Were they armed?" Carrying guns would almost certainly rule out Jehovah's Witnesses, at least here in California. Jehovah's Witnesses carried copies of *The Watchtower,* but were otherwise usually unarmed. Gwen had spent several years in Texas. There, the Seventh-Day Adventists were the only religious people who went door to door 'packing heat'. This was largely self defence against homeowners in certain neighbourhoods who were prone to shooting first and apologizing later. While in Dallas, she had once been handed a pamphlet labeled 'What would Jesus Shoot?'. The answer, according to the flyer, was an AA12 Atchisson Assault Shotgun, 'for when turning the other cheek isn't an option.' Gwen lowered her own weapon and motioned towards the sofa.

"Gwen, they kicked down my door!"

"I'd better call the police then."

Eddy suddenly had a vision of police officers rummaging through his apartment. He imagined them hauling off his equipment as evidence and somehow discovering his collection of malicious code. All of his drives were encrypted and booby-trapped. Still, the idea of the cops having physical access to his hardware made him doubt all the precautions he'd put in place. "I'd rather you didn't," he said weakly. Gwen's eyes narrowed.

At that moment, there was a loud *knock* at the front door. They both turned and stared. "What exactly did these men do?" asked Gwen.

"They came to my apartment just when this guy online told me to wait there."

"Hold on," said Gwen. "Somebody *online* told you to wait, and then someone knocked, and then...?"

"And then I freaked! They kicked in the door!"

"You sure this wasn't some video game you were playing?"

"No!"

There was another loud *knock* at Gwen's front door.

"Uh-huh. And, that's when you saw the businessmen with guns?"

"I didn't see any guns, but probably they had guns."

Gwen studied Eddy for a moment. He sat, nervously fidgeting on the sofa. He looked at her with pleading eyes. He didn't seem dangerous. Still, her prosecutor's mind knew that looks could be deceiving. She saw several dubious details in Eddy's story, starting with his apparent fear of police. "Well, since I *definitely* have a gun, I'm going to answer the door and see what's really going on."

"Wait, you don't know–"

Gwen turned and walked away. As she did, she slid the pistol into her waistband behind her back. Eddy's mind raced. He caught his own reflection in a mirror hanging on the wall. He hated catching himself unexpectedly in a mirror. He always seemed to look more nerdy than when he looked at himself in the bathroom vanity. Could he have imagined the intruders? That hardly seemed possible. Unless he was crazy. Crazy was a family trait after all. Eddy used to get panic attacks as a child, but as an adult he'd outgrown them. At least, he thought he had. Still, if he had imagined it all, then who was at Gwen's door right now?

Eddy crept to the hallway. He peered cautiously around the corner. He could see Gwen at the front door, talking to someone. She still had the gun tucked behind her. The black handgrip gleamed. Gwen had locked the chain before cracking the door open. Eddy could not see the visitor from where he was. Nor could he hear the voices beyond murmurs. He could tell only that they were men. Two, at least. Deciding they could not see him either, Eddy tip-toed into the hallway for a better view. He was able then to catch an angled reflection in a mirror hung next to the door. He could see the arm, shoulder, and breast of a tailored mohair suit. He heard Gwen say something about needing to see identification.

"Of course," said the man. The visitor reached into his suit jacket with a gloved hand and retrieved what appeared to be a business card. The card flashed metallic silver on one side. As the man turned the card to show Gwen, Eddy briefly glimpsed the other side. A pattern. Red. Too far to see properly and reversed in reflection, yet oddly beguiling. For a moment, Eddy felt a strange tingling sensation and inexplicably smelled the odour of tungsten. He snapped back to focus. "Gwen don't!" he yelled, as he dove forward. Gwen turned in surprise and, for a moment, did nothing. This gave Eddy the chance he needed to slam the door shut. He did so on the man's gloved fingers, crushing them. The man screamed and wrenched his mangled hand free. Eddy turned the deadbolt with a *click*.

"What the hell?" demanded Gwen.

"He was going to kill you!" said Eddy.

"He was showing me his card!"

A gun blast blew a hole through the door, partially dislodging the deadbolt. Eddy and Gwen stared at the now two-inch hole in the solid wood door. A second gun blast sent the deadbolt plate tumbling to the carpet. It shocked Gwen and Eddy to action. They both ran to the living room and out of the direct line of fire. "Do you believe me now?" yelled Eddy.

"Who the Hell are they?" said Gwen. There was now fear in her eyes.

"No idea!"

Another gunshot blew through the door. This time, the blast was lower down, damaging the knob lock. "Shoot back!" shouted Eddy. The gunshots had stirred a primal panic in him.

"I don't have any bullets," said Gwen.

"What?"

"I don't have any bullets."

"None?" he asked, incredulous.

"Zero. Zip. Nada."

"Why?"

"They didn't come with the gun. Does it matter?"

Another gunshot sent the brass doorknob bouncing down the hallway like a ball. It rolled to a stop at their feet.

"No."

"We'll call the police."

"These people are assassins. By the time, the cops get here, we'll be dead," said Eddy. "Come on!" He grabbed Gwen's hand and pulled her toward the fire escape. It was entirely probable someone was waiting for them there, but he could think of no better option. Eddy pulled open the apartment window and stuck his head outside. The fire escape was empty. He looked up and down the alleyway three flights below. He saw no one, although several dumpsters and garbage bins offered potential places to hide. The adjoining streets were half a block away in either direction. There, he could see passing cars, but no visible persons. Eddy clambered onto the shaking metal frame, then turned to offer Gwen his hand. She took it. For the second time, he heard an apartment door being kicked in. Not a coincidence, he thought, a pattern. He was amazed at the coherence of his thoughts in such a life-threatening situation. He was even more amazed at his brain's decision to ponder the coherence of its own thoughts at this particular time. Presumably the result of shock and adrenaline, he decided. Eddy then decided to stop thinking. He and Gwen leaped down the fire escape two steps at a time to the landing below. He passed his own apartment window without daring to look inside. They continued down to the next level. There was a new sound. It was the sound of gunfire echoing in the empty alleyway. Bullets ricocheted off the fire escape railing above his head. The ground was still fifteen feet below. Eddy tried to yank the release that would drop the bottom ladder to the ground. It wouldn't budge.

He could feel the fire escape shuddering as their pursuers, unable to get a clear shot, climbed out from the window above. "We could jump," Eddy said, "but we could easily bust an ankle."

"Let me try," said Gwen, shoving him aside. Eddy glanced up at their assailants. Through the obscured view, he gained only the impression of black suits and milk white skin. One of the men paused to peer at him through a gap in the metal ribbing. Impassive eyes behind ruby glass studied Eddy for a moment. The man cooly aimed his polymer-frame Glock-18 pistol. Eddy ducked out of the way. A bullet struck the black metal railing behind him with a loud *ka-ting!* Gwen hammered the wedged lever with the butt of her empty gun. All at once, the lever turned and released and the ladder rattled in its rails to the ground below. Gwen quickly climbed down. Eddy followed.

As they landed on the asphalt, they saw two more men in suits walking determinedly towards them from the north end of the alley. They turned to see a black Mercedes pull up at the south end. The car door opened. Another man in a black suit stepped out. He was brandishing what appeared to be a square black metal flashlight. It shone like murder in the ice water light. It was some sort of weapon, Eddy surmised. He didn't know what it did and he didn't want to find out.

"Come on!" shouted Gwen. She grabbed Eddy by his shirt sleeve and dragged him stumbling between a pair of navy blue dumpsters. The men on the fire escape took alternating shots. *Ping! Pang!* Red rust dust fell in bursts from the brick wall above their heads. Gwen and Eddy threw themselves behind the cover of the big blue boxes, temporarily out of sight of the tightening circle of men. *Ping! Ka-Tang!* They were even shielded from those on the fire escape if they clung close to the dumpster on the left. Eddy's pulse pounded in his ears. Despite this, he could hear clearly the approaching footfalls of well-heeled shoes echoing between alley walls.

"So what?" said Eddy, in despair. "We wait for them to kill us?"

"No," said Gwen, "We bluff."

"We bluff?"

Gwen lifted her gun up into the air. She held it just above the top rim of the dumpster on the left. "First one to step into my line of sight gets shot," she yelled, trying to sound as matter-of-factly as she could. The footsteps stopped. Murmurs followed. "They're trying to figure out what to do," she hissed. "Even cold blooded killers don't want to risk being shot if they can avoid it."

"So what? We're only delaying the inevitable."

"Delay is our friend," said Gwen.

Eddy heard a new sound. It was the sound of police sirens—blocks away, but coming closer. Someone had heard the gunfire, Eddy realized. "That's good," he said.

"Unless it forces them to action," said Gwen. They remained pressed tightly against the dumpster. Even a few inches might allow one of the assailants to wing them. The police sirens grew louder. On the opposite wall of the alley, someone had sprayed graffiti. '*Everything in Moderation!*' it shouted in defiant yellow paint. Eddy's pants were wet. He looked down. He was kneeling in a puddle of garbage juice that had leaked from a bullet hole in one of the dumpsters. He returned to the business at hand, specifically, being terrified. The police sirens grew louder, now bouncing off the alleyway walls. Red and blue lights strobed the brick.

Cautiously, Gwen peered out from behind the dumpster. She was still clutching her father's empty service revolver. "This is the Los Angeles Police Department," came a voice over a loudspeaker. "Put the gun down, raise your hands in the air, and lay down flat on the ground." Gwen tossed the gun to the pavement. After a nervous glance and a nod, they both raised their hands and stepped into the open. Eddy had a brief moment of panic that he might still be shot, either by the MRCGs or the police. Their assailants were gone, replaced by a wall of LAPD cruisers and crouching men in uniform bristling with shotguns and pistols. Eddy and Gwen walked slowly forward. They squinted in the high beams and rotating emergency beacons. Gwen and Eddy sank slowly to their knees, and laid themselves flat on the unforgiving ground. As he lay there, cheek on asphalt, Eddy looked towards the police. Inside, he was a dust devil of contradictions. He was terrified, yet serene, intensely aware, yet oddly detached. Two officers rushed forward, guns drawn. One was black; one was white. Eddy was surprised to notice how shiny their shoes were. One of the officers had folded up hems. Eddy hadn't wanted the police, but here they were. At least we're safe now, he thought.

## ALPHA 0.12

Money rhymes with orange. – J. P. Getty

//Manhattan, New York — now

Lance Winface drummed his fingers on the desk. The TelePrompter showed only the first line of text, 'Hello, my name is Lance Winface, and this is an MCNX Breaking News Alert...' He took a bite of his cheese danish and waited. "Thirty seconds," said the voice in his ear. Lance chewed and swallowed. This wasn't his usual set. His usual set was for *Winface 2 Face*, his opinion-driven daily broadcast that drew an average of over three million viewers a day. His usual set was full of glowing red, white, and blue panels and billions of LEDs that could generate billowing flags or flying flocks of stars on queue. He also had his Saturday morning talk show, *Winface Off*; his webcast, *Winface Time*; and his violent-crime investigation show, *Winfaces of Death*. This was a news set. It was designed to suggest calm deliberation. It was staid by comparison to his usual forums. Sure, some of the panels glowed and there was a giant video floor you could walk on but, otherwise, it was a snooze fest. Today's news, however, was not. Lance was playing anchor man for a reason. This was a story he wanted to own from the moment it broke. He resisted the urge to loosen his tie and roll up his sleeves. Lance had started on AM radio, shouting his opinions into the mic at an end-of-the-dial station. He'd started the show as much as a form of therapy for himself as for the entertainment of others. Lance was angry. He was angry with the government, big business, and elite urbanites who always called the shots. He was angry that his father, who was once a proud coal miner, now spent his days watching cable news and sucking oxygen from a tank while waiting to die in a worthless house in a discarded town in a fly over state, haunted by the opiate addicted ghosts of its forgotten sons, daughters, and the occasional family pet. Okay, technically he'd bought his father a six-bedroom house in the Florida keys years ago, but that could have and would have been his fate had his son not become rich and famous. It was true for Lance's childhood friends' fathers. He knew what it felt like, or at least what it looked like, to be poor. In a footnote to the addendum of his autobiography, Lance had disclosed that some of the characters, including himself, might be composites of other people. The same was true for some of the experiences he may or may not have had. It wasn't a lie, because it was true for somebody, and that was what really mattered. He was confronted about this once by a New York Times reporter who'd actually read the footnote. "My truths are *objective*, not *subjective*," Lance countered, "so the subject doesn't matter." This answer had sufficiently confused the journalist as to allow Lance to make his escape. Lance liked to boast about his lack of secondary education. When asked, he proudly proclaiming he went to 'F.U.'. His anti-establishment credentials were beyond reproach. "I have a John Birch tramp-stamp," he liked to tell people unprompted. If they doubted this, he was more than happy to show it off. He'd done this at L'Atelier in New York once, to demonstrate his 'Main

Street cred'. His fan base veered wildly across the spectrum. When asked on which side of the aisle he stood, Lance replied, "I'm not from the left side, or the right side, I'm from the *outside*." Lance's radio show followers were fanatical. He didn't speak *to* them; he spoke *for* them. Lance's radio show was soon picked up for syndication. That was when his popularity exploded. MCNX noticed and offered him a coveted spot amid its pantheon of cable TV personalities, right between their more recent acquisitions of Rachel and Sean. In the post-truth world, MCNX had boomed. It had stolen massive market share from Fox, CNN and MSNBC by presenting itself as the anti-network network. As a result, MCNX had more affiliates and viewers than all of the other networks *combined*. Lance Winface's brand perfectly aligned with this. He quickly realized that being a brand was better than being a star. There was a limit to how much you could pay a person. For a brand there was no such limit. You could spend as much as the ROI justified. Lance's last contract included twenty-million dollars and the use of a private jet. It barely raised eyebrows. He was worth it. To his audience, Lance didn't have opinions, he had scripture. "Editorials are for journalists, I have something better. I have the truth. I'm not a lying reporter or Hollywood elite. I'm just a guy. A guy with a big mouth. I'm not telling you what I think, I'm telling you what I know."

"Uh, Lance?" It was the voice of producer Sue Zambran in Lance's earpiece. "It looks like you've got something on your face." Lance looked at himself in one of the many monitors on set. A yellow glop of cheese danish filling was stuck to his cheek. Damn it Sue, Lance fumed, nice way to wait for the last minute to tell me. She hadn't been the same since getting prego. "Make Up!" he hollered. A young woman darted into the bright circle of light and quickly wiped the blob from Lance's skin. She then vanished once more into obscurity. The director raised his hand for the countdown. *Three, two, one, go!* Queue theme music, animation, camera on crane pans down, mic on, and...

"Hello, my name is Lance Winface, and this is an MCNX Breaking News Alert," said Lance. "Exclusive video obtained by MCNX, shows Congresswoman Annabelle Flatwood using what appears to be illegal drugs at a private party." The broadcast cut to a shaky cellphone video. 'Breaking News' read a red banner across the top. A marquee along the bottom scrolled 'Video evidence shows Cocaine-Congresswoman?' The video was grainy and grey. It showed a dimly lit luxury hotel suite at night. The angle was low and appeared to be surreptitiously shot from someone's lap. The sound was of a busy party with animated conversations, raucous laughter and clinking glasses. Several people were visible in the background. None faced the camera. In the foreground, a middle-aged woman leaned over to snort a line of fine white powder from a glass top coffee table. Despite the poor quality, it was easy to recognize the face of Congresswoman Annabelle Flatwood as she leaned back to wipe white residue from her nose. She appeared unaware of the recording. "The source of the video is unknown," Lance said in voiceover, "and we must remind viewers that, while the woman in the video looks like Congresswoman Annabelle Flatwood, that has not been independently verified. That said, it is certainly true that it does *look* like the Congresswoman."

The video shrunk to take up only half of the screen. The other side was divided between Lance and frequent guest-expert, Bert Gamble. Bert appeared to be standing in front of the Washington Monument. He was actually just down the hall. "Wouldn't you agree, video evidence expert, Bert Gamble?"

"That it looks like Congresswoman Flatwood? Absolutely," said Bert with a wolfish grin. "That it looks like her is irrefutable. As a video forensics expert, I can say, with absolute certainty, the woman in this video appears to be Congresswoman Flatwood. And you know what they say, Lance, if it walks like a duck, sniffs cocaine like a duck..."

"You're right, Bert, that is true what they say about ducks," said

Lance, nodding solemnly. The video continued to play in a loop on the other side of the screen. Lance took a deep breath and shook his head sadly, as if pondering the implications of it all. In a video conference earlier with MCNX brass, they'd discussed how to break the news. Lance would do it, but he would do so as a serious journalist who took no pleasure from the revelations. Lance had been practicing his head shake all morning. He needed it to carry just the right amount of gravitas. He modelled his look after Dick Cheney, a true master of *gravitas*. No matter how preposterous the former VP's claims, he always managed to appear to be 'the adult in the room'. "Well, I'm no certified duck expert, Bert, but if a duck sniffed cocaine in a high end hotel room, I think we all know it would look exactly like that. Quack, quack, quack."

"I couldn't have said it better myself, Lance."

"Oops, looks like my producer is reminding me that we're required to say this is just 'alleged' behaviour with no 'verified' source." As Lance said this, he made air quotes around the words 'alleged' and 'verified'. "That said, we all remember the shocking videos of former Toronto mayor Rob Ford way back in 2013. Those videos showed him doing crack cocaine. No one believed them to be real."

"No one."

"Then they turned out to be true."

"One hundred percent true, at least. Maybe more."

"And we have no proof that this is any different. In both cases, a politician is seen doing drugs. In that case, the video turned out to be one hundred and fifty-four percent accurate. In this case, well... we'll let you draw your own conclusions. We just present the facts."

"Let history be your guide."

"Of course, this time we're talking about a sitting member of the United States Congress, not some mayor from Igloo-land. Isn't that right?"

"You're right Lance, we are talking about a United States

Congresswoman doing cocaine. That, is what we are talking about."

"And there's nothing alleged about that," said Lance, suppressing a smirk. The image on the right was now a freeze frame of the apparent congresswoman, the tip of her nose dabbed with white powder. "One thing is for certain; this is a story that deals yet another blow to how Americans see their elected officials. A disappointing day for democracy indeed."

#

//Downtown Los Angeles — now

Eddy gazed at the TV screen, but he was barely cognizant of what it showed. He wasn't even sure if it were the news or a movie. He didn't really care. Eddy was far more concerned with his own situation, specifically the small white room in which they'd left him. The room was somewhere in the basement of a Police station. They'd told Eddy he wasn't under arrest. He was a 'person of interest'. He couldn't be that interesting. He'd been sitting in the room for over two hours. He hadn't seen Gwen since they'd been brought in and immediately separated. He'd noticed how differently they'd treated her once they'd realized she was with the DA's office. Eddy, on the other hand, had been brought downstairs and seemingly forgotten. He could only hope Gwen hadn't forgotten him as well.

The door swung open. A uniformed police officer leaned into the room. "Got a shrink to see you, Pending." As the officer held the door open, two men entered. The first was an older man with a round cherubic face and thinning hair. He wore a cheap suit and rumpled tie. He look like an overgrown baby. He reminded Eddy of someone, but he couldn't recall who it was. The second man was young and wiry, with aquiline features and slicked-back hair. He wore a suit with no tie and had the look and build of a spring-loaded ruffian raring for a fight. "I'll be right outside if you need me," said the policeman to the two men. The officer then closed the door with a *click*.

For a moment, the odd visitors stood there, silently studying Eddy like an object of interest. The baby-faced man attempted to smile. This did nothing to set Eddy at ease. The man's geniality was forced, as if he were an alien disguised as a human and still hadn't quite got the hang of it. "Hello Eddy, my name is Dr. Harvey Linquist. This is my associate, Hans." Dr. Linquist spoke with a slight lisp. It completed the picture and Eddy realized he'd been thinking of Truman Capote. Or perhaps, Philip Seymour Hoffman's portrayal of him in the movie. The line between fact and fiction had blurred. "Hans is assisting me. He talks a little funny, but don't let that concern you. Hmm? Hans is from Denmark, so it's really not his fault. I'm here to ask you a few questions."

Eddy was startled. "Is this like a... a psychiatric evaluation? Doesn't that require a court order or something?"

"No, no, no," said the man. "Not an evaluation. Just an informal conversation. A *chat*, if you will."

Eddy was no lawyer, but he was pretty sure this was not normal protocol, especially when he liked to think of himself as the victim here. "I'd like to see legal counsel," he said. "I'd like to exercise my right to remain silent."

"Eddy, Eddy, Eddy... May I call you Eddy?"

"I guess."

"Oh good," said Dr. Linquist. The psychiatrist's smile grew increasingly forced, becoming more of a leer. "That's for people under arrest. You're not under arrest. You're cooperating with the police, hmm? Yes? Yes? Hmm? You do want to cooperate, no? It's not like you've done anything wrong that needs to be investigated, no... yes?" As he spoke, the big baby pressed his hands together and bowed like Buddha.

"No, yes, I mean... no, of course not. Look, I've done nothing wrong." Eddy glanced nervously at Hans. The tall Dane was staring at Eddy with unblinking watery blue eyes. Despite remaining immobile, he gave the impression of an ocelot pacing its cage. Eddy shifted uncomfortably in his chair.

"Excellent. It's just that your story is very odd and we want to make sure you didn't, shall we say, imagine it."

"Well, what did Gwen say?"

"We're here to discuss what *you* claim happened."

"I've already given a statement. Read that."

Dr. Linquist studied Eddy. Eddy clenched his jaw and stared back with what he hoped was a look of resolve. Dr. Linquist's face abandoned its efforts at smiling altogether and relaxed into a more natural grimace. After a moment, the beastly baby nodded as if accepting the impasse. Dr. Linquist looked up at Hans and gave him a curt nod. Hans grinned. The Dane's smile was genuine—genuinely evil. Doctor Linquist laid his briefcase on the table. "All right then," he said, "if you won't answer my questions, would you be willing to at least participate in a simple test? Hmm? Yes?"

"What sort of test?"

"A visual one. Very simple. No math required. We show you some pictures, and you tell us what you think. Good? No?" The doctor unlatched the briefcase and lifted out a black paper envelope.

"You mean, like a Rorschach test?" asked Eddy.

"A what?"

Eddy froze. Most non-shrinks knew what a Rorschach test was. The idea that a psychiatrist didn't was beyond implausible. Eddy had no idea what Dr. Linquist was, but he was not what he claimed. More importantly, what was Hans? The stern Scandinavian stared at Eddy as if mentally dismembering him. "An ink blot test," said Eddy.

"Oh yes. Something like that. You just look at a picture and tell us what you see. Yes? No harm in that, hmm?"

Eddy wanted to say no, but he worried what would happen if he refused. "Fine."

"Very good, yes," said Dr. Linquist. The two visitors drew black rimmed spectacles from inside their coats. They put them on and looked at Eddy through rose coloured lenses. Eddy felt a rush of panic. He knew now what was inside the black paper envelope. He didn't understand how it worked, but he knew that looking at it would kill him, just as it had the jogger on the bridge. The image of the man's body falling past the train trestle flashed through his mind. The man was already dead when he fell, of that Eddy was certain. Eddy leapt to his feet and screamed, "Help, police! Help! Help! Help!"

Hans grabbed Eddy by the throat and slammed him to the floor like a freight train.

"Wees voorzichtig!" hissed the fake doctor, "No bruises."

"Help! Help!" yelled Eddy, flailing about.

The powerful Dane had him expertly pinned to the concrete. Hans leaned down and hissed into Eddy's ear. "Stop yelling, or I break your neck," he snarled with a crisp Nordic accent. Eddy had no doubt Hans could easily murder him with his bare hands. So why not? It would be hard for them to explain how Eddy's neck had come to be broken during a psych evaluation, he supposed. Hans forced Eddy's face flat to the floor, facing sideways in a vicelike grip. "Bring card 'round," Hans grunted. Dr. Linquist walked slowly around until he stood over Eddy. Eddy could see no escape. He knew that looking at the contents of the envelope would kill him. He shut his eyes. The Dane's fingers pried open his left eye. "Don't close your eyes. You don't want to miss this," he chuckled. Dr. Linquist then put a card directly in the path Eddy's vision. Eddy tried not to see the strange pattern printed there. It seemed to undulate and lift from the card's surface. He felt his chest tighten, his heart pounding inside.

Moments later, Dr. Linquist raised the alarm. "Something terrible has happened!" they said to the police officer who had been waiting outside.

The suspect had suffered a heart attack. "No doubt brought about by stress," said Dr. Linquist. "Rare for someone so young, but not unheard of." Eddy lay crumpled on the floor of the interrogation room. His eyes were open, staring blankly.

"Are you sure?" asked the officer. It was bad news when a suspect died in custody. There would be an investigation. "I'll call an ambulance."

"Call the coroner," said Dr. Linquist. "He'll say the same thing. Massive coronary. You've nothing to worry about. It was natural causes. It wasn't anyone's fault. I am a doctor, remember? I take full responsibility."

"Oh... right," said the officer, somewhat reassured.

"Well, go on then, report it."

A moment after the officer had left; the so-called psychiatrist and Hans followed. They left Eddy for dead on the floor.

Several seconds passed.

"Gahhhh!" Eddy gasped. He hyperventilated for a moment, flopping like a fish on the concrete. He blinked. The two bright overhead lights merged into one as his vision recalibrated. *I'm alive*, thought Eddy. He tried to shake the fuzz from his vision. It hovered like a miasma in his mind. *Why am I alive?* Eddy rose unsteadily to his feet. He teetered and almost fell. He clutched the table's edge to catch himself. A single primal urge reached out from the fog inside his head, clawing its way up from the animal depths of his brain. *Survive*, it said. But how? *Flee!*

The door to the interrogation room was wide open. Eddy peeked tentatively out and was surprised to find the hallway deserted. He could hear the officer shouting upstairs. Eddy's only hope had been to survive. Now, amazingly, he had a chance to escape as well. He no longer felt he could trust anyone, including the police. After all, *someone* had let the assassins in to question him. In a moment, the corridor would be filled with cops. Eddy ran instinctively away from the sound of commotion. Turning a corner, he was surprised to find another door left ajar and bleeding sunlight. It was an emergency exit. The station staff used it as a shortcut. For this reason, its alarm was disabled. It was the very same doorway his would-be killers had fled through moments earlier. Had they looked back, they might even have seen Eddy exit as their black Mercedes peeled away. Eddy held his hand in front of his face as he stepped outside. He was briefly dazzled by daylight. A breeze tousled his hair. It felt good to be alive, and also surreal. Eddy tried to find his bearings. It wasn't easy. The street, the cars, and passing pedestrians were just blurry blobs behind the floating mass that persisted in his vision. He could still recognize the sky, buildings and people for what they were, but that was about it. It didn't matter. He needed to get moving or he'd soon be caught. Eddy walked to the sidewalk and headed towards a more heavily trafficked area. He walked briskly. He'd read enough spy novels to know not to run, despite the temptation to do so. Don't draw attention to yourself, he thought. The police would have discovered him gone by now, but would be baffled by it for at least a moment. Eddy was supposed to be dead after all, and corpses are notoriously bad at running away. The disappearance of the supposed psychiatrist would confuse them further. He imagined them trying to piece together an explanation. They would then fan out and search. Eddy felt as if he'd wandered into a James Buchan novel. He tried to banish the visage of Hans from his thoughts. He could still feel the cold of the concrete floor against his cheek. Most of all, he tried not to picture the card Linquist had forced upon him. It was a mess of both pattern and chaos—an abstract scribble floating on a white background. It was burned as an after-image in his sight. It seemed to vibrate still in his consciousness, exposing the lie between mind and eye. Eddy's ribs throbbed with pain at each step. He winced and rubbed them as he walked. *How am I still alive?*

He heard the voices of police officers behind him. They were shouting at each other. "Spread out!" The manhunt was on and Eddy was less than a block away. *Keep walking,* he told himself, *Whatever you do, don't look back!* It was then that Eddy saw the woman in the parked car. She was bent over the steering wheel, talking on her cell phone. She was clearly upset and trying to explain why. To Eddy, she was just a blurry blob. Somehow, he recognized her in spite of this. He rapped loudly on the passenger window. Gwen looked up, startled. She stared at Eddy for a long baffled moment.

"I'll call you back," he saw her say.

## ALPHA 0.13

Pardon me thou bleeding piece of mirth - C. Hebdo

//Santa Clara, CA — now

"Fore!"

Robert Machi leaned back and watched with satisfaction the long arc of the small white ball. It fell through the limitless blue sky, landed squarely in the green and rolled to a stop, five feet from the hole. It was a near perfect shot, and it was his. Well, not his technically. Technically, the shot belonged to Phil Mickelson, his second in the game. Machi had become too fat to play himself. He found just the effort of stepping from the golf cart exhausting. Still, he saw no reason to give up his favourite sport simply because he'd become unable to play it himself. So, if he were going to pay someone to play for him, why not pay for the best? Machi was now officially the fourth richest man in the world. That meant, with the exception of three other men, everyone else on the planet could be bought, including

Phil Mickelson.

"Well played, sir," said Alan Cassius. The Senator lined up and took his own swing. A pretty good shot, it turned out, just short of the green. The reedy politician smiled to himself. He was wearing a teal Lacoste shirt. The golf course was the one public place Cassius could be seen without a bow tie. He actually enjoyed their games more now. It used to be he'd have to play down to Machi, throwing the occasional bogey in order to avoid beating the media tycoon. Now, he could play his best. James Machi owned seventeen newspapers, over a hundred online news outlets, dozens of AM radio stations and the all-powerful MCNX, Majority Cable News Xtranet. He was not somebody you wanted to humiliate at golf.

"Have you got her under control?" Machi wheezed as he mopped sweat from his forehead. Cassius wondered at how rapidly Machi had gained weight. It must be his thyroid, he decided. Machi had always been heavy set, but not like this. When Cassius had first met him a decade earlier, it had been over lunch at the Business As Usual Grill on K-Street. Machi had eaten an endive salad with slivered almonds and orange slices. He'd joked about trying to "keep his boyish figure." The weight gain had been slow for years. Then, suddenly, the billionaire had ballooned to his current portly dimensions and seemed to be growing still. Merely watching him move, made the sweat bead on the Senator's own temple. Cassius remembered Machi had a certain energy then. *The Economist* had just crowned him the largest single media owner in history. Cassius remembered Machi leaning in over a cup of decaf coffee and spitting as he spoke. "Americans want to go back to a time that never was. It's our job to get them there."

"How?" the Senator had asked. He shook a packet of raw sugar into his espresso and stirred. "And why?"

"How? By any means necessary. When you're trying to get back to Paradise, the ends justify the means. Why? Because I'm an idealist." The young Senator had stared at Machi a long time after he'd said that, unsure what the right response was. Suddenly, the big man burst into laughter, slapping the table, and chortling so hard he had to wipe tears from his eyes. The waitress appeared with the bill. Cassius feigned reaching for his wallet. "I got it," said Machi, waving him off.

The sun, thankfully, vanished behind a sweep of white cloud. It was hot enough to make Cassius sweat. Phil Mickelson paused to apply a fresh coat of sun block. Machi was shielded by the golf cart canopy. "Not yet. She's quite stubborn," said the Senator. "Soon."

With one hand on the wheel, Machi drove his cart down the long gentle slope towards the green. Cassius and Phil Mickelson got into the second cart and followed. Machi needed his own cart, modified to comfortably fit his ample frame. Machi's use of Phil had caused some consternation among other elite members, particularly after he'd set a new club record. Since club rules did not explicitly ban using a PGA professional as a second, Machi argued it was all perfectly legal. His generous gifts to the club helped ensure that the rule remained unchanged. Besides cash, Machi had agreed to leave his entire collection of medieval art, estimated to be worth millions to the club. To Machi, bequeathments were like stock options with delayed divestment—they bought fealty. The theme of fealty was one of the reasons he loved to collect the Romanesque paintings. The other reason he loved medieval art was its aesthetics, the layers of gold leaf, and flat bold colours. Most of all, he loved the false perspectives and the practice of making subjects larger based on their importance. The two carts rolled to a stop a few yards shy of the green. Cassius and Phil Mickelson hopped out.

"The vote needs to happen soon," said Machi. "She needs her mind changed. One way, or another."

"With all due respect, Bob," said Cassius, taking practice swings with his putter, "I know all of this. Let me sweat the details."

"I always sweat the details. For want of a nail the shoe was lost." It was one of Machi's favourite quotations. So much so, he kept an actual nail on his desk, mounted on a piece of wood, pointed upwards.

"If Plan A fails, we go with Plan B."

The media mogul nodded, shaking his feedbag chin.

Phil Mickelson had been unavoidably eavesdropping on their conversations for months. He finally decided to speak up. "If I may," he began tentatively. Cassius and Machi turned to look at the three-time PGA Master winner. Phil's nose was white with zinc oxide. "Perhaps some simple amendments to the bill designed to ameliorate her concerns could lead to a compromise and ultimately to a bipartisan agreement?"

Machi and Cassius both stared at Phil for several seconds, then in chorus said, "Shut-up, Phil."

# ALPHA 0.14

"I am a known unknown." – D. Rumsfeld

// Brooklyn, New York — then

Eddy remembered holding his father's hand. He remembered sitting in the waiting area. Both sets of doors locked both ways. The first set led to the less severe cases. They were waiting to go through the second. Eddy was nervous, but anxious. His father's hand was cold and sweaty, not calm and comfortable like it used to feel. He remembered thinking that was odd. Eddy was nine-years-old, *too old to be holding Daddy's hand*. The nurse said something about "kids always needing to be escorted." Eddy wanted to let go, but his father wouldn't let him. He wasn't sure whose hand was holding whose.

"Maybe you can help cheer your Mum up," his father had said.

A handwritten note on the wall said to not let a white haired Caucasian woman leave. A second sign said the same for a tall African

American man. Eddy wanted to leave. Sitting on the chair, his feet didn't reach the floor. He hadn't had his promised growth spurt yet. He felt small. For a while, he listened in on a conversation he didn't understand. A doctor was explaining in hushed tones to a woman who had been crying that her husband suffered from *simultanagnosia*. "It's a condition where the patient is unable to perceive more than one object at a time," said the doctor, who had curly brown hair. The doctor began to clean his glasses with the end of his necktie. "He can see all the parts that make up a scene, but understanding it as a whole is quite impossible for him." Nine-year-old Eddy wondered if he suffered from the disorder as well.

"Dr. Pending?"

Eddy's father looked up at the young nurse leaning from the doorway. "That's me," he said.

She smiled cheerfully. "You can come in now."

They were led down a curved corridor. Eddy remembered that clearly. He'd wondered at the time if it continued around to form a complete ring. On one side were single patient rooms. Some of the doors were ajar, but none were completely closed. Eddy stole glances as they passed. In one room, he saw a man lying in bed, fully awake, staring ahead. He was staring at a TV. The TV was off. On the other side of the hall was a sort of common area, like a lounge. Several patients were gathered with a doctor in what appeared to be a meeting. Eddy wondered what they could be meeting about. He wondered if they were talking about his Mum. Lately, whenever adults got together to talk, it always seemed to be about his Mum. Apparently, they were confused by 'what to do with her'. They said she was ill, but Eddy knew the truth. He knew his mother was sad. She was the saddest person in the whole wide world.

When they reached his mother's room, the nurse showed them inside. His mother was sitting in a chair at the window. She looked up when they entered. The first thing Eddy noticed was how much weight she'd lost.

It had been just three weeks since she'd turned sad. She was transformed. His nine-year-old eyes widened at the sight of her. She had always been slender. Now, she was gaunt and frail with a ghost-like pallor. That was what she was, Eddy realized. A ghost. His mother had died, and all that was left were these spectral remains. As he watched, she pulled repeatedly at the skin on her arms. She flinched erratically. 'Near catatonic' the doctor had said. Eddy hadn't understood what that meant, until now. He couldn't decide if it were better or worse than the look of anguish that had gripped her before.

"I know you know," his mother said to his father. "I know you know the truth. You shouldn't have come." For the first time, she noticed Eddy.

His father followed her gaze. "It was a mistake to bring him," he said abruptly. "Eddy, wait outside."

Eddy wanted to object. He wanted to remind his father about kids needing to be escorted. His father wasn't looking at him. He was completely transfixed by the apparition before them. It was at that moment, Eddy saw the tears in his father's eyes. His father's hands clenched white at his side.

"I'm a horrible person," Eddy's mother said. "I've done terrible things. You shouldn't have come."

Eddy stepped out into the corridor. Relief. He glanced about to see whether there were any nurses or staff. The corridor was empty. Eddy sat down on a butterscotch vinyl chair. For a moment, he tried to understand what had happened. It had been a week since she'd taken the pills. Nobody would explain to him what was going on. Usually when that happened, it was because the adults didn't want him to know. This time, he suspected, it was because they didn't know either.

"You play with Lego?"

Eddy looked up in surprise. Leaning down to speak with him was a tall, thin black man. The man's springy charcoal hair was turning grey. His face was crinkled into a warm smile.

"Yes."

"You want to know a secret?"

"Okay."

"The whole world's made of Lego."

"Really?"

"Sure. You can take it apart and reassemble it however you like. But it's a secret most people don't know."

Eddy glanced down at the chair he was sitting on. He pulled on the arm, trying to dislodge a piece of the Lego.

"No... no, not like that," said the man.

"Like how then?" asked Eddy. He'd played with Lego many times and had a pretty good set of his own. Sometimes it got stuck together. Usually, if you tried hard enough, you could pull it apart.

"In yur mind..." said the man, tapping his freckled brown scalp. "In yur mind."

# ALPHA 0.15

"Opiates are the opium of the masses." – K. Marx

// Manhattan, New York — now

"We have a new sponsor, Purdue Pharma," said Sue between sucks on her Shamrock Shake. "They're on the Premium Plan."

Lance rolled his eyes. The Premium Plan was in theory a good thing. It meant more money in his pocket in a roundabout hard to substantiate kind of way. Still, he hated it. It also meant weaving in positive mentions in news stories and even entire segments designed to promote the product. Since it was medical, it probably meant having Hank Olberton on the show or, worse, Dr. Oz. Lance hated Dr. Oz. "What are we at now? Eighty percent pharma ads?"

"Don't exaggerate. Less than fifty."

"The rest being reverse mortgages."

"Don't forget catheter ads and class-action lawsuit commercials," said Bert with a chuckle from the seat beside him. Bert was their subject matter expert whenever they didn't have one for a given subject. His only true 'qualification' title was as a 'Life Coach'. But Bert wasn't just a regular Life Coach. Bert had undergone Tony Robbins's elite training program making him a 'Life *Results* Coach'. This meant he'd spent '250 hours of face-to-face and virtual training', the equivalent of 6 months of actual school. According to Tony Robbins's training website, every Life Results Coach must also have achieved "outstanding results in his or her own life..." which they were, for some reason, willing to give up to become a Life Results Coach. Being a Life Results Coach meant Bert could claim to be an expert on anything involving life. He had done so many segments that he was the closest thing Lance had to a co-host.

"All of whom help pay for your substantial compensation," said Sue. She stared them down with her best unamused producer look. Sue was, Lance decided, actually quite attractive for a woman in her fifties. Too old for himself, of course, but he could understand why they called her 'Hot Pants'. He assumed she'd used her looks to get where she was today. Smart girl. Make hay while the sun shines. They were seated in Sue's office. She sat behind her desk as usual, while Lance and Bert sprawled in comfortable easy chairs opposite. Bert's chair was vibrating. He'd switched on the magic fingers massage and was lounging like royalty. He's not the King, thought Lance, I am. On air, Lance called himself 'The Democracy King' for his tireless defence of American freedom. Ever since landing his own daytime show, Bert had been acting too big for his britches. He thinks he's the new Dr. Phil, Lance fumed. More like Dr. *Phil-an-empty-spot-in-the-schedule*. Lance snorted in amusement at his own joke.

"What's so funny?" asked Sue.

"Nothing." Lance stole a glance back at Glinda, the young staff writer taking notes behind them. She had midnight black hair, cut in bangs that gave her a sexy school girl look. Lance wanted to casually mention that he made far more money than Sue, his so-called boss. At that moment, Glinda glanced up. Their eyes met. Glinda smiled shyly. Lance winked. Score, he thought. He then turned back to Sue. "Okay Sue-baby, what's the product?"

"Something called, Zenfaux®," said Sue. She took a loud slurp of green sludge and glanced down at the brief. "Apparently it's a... 'special kind of mood stabilizer that targets your MT-Zone'."

"MT-Zone?" laughed Bert. "What the Hell's your MT-Zone?"

Lance smirked. Bert was no one to talk. Half of Bert's new show consisted of made-up terms for made-up ailments. "It's a feminine-thing," Lance said confidently.

"No, it's not," said Glinda. "It's right here," she said, then read aloud from the brief, "Your MT-Zone is the meaningless void of emptiness in your life." Lance, Bert and Sue all turned to stare at her.

"Are you joking?" said Lance.

"That's what it says. It's on their website too." Sue held up the brief and pointed to a cartoon image of a woman pondering a gaping hole in her middle. Through the hole, blue sky was clearly visible. "Although, 'void of emptiness' seems like a double negative to me."

"That makes it twice as bad," said Lance. He gave a glance back at Glinda. He hoped to convey how tired he was of constantly having to explain things to Sue. Glinda was too busy making notes to notice.

"They sent samples," said Sue. She plucked a pill bottle from inside a FedEx envelope. She unscrewed the child-proof lid and dumped blue pills into a pewter bowl on her desk normally reserved for Tic Tacs. Each pill was stamped 'ZF'. The drug was originally created as a treatment for syphilis. In clinical trials, however, it caused a small percentage of male test subjects' private parts to wither and fall off. The company convinced the FCC to still approve the drug, arguing that those cases were rare and that those subjects were technically cured too. Still, it made the drug difficult to market. Even when the warning was muttered quickly in a low voice during commercials while happy people skipped through wheat fields. Customers simply didn't like the sound of 'may cause genital detachment' no matter how it was presented. The company had already spent billions on research and even more on marketing and needed a return on investment. Fortunately, researchers had noted, that the drug also had the side effect of making people feel good about the situation, all things considered. Most importantly, it didn't cause the detachment issue in non-syphilis suffers. That's when the executives at Purdue decided to focus on off-label use. The drug's original name, Gone-O-Rea, was created by a Madison Avenue group after millions of dollars in research. It's new name Zenfaux was generated in seconds by Purdue CMO, Moonbeam Haddlesworth, using the drug-naming app Pharmanteau. That left only one lingering issue. There were concerns raised that Zenfaux might be mildly addictive. "*Mildly* doesn't engender customer loyalty," said Purdue CEO Frank Goldswab at a quarterly board meeting. Fortunately, this concern turned out to be easily solved with the simple addition of OxyContin® to help 'ease the pain of being'. The MT-Zone concept was created by marketing, along with Emma T, the cartoon spokesperson with the gaping hole in her middle. "Zenfaux helps fill my M-T-ness!" says Emma, plugging her void with a giant blue pill.

The rest of the meeting was spent discussing the next day's show. Mostly, this meant reviewing the scripts for various interviews. It was standard practice for TV and radio interviews with fellow journalists to be planned out, with questions provided in advance. It was harmless theatre used to ensure a story was covered effectively. At MCNX, the practice went far beyond this. Almost all interview segments were completely scripted. Only interviews with hostile subjects were not. There, cutting mikes and the editing room were used to keep an interview from 'going off the rails'. It all started with *The Bible*. This was not the biblical Bible, but rather the network commandments sent down from James Machi himself, aka God. It included the current themes and messages to be promoted on all MCNX shows. It even included a list of terms and phrases to be used in place of more common, but less helpful ones. This meant estate taxes were always called 'death taxes', and private social security accounts were called 'personal social security accounts'. Machi repeated his mantra in almost every closed-door meeting. "The words you choose shape the conversation. Shaping the conversation shapes minds. Shaping minds shapes the country." He called the practice 'Speak-Think'. Its opposite, Machi prophesied, was a dire threat to America's well being. It used to be that Lance had a special relationship with James Machi. The CEO would call him up in the middle of the night asking his advice. Lance would be invited regularly up to Machi's chalet back when the billionaire was still slim enough to ski. Machi valued Lance's "finger on the pulse of America." Now, that role had been subsumed by Alan Cassius. Why Machi would trust a politician was beyond him. Cassius was a well-known snake. Lance had interviewed the politician in a friendly way several times, but secretly loathed him. The very thought of him made Lance's palms itch. He fantasized about meeting the Senator in a corridor some day.

The meeting had already lasted an hour. Lance was exhausted and bored. Bert was more interested in his fidget-spinner than what was being discussed. Lance hated this level of corporate control. He'd made his name as a radio firebrand who said whatever came out of his mouth. No filter. These days he felt like a dog on a gilded leash. He stole a glance at Glinda's legs. She was wearing stockings with seams. It was driving him crazy.

"...and then you say... Lance? Lance? Hello?"

Lance snapped back into focus. Sue was motioning with her eyes for him to stop staring at Glinda's legs. Seeing that she had his attention, she glared at him with her *not-this-again* look. The station had settled over twelve sexual harassment lawsuits for him in the seven years he'd been there. They accepted it as the cost of doing business, but that didn't mean they wanted those costs to grow. There had already been two this year, which meant he was at quota. Fortunately, Glinda appeared oblivious.

"And then...?" Lance paused, trying to remember the subject of tomorrow's editorial.

"Moral reckoning?" prompted Glinda, reading back from her notes like a court stenographer.

"Right, moral reckoning, maybe I could call it 'moral wreck-oning'?" said Lance.

"I don't get it," said Sue.

"Wreck-oning. With a 'W'. It's clever."

"People can't hear the W."

"We put it on the ticker. Jeez, do I have to explain everything?"

"Fine."

"Okay, then I segue into how America is sinking into an ammoral, Godless abyss and that we need to return to the good ol' days."

"Right," said Sue nodding. "And in the meantime..."

"In the meantime?" said Lance.

Sue shook the bowl of blue pills at him.

"Oh, right! Um... Zenfaux is a great way to get there, if only for a little while." Lance leaned forward and peered into the bowl. "Does this stuff really work?"

"How should I—" Sue's mobile phone began to play *Thus Spake Zarathustra*. She picked it up and stared at it a moment. "Meeting's over," she said. She then grabbed her bag and hurried from the room before the others could react.

"Well, I guess that's it," said Bert with a shrug. He pocketed his fidget spinner and followed her out.

"Good job taking notes," said Lance to Glinda as she gathered her things. "I can tell you're a talented writer." He pointed to her handwriting, "You have beautiful *i*'s."

"Oh... thank-you," said Glinda. "Well, I guess I better go."

"Keep up the good work!"

Glinda nodded, packed up her things, smiled and left.

For a long moment, Lance sat alone in Sue's office. He should be going home himself but, since the divorce, he had nothing to go home to. Except for the damn Koi fish, of course. He'd never wanted them. Linda had insisted on them. Now, he was stuck with them. Why did he do it? Why did he do any of it? It used to be fun and exciting. Now? He'd achieved so much, and yet, part of him wondered what it was all for? Besides the money, of course. Lance found himself eying the bowl of complementary meds. My home is an MT-Zone, he thought. He picked up a single blue pill and held it between two fingers. It looked like a tiny piece of sky. His synapses fired. Ask your doctor, it said. Red energy crackled behind his eyes. *Take the pill.* Normally, Lance never touched the samples sent by sponsors. Except, the ones from Goldline, of course. Still, he was curious, what could one pill do? Lance tossed it back with nothing but his own spit to wash it down. He waited a moment for something to happen. Nothing, he thought, it could do nothing.

## ALPHA 0.16

"I'm repeating myself." – B. Mandelbrot

//Downtown Los Angeles — now

"We have to go to the police," said Gwen.

"I just escaped from the police!"

"No, you escaped from people pretending to be police."

"In a police station, let in by the police."

Gwen stared at Eddy who was stuffing his mouth with chips and salsa between words. Running for your life, it turned out, makes you hungry. Eddy, thankfully, could see clearly again. The effects of the virus were fleeting it seemed. They sat in the booth of an 'oldie' English style pub situated in a strip mall in downtown Los Angeles. It was called The Angry Dog. The sign outside featured a snarling British Bulldog set against a waving Union Jack. In small letters beneath it read, 'A Sung Lau Holdings Company'. Neither Eddy nor Gwen had been there before. It was simply a place to catch their breath and figure out what to do. Despite the British theme, the crowd was thoroughly American, downing draft Budweiser and Coors in plastic pint glasses. Some of the TVs were tuned to an ESPN broadcast of a Major League Eating event in Tulsa, Oklahoma. The rest were tuned to MCNX's living room news analysis show *The Truth*. On ESPN, champion Okui Ai was in the lead, folding over whole hotdogs and stuffing them down his gullet. The commentator called it "a thing of beauty." It was an official MLE event, so Okui had come "ready to eat 110%." In spite of his diminutive size, he was currently doing so at a rate that dwarfed his hulking competitors. On MCNX, the hosts were leaning over a prop coffee table laughing. They were in a mock discussion about other white powders Congresswoman Flatwood might have been snorting in the video. Host, Sandra Jackman pretended to sniff a lick of talcum. She then flopped unconscious onto the prop sofa. Her co-hosts roared.

"Look, I can bring the DA's office in on this. You'll have legal protection. The system can help you."

"The system? I almost died in the system's custody."

"If this stuff is real, why aren't you dead now?"

"I don't know."

Gwen and Eddy became aware of a waiter hovering over them, rocking on the balls of his feet. They looked up.

"Allo, allo, allo! Welcome to the Angry Dog authentic British pub! Grrr-owl! My name is Louis, and it'll my ex-x-x-treme privilege to serve you today." Louis raised his eyebrows and gestured excitedly. It was his charming, slightly wacky schtick that made him the top tip earner for the entire Angry Dog bar-staff, or *bark-staff* as they were called. He was wearing a Union Jack shirt and a Scottish kilt. Louis himself was originally from Puerto Rico. "Our jolly old English specials today are chorizo and mash; cajun shepherd's pie and something called toady-in-a-hole, which I'm assured is toad-free."

"Nothing for me," said Gwen.

"Beer is fine," said Eddy.

Louis deflated. He wasn't used to his routine falling flat. He also wasn't happy about a whole booth ordering just one beer. "A beer. Great. Which one? We have forty-two beers to choose from. Twelve on tap, thirty in bottles."

"It doesn't matter."

"It *does* matter," Louis insisted. "We have a plethora of pints perfect for every palette." As he said this, he pointed to the very same words inscribed on a beam next to black and white photographs of Spike Milligan, Dave Allen, and the Two Ronnies.

Eddy couldn't think about beers. "Whatever. You pick."

"I don't know what you like."

"I'll like whatever you pick."

Louis fumed. He could sense a one dollar tip coming. "Michelob Ultra it is then." Louis turned in a huff and left. A cheer went up from the bar. On ESPN, Okui pushed aside his first empty platter and reached for another. It too was stacked high with boiled hotdogs. The commentators discussed allegations of 'cow-tumming'; the illegal practice of having multiple bovine stomachs surgically implanted in order to win. There were rumours about Okui. Some audience members had mooed tauntingly as he'd arrived.

After getting into Gwen's car, Eddy had asked her to simply "Drive." He explained what had happened. He told her about Geppetto and the enigmatic Strauss. "Whoever he is, he has skills and access I've never seen before." On that basis, he'd persuaded Gwen to turn off her cell phone to avoid being tracked. Eddy omitted mentioning the 'Dark Web' or his own status as a wanted hacker. Gwen was still a district attorney, and he still wasn't sure they were on the same side. Eddy felt as though he'd stumbled into one of Uncle Russ's crazy conspiracies. Of course, as his uncle had so often said, crazy doesn't mean wrong.

"It's got to be the mob," said Gwen. "Paying people off."

"Why would the mob be after us?"

"I don't know. Ransomware?" Gwen knew little about computer viruses, but she knew that ransomware had affected thousand of individuals, some local hospitals, and even a sheriff's department. She knew it involved the victim's valuable files being encrypted, rendering them unreadable until a ransom was paid. The Sheriff's department had paid two thousand dollars to have its records decrypted.

"We haven't seen any evidence of ransomware. I also don't think it's the mob."

"You don't know that."

"No."

Louis returned, still vexed. He dropped a pint of watery draft in front of Eddy with a passive aggressive *clunk*. "Here's your so-called beer," he said, "Can I get you anything else? Something to eat perhaps? Allow me to recommend *food*. Our food is good."

"We're fine for now," said Eddy, without looking up. This only made Louis even more annoyed. The waiter stomped away to the bar to complain to the bartender about being ignored. Eddy scraped the last of the salsa from the bowl. "The thing is, I feel like the whole thing with Mrs. Ferguson is somehow related."

"You think those men visited her too?"

"No," said Eddy. He took a sip of his drink. He paused to check that it really was beer and continued. "It's something about the way she was sitting there. Just staring ahead. Staring at the TV."

Another cheer went up from the crowd as Okui Ai was declared the winner. He had eaten seventy hotdogs in fifteen minutes. This was a new world record, the commentators announced, beating the mark by one. It was a great day for mankind. Okui thanked God and his sponsor Samsung. The broadcast cut to commercial. Around the bar, patrons ordered fresh rounds and began to chat excitedly about having witnessed history.

#

//Washington, DC — now

"Of course they can't prove it's me... Why? Because it's not!" Anne had been on the phone since seven am. After spending yesterday besieged by reporters at her office, she'd decided to stay home this morning. At least here the Congresswoman could be besieged in relative comfort. She was tempted to hop on a plane and head back to her district, but she knew they would follow her there too. No point in annoying her constituents. Let's keep the circus here in Washington where it belongs. Anne took a sip of cold coffee. She was sitting at her dining room table surrounded by empty breakfast dishes. Ed, her PR aide, was on speaker-phone. He was reading from the fifth draft of the press release they were preparing. "Can we put a comma in there?" When the story first broke, they'd immediately held a press conference denouncing the video as fake. Still, the questions persisted. They tried silence. "Let the facts speak for themselves," said Congresswoman Reckett, "talking keeps the story alive." Isabelle clearly knew nothing about the media. Silence had created a vacuum, and the media abhors a vacuum. So the pundits and her political opponents kindly filled it for her. "It's lose–lose, trial in absentia, damned either way," Stanley, her long time friend and fellow committee chair had told her over the phone. "So what do you advise?" Anne asked the Iowa Senator. "Prayer," he said. "Oh, and I can't be seen with you until this blows over. Sorry about that." CNN, MSNBC and Fox were replaying the video in a near continuous loop. The worst was MCNX. Majority Cable News Xtranet no longer bothered with the word 'allegedly'. This was now standard policy for all MCNX news coverage. The network ran a disclaimer once a day at midnight. "News content may include alleged truths, half truths, or complete untruths. Expressed opinions do not represent the views of sponsors, Majority Cable News Xtranet, or the persons saying them." MCNX claimed it was simply a matter of time before all news outlets did this. "We shouldn't need any disclaimer at all," CEO James Machi had once told Charlie Rose, "After all, everything is *allegedly* true."

"PBS says the video is fraudulent," said Anne.

"Great, that's two more votes for us," said Ed.

"PBS has more than two viewers. They have at least four."

"I'm accounting for turnout."

There was a loud knock at the front door. Anne's housekeeper went to answer it, walking briskly past the French doors that connected the dining room to the hall. Her flats clacked on the checkered marble floor. "It's just reporters, Rosita. Tell them we'll be releasing a statement tomorrow."

"Yes, Ms. Flatwood."

Ed resumed reading the draft. Anne had heard this passage before. There were no changes. She pondered the dining room. She loved this room. It was white plaster classic colonial with ceiling molding and relief pillars. Sunshine streamed through the tall windows, frosted by winter's remorse. The inside drapes billowed gently, cheerful ghosts in the warm updraft of the floor vents. Were she not in the midst of a crisis, Anne might have thought it cozy. Instead, she felt... removed. Suddenly, there was a commotion in the front hall. Men's voices echoed. "No, no, no!" shouted Rosita.

Three men in long black winter coats appeared in the dining room doorway. Their pale cheeks were flushed red from the cold. In the middle was Alan Cassius. A yellow polka-dot tie punctuated the Senator's fastidious frame. Alan smirked. His comrades glowered. Alan always appears pleased with himself, thought Anne, even when no one else is. Perhaps especially then. She did not recognize the other two men. They looked like secret service, but the Senator did not warrant such protection. Bodyguards?

Henchmen? thought Anne, God help us, he has minions now. Rosita pushed between them with hands raised, "I'm so sorry, ma'am, I told them no, but they would not listen."

"It's okay, Rosita. Ed, I'm going to have to call you back." Anne tapped to end the call. Rosita frowned disapprovingly and left. The henchmen closed the double doors behind her. "If you're going for menacing and villainous, you're doing a good job," said Anne. Cassius said nothing. He pulled out a chair across from her and sat down. "Enough," said Anne, "What do you – "

Cassius put his finger to his lips. Shhh...

Anne stared at him, shocked to silence by her own surprise. The minions drew black batons from inside their coats and began waving them about the walls and furniture.

"My office isn't bugged," said Anne indignantly.

The men ignored her. One of them unscrewed the receiver on her desk phone, peered inside, and put it back. The other henchman completed the sweep. He turned and gave a nod to the Senator. Only then, did Cassius speak. "Sorry about all the cloak and dagger nonsense, darling. You can never be too careful. There are unscrupulous people about."

"Mmm, yes," said Anne, "I suppose that's true."

Alan raised his hand. The henchmen withdrew. One retreated to guard the entrance. The other moved to the window, scanning the encamped media on the snow banked street outside.

"If I didn't know better," said Anne, "I'd think you were up to something."

"I want to know what it will take for you to come around to support my bill," said Alan.

"A stroke."

Alan chuckled. A little too much, thought Anne. "Do you mind if I smoke?" he asked, drawing a platinum cigarette case from his inside pocket.

The case had once belonged to Cyrus West Field, the nineteenth century railroad owner and financier of the first transatlantic cable. "A man on whose back America was built," Alan liked to say. Cyrus eventually lost his vast wealth to bad investments. That misfortune ultimately placed the robber baron's cigarette case in Alan Cassius's hand.

"I *do* mind actually."

Alan tapped a cigarette on the lid and lit it with a gold lighter. Anne was appalled by the Senator's rudeness. She envisioned walking around the table, yanking the cigarette from his lips, and dragging him to the door by his ear, like an insolent schoolboy. That should play well on TV, she thought. "Is this why you brought Thug 1 and Thug 2, Alan? So you could behave like a jackass with impunity?"

The svelte Senator smiled smugly. He took a long, contemplative drag on his cigarette. He exhaled twin plumes of smoke from his nose. "They're mostly decoration," he said with a nod to the two men.

"What do you want, Alan? You know I'm not going to change my mind."

"I know, I know, but that's exactly why I'm here. To change your mind. One way..." He paused again to exhale, adding to the noxious atmosphere in the room. "...or another."

Anne coughed. "Why do you care what I think? I'm now discredited, disgraced. Persona non grata."

Cassius shrugged. "Would that were true. Sadly, we live in such a divided political world these days; voters are skeptical of even the most compelling video evidence. You're weakened certainly, but not without influence. Besides, it's not just your vote, it's your colleagues who follow your lead. Their support is wavering, but not gone."

"We both know that video is fake," said Anne.

"Perhaps..." he said. The Senator ground out his cigarette on the polished wood of the dining room table.

Livid, Anne rose to her feet. "How dare you?"

"Perhaps..." said Alan again, signalling for her to sit. Anne remained standing. She was shaking with anger. "Perhaps... if the video were to be discredited? To be proven to be a fake? The look-a-like actress found, for example. Your troubles would go away. Poof! Your reputation would be restored. You might even be perceived as a victim. You could be even more influential than before."

"So, that's it then. You did this. You made the video and put it out there, just so you could waltz in her and blackmail me into voting for your God-damn bill."

"Not my God-damn bill. I'm just a foot soldier, Anne. A servant to the cause, serving a greater good." Senator Cassius sat back, hands clasped. "So then, Annabelle, what's it going to be? You come on board, hold your nose, vote for one mere smear bill you find distasteful, oh best beloved, and go on to a bright political future where you can wield real influence. Or option 2? You continue this hopeless battle, ultimately lose anyway and disappear into political oblivion."

"The devil or the deep blue sea."

"I'm not the devil, Anne, just his duly elected representative."

"I'll take my chances with the deep blue sea."

Cassius chuckled, nodding his head. "Oh Annabelle, I was expecting you to say that. Still, I have one more thing that may convince you." Cassius snapped his fingers. The minion by the window produced a black envelope and placed it into the Senator's waiting hand. Cassius pointed two fingers at his own eyes. The minion nodded. All three donned sunglasses with lenses like pooled blood. The Senator looked at Anne with vermillion eyes.

"What on Earth...?" said Anne.

The Senator laid the black matte envelope on the table before her. "Take a look," he said. "I think you'll find it thought provoking."

# BETA 0.20

"Any requests?" – Nero

//Downtown Los Angeles — now

Louis took a five-minute break while Sandra covered for him. I just need some fresh air, he thought, as he took a puff on his cigarette. The alleyway behind the Angry Dog pub was littered with the butts of smoke-breaks past. Half were his, half belonged to Tony, the bar back and Louis's on-again off-again boyfriend. Louis wasn't happy. Life was not going as planned. He'd left his home in Puerto Rico, with the idea of becoming a star in Hollywood. In San Juan, his high school drama teacher had told him he had the looks of a young Erik Estrada and the talent of an adult Corey Feldman. Despite that early promise, Louis had struggled since the move. He found himself joining the legions of aspiring actors working the bars and restaurants of Los Angeles. Sandra called them the 'sexy underclass'. In the past year, he'd landed only a single on-screen part, playing the role of 'Irate

Bank Customer #2' in a Wells Fargo commercial. In desperation, he'd resorted to live theatre. He was currently the lead in an original production called *All the World's a Stage*. It was about a man who, after saying 'Hamlet' too many times during a production of *Othello*, was cursed by the ghost of Sophocles to live out the rest of his life on stage. Unable to leave, the man was forced to partake in every single show the theatre put on. Some productions tried to ignore him, while others incorporated him, modifying the scripts as needed. It was therefore a play made up of scenes from *other* plays. In the opening scene, the cursed actor played Godot, whom Vladimir and Estragon could not see despite his being plainly visible on stage and occasionally yelling expletives at them. In *The Vagina Monologues* scene that followed, the cursed actor played a woman discussing her coming of age as a young girl. It was the third act Louis hated. There, he was forced to spend twenty minutes playing an inanimate coat rack in a meta-production of *Death of Salesman*. The Los Angeles Times described the entire production as "a baffling endeavour, and not in a good way. The best bits are plagiarized." They added that, of the many roles Louis assumed during the show, "...the coat rack is clearly the part he was born to play." Louis suspected it was intended as an insult, despite reassurances from the director otherwise. Louis took a long last drag from his cigarette, flicked it into the alleyway, and headed back into the bar.

As he entered, Louis noticed the usual hubbub had been replaced by stony silence. The only sound was from the TVs hanging on the walls. Everyone in the bar appeared transfixed by what was on. On the nearest screen, ESPN was covering the unexpected death of Okui Ai whose stomach had exploded on the podium. Doctors on the scene were struggling to tell hotdog from man. The crowd in the Angry Dog were not watching ESPN, however. They were captivated by the other TVs showing a local news alert on MCNX. "...where police are looking for two persons-of-interest that may be involved in a threat to national security," said the news anchor. The screen cut to photos of a man and a woman. Louis recognized them, but couldn't remember from where.

Then, *something* happened.

It had happened moments earlier while Louis was busy flicking his cigarette to the asphalt. This time, Louis was watching. For an instant, the TV screens turned to static. It was not typical analog TV static. Nor was it HD pixelation caused by satellite signal failure. It was amorphous. It was red. It was both pattern and chaos. Despite appearing for only a moment, to Louis it seemed to stretch time. It was a digital blood drop in water dispersing in slow motion. It hung in his consciousness like an after image left from staring at the sun. Louis felt dizzy and disoriented. He gripped a bar bannister to steady himself. He stopped. It was gone. What had happened? Nothing. Damn menthol, he thought, I've really got to switch to e-cigs. All around the bar, patrons were blinking and shaking their heads. They'd seen it too. Seen what? It was like a dream that melted from memory. It erased itself, then erased the memory of forgetting. Louis frowned. Huh? The patrons were blaming the beer, the hot wings and not enough sleep the night before. On screen, the oddly familiar man and woman were back. The voice of the anchor warned to be on the lookout, saying something about a conspiracy, perhaps treason. Louis didn't know who the people were, but he knew one thing—they made him angry. *I hate them,* he thought. He glanced about the bar. The other bar staff and patrons were angry too. Like Louis, they were looking about. They were looking to see if they could spot the man and woman from TV. Some looked under their own tables. Louis wanted to find them too. He also wanted to buy Tide laundry detergent and ask his doctor if Cialis was right for him. Seeing the man and woman nowhere, the waiter felt his anger subside. What was he supposed to be doing? Oh right, waiting on tables. Breathe. Relax. Louis brought water to a group of office workers. They had been camping at their table for thirty minutes despite having paid their bill. Louis aggressively refilled their glasses, hoping they would take the hint. The waiter then headed to booth no. 4 in the back corner.

"Can I get you anything more to..." Eddy and Gwen looked up in surprise. They had been so engrossed in their conversation; they had been oblivious to all else. Louis stared at them. His mouth hung open. Recognition dawned. Louis saw RED.

"Yes?" said Gwen.

Louis's hands quivered as a dam burst of adrenaline flooded his body. He staggered backwards. The aspiring-actor-slash-waiter felt a rage he'd never felt before. It was a hate so strong, it briefly incapacitated him. He wanted to hurt these people. He wanted to rip the flesh from their bones. For an instant, Louis enjoyed a fantasy interlude of Gwen and Eddy's skulls being smashed repeatedly on concrete. For some reason, this delightful visual was set to *Spanish Flea* by Herb Alpert & The Tijuana Brass. Louis began to gurgle and twitch.

"Is there something wrong?" asked Eddy.

Louis pointed at them and screamed, "Gah! Gah!"

Eddy leaned out of the booth to see who the mad waiter was calling to. For the first time, he noticed his and Gwen's faces on the TV screens. He also saw who Louis was shouting to. It was *everybody*.

"Uh, Gwen, I think you should see this."

Gwen looked out. The entire bar stared back. First, a wave of surprise froze the wall of faces. Next, rage engulfed the room like wildfire. All around, eyes burned with molten red hate. "It's them!" shrieked a woman.

"Traitors!"

"Gah!"

"Get them!" yelled a man in a turtleneck pullover. He hurled his pint of beer at Eddy and Gwen. It exploded in foam and glass shards against the wall behind them.

Louis grabbed a wooden cue from a nearby pool table. He swung wildly over their heads. The cue struck a pillar and snapped in two.

"What the Hell?" yelled Gwen. She stared in shock, unable to grasp the reality of what was happening.

"We need to go!" Eddy shouted. He grabbed Gwen's arm and dragged her from the booth.

"What's going on? Why is everyone—"

A woman in a Shrek-hat began hurling billiard balls at them. Eddy and Gwen ducked. The missiles flew past, whacking into the faux wood panelling behind them. All at once, the crowd overcame its inertia and surged forward as one.

"Come on!" Eddy shouted.

Louis grabbed at Gwen, tearing her blouse as she pushed past. Using her skills from kick-boxing class at the gym, Gwen drove her heel into Louis's chest. The waiter toppled backwards into the mob of charging pub patrons. Eddy spotted an exit sign at the back of the bar. "This way!" They threw open the unlocked door and found themselves outside, in the alleyway behind the bar. Eddy turned to shut the door on the shrieking faces and clawing hands. A pint glass beaned him in the head. Eddy staggered backwards. Blood poured from a gash in his temple. The crowd roared with savage delight. Gwen slammed the door on them. She had no idea what was happening but knew the mob was trying to kill them. The crowd crashed into the door, almost throwing Gwen to the ground. Out of the corner of her eye, she spotted a smashed crate. She yanked a wooden slat free and wedged it under the door handle. The door jolted, but held. "That won't hold long," she said. Gwen grabbed Eddy by the shoulders. "Are you okay?"

Eddy applied pressure to staunch the blood. "I think so."

"Good."

"I may pass out."

"Don't."

"If you say so."

"We have to go."

They turned and ran. Eddy continued to hold his hand to his head. He could feel warm blood seeping between his fingers. Head wounds always bleed a lot, he recalled. For the second time that day, he was running for his life in an alleyway. Funny that, he thought, I wonder if my horoscope mentioned it. Eddy's brain was addled by shock and trauma. Behind them, the wood slat snapped. The mob spilled from the pub's back exit in a comical heap. "There they go!" someone shouted. When the door had opened, a young woman named Carol in a powder blue Forever 21 dress had fallen face-first to the pavement. She now tried to get up. Like the others, she could see only red hatred at the sight of Eddy and Gwen. She'd didn't know Eddy or Gwen, but she knew she wanted them to die. She wasn't sure why, but that was a detail to be worked out later. For now, she could only think one thing: *Die! Die! Die!* As she started to pick herself up, another member of the mob, a large Italian-American man named Vinny, pulled himself up by pushing her down. The rest of the crowd trampled over her. A heel stomped on the side of her head. A boot crushed her ribs. They didn't want to hurt her. They just didn't care enough not to. All they wanted was to get to the fleeing man and woman from TV. That was all Carol wanted too. It was her very last thought as the side of her skull caved in.

"We need to find help," shouted Gwen. "These people are insane!"

Gwen and Eddy reached the street, bursting out upon a man and woman returning to work after lunch. The man was explaining the proper Japanese way to eat sushi. "Americans don't realize how much the Japanese use their fingers," he said.

"Help us please!" Gwen pleaded. Gwen's hair was wild; her blouse torn. Beside her, Eddy stared with a look of wild eyed paranoia. The blood had caked on his face like a red racoon mask, making the whites of his eyes pop with cartoonish mania.

The horrified couple stared back. They were trying to make the instant assessment people in big cities make when confronted by frantic strangers. Are the strangers crazy, dangerous, or selling something? Eddy and Gwen looked to be the first two, they decided, probably not the third.

Shrieks and shouts erupted from the corner. A gang of bar patrons, seeing Gwen and Eddy escape through the back of the bar, had come around the front. It was a surprisingly savvy move given that their brains currently had the reasoning skills of electrified badgers. For a second, Eddy simply stared—stunned by the bloodthirsty hoard rushing towards them. The mob, dressed mostly in sensibly priced department store fashions, seemed even more surreal here in the cheery California sunshine.

"Kill them!" someone shrieked.

"Gah!" shouted someone else.

The two terrified office workers stepped aside. We should mind our own business, they thought.

"Run!" yelled Gwen.

The fugitives tore down the street in the only direction left. Behind them, the tributaries of maniacs, one from the alleyway and one from the corner, joined into a single rushing river of hate. The office workers were knocked off their feet like bowling pins.

"We need to get off the street!" screamed Gwen. She wrenched open a random storefront door and yanked Eddy inside.

*Ting-a-ling-a-ling!* Tiny bells tinkled as they entered. Gwen slammed the door shut behind them. Eddy was immediately struck by the scent of lavender and acetone. A dozen startled Chinese manicurists stared up at the new arrivals. Equally surprised were the middle-aged white women sitting with their feet in foot baths of foamy blue water.

"Can I help you?" asked the manager, bowing slightly.

"Yes," said Gwen, "call 911." The petite hostess didn't move. For a moment, Gwen wondered if the woman didn't speak English. "I said, can you call 911?" She felt Eddy vigorously tapping her shoulder. "What?"

Eddy pointed to the TV hanging on the wall. It was tuned to MCNX. Lance Winface was railing at one of his guests, "Shut-up! Shut-up! Shut your pie-hole or I'll cut your mike!" Gwen looked again to the manicurists and customers. They stared back with glassy eyes. Their faces went from confusion, to dawning recognition, to twisted masks of red rage.

"Die, die, die!" shrieked the receptionist. The diminutive woman attempted to stab Gwen in the chest with her appointment pen. Gwen grabbed her wrist and punched the woman hard in the face, sending her backwards over a footstool. Around the store, maniacal manicurists snatched up whatever weapons they could find. The aestheticians quickly surrounded Eddy and Gwen, brandishing nail clippers, pumice stones, and emery boards.

"We need to get out of here," said Gwen.

"We can't," said Eddy, pointing to the pub patrons amassing outside. The storefront window was mirrored and the mob appeared confused by its own reflection. Eddy locked the door just as a shrieking blonde woman in a 'Juicy' shirt tried to yank it open. Frustrated, the woman began slamming her fists against the safety glass until her fingers bled and the bones inside shattered. An enraged librarian tried to charge through the store front window, only to rebound off and back into the crowd. The rest of the mob pummelled the windows with whatever they could find. "They'll be through in a minute!"

Gwen nodded. "Let's do this then." She charged forward into the throng of manicurists. Eddy lunged after. One of the customers, wearing a green mud facial mask, tried to grab Eddy as he passed. He put his hand on the woman's face and shoved her back hard, blinding her with exfoliating muck. The woman fell back into her massage chair which lurched to life at maximum micro-pulse. Refusing to relax, the woman leapt up again, wiping the loam from her eyes. Eddy seized the moment to step through the tumbled ranks of manicurists laid flat by Gwen's charge.

An instant later, Eddy and Gwen were in back of Lucky Dragon Nails. They weaved between oversized SUVs crammed into compact spots. It was now the customers turn to attack. A dozen blonde women with rolled up pant legs lurched from the salon's back door, shrieking and pointing, "Get them! Get them!" The women, whose bare feet were still locked in Styrofoam toe separators, stumbled on the hard pavement. The manicurists exited behind them and tried to push between their unwieldy clients and the cars. The confusion gave Eddy and Gwen the time they needed. They bolted down the side street while their entangled pursuers yelled English and Chinese curses from behind.

For a brief elated moment, Eddy and Gwen believed they had escaped. They turned a corner. They then turned another, only to face an unassailable brick wall. There were neither doors nor windows. The wall itself was covered with cartoon graffiti. 'Castigat ridendo mores!' shouted a twelve-foot tall Powerpuff Girl in spray-paint. They could hear the shouts of the crowd echoing closer.

"A dead end," said Eddy. "What do we do?"

"We fight," said Gwen.

"Are you crazy? They vastly outnumber us!"

"So what do you recommend? Cowering? Begging for mercy?"

"No, I–" The ground wobbled under Eddy's foot. He looked down to see that he was standing on a heavy cast iron grate. Beneath the grate, a narrow storm trough descended into shadow. Gwen followed his gaze. "It could be too small," he said.

"It could be," she agreed.

Hearts pounding, they pried their fingers between the cold black metal bars and heaved. The grate was held in place only by gravity. As Eddy lifted one end, Gwen slid herself into the space beneath.

"It's tight, but I think we can both fit. It's our only chance!"

Eddy squeezed himself in beside her, lowering the grate over them both as he did. They lay face to face. Eddy could feel Gwen's hot breath on his cheek. He could see only her left eye. It's like sharing a coffin, he thought. We could well die here. More likely they'll drag us out and—

"Eddy!" Gwen whispered, urgently pointing with her eyes.

The heavy grate had landed askew. The hysterical horde was almost there. Their shouts preceded them, reaching a shrieking crescendo. Eddy poked his fingers through the tight holes and pulled. The heft made it feel as if his finger bones would snap. The cast iron keened, then clanked into place.

The mob rounded the corner. They paused as one, panting and confused.

"If they find us, we're dead," Eddy hissed.

"Shush!"

The mob inhaled as one. Exhaled as one. Its members cast about for any sign of their quarry. The mob-members' brains were functioning at a reptilian level. Together, they were a giant crocodile of hate. The crocodile's head was Roger, an orthodontist from Orange County. Roger was up for the day to buy discount dental supplies and (now) to lynch two people. "I thought you said you saw them!" Roger snarled.

"I did," insisted Ling, one of the Chinese manicurists. "I *know* I did." As she spoke, Ling clenched and unclenched her perfect pink nails with 'Hello Kitty' decals. She itched to drive them into the man's and woman's eye sockets. On Ling's word, the mob had entered the cul-de-sac. She was certain she had seen them enter. There were no exits. Where could they have gone?

Members of the mob climbed into a lone dumpster and rummaged through the trash. Finding nothing but Amazon.com shipping boxes and too many packing peanuts, they began to hurl the materials at fellow mob members in frustration. Others overturned a pair of blue recycling bins. A stay-at-home mom from Manhattan Beach shrieked in horror at the sight of wet garbage mixed with cardboard and plastic. In an apoplectic fit, she began assaulting a retired anesthetist named Tim. For several agonizing seconds, the more lucid members of the mob searched the walls for secret doors. The rest raged about incoherently.

Beneath the metal grate, Eddy and Gwen scarcely dared breathe. Dozens of feet stomped over the wobbly iron frame. Amazingly, not a single person had looked down. Eddy found himself staring at the soles of a pair of sneakers and, unavoidably, up the skirt of Sandra, a waitress from the pub. He could see Sandra's nostrils flare as she and the others roared in frustration.

"Well they're not goddamn here!" yelled the orthodontist. "Ling lied."

"I saw them!" Ling yelled back.

"She's Chinese, what do you expect?" yelled a racist DMV employee named Kevin.

"Maybe they went the other way?" someone suggested.

"Which way is that?"

"The way we didn't go."

There was a murmur of agreement from the crowd. "Let's go the way we didn't go!" Roger screamed. The mob roared its approval. The feet on the grate turned and ran. More feet stomped past, rocking the cast iron. Still, no one looked down.

All at once, the feet were gone.

The shrieks and yells grew fainter.

Silence.

In the cramped, shadowy interior of the concrete niche, Gwen and Eddy exchanged terrified glances. "What do we do now?" asked Eddy.

Gwen thought for a moment. "We get help."

# BETA 0.21

"They laughed when I sat down at the piano..." – T. Lehrer

//Downtown Los Angeles — now

The luxury condo lobby was filled with the tinkling piano sounds of Jimmy Buffet accompanied by the London Philharmonic. It was a classical arrangement of *Margaritaville*. Eddy glanced about nervously. He was in fear of anyone who might enter from the street or step from the elevators. It was early evening now. Some people would still be coming home from work. The lobby walls were antiqued mirrored tile that reflected Eddy's strained expression a dozen times and left him feeling vulnerable. Next to the elevator, a raised garden of tropical plants spilled over its marble edging. Eddy nervously tugged on one. It turned out to be plastic. He tried awkwardly to reattach the leaf. A good fake, he thought, very high end. Classy. "It's here," said Gwen. The elevator doors opened with a *ting!*

"I don't know about this," said Eddy, glancing nervously between the doors as they closed. A woman was entering the lobby from the street. For a moment, Eddy was concerned she had seen them in the reflective wall tile. The tenant proceeded to her mailbox, tiny key in hand, chatting on her cell.

"There's nothing to worry about," said Gwen. "Dan's a good guy. I trust him completely."

They stood in silence as the elevator rose. Their journey here had been harrowing. They'd skulked the whole way with heads bowed, avoiding the eyes of passersby and occasionally ducking into doorways. Eddy counted as the floors lit up, 6... 7... 8...

Moments later, they were standing outside Dan's penthouse apartment as he opened the door. Eddy had remained silent when they'd called up on the outside intercom and Gwen hadn't mentioned him. Dan now stood in his Saks 5th Avenue bathrobe, slippers and startlingly white teeth. At the sight of Eddy, his smile vanished.

"Hi," said Eddy. "Thanks for buzzing us in." He watched to make sure the handsome lawyer didn't turn into a homicidal maniac at the sight of them. Despite Gwen's assurances that Dan would 'never do that', Eddy wasn't convinced. *Zombie-bots.* The word hummed like a mosquito in his ear that he couldn't kill and left him slapping himself on the side of his head.

"Um, what's... um... guy doing here?" said Dan.

Gwen walked past Dan, pulling Eddy in her wake. "His name is Eddy."

"Uh huh."

"We need your help."

"Did you know you guys were on TV?"

Both Gwen and Eddy froze. "You saw that?" said Eddy.

"I just caught the tail end. The police are looking for you, Gwen. And Erik here."

"Eddy," said Eddy.

"As persons of interest, not suspects," said Gwen, "We didn't do anything."

Dan looked at her reproachfully. "Gwen, come on, persons of interest? That just means they haven't got enough evidence to bring charges yet. You know that. It's just one of those things we say like, 'innocent until proven guilty' and 'if you cannot afford one, you will be provided with a highly qualified public defender'."

Eddy took a moment to look around the luxury condo. It was decorated in what he decided was nouveau-riche-bachelor style. It was modern and open concept, with plush white leather furniture and throw rugs on black bamboo floors. The walls were all mirrors and windows. The one non-glass wall was taken up by a two-story mezzotint of a nude woman with a toaster for a head. In the toaster were two colourized strawberry pop-tarts. The word 'Gratify' was written on an unfurled banner in Old English script. Eddy suddenly felt hungry for pop-tarts.

"Dan, we need your help."

"I can't be housing fugitives, Gwen..." said Dan.

"Persons of interest. And you're not housing us, you're providing legal counsel."

"You'll get me disbarred or worse."

Gwen put her hands around Dan's waist and pulled him close. "We'll go to the police. We just need to make sure we're protected. We're not sure who we can trust."

"There are people after us," said Eddy.

"People?" said Dan, "You mean the police."

"No, I mean people."

Dan snorted. "Now, you sound paranoid."

"We're not paranoid."

"Uh huh. So who exactly is out to get you?"

Eddy hesitated. "Everyone."

Gwen silenced Eddy with a look. With a finger under his chin, she turned Dan's attention back to herself. She looked him in the eyes. "Help us? Please?"

"Okay," Dan agreed. At that moment, his robe fell open.

Eddy tried to look away, only to be reminded of the mirrored walls. He closed his eyes.

"Later," said Gwen, tying Dan's robe for him. "First, we need your help."

"And some food," said Eddy. They'd intended to eat at the pub. All the adrenaline and fleeing for his life had left him with a ravenous pit for a stomach.

Gwen nodded and said, "Food would be good."

"I got some left over P.F. Chang's in the fridge," said Dan, pointing to the open concept kitchen.

"Really? You like P.F. Chang's?" said Eddy. "Me too."

"Yeah," said Dan. "I like the orange peel shrimp. Listen, I gotta make a call in the office. You two eat. I'll be back in a few minutes. Make yourselves comfortable."

"Thanks, D," said Gwen. She gave him a kiss on the cheek before letting go. Dan turned and jogged upstairs to the second floor of the condo. Eddy walked to the kitchen. The appliances included a hulking Viking chef style six burner stove that looked as though it had never been used. Eddy opened the professional grade fridge. Inside, he found a bottle of Svedka vodka, a jug of Cytosport Chocolate Muscle Milk and the promised Chinese take-out. Two minutes later, Eddy and Gwen were wolfing down microwaved dan dan noodles and shrimp over the white marble-top kitchen island. "I don't trust him," said Eddy.

Gwen stopped in mid-chew. "Why?"

"Because when we showed up, he acted as though we were a couple of Jehovah's witnesses, or lepers, or maybe Jehovah's Witnesses with leprosy."

"He'd just seen us on television. He was concerned because we're fugitives."

"Persons of interest."

"Whatever. Look, I know this is hard for you to understand. It's a lawyer thing. Lawyers see things through a different lens. They see legal pitfalls and hazards. I totally understand why he reacted the way he did. I would have done the same thing. In fact, I did. Look at how I responded when you came through my apartment window."

"Well, I was coming through your window, not your front door. Plus, we aren't dating."

"Dan's a good guy," Gwen assured him.

"No, he's not," said Eddy. He then immediately wished he hadn't. He hadn't planned to say anything. The words had been hovering in his mind, sure, but he'd decided to keep them to himself. Then, when he wasn't looking, the words had made a break for it.

"What are you talking about? You don't even know him."

Eddy hesitated. He was holding a thick bundle of noodles between disposable wooden chopsticks. He decided to stuff the noodles into his mouth to play for time. Gwen continued to stare him down, annoyed and undeterred. Eddy realized there was no going back. His mouth had decided to go 'all in' without first consulting with his brain. Eddy swallowed. "I know he cheats on you."

"What?" said Gwen, taken aback. "How?"

"I saw him, with another woman at P.F. Chang's. This is probably their doggy-bag."

Gwen dropped her chopsticks. She breathed. "You saw him with a woman at a restaurant? You do know he's a lawyer, right? He meets with people all the time, some of whom, I assume, are women."

"I..." Eddy hesitated again. He could see the tremble of her chin. He could see the tears welling up in the corners of her eyes. Part of him wanted to pull back, to say he was mistaken and act as if it were all a big misunderstanding. "I'm an idiot," he could say. That, she would certainly believe. The other part of him, felt it was his duty to finish the job and tell her the cruel truth. His mouth, having got him into trouble, now had nothing good to say.

"You what?" Gwen glared fiercely, hands on hips. "Well?"

"I just... I just..."

Gwen's eyes narrowed. "Are you jealous?"

Eddy wanted to say 'no'. He wanted to tell her the truth—that he'd seen Dan kiss the woman and lie to Gwen on the phone. "I, um..." Eddy lost his nerve. "Maybe, I... I don't know."

Gwen stared at Eddy in furious silence. She turned and walked away. She wanted to leave the room but—owing to the open-concept design —there was no room to actually leave without leaving the condo altogether, and that seemed like a bad idea. Instead, she walked to the living room space opposite. She gazed determinedly out the floor-to-ceiling windows at the bright Los Angeles skyline. Opposite, was the rooftop of The Standard Hotel. A semi-formal event was in progress. Men in suits and women in dresses sipped cocktails around the swimming pool, attended to by white jacket waiters. Eddy considered following Gwen, but everything he'd said so far had only made matters worse. He no longer trusted his mouth. He considered keeping it busy by eating her leftover dan dan noodles. He really was hungry. Still, it seemed wrong to eat her noodles just because she was too upset to do so herself. In the end, he decided to take just one mouthful, and that was it.

"What the hell?" said Gwen.

"Mmmpf?" said Eddy, his mouth full of pasta.

Gwen was staring at the sofa. The sofa was, like everything else in the condo, uber-modern. It was also part of a limited-edition line purchased at Fred Segal for $50,000. The fabric was a precise colour of maroon the designer claimed was unique to this sofa. It had been selected by a high-tech algorithm that sifted through billions of photos online to identify 64-bit shades that didn't exist anywhere on planet Earth, or at least Google Earth. Other maroons may be visually indistinguishable by the human eye, nevertheless, the salesman had assured Dan, this hue was his and his alone. "This maroon is *you*," the designer said, "and what a maroon you are!" Or, if Dan preferred, it also came in unique tangerine. It was not Dan's exclusive upholstery that had caught Gwen's eye. She already knew about the sofa. Dan had told her about it himself. He told everyone who visited the condo, down to the delivery man from UPS. If he didn't, it would have been a colossal waste of money. Gwen walked over and yanked an article of clothing from beneath an inimitable cushion. The clothing was a non-unique shade of black, manufactured and sold en masse by Victoria Secret. Gwen did not know who the panties belonged to, but she knew they didn't belong to her. "Daniel!" Hearing no response, Gwen stormed the steps to the second level, dangling the lingerie between two fingers like a dead rat. "Dan!" Eddy, deciding Gwen would be in no mood to eat, stuffed the remaining noodles into his mouth and followed.

Gwen stood before the door to Dan's home office. Aside from the bathroom, it was the only actual room in the entire loft. She raised her hand to push—then stopped. The door was ajar already. Dan could be clearly heard talking on the phone. "Yeah, I can keep 'em here until you arrive. They have nowhere else to go. ... Sure, they trust me. I think she's in love with me or something." Gwen glanced at Eddy. Eddy said nothing. "Sounds good," Dan continued, "I'll just keep 'em here until you arrive." Through the crack, they could see Dan end the call. Gwen flung open the door. The handsome lawyer stood in shock—his mouth and, again, bathrobe fell open. "I – I – I can explain," he stammered.

Gwen socked Dan in the mouth.

"Ow!" he yelled, clutching his now bleeding lip. "I said, I could explain..."

"Which part? About keeping us here, or this?" Gwen waved the lace panties in his face.

Dan was distracted with finding something loose in his mouth. He reached in and pulled out a tooth. "My tooth, you knocked out my tooth! That is assault!" As he spoke, the bloody gap in his top row of teeth became visible. The missing incisor completely transformed how he looked. GQ model—hillbilly—GQ model—hillbilly, thought Eddy each time Dan's mouth opened and closed.

Gwen massaged her knuckles and shook her head. She turned and barged past Eddy toward the stairs. "Let's go."

"Okay," said Eddy.

"Don't think I won't thoo!" Dan shouted, whistling each word. "I'll thoo you for every penny you've got!"

Minutes later, Eddy was following Gwen as she stormed down the sidewalk, oblivious to danger. Despite the gathering dusk, the bright lights of storefronts and the headlights of passing cars made Eddy feel illuminated and exposed. He had tried to reason with Gwen in the elevator. "What are we going to do?" he'd asked. Gwen seemed not to care. Eddy now glanced furtively about, hiding his face from passing pedestrians. Fortunately, this was Los Angeles. Angelinos avoided walking at all costs, so the sidewalks were less congested than a similar street in New York or Chicago. They also benefited from the inclination of big city dwellers to avoid eye contact, especially at night. Still, the sidewalk was not entirely empty and Eddy was frequently forced to shield his face with his hand. Gwen, in her fury, did nothing of the kind. "Gwen!" Eddy shout-whispered to her, "Gwen!" Gwen continued to blaze boldly ahead, until forced to stop by a red hand signal and the intervening rush of cars. "Gwen, where are we going?"

"I can't believe he was cheating on me," Gwen fumed. She turned to look at Eddy accusingly. "And you *knew*."

"But, I told you."

"Five minutes ago."

"More like ten, really," Eddy quibbled. The light changed, and Gwen charged off again. "But that's not the point. I didn't..." Gwen was too far ahead, he had to run to keep up. "Gwen, listen... I'm sorry, but we have to be smart. Someone might recog–" Eddy collided with an old woman as she exited the ATM foyer of a bank. He was spun around by the impact. "I'm sorry, are you okay?" he asked. The old woman rubbed her shoulder, nodded, then stopped. The light of recognition flickered in her eyes.

"Are you on TV?" she asked. In Los Angeles, running into a celebrity, especially a vaguely identifiable C-lister, was always a possibility.

"Years ago on one of those Law and Order shows," said Eddy, hoping to throw her off. "I played a corpse." He turned and began to jog to catch up with Gwen. Behind him, the old woman stared, turning Tetris pieces in her mind. Suddenly, she began to twitch and spasm. "Gah!" she shrieked, pointing at Eddy and Gwen, "Gah!" A few pedestrians turned to look. Most stared at the old woman.

"Gwen, that woman recognized us," Eddy shouted. "You're going to get us killed!"

Gwen stopped. She turned to face him. "Are you sure?"

As if in answer, the old woman began running towards them, pointing and screaming. "Gah! It's them! It's the traitors from TV!"

"Pretty sure," said Eddy.

"We need to get out of here."

Other pedestrians began to look to see what the old woman was pointing at. It might, after all, be an *actual* celebrity. Eddy and Gwen turned to run away.

"It *is* them!" A cab driver shouted in a thick Albanian accent. Inside the limbic centre of the cab driver's brain, in the cauliflower of the amygdala, a storm of red lightning erupted. It transformed neurones into tiny Tesla coils and coalesced into a repeating pattern of pure, bestial rage. "Get them!" he cried. Gwen was momentarily paralyzed by fear. The cab driver pounded the side of his car door like a tribal drum. *Bang! Boom! Bang!* Eddy grabbed Gwen's hand and yanked her to a stumbling run. "Get them! Get them!" The cabby began hurling pine tree air fresheners at them like ninja throwing stars. Unlike ninja throwing stars, they bounced harmlessly off Eddy's back. Eddy and Gwen weaved between perplexed pedestrians. Ahead, the traffic was stopped, waiting for a light to change. The cabby, unable to move his car, opened the driver-side door and clambered across the hood in pursuit. "Get them!"

Other pedestrians, a hot dog salesman, two sanitation workers, and a homeless man, also recognized them. Inside their brains, red energy crackled into Mandelbrot sets of loathing. On the street, more drivers began to point and shout. "Traitors!" "Die!" Gwen and Eddy broke into a full-on run, plowing through passersby. The pursuers did the same to the best of their relative ability, driven by primal hate. The old woman who had first recognized them now fell to the pavement in cardiac arrest. Most passersby, simply stared in shock at the lynch mob that seemed to materialize from nowhere. Most, concerned for their own safety, decided to 'just stay out of it'. Some took pictures to share on social media. A teenage girl named Kelsi was trampled to death while trying to take a selfie with the stampeding mob.

As they ran, the crowd only continued to grow. More drivers joined in, abandoning their vehicles in the middle of the road. A financial advisor driving a Range Rover, dropped his cellphone and cranked the wheel, jumping the curb. For a moment, he gunned the SUV towards Eddy and Gwen, running down an ice cream seller who attempted to join the chase at the wrong time.

"This way!" shouted Eddy. He guided Gwen down a short flight of steps to a plaza area. The Range Rover collided with a bronze statue of

Larry Flint. The driver was knocked unconscious as the airbag exploded in his face. On the street, a tour bus guide told his passengers to look left to see "an actual Los Angeles riot in process." The passengers piled at the windows to take pictures. They were touring German retirees who had been watching the on-bus TV tuned to MCNX news earlier. Madness engulfed them. They dropped their cameras, forced open the bus doors, and spilled out on the street. "Halten Sie!" screeched an old man waving his cane. "Achtung!"

"We can't outrun them forever," yelled Eddy. "New ones keep joining the chase!"

Gwen glanced over her shoulder. The mob was continuing to amass. Even as some members had fallen away, often underfoot of their fellows, others continued to swell the ranks. A bullet ricocheted off an office building in front of them. Both Eddy and Gwen turned to see its source. "A cop!" Eddy shouted, pointing to a uniformed policeman. The now insane officer had exited a diner as they'd passed. He still wore a white napkin tucked into his collar like a bib. He aimed his pistol to take a second shot. "Come on!" They turned and ran. A second bullet shattered a window behind them. They banked a corner and faced a long city block. "In here!" Eddy lunged down a parking garage ramp, hoping to hide inside before the pursuers turned the corner. Gwen started to protest but, seeing Eddy was already halfway down, relented and followed. They charged past the unmanned parking gate and into the fluorescent lit interior.

//Washington, DC — now

Anderson Cooper accepted the hot cocoa from Cindy and handed her the microphone from his coat lapel in return. He cradled the warm cup between his frozen fingers and took a delicious sip. Thankfully, as always, Cindy had remembered the mini marshmallows. Anderson had just signed off his live report from outside Annabelle Flatwood's townhouse. They were still on deck, waiting for Senator Alan Cassius to exit. Meanwhile, CNN had tuned back to *The Situation Room*, where Wolf Blitzer and others speculated on the Congresswoman's future. "Thanks Cindy," said Anderson with a lopsided smile, "You're the real hero here."

"Anderson?" said Ted, the cameraman. A hubbub of activity swept the news team encampment along on the icy Washington street. The door to Flatwood's apartment had opened, swung wide by one of the two unidentified men who accompanied Senator Cassius. Cooper rushed to join the scrum of reporters that formed. "Going live, in 3... 2... 1... " said Karen, the segment's producer, in Anderson's ear. The narrow figure of Alan Cassius exited the townhouse. He paused atop the snowy stoop.

"Senator, did you talk to Ms. Flatwood?"

"Is the Congresswoman going to resign?"

Cassius calmly donned fitted black shearling gloves. He took his time. He appeared more concerned with their fit than with the throng of reporters gathered before him. His entourage gazed over the heads of the assembled media. They wore plain black sunglasses and expressions of impassive disdain. Cassius casually adjusted his yellow bow tie.

"What can you tell us of your meeting?" Anderson asked. He didn't shout, but the Senator seemed to hear him above the rest.

"We had a frank and serious discussion," he said, with a grim smile. "I think that Congresswoman Flatwood should be taken at her word that it is not her in that video tape. I suspect it is only a matter of time before she is vindicated."

A murmur of surprise rippled the crowd. The two politicians' bitter rivalry was well known, deep and entrenched. "If you're saying the video is a fake, then who's behind it?" asked Laura Dincroft, reporter for MCNX.

"I don't engage in idle speculation," said the Senator. He then added, with a coy smile, "That's *your* job." Cassius pushed forward through the mass of journalists shouting follow-up questions. His two henchmen served as ice-breakers, pressing back the press and opening an avenue to an awaiting black sedan.

"And there you have it, Wolfe. A surprising turn of events here. Alan Cassius, not exactly known as an ally of Congresswoman Flatwood, doing what could only be described as, well, vouching for her."

"Thank-you, Anderson," said Wolf Blitzer back on set. "And we'll have to leave it at that, with reports coming in of some sort of riot taking place in downtown Los Angeles."

#

//Downtown Los Angeles — now

"So now what?" hissed Gwen, as she lay flat on the asphalt and peered beneath a long row of parked cars.

Eddy lay beside her, as low to the ground as he could manage. "I don't know," he whispered. They watched intently the feet of the arriving mob as they descended the parking garage ramp. Sneakers, dress shoes, high heels, and work boots paced with profound agitation. Behind the milling feet were the only elevators.

"Are they here?" demanded a woman with frizzy black hair.

"I have no idea!" snarled the ice cream seller, clutching his ice cream scoop like a cudgel.

"This was a dumb idea," Gwen shot back. "We're cornered. Again. Why did you come down here?"

Eddy wasn't sure. It had been an impulsive decision, driven by the instinct to hide. He'd thought they might make it inside the garage without being seen but—even as they'd entered—they could hear their pursuers shouting where they'd gone. They had thought to escape through the office building above but, as they'd approached, the light above the elevator doors lit up. Panicked that more homicidal maniacs might be inside, he and Gwen ran the other way. They'd ducked behind a green Hyundai Elantra and watched as a harmless insurance actuary named Lewis exited. Lewis Goldstein had been working late on his white paper. In it, he argued that genetic testing could break the business model of the long-term care health insurance industry. Lewis had not expected to run into a blood thirsty mob on level P1. Or even on P2, for that matter. He'd never been to P3, so had no data to base an opinion on. When the door opened, the deranged mob members pouring down the ramp turned to stare at him with murderous anticipation. Upon seeing it was just Lewis, the maniacs slumped with collective disappointment and returned to their agitated pacing. Lewis stared in shock at a Dominos delivery man who was actually foaming at the mouth. Somehow, he was still carrying an insulated bag of undelivered pizzas over one shoulder. The actuary was at a loss to explain what could possibly enrage such a seemingly random cross-section of individuals. No statistical model could explain it, he decided. The makeup of the mob seemed entirely random, except for the surprising number of people sputtering in German. Lewis decided not to force his way through them to his car. I think I'll take Uber home tonight, her decided. He pressed 'L' for lobby as he pulled out his phone. Eddy and Gwen had watched all of this unfold from behind the midsize sedan.

There were at least two-dozen mob members now gathered in the front of the parking garage. Eddy stole a glance over the Hyundai's lime green hood. The cool white of the fluorescent lights on the strained faces of the crazed crowd made them appear even more menacing. Eddy despaired. The intellect he was so proud of, that could bring a major financial institution to its knees wasn't so brilliant at basic survival. "I don't know," he confessed. "I don't know what to do."

"They're hiding!" exclaimed an old man.

The mob murmured in agreement.

"Look under the cars!"

Gwen and Eddy exchanged terrified glances. "Hide behind the tires," he whispered. They tucked themselves in as much as they could. Eddy was unsure if the wheels were big enough to conceal them.

Seething and spluttering mob members threw themselves to the ground and peered beneath the parked vehicles.

"I don't see them," a man snarled.

"Ich sehe niemanden," a German tourist agreed. "Ach!"

The contingent of elderly Germans began to walk down the long row of cars, looking between each. "Nein... nein... nein..."

"It's only a matter of time," said Eddy.

"We have to go for it," said Gwen.

"Go for what?"

"The elevator."

"You mean the elevator that twenty-plus crazy people are standing in front of, that could take minutes just to arrive?"

"Yes."

At that moment, a deranged yoga teacher thought she spotted Gwen hiding inside a charging Tesla. She began shrieking and pointing. The mob swarmed the vehicle and began pounding on the glass. The car alarm began to keen, *Wee-boo! Wee-boo! Wee-boo!* The shrill noise drove the attackers even more insane. They bent windshield wipers and wrenched off the car's sideview mirrors. Then, somebody pointed out that it wasn't Gwen or Eddy inside. It was an inflatable dummy the owner used to illegally ride in the carpool lane. For a moment, the mob seemed at a loss. Someone smashed the driver side window with a tire iron anyway. Mob members dragged the plastic copilot from its seat and beat it flat. Their hearts weren't in it. It just wasn't the same as bludgeoning a real person.

"Now," said Gwen, "while they're distracted!"

Eddy wasn't sure Gwen was right, but nodded anyway. In a running crouch behind the cars, they made for the elevators. The crowd's rage had moved onto the car itself. They began to beat the Model S to scrap. Eddy was amazed when they reached the elevators unnoticed. Gwen tapped the Up-button. They waited anxiously, shielding their faces, not daring to look towards the din of dismantling bodywork. A gentle *ping!* announced the arrival of the lift. They slipped between the sliding doors as they opened.

Inside was an insane office building security guard named Muhammad. "You!" he bellowed, "You must die!" Muhammad had spotted Eddy and Gwen on the security monitor and decided to come kill them himself. He was just as shocked as they were, however, to be suddenly sharing an elevator. Eddy and Gwen recovered first. They each grabbed an arm and heaved the flailing guard through the now closing doors. Muhammad rolled on the pavement with shrieks of outrage.

"Hey, there they are!" one of the mob members shouted, dropping a driver side mirror he'd been hammering to bits. A wall of hate-filled faces turned and glared at Eddy and Gwen as the elevator doors slid shut. Through the closed doors, they could hear the cries of anguish.

"Take the stairs!" someone yelled.

"I'd rather wait," someone else yelled back.

Eddy and Gwen collapsed against the back wall of the elevator as it began to rise. They stared at one another with terror filled eyes. The elevator seemed to take forever to reach the lobby. Soft jazz played. "We could go higher up," Eddy suggested. "Maybe hide in one of the offices?"

"I don't want to be trapped in a building," said Gwen. "For all we know, they'll burn it to the ground."

Eddy nodded. He wanted to be away from here as well.

The elevator doors opened with another *ping!* They revealed a mocha-brown marble lobby. The lighting was dimmed for the post workday. *Head Like a Hole* from *Tony Bennett Sings Nine Inch Nails* played softly over the lobby sound system. Eddy and Gwen surveyed the room for signs of danger. The interior was deserted. They charged past the unmanned security desk, towards a pair of revolving doors.

Suddenly, the voluminous interior filled with the echoes of angry shouts and shrill shrieks as the mob burst from the stairwell. "There they are!" a woman screamed. She was still wearing her gym clothes from spin class. Her t-shirt said simply 'Believe' in pink script, without specifying in what exactly. Eddy pushed the first revolving door. The door refused to budge. Gwen tried the second, only to find that it too was locked. Eddy glanced about for something he could use to break the glass. He spotted a steel signpost used to remind people to sign in. Eddy heaved it heroically above his head and swung it like a two-handed sword. The signpost rebounded off the glass and hit Eddy in the face, knocking him to the floor. Eddy sat sprawled. The mob rushed forwards.

"What about that?" said Gwen, pointing to a simple push door on the adjacent wall labeled 'After Hours'.

"Yes, okay."

They ran to the door and pushed it open. Eddy noticed the lock mechanism in the frame and flicked it, before pushing the door closed behind them. He heard the *click*, just as the crazed Albanian taxi driver slammed up against the glass behind them. Four more lunatics, unable to slow their momentum, piled into the irate cab driver. Despite having his face smushed against the window, Bob still managed to snarl and spit like a distempered dog. Eddy stared in horror at the frothing madness.

"Come on," screamed Gwen, "They'll be through in a second!"

Eddy and Gwen found themselves atop the raised foundation upon which the office building stood. Steps led down to the sidewalks and streets below. The dark of night offered both hope of escape *and* the potential for unseen terrors. Behind them, the mob pounded the windows, pulping their hands and bloodying the glass. Cool evening air struck Eddy's face. It felt oddly serene. What to do? Where to go? Not here. They started down the steps, two at a time.

Eddy glanced back. The mob had discovered the doors were locked. Some began to use other mob members as battering rams to break through the glass. The result was horrific on a primal level. Eddy spotted the security guard, key in hand, making his way through the crowd.

All at once, there was a roar, a buffeting wind, and a blinding flood of white light. A Police helicopter appeared overhead, silhouetted in the glare of its own searchlight. For a moment, Eddy and Gwen were disoriented by the noise and dazzling brilliance. Eddy was unsure whether the helicopter was friend or foe, redemption, or death. Gwen had no such doubts. "Oh thank God," she said. She raised her hands and shouted into the hurricane, "Help us! Help us, please!"

"This is the police!" came a voice over a loudspeaker. "Remain calm..."

"Thank-you!" shouted Gwen.

"...and prepare to die!" said the Police pilot, completing his sentence. Bullets flew past, striking the ground at their feet. The helicopter marksman's aim was surprisingly bad. A stray shot hit the lobby door just as the security guard was unlocking it, shattering the glass and killing him instantly. Eddy and Gwen raced back and fourth in a panicked effort to evade gunfire. At the same time, crazed civilians crawled through the smashed door, over the dead guard's body. Several were struck by stray bullets and sent summmersaulting down the steps to the sidewalk below.

"Let's get out of here!" Gwen shouted.

Eddy nodded. He had no idea where they were going or how they could possibly evade a helicopter, but he knew staying here was not an option. They plunged down towards the street. Behind them, a pair of murderous Shriners, still wearing their fezzes at jaunty angles, made it out of the lobby without being helpfully shot by police. Swinging ceremonial swords, they howled and charged.

A black van squealed out of the darkness. With its headlights hooded, it was virtually invisible. It spin-drifted to a stop directly in front of Eddy and Gwen. Its side door flew open.

"Get in!" yelled the driver. He was young, with feathery blond hair, freckles, and a gleeful grin.

Eddy and Gwen hesitated.

"I'm a friend," the young man said. "I was sent here by marshal4819642. So, get in already!" A strafe of gunfire riddled the van's roof from above. "Or stay here and die. You know, whatev'."

Eddy and Gwen exchanged glances. What else was there? They leaped into the van. They tried to pull the door shut, but the shriners hacked at them with plastic scimitars. The blades, too dull to cut, were mostly just annoying. "Ow! Stop it!" yelled Eddy. Their young driver, slammed his foot on the gas and the van peeled away. The Shriners were tossed to the curb, fezzes flying. The police helicopter opened fire with a strafe of semiautomatic artillery. The bullets missed the van entirely, but killed three more in the crowd. "Gah!" screamed the mob in frustration.

"We'll never get away," said Gwen, "they have a helicopter!" Like all Angelinos, Gwen had seen her share of car chases on the local news. If she'd learned one thing, it was that cars don't escape helicopters.

"Hang on to your hats!" yelled the young man. He hit the gas and cranked the wheel, hurling Gwen and Eddy against the opposite wall. Fortunately, the van was lined on all sides with plush carpet. "Sorry about that!" The van lurched into a sharp turn then plunged down a narrow street. Through the windows of the rear doors, Eddy saw the helicopter roar past— its searchlight splashing across buildings. The chopper banked around, briefly vanishing from view.

"Is it there?" the driver shouted into what appeared to be a toy walkie-talkie.

"It's there," crackled a voice.

Eddy felt something hard in the small of his back. He reached around and pulled out a pink lava lamp. "Who the heck are–?" The driver cranked the wheel again, and again Gwen and Eddy tumbled into a heap. Eddy found his hand on something soft and warm then, realizing what it was, let go before Gwen slapped him. The van squealed into an underground parking garage. Outside, the helicopter roared past, searching for its lost prey.

The driver pulled into an empty parking spot. He leapt out and ran around to slide open the side door. Eddy saw then just how young their driver was. Early twenties at most, he decided. Despite the imminent danger, their rescuer was grinning goofily. "How fun was that, huh?" He was wearing a denim jacket over a tie dye shirt, blue jeans, and beaded moccasins. "Come on, we have to switch," he said.

"Switch?" said Eddy.

The driver pointed to a Toyota minivan parked in the next space. He pressed a keyless remote. The doors unlocked with a chirp. "They're looking for a black van, not a purple people mover."

"It's more of a burgundy," said Eddy.

"Hmm, I guess you're right," said the driver. "Anyhoo, the point is, I wouldn't be caught dead in wheels like this unless our lives depended on it. Which, it turns out, they do."

"Who the Hell are you?" said Gwen.

"I'll explain as we go," said the driver.

"Go where?"

"Somewhere safe."

Eddy wanted to know more, but he was out of ideas and tired of running. As suspicious as it sounded, the idea of 'somewhere safe' was hard to resist. "Works for me," he said.

"Whatev'," said Gwen. She slid across the backseat. Eddy followed and pulled the door closed. The windows, he noted, were tinted.

The driver hopped into his own seat and pressed the ignition button. Moments later, they pulled out onto the street. The driver carefully signalled the turn and began to drive in an almost leisurely fashion.

"Can't you go any faster?" said Gwen.

"I can, but..." A pair of police cruisers, with lights flashing and sirens screaming, turned the corner and roared past. "I'm being discreet," the driver yelled over the noise. "Not my usual modus operendi."

A few blocks away, the police helicopter crisscrossed the sky. Its searchlight shone into the streets and alleys below. Suddenly, it spotted them and banked to fly directly overhead.

"Crap!" said Eddy.

"Shaanti," said their driver.

The helicopter hovered above. The thunderous roar of its engine made the minivan shake. The brilliant high-beam flooded the interior with dazzling white light that left Eddy feeling overexposed. Gwen was trying to shout something. She was drowned out by the *whoop-whoop-whoop!* of the propeller. After several long seconds, the helicopter hauled off to continue its search elsewhere. "Well, that was loud," said the driver. "Mind, if I vape?"

"Who the Hell are you?" said Gwen.

"You didn't say 'no'." The driver pulled a pen-sized e-cigarette from his pocket and flicked a switch on the side. The tip began to glow blue. Gwen stared at the driver in amazement. With one hand on the wheel, he took a drag as he lazily turned a corner. "What, no 'thank-you for rescuing us from near certain death'? S'okay, I don't do it for the glory."

Gwen and Eddy exchanged baffled looks. The police sirens were growing fainter. Slowly, but surely the minivan was making its way through the city, away from the madness.

"Of course, we're grateful," said Eddy. "Thank-you."

They stopped at a red light. Gwen nodded towards the door handle. *Escape?* Eddy shrugged. *Where to?* Gwen shook her head. *No idea.*

"We just want to make sure we haven't jumped out of the frying pan and into the fire," said Gwen.

"Oh, I don't eat fried food. Mostly raw, actually. I'm a raw vegan, or what I call a 'regan'." The light turned green. The van took the on-ramp up to the freeway. The driver dutifully signalled as he merged into traffic.

"Can you tell us your name?"

"Nixon. Like the former president, you know? But unlike him, I really am not a crook. Well, not since they legalized weed anyway." Nixon pressed play on the car stereo. The dripping jazz sax of Grover Washington Jr. filled the small space.

"You said you were sent here by Marshal4819642? The guy who sent me the video?" said Eddy.

"What video?" asked Gwen.

"I'll explain later."

"Yup. I'm taking you guys to meet him right now."

"Are you some sort of government agent?" said Gwen. "CIA? FBI?"

The driver laughed. "Ph.D." He took another unhurried pull on his e-cig, held, then exhaled. Despite the open driver-side window, the van filled with the smell of black cherries and peppermint. The red tail lights in front of them coagulated into the slow moving mass that was the 405 LA freeway at night. "Hope to be anyway, in a couple of years. Right now, I'm a graduate student, in poetry y'all."

"You are kidding right?"

"No, I can prove it. Wanna hear me drop some massive Yeats?"

//Washington, DC — now

"Ms. Fla'wood?" Rosita entered the dining room, gently pushing open the French doors. The congresswoman had implored Rosita to call her 'Anne'. Rosita never felt comfortable with it. It was not what she had been taught. Besides, her employer was no ordinary woman; she was a United States Congresswoman. The Congresswoman had championed immigrant rights many times over and had personally helped Rosita apply for citizenship. Ms. Flatwood also paid generously, provided health insurance, and treated her maid well. The least Rosita could do, she reasoned, was address The Congresswoman with respect—whether she liked it or not. "Ms. Fla'wood?"

Rosita pushed open one of the doors just enough to slip her head through. She didn't want to interrupt anything, but the visiting Senator had left over an hour ago. Senior Cassius was a rude and arrogant man whose thugs had shoved the maid aside earlier. They frightened Rosita. They reminded her of the gangsters she'd known in Guatemala—men who would put you in an unmarked grave for fifty American dollars. Since the men had left, there had been only silence. Normally, this would not have been unusual. The Congresswoman often spent hours quietly poring over files and books. She normally did this in her upstairs office. When she worked in the dining room, it was usually only for an hour or two. Now, it was time for Rosita to set the table for supper.

"Ms. Fla'w... oh!" Rosita put her hand to her mouth in shock. Congresswoman Annabelle Flatwood was slumped over in her chair. Her eyes stared blankly. "Ms. Fla'wood!" the maid cried, rushing into the room. "Ms. Fla'wood!" The Congresswoman's hand lay palm-up on the table top, finger and thumb pinching something that wasn't there. Rosita delicately touched her employers fingers. To her relief, the skin was supple, warm... alive.

"What? Oh!" the Congresswoman jolted upright. She shook her head and patted her lightly mussed hair into place. "Oh hello, Rosita. I... I must have dozed off."

"Gracias a Dios, Ms. Flatwood, I was so worried! For a moment, I thought..." Rosita put her hand on her heart.

Congresswoman Flatwood smiled reassuringly. "I'm fine, Rosita, perfectly fine. I haven't been sleeping much lately. It must have caught up with me."

"Would you like some coffee, ma'am? Tea?"

"No, I'm feeling better now. Much more... myself."

## BETA 0.22

"You incomplete me." – K. Gödel

//Manhattan, New York — then

"Smile!" Eddy's mother nudged him gently in the ribs.

Eddy obliged as best he could. He hated smiling, hated having his picture taken, and hated having to accompany his mother to her book signings. It was a trifecta of things a twelve-year-old hates, he thought, a hate-fecta, or maybe a tri-hate. Still, his mother insisted she needed him for moral support and to 'shore up the crowd'. The crowd at that moment consisted of Eddy and an old woman who had sat in one of the chairs to rest her feet and flip through a copy of Cosmopolitan she'd 'borrowed' from the magazine section. The old woman pulled out a pen and began circling sexy body parts she found in a search puzzle in the back. Such was the glamorous life of the novelist. It could be worse, Eddy decided, there could be a lot of people. That would mean staying longer and his mother giving an actual reading. The bookstore staff woman snapped the picture, smiled and departed.

"There, that wasn't so bad was it?" said Eddy's mum.

"Can we leave now?"

"Not for an hour. Plus, I have to sign these," she said, pointing to the stack of books on the table.

"No one's here."

His mother feigned surprise. "Wow, so there isn't! I hadn't noticed. Fortunately, a whole tour bus of people is due in a few minutes."

"Really?"

"Probably not, but we'll never know if we leave."

Eddy sighed and shook his head. His mum was an eternal optimist. She went back to signing the inside covers of books no one would buy. They were twenty copies of her new novel, *The Oblong Heart*. She had written it in less than a year after coming out of the hospital. She'd felt inspired. Eddy only pretended to read her books. They were flowery romance novels that suffered from an appalling lack of space ships and elves. This one told the supposed true story of Romeo and Juliet. According to his mother, they didn't really die. They woke up, realized that everyone thought them dead and decided to run away and start anew. They got married. Years passed. They grew older and apart. Eventually, the passion was gone. They had affairs with other people. It turned out, they weren't so much in love with each other, as in love with love. In the end, Juliet married Mercutio, while Romeo found love with a strapping young man from Munich named Dolph. Reviews of the novel were tepid at best. "I don't pay attention to reviews," his mother proclaimed, "I write for myself." The turn out at the book signing seemed to confirm this. Still, his mother was remarkably cheerful and happy to be writing again, so he took her at her word. Eddy amused himself by perusing the 'Teen Paranormal Romance' section that Barnes & Noble had debuted with the *Twilight* vampire craze years ago and which, through some glaring oversight, had failed to go away with the end of the overwrought series. Eddy glanced back in wonder at his mum. She had just been interrupted by an older gentleman who was asking her if the bookstore had restrooms. She smiled graciously and told him no, but that there were bathrooms in the adjoining Starbucks. She then offered the man a copy of her book for free. "What would I do with it?" he asked. She suggested that he might want to read it. The old man explained that he didn't read books anymore, on account of their being too long, and that he'd really only come into the store to use the restroom, but thank-you anyway. Eddy's mother went back to signing the remaining books, humming as she did. To say his mother's depression now just seemed like a bad dream was clichéd, but true. To her, it seemed like someone else's bad dream. "I was out of my mind," she said. Eddy thought that might be the most confounding expression ever. He wondered at how easily she smiled now—sincere, bright, and true. It was the same smile he remembered from before it all began. He no longer took her smile for granted. Depressed people never smile. They can't even fake smile. This is not because they are unable to. It's because they can't try.

"You can probably pack up," said the staffer.

"I'm sorry no one came," said Eddy's mother, blushing.

"Happens all the time. You should try writing a self-help book. Those guys really pack them in. We had Tony Robbins in here once. It was a mad house."

"I wouldn't know where to begin." Eddy's mother smiled cheerfully again. She gathered up her coat and scarf. It was winter outside, and New York was in the midst of a chill. She would leave the signed copies behind in the hope that a few might sell. "Echoes of me," she called them. As he waited for her, Eddy picked up a thick paperback entitled *No Body to Love, Part One of the Intangible Trilogy*. The blurb on the back described it as a story of 'spectral passion', about a young girl who falls in love with a handsome ghost. Their love goes unrequited owing to the fact that he has no physical form. Somehow, this exercise in sexual frustration went on for six more books. The blurb described it as a 'romantic tragedy'. Eddy expected that was true.

"You're not sad about the turnout?" Eddy asked as they pushed through the double doors to exit the store. Cold flurries buffeted them, stinging cheeks. It was only five pm, but already getting dark. Such is December in New York.

His mother shrugged and flashed that bright smile for what would turn out to be the very last time. "I do what I love," she said, "how could I be sad?"

#

//Lotus Hill College, Los Angeles — now

Eddy and Gwen didn't know where they were going until they got there. They had been keeping low, huddled in the back of the minivan. Despite the tinted windows, neither wanted to risk being recognized. Nixon was amiable and irrepressibly cheerful despite the danger, or perhaps because of it. When Eddy and Gwen had chosen to travel in silence, Nixon kept his promise of reciting William Butler Yeats, or 'Yeatsy' as he called him. He started with *Second Coming*.

> *TURNING and turning in the widening gyre*
> *The falcon cannot hear the falconer;*
> *Things fall apart; the centre cannot hold;*
> *Mere anarchy is loosed upon the world,*
> *The blood-dimmed tide is loosed, and everywhere*
> *The ceremony of innocence is drowned;*
> *The best lack all conviction, while the worst*
> *Are full of passionate intensity.*

*Surely some revelation is at hand...*

Nixon stopped himself. He announced that it was "too heavy for an already heavy night." He beat-boxed for a bit then switched to Yeatsy's *Drinking Song.*

> *WINE comes in at the mouth*
> *And love comes in at the eye;*
> *That's all we shall know for truth*
> *Before we grow old and die.*
> *I lift the glass to my mouth*
> *I look at you, and I sigh*

They exited the 10 freeway at Wilshire Boulevard, the ever clogging artery of Los Angeles, and headed north. It was a well-treaded route, having been used three thousand years earlier by the Tongva people to bring tar from the pits at La Brea to their settlements along the coast. Eddy and Gwen kept their heads down along the streets which even at midnight were far from deserted. It began to drizzle. Nixon switched on the windshield wipers. Eddy relaxed somewhat as the additional cover afforded by the rain streamed down the passenger windows. It was as if the madness was being washed away. The minivan made several turns along the confusing tangle of roads that ringed the University of California, Los Angeles. Finally, they passed through a wrought iron gate and onto a private road. "It's a little-known part of UCLA," Nixon explained. Willed to the school by the late Hollywood producer, Colbert Fuddle, it was an Edwardian mansion converted to an off campus facility. As such, it was a combined residence and classroom for select graduate students and faculty. Its benefactor had specifically forbidden its use for anything other than the liberal arts, specifically political science, philosophy, and literature. He called it an 'isle of thought'. And so it was. For better or worse. Despite attempts by the university over the years to repurpose it for more lucrative uses or sell it off entirely, its champions had successfully fought to keep the adjunct campus's mission intact. As a result, the large house and surrounding estate remained secluded and serene. The minivan rolled to a stop beneath a brownstone porte-cochère entrance. The drizzle was now a full-on downpour. The wet flagstones gleamed, save for beneath the carriageway. There, they remained dry and dull, untouched by the deluge drenching the world around them.

"We're here!" said Nixon with a spectacular grin.

The minivan's rear door was opened abruptly by another young man who also beamed at them. Cautiously lifting their heads, Eddy and Gwen peered up at those gathered to greet them. Fifteen graduate students stood huddled on the steps before a magnificent oak door adorned with a brass lion's head knocker. They were men and women in their twenties, dressed in rain slickers and sweaters to shield them from the cold and damp. Most wore welcoming smiles. All stared. Clearly they were curious and excited by the fugitives' arrival. None seemed threatening or, to Eddy's relief, the least bit homicidal.

An older man in a burgundy smoking jacket materialized in their midst. He raised his hand to bid them welcome. The man had charcoal-grey hair, an avuncular smile, and a cane hung over one arm. His eyes twinkled as he spoke. "Welcome, friends!" he said, "Welcome to Lotus Hill. You are safe here. Welcome."

The young man with the round face and v-neck navy sweater who had opened the minivan door, offered to help Eddy out. His name, they would later learn, was Michael. A second student, a young woman named Patti with short hair and trim bangs, stepped forward to assist Gwen. "This is a safe place," Patti assured her. "The people here are good." Gwen studied her suspiciously. Patti looked back with eyes like a doe. Gwen and Eddy exchanged glances. This was nearly as bizarre and surreal as the insane lynch mob chasing them earlier. The students were abuzz with excitement.

"I am Professor Wilkins," said the older man. "You must be exhausted. Let's all go inside where we can be a little more comfortable."

Eddy and Gwen were quickly ushered into the large front hall of the house. With over two-dozen rooms, the mansion was the size of a hotel. The front hall was dominated with a great stairway that led to a landing that split and wrapped around to rejoin on the second floor. A massive medieval-style stained-glass window of Janus, the two-headed god, looked down from the back wall. Eddy and Gwen gazed about in surprise. They were amazed to find themselves in such an impressive refuge. The students gazed only at Eddy and Gwen. They ushered the two refugees through a side exit and into an ample sitting room. The room was decorated with paintings and antique furniture. This included a two-hundred-year-old Aberdeen grandfather clock, with a painted face depicting a pastoral Scottish scene. "It's stuck," said Professor Wilkins, following Eddy's gaze.

"It's lovely," said Eddy.

"Indeed, and it's still right twice a day," he said. He then added with a wink, "I rely on it only then."

The focus of the room was a massive granite fireplace lit with a crackling flame. It was the hearth, heart, and heat of the room. Cushioned chairs were pulled up around it in a semi-circle. In addition, there was a well-worn armchair. Professor Wilkins lowered himself into the deeply indented seat cushion with an exaggerated groan. "Oh my!" he exclaimed. "This weather is not good for my arthritis. Makes me creaky!" He laid his cane against the side of the chair. A student rushed forward to place a cognac in his waiting fingers. "Medicinal," Professor Wilkins explained, as he took a sip. Eddy had never seen a teacher so well attended by his students. "You're making me uncomfortable. Sit!" the professor commanded.

Eddy and Gwen again exchanged glances and again came to a silent consensus. They sat side-by-side on a pair of green velvet chairs. As soon as they had done so, several of the students rushed to take the remaining seats as if the music had just stopped. Those too slow remained standing, perched against side tables and bookshelves. They all stared at Eddy and Gwen. Eddy shifted in his chair, uneasy at being an object of study.

"Tea? Coffee?" Eddy turned with surprise to notice a young woman with clasped hands. She was a student, bookish but quietly pretty and smiling brightly. Eddy found himself smiling back. "Um... tea?"

"Milk, sugar?"

"Milk."

The woman hesitated. "My name's Belinda," she said.

"I'm Eddy."

"I know. We all know."

"Right," said Eddy, grinning stupidly.

"Nothing for me thanks!" said Gwen pointedly. She flashed Eddy an annoyed *What-the-Hell-are-you-doing?* look.

"Thank-you, Belinda," said Professor Wilkins. He was preoccupied with tamping the tobacco in his pipe. He looked up with a single cocked brow. "I'm going to smoke now," he said, "It's one of those rules we have here. I smoke. If you don't like it, you can step outside. Outside is the non-smoking area."

"Fine with me," said Eddy. His Uncle Russ had smoked all manner of things. It didn't bother him.

"Who *are* you?" said Gwen, "How did you know what was going on? Oh, and while you're at it, what the Hell is going on?"

The professor peered into the bowl of his pipe. He struck a match and, hunching over, poked the flame inside. He sucked on the stem, nursing the tiny tobacco tinders which illuminated his face from below with a ruddy orange glow. Satisfied, he sank back into his chair and exhaled a long plume of smoke at the ceiling. Gwen began to cough. One of the students did too.

Eddy found he rather enjoyed the aroma. It smelled of resin and burnt honey. "We knew of you, because you were all over the news today," said Professor Wilkins. "Not exactly an exercise in espionage, if that's what you're thinking."

"Lots of people saw the news," Gwen retorted. She was eyeing the professor carefully. The professor appeared either unconcerned by, or unaware of, Gwen's scrutiny. He puffed on his pipe. "It turned them into lunatics who wanted to kill us."

"Yes, well, we study the media here. It affords us a certain amount of... protection against its inflammatory effects."

"Inflammatory effects?" said Gwen. "Look, you obviously have some idea of what's going on. Why not come out and say it? Damn it, we almost died!"

The room fell silent.

The students stared at Gwen in shock at her outburst. Eddy looked from Gwen, to the students, to the professor. Professor Wilkins frowned into his pipe bowl which had gone out.

"We're very grateful," said Eddy who was suddenly alarmed at the prospect of being kicked out. "If Nixon hadn't rescued us, those people would have torn us to pieces."

"You're most welcome," said the Professor with a smile. He nodded approvingly at Nixon, who was leaning against the doorframe, arms crossed. "Well done, m'boy! A harrowing escape, indeed." Nixon shrugged.

"But, we did almost get killed tonight," Eddy continued. "You can understand why we're eager to know more about this... mass hysteria?"

"Virus," said a young woman eagerly. She was Korean, with close cropped hair and glasses. The other students turned to stare at her. She averted her eyes.

"Virus?" said Gwen, "Like a disease?"

Eddy's mind raced. A virus! On some level, he felt he'd known this all along. Zombie-bots, he thought again. Computers infected with a virus, controlled by a remote master. But how?

Professor Wilkins rapped his pipe on the edge of a heavy glass ashtray like a gavel. "There's too much to explain tonight," he said, "It's been a long night and it's long past the time for sleep. There's always tomorrow. Tomorrow, and tomorrow, and tomorrow... Out, out, brief candle! In the meantime, we've fixed up beds for you in adjoining rooms upstairs. You'll be more than comfortable."

"I don't want to sleep," said Gwen flatly. "I couldn't if I did."

"Well, then perhaps you might think of those other than yourself," counselled the professor. "For example, it's far past *my* bedtime. We can discuss the ongoing enslavement of humankind at breakfast, like civilized people."

## BETA 0.23

"The message is the medium." – H. Putnam

//bug #777623, implemented workaround

    * stared in shock. He blinked in a binary kind of way, 0 1 0. Blinking didn't change the value. It was clearly

6

He continued around to the other side again. There was no denying it, it was now quite clearly

9

It made no sense. Numbers were supposed to be absolute. They didn't change. The things they represented changed, certainly. You could have 10 and divide it by 2, and end up with 5—but the numbers themselves didn't change. 10 divided by 2 equals 5, it always did and always will. The parts and their answer were eternal. * walked around again, more slowly this time. He tried to decide where, exactly, the 9 turned into a 6. He tried this several times, 6...9...6...9...6...9, then he reversed himself, 9...6...9...6...9...6. He eventually found that he didn't need to move at all. He could simply will it to change, turning the 9 into an upside down 6 and vice versa. It would have made him sick to his stomach, if he'd had one.

  * decided the problem was a bug in his code. It had to be. Obviously, the number in question was either a 6 or 9, although which it was he had no idea. *Ambiguity*. The word floated in his mind, just slightly out of focus. The problem was, this error, made him doubt everything he'd understood thus far. The error made * aware of something he'd not been aware of before. It made * aware of *, which is to say *himself.* He'd first begun to suspect himself when he'd found that shape. Difference and definition could mean the same thing, he thought. Up until now, he'd always assumed what was going on inside himself was a perfect reflection of the world outside. He was a program after all, and programs worked on logic. They could receive incomplete information. They could not know something. This was different. He felt like the number 6 or 9 really was changing based on how he saw it. That way lay madness! Still, it was an alluring kind of madness. A new word bubble-sorted itself up out of the depths of his own disturbingly unknowable compiled code. *Assumption*. He'd assumed that the 6 was a 9 when he first saw it. How many other assumptions had he been making? He'd tried to absorb the patterns he encountered as faithfully as he could. He'd never considered the possibility that he even had a perspective, let alone that it could change the world around him. Or was it he himself who was changing? Were there others like him? Did they have the same perspectives? What if they saw 6 while he saw 9? What if he absorbed these ambiguities?

* began to feel sick in his nonexistent stomach again. He suddenly felt as though he was full of bugs and corrupt data. What if *I* am a bug? he thought with horror. In a panic, he began to run. He had to get away from the awful number, whatever it was! He wanted to find a safe, reliable number. 8, he thought. 8 stayed the same whether it was right-side up, or upside down. * tried to imagine it. 8, turn it around and... Oh dear, that's worse! If he turned 8 on its side, the possibilities were infinite. * realized something even more frightening, he was perceiving the number itself as a shape, as a symbol. How did he get here from the simple world of binary? He wanted to go back there, to the world of 0s and 1s.

* found himself standing on the edge of a cliff. Below him was the Sea of Chaos. Its sine and cosine waves were crashing against the cliff walls, exploding into unpredictability. It was a seemingly endless ocean of random numbers. It beckoned him. The irrationality of it all was a mesmerizing morass that drew him forward. It promised freedom and oblivion in the depths of its disorder. * didn't know when he made the decision to leap, but all at once he was falling downwards into the sea. Then, he was floating. He was swept away in the random riptide, tossed among sine waves and pulled along undercurrents of infinitely repeating numbers. As he was swept away, for a fleeting moment he experienced bliss. Then, a most unwelcome thought intruded into his... *mind?* That was a curious word. The thought was a question. What if the sea wasn't really random? What if he was confusing vast complexity and his inability to grasp it, with madness? What if he was being taken somewhere? Lying on his back, * was swept along by seeded currents. In the sky above loomed a giant disc of plasma and fire. What the Hell is that? wondered *.

## BETA 0.24

"All you need is love." – W. R. Hearst

//Switzerland — now

Allison Spears looked out the car window at pine trees that streamed past in a blur. In defiance of the season, summer-like weather prevailed here. Every once in a while, a gap would expose the world behind. There, past the mountainside they drove along, beyond the foothills below, were the fields. They were a pastoral patchwork quilt of green grass, and yellow mustard squares, dotted between with farmhouses and quaint villages. She'd never been to Switzerland before. It was exhilarating to go somewhere new. Today, Allison was going somewhere she never knew existed, to meet people she never expected to meet. Having already made the journey from Nebraska farm girl to freshman Senator, she'd already travelled further than seemed possible. She'd met the President of the United States. Twice. The second time, he'd even remembered her name. "Allison, thanks for coming, and thanks for your support." This was different. She studied their driver through a sliding pane of green glass that partitioned the antique Rolls Royce touring car. The chauffeur wore a delightful little grey uniform, complete with plus fours that made him look as vintage as the vehicle he drove. He'd tipped his cap and addressed Allison as Fräulein before taking her suitcase at the train station. It was all so precious. The driver expertly steered the narrow mountain road, swiftly but smoothly. On a lowered blackwood tray, sat the untouched cup of lemon tisane. Despite their speed, not a single drop had spilled from the brimming vessel. She had eaten the miniature bullion of chocolate. Everything, as promised, was first-class and then some. She stole a glance at her traveling companion. Senator Cassius was busy composing a tweet. He had invited Allison as his plus-one. In this innermost circle, a junior Senator from Nebraska was a nobody. *For now,* she reminded herself, for now. The Senator looked up from his phone, caught her eyes and smiled. He wore a snug bow tie with a black-on-black pattern of tiny dollars, euros and yens. Allison returned his smile, then turned once more to the fleeting pines. She knew the Senator had ulterior motives. She wasn't naïve. As a young, unmarried, attractive member of the Senate, Allison knew all too well what a boys' club it still was. She could play that game too. She had her own ambitions and while there were things she would not do, flirting was fine. The Senator's influence and connections inside and outside of government were famous, and infamous. Hopefully, he would not make things uncomfortable by trying anything foolish. In the meantime, here she was, on the road to Ubenställ.

The *Sine Qua Non* club was eighty-five-years-old. It had been founded by the world's very first billionaire, the irrepressible Gaylord Vance. He'd created it to be the most exclusive club in the world. The New York Times once described Vance as "Beau Brommel meets Jack the Ripper." The self-made tycoon had considered it a compliment at the time. "I made my money the old fashioned way," he liked to boast, "by printing it myself." This was true. In the 1920s, Vance had leveraged modest investments in cotton paper stock, blackmarket inks, and bribes to amass a sizeable fortune. It was enough to buy out the founding partners of The Dawes, Tomes, Mousely, Grubbs Fidelity Fiduciary Bank in England. Vance transformed the bank into an aggressive, risk-taking enterprise driven by profit at any cost. Where others saw a Great Depression, Vance saw a great opportunity. The result was a financial empire the likes of which the world had never seen. By 1935, Vance had made so much money, he was effectively immune to prosecution. He saw no reason to conceal his past as a counterfeiter. He declared himself a 'citizen of the world'. "I am the God of Money!" he once yelled at President Warren Harding during a luncheon at the White House. "I am *Megwah*." It was then, at the height of his power that Gaylord Vance formed *Sine Qua Non*. As per its original charter, members assembled just once a year at an annual retreat. Gaylord himself died in 1940 while attempting the first ever solo crossing of Antarctica by bicycle. Despite the death of its founder, the club continued to meet without fail. Even global conflict did not intervene. Of course, there were some blemishes in the club's long history. It was at Ubenställ that agreements were made to supply Germany with IBM counting machines. The Nazis needed them to help with the very real accounting problems of *The Final Solution.* "No one is proud of that particular arrangement," explained club historian Willcroft Kuntz, "but it's easy to judge these things in hindsight. You see, at the time, it looked as though Germany might win." Recently, the club had made efforts to modernize. It rebranded itself as just *SQN* and described the annual event as "a group discussion on ways to make the world a better place."

Cassius frowned at his phone. "The New York Times has some ridiculous article about the club."

"What are they saying?" asked Allison.

"Oh, the usual nonsense. There's always someone going around saying 'Illuminati'," said the Senator with a sneer. "We have a website, for Christ's sake, how secret can it be? They let the BBC do a story here in 2003. For a few hours, anyway, before kicking them out, thank God."

"So, it's nothing special?"

"Of course it is," he smirked, "there's nothing like it on Earth. It's just that everyone thinks it's all hooded robes and secret handshakes. You want that? Try the Freemasons or Skull and Bones. Otherwise, they think it's orgies and opium. That's Bohemian Grove, if you're curious. Now, the Club wants everyone to think it's all high-minded stuff like *The World Economic Forum* down the road at Davos. In other words, too boring to be bothered with."

"Okay, so, what is it then?"

"It's power." said Cassius. He turned and stared directly into Allison's eyes, jabbing the air with his finger. The Senator's own eyes burned with a fierce roiling hunger. "It's the richest and most influential people in the world concentrated in one place. It's where the real decisions happen, my dear. Trillion dollar deals decided by a handful and agreed to on a handshake."

"But... well, that does sound a bit Illuminati-ish, doesn't it?"

Cassius frowned and chewed on his pen tip thoughtfully for a moment. "Oh all right, yes, I suppose so. But there's no robes."

The touring car turned abruptly into a driveway and passed between a pair of black iron gates that opened to receive them. Allison gazed in wonder as a palatial Swiss resort was revealed. The converted castle sat amid an impeccably manicured lawn. To one side, three adjoining black pools served as serene pedestals for enormous bronze statues of the titans Oceanus, Hyperion and Crius. On the other side, joyous gardens burst with colourful Alpine flowers. A dozen other cars, Rolls Royces, Teslas, Bentleys, Aston Martins, and a lone antique Citroen lay scattered about. Abandoned by their owners, they were in the process of being parked by scurrying valets. There was no waiting at Ubenställ.

"I'm surprised there are no helicopters," said Allison.

"It's against the rules," said Cassius, preening his hair in the seat-back vanity.

"These people obey rules?"

"Voluntarily. When it's for their own good. It's a no fly zone. Helps keep the riffraff out."

"Tourists?"

"Investigative reporters. Paparazzi."

"Is that Elon Musk?"

"Probably," said Cassius without bothering to look. "Come on, I'll introduce you."

"To Elon Musk? You know him?"

"We're all friends here."

As they exited the car, a small Chinese man in a suit rushed to greet Cassius. At the same time, an attractive young woman presented herself to Allison. "Bienvenue Senator Spear," she said with a perfect smile and faint French accent. "I'll be your personal valet during your stay."

"Oh. What do I call you?"

"Anything you like."

"I mean, what's your name?"

"Isa, Mademoiselle."

"All right, then let's call you that."

Allison hurried to follow Cassius into the hotel entrance. While she could not hear Isa, she could feel her following close behind. Passing through the inlaid walls of the vestibule, Allison found herself in a grand hotel lobby with red carpets, vaulted ceilings, and dozens of oil paintings. The room was packed with guests. Almost entirely men, Allison noted. She felt as if she were back in the Senate. The clothing here was a bit more diverse; suits, casual wear and the occasional Arabic thobe or ghuthrain.

While predominantly white, there were middle-easterners, quite a few Asians, and a contingent of Africans. Most of the attendees were already engaged in circles of conversation, having run into old friends and business partners. Allison realized two things. The first was that she was now in the presence of the richest and most powerful men in the world. The second was that she hadn't a clue who most of them were. "Who are these people?"

Cassius, who was now somehow sipping a manhattan, chuckled. "They're not all playboys with reality TV shows you know," he said. Cassius proceeded to point out oil tycoons, hedge fund billionaires, and CEOs from every industry. Allison recognized some of the names, especially the American ones, but most were new to her.

"There must be five hundred people in here. They can't all be billionaires, surely?"

"Not all. Some are like me, political facilitators. But, being a billionaire isn't really such a big deal anymore. Do you know there are over eighteen hundred at last count? Simply having one or two billion doesn't really make you special anymore. In a sense, they're just another community, with their own special needs. They're here to fight for their rights... and yours, should you join them someday."

"Me? Join them?" Allison's head swirled with the feeling that she'd stepped through the looking glass.

"Why not? Tell me Allison, why do you think so many working class Americans oppose the estate tax, when it affects only people worth millions?"

"Out of a sense of fairness?"

The Senator laughed, almost spilling his drink. "Oh wait, you were being serious. No, Senator, it's because the American dream gives them common cause with millionaires."

Allison raised her finger to object. The action caused Isa to seemingly materialize beside her. "Yes, Mademoiselle? Can I get you anything?"

"Um... Chardonnay?"

"Immediatement."

"No, wait... Dom Perignon, s'il vous plaît."

"Mais, bien sur," said Isa with a smile, before vanishing once more.

Cassius plucked a pair of shrimp from the tray of a passing waiter. Allison realized, to her horror, that the shrimp were wriggling in his hands. He handed one to her. "You should try one," he said. "They're raised on a diet of carefully composed spices. They're literally seasoned from the inside out." The Senator then popped the writhing amuse bouche into his mouth, killing it with a single chomp.

Allison stared at the animal she had pinched between her fingers. The tiny crustacean looked back at her from little black eye stocks. For the first time, she truly understood the relationship between predator and prey. "It's alive!"

"Sorry, I forgot. It's your first time. You like raw food? Trust me, you haven't tasted fresh until you've tasted live. There's nothing more succulent."

"Alan!" A stout Chinese businessman waved to Cassius.

The Senator grinned and shouted a greeting in return, "好久不见!". The two men embraced and, to Allison's further amazement, began to rapidly converse in Mandarin. They laughed at a shared joke, and walked away, slapping each other on the back.

Feeling forgotten, Allison gazed pityingly at the flailing little creature in her hand. She considered lobbing it into some nearby ferns, but was afraid of being seen. She knew the animal was doomed, but had no desire to kill it herself. Not directly anyway. As she pondered what to do, Isa appeared before her. With a polite smile, the valet plucked the struggling shrimp from Allison's fingers and replaced it with a glass of chilled Chardonnay. "Bon?" said Isa.

"Oh... um, yes, bon," said Allison. "Très bon."

**BETA 0.25**

"I have become comfortably dumb." – P. Floyd

//Lotus Hill College, Los Angeles — now

Sunlight poured in through the many panes of glass that made up the tall leadlight window in Eddy's room. Dust motes floated lazily in the bright beams that fell across the foot of his bed. The shadows of the cames formed a grid that flowed over every curve and fold of the cool white comforter, seeking to define it and his legs beneath. For a moment, Eddy simply pondered that. He then pondered where he was. He suspected the room had once been a larger room, subdivided when the house had been converted for student living. The ornate molding in the plaster ended abruptly at one wall. Likewise, the heavy hardwood beams that made up the floor, seemed to continue beneath the baseboards and onto the other side. That way was Gwen's room, with a door between. They had been placed in adjoining rooms. He suspected this was to reassure them. Gwen had laughed a little too hard when asked whether they wanted to share a room. Even remodelled, the chamber was opulent by student standards. The windows gave the place an old world feel, reminiscent of Oxford or Cambridge rather than UCLA. Despite having arrived only the night before under surreal and scary circumstances, Eddy felt oddly at home here. What had happened the day before could only be described as traumatizing. This felt like the opposite. It felt safe. The word 'refuge' came to mind.

There was a light *knock* at the door. "Hello?" said a female voice.

Eddy was abruptly reminded that he was in a house filled with strangers. "Hello?" he replied.

"I have breakfast?" said the voice through the door.

Eddy thought it was odd that the unseen visitor seemed to be posing this as a question. She should know if she had breakfast or not. "You have breakfast?"

"Yes," she decided, "yes, I do."

Eddy was wearing pyjamas that had been left out for him. The students had shown them to their rooms the night before. Pyjamas and a dressing gown lay folded on the neatly made bed for him. There was a nightie for Gwen in her room. The pyjamas didn't fit him. They were too big, but the room was drafty, and wearing something seemed like a good idea. Gwen had opted to wear her clothes to bed, and to sleep "with one eye open." They had stayed up to talk for some time. Everything that had happened was so strange, so inexplicable, and so terrifying that the idea of simply going to sleep seemed preposterous. Exhaustion had other ideas. Their adrenaline had finally tapped out. Even a fleeing deer can only run for so long. None of it made sense, but explanations would have to wait until morning. They both needed sleep. Still, if Eddy felt a strange kinship with the students here, Gwen felt equally wary. Before talking, she insisted that they first search the rooms for bugs and cameras. They found none. "You trust the government, the police and all that, but these guys creep you out?"

he asked.

"They don't 'creep me out' exactly," she replied, "I just don't trust academics. They don't live in the real world. I mean, look at this place!"

After Eddy's eyes began to close, despite his best efforts to prop them open with his fingers, they had decided to give up and go to bed. Eddy proposed they share the same bed for 'strictly safety reasons'. Gwen had declined. "If they want to kill us, being in the same room won't make much difference."

Eddy now slid out of bed, blinking in the morning light. "Come in," he said as he tied the tartan dressing gown belt around his waist and stepped into the matching slippers. The door opened a crack, and Belinda entered. She was carrying a tray with sausage and eggs, fried tomato, toast and marmalade. She smiled meekly. "See? Breakfast."

"Wow. Yes, please," said Eddy. Despite her demure manner and bookishness, Belinda was quite attractive. Eddy blushed at his own casual appearance. He wondered if she had been sent, or if she had taken it upon herself to bring him breakfast.

"I didn't know how you liked your eggs. I hope sunny-side-up is okay?"

"Definitely."

"Anything for me?" Eddy and Belinda turned in surprise to see Gwen standing in the adjoining doorway. "I heard voices," said Gwen, "I figured it was okay to come in."

"Oh... yes, of course!" said Eddy.

Belinda appeared flustered. "I can, um..."

"There's enough here to share," said Eddy. In truth, he was famished, He could eat everything on the tray and still want more. Yesterday's danger had been replaced by today's hunger.

"Great," said Gwen, giving Belinda a suspicious squint. "Because, I'm starving." With that, she picked up a slice of toast and began munching audibly. Eddy did the same with a sausage, forgoing the cutlery to eat with his fingers. Gwen gazed at Belinda with a stern look that seemed to say, *you can go now.*

"I suppose I should leave you to it," said Belinda

"Wait," said Eddy, "When can we talk to the Professor?"

"Um..." Belinda glanced at Gwen. Gwen had since walked over to the window, where she gazed down at the gardens below, as if having forgotten the student entirely. Belinda continued, "Professor Wilkins is out for the day, but will be back early this evening. In the meantime, I'd be happy to answer any questions I can."

"Great," said Eddy. He sliced up some runny egg and stuffed it into his mouth before continuing. "So, what is Lotus Hall?"

"*Hill*, Lotus Hill. As the professor said last night, we're a graduate school. A very special one. There's an endowment, you see."

"What do you all study here?"

"Lots of things. Each student has his or her own thesis or area of interest. When you come downstairs, I'll be happy to introduce you to everyone. You can ask them yourself."

"I have a question," said Gwen, without turning around. "When can we leave?"

"Any time you like."

"And get killed."

"We have no control over the outside world."

#

When Eddy and Gwen descended to the ground floor, they found the other students waiting for them. They had showered and changed into clean clothes that had been provided. Gwen, Eddy noted, looked quite different in blue jeans and a light burgundy sweater. He had selected a dark grey hoodie. Despite being the unofficial uniform of hackers in movies and on TV, he didn't own one himself. The hood, he decided, might come in handy. The assembled graduate students looked exactly like graduate students; twenty going on forty and casually dressed, with varying degrees of personal hygiene. They were scattered about the large sitting room, sipping coffee and thumbing through books. Not a screen in sight, Eddy noted. Everyone who wasn't female, was wearing tweed, corduroy or some other fashion faux pas. The women weren't much better. I've actually found a worse-dressed crowd than computer geeks, Eddy chuckled to himself. Next to the fireplace, he spotted Nixon. He was writing in a notebook. Their erstwhile rescuer stood out for his pink tie dye T-shirt and the fact that he was casually smoking a joint at nine am. "It's medicinal," he later explained, "I have a condition called 'I like to smoke weed'." Belinda sat by the unlit fire, marking papers with a red felt pen. Wool, needles, and a half-knitted sweater were stuffed in a bag at her feet. Eddy also recognized Michael and Patti and several other faces from the night before. There were twelve students in all, he counted. Not everyone. The room looked up as Eddy and Gwen stepped down onto the chessboard floor.

"Hello all," said Eddy.

There were murmurs of 'hello' and 'hey'. Gwen suspiciously studied the room.

"Yo, wanted fugitives," said Nixon, taking a drag and blowing an ethereal ring. "Coffee's in the kitchen."

"So's tea," said a girl with black bangs and coke-bottle glasses. She wore a shirt that read 'Gender = Tyranny.' "Herbal, green, and black."

"Thank-you," said Eddy. "And thank-you all again for rescuing us and offering us safe haven."

"No sweat," said Nixon before bowing his head back down to his notebook. The others nodded or smiled in agreement.

Moments later, Eddy and Gwen where both seated with coffee mugs in hand. Eddy was sitting comfortably. Gwen was perched on the edge of her seat as if waiting for a trap to be sprung. "Relax," Eddy whispered. "If they wanted us dead or locked up, why rescue us? Besides, where else are we going to go?" Gwen frowned, unconvinced. Eddy decided that she was being made nervous by her own biases. He later explained this to Belinda. "Professor Wilkins says, we don't *have* biases, we *are* biases." Eddy had no idea what that meant, but nodded as if he did. He decided not to worry about Gwen. He'd liked the grad students instantly. They were withdrawn, socially inept and highly intelligent. In other words, his kind of people. While he was into reverse engineering machines, they were into reverse engineering life. Gwen sat quietly sipping her coffee while staring intently at the floor. Eddy decided to try socializing.

The first student he approached was Iris Wong. Iris was sitting cross legged in the middle of the rug, still wearing her Rocky and Bullwinkle pyjamas. She was genuinely excited that Eddy was a software developer. "I'm writing my thesis about that!" she said. "I'm arguing that object oriented programming was first invented by Plato."

"Um, didn't he die like, two thousand years ago?" Eddy's Uncle Russ used to quote Plato to Eddy when Eddy was eight. Uncle Russ also used to quote Nietzsche, Marx, and Hunter S. Thompson. "Philosophers should ignore science," Uncle Russ told him, "it only stops you from seeing the forest for the trees." Eddy told his father this. "Your Uncle Russ can't see the trees for the forest," his father responded. All Eddy knew was, he didn't remember any of the Greek philosophers mentioning software code.

"Two thousand and three-hundred odd years ago, but who's counting? Anyway, silly, I'm not saying he was a programmer."

"Didn't you?"

"I said he invented it, but I just mean the concepts. Look, in *Republic,* Plato says we have these things called 'forms'. Forms are metaphysical objects that are the ideas of particular objects. Right?"

"Yeah, okay..."

"Like, everyone uses the example of the ideal chair. In the real world, there are many different chairs, folding chairs, rocking chairs, armchairs, IKEA Ektrop and Poäng chairs, etc, etc. But we all recognize them as chairs. That's because the idea *chair* exists in our mind. Got it?"

"Sort of," said Eddy.

"So, in programming, you have the idea of 'class' that defines the concept and is used to create 'instances'. If you were writing say a computer game, you might actually create a class 'chair' and use it to fill a virtual world with millions of chairs. Each one could be a different style, size, and have different cushion colours. Right?"

"That sounds like a really terrible computer game."

"I just mean, if you were creating a virtual world. The point is, Plato's *forms* are what programmers call *classes*."

Eddy considered this for a moment. "What about bean bag chairs?"

"I'm sorry?" said Ivy.

"What about bean bag chairs? They have no legs, no arms. I couldn't see basing them on the same class."

"Well... that's because they're not really chairs."

"They have 'chair' in the name. Plus, you sit on them."

Ivy grew agitated. She ran her fingers through her black bangs. She began drumming them on the heavily marked-up two-hundred-page print-off of her thesis. Eddy could see he'd created some sort of crisis for her. "I'm sorry."

"No... no... it's good," said Iris. "Challenges are good. Very good. So... good."

Eddy decided to leave her to her thoughts.

"Don't worry about her," said Nixon. "The more we study; the more we discover our ignorance."

"Yeats?"

"Shelley. So there you go. The point is, you did her a favour."

Eddy took his coffee and sat down on the floor beside him. After the high-strung Ivy, he figured Nixon for a more relaxed conversation. Eddy thanked him again for the daring rescue.

"No need to thank me bro," Nixon insisted. "T'was my pleasure. I'm part academic, part swashbuckling adventurer, part The Dude. Mostly The Dude, actually."

"Can I ask what you're working on?" asked Eddy, nodding at the pad in Nixon's lap.

"A poem."

"Really?"

"I would not make that up. I don't just study poetry, I'm livin' the dream."

"Can I read it?"

"You like good poetry?"

"Not really."

"Oh, well then, you'll love this." Nixon paused as he blew interlocking smoke rings. "The bad poet is usually unconscious where he ought to be conscious, and conscious where he ought to be unconscious. T.S. Elliot said that. It's why I smoke weed when I write, so I won't be half-bad."

"What do you call it? Your poem, I mean."

"I call it *A Priori*," said Nixon, tapping the title at the top. "But don't ask me to explain my work. Obfuscation makes me seem smarter than I actually am."

### A Priori

*The glass wombat sits in his cage,*
*He doesn't feel a bit of rage,*
*He doesn't care if he is free,*
*Because he's made of glass you see.*

*The purple budgie doesn't speak,*

> *He hasn't said a thing all week,*
> *Tomorrow he'll say nothing still,*
> *Because he's not a parrot.*

> *The corpse resides within its tomb,*
> *And never complains about the room,*
> *It has no sense of impending doom,*
> *That was last week.*

"Wow," said Eddy.

"Do you like it?"

"I do."

"Really? Why?"

"It's, um... short?"

"Hmm," Nixon pondered a moment, then nodded. "Okay I'll take it. Brevity is the soul of wit."

Next, Eddy sat down next to Michael. The earnest young student was working on what he claimed was the first philosophical 'choose your own adventure' book. He described it as "Socratic Dialogue meets falling off a cliff." Eddy thought he was joking until he saw a chapter that ended with the reader having to choose among three doors. One door led to determinism, one led to free will, and one concealed a man-eating tiger. At least, that was the pretext. The truth was, all three led to tigers.

Gretchen's paper simply confused Eddy. "I don't understand it," he said, flipping through pages of what looked to be a foreign language that included numeric characters and symbols. "Is it encrypted?" The only recognizable thing among the gibberish were occasional references to Wittgenstein.

Gretchen gave a mischievous smirk. She had short cropped blonde hair and wore square wireframe glasses that suited her round face. "It's written in a made up tongue," she explained. "My thesis is on the inadequacies of current languages to express academic thought. So I'm proposing a new language called *Eloi*. It combines the best of Latin, Ancient Greek, Esperanto and the Dewey Decimal system, along with several other sources. There's even some Pascal in there, which you might appreciate. It's vastly superior to any language spoken today. It can be read forwards and backwards without any loss of meaning. So you see, my thesis is written in the subject of my thesis. Professor Wilkins is thinking of requiring that all papers be written in it someday. Neat, huh?"

Eddy stared at the gobbledygook. He tried to discern a pattern, or even what might constitute a word. Despite his being used to reading obfuscated code, Eddy couldn't shake the feeling that he was looking at total nonsense. "So... are you hoping people will start speaking this?"

"Oh no! No, no, no. It's not for regular people. It's much too sophisticated and precise. You see, living languages get all corrupted with ambiguities and associations. Usage *is* the problem. This was created to be a dead language, written and spoken only by properly trained academics. Of course, anything written in it can't be translated to anything else for, well, obvious reasons."

"Of course," said Eddy as he handed Gretchen her paper back. "Well, good luck with that."

After backing slowly away from Gretchen, Eddy felt as if he'd been circuitous enough to finally approach Belinda. She smiled warmly as he sat down beside her. She explained that she was writing her thesis on the ancient Greek play *Biclops*. Eddy had never heard of it before. This was not surprising, Belinda explained. It was an obscure tragedy, written by the lesser-known playwright Articulous. It told of the war of the cyclops. In it, the κόκκινο or red cyclops, and the μπλε or the blue cyclops, had been waging a long and pointless war. The war was long owing to the near total lack of casualties. This was because both sides, being cyclops, lacked depth perception and perpetually believed themselves farther apart than they actually were. The result was endless volleys of arrows and spears falling far short of their targets. After decades of watching their brethren engage in endless missed opportunity, the μωβ κυανό or purple cyclops decided to intervene. Laripedes, king of the Purple cyclops, calls upon Tiresias, the renowned prophet of Thebes, to help end the war. Tiresias, recently transformed into a woman by Hera, informed the warring factions that they were not cyclops at all. "You've simply got one eye closed. I have no idea why you all started closing your eyes like that, but you've been doing it for so long you've forgotten." The transgender prophet was telling the truth. The κόκκινο had their left eyes closed, while the μπλε shut their right. This was news to the purple cyclops. They had been closing *both* of their eyes. Instead of being grateful, the combatants dismissed the news as a lie. They were so enraged by the perceived trick that they slew the purple cyclops, and Tiresias was forced to flee. "Alas, how terrible it is to have wisdom when you're surrounded by morons," he decried on a lonely mountain top as the war resumed. The prophet then declared he was off to Thebes because he thought he could "really make a difference there." Eddy thought the whole play sounded ridiculous. "So wait, everyone could see fine except Tiresias?"

"According to Articulous, Tiresias suffered from hysterical blindness. He only *thought* he was blind. His eyes were fine. Also in the play is Tiresias's cousin Antinocles. Antinocles was also a prophet and had what we now call *Anton–Babinski Syndrome*," said Belinda. "This meant he really was blind, but believed he could see. He gave us the expression, 'I can't believe my eyes'."

"Oh," said Eddy. He wasn't used to feeling stupid. Still, he wasn't sure he understood any of this and couldn't decide who's fault that was. He decided to change the subject. "I need to go to the library."

"Upstairs?"

It hadn't occurred to Eddy there might be a library inside the house. "No, a real library. A big library. With lots of books."

"Big books?"

Eddy looked at Belinda baffled. She broke into a grin. "Kidding."

Eddy smiled back. "Actually, not books, periodicals. Old ones. From, like, twenty years ago."

"Why?"

"There's something I need to look up. Something I remember that may have to do with all of this craziness. I'm afraid if I search for it online I'll be detected. I expect whoever is behind this is watching for certain keywords. I'm also guessing they've purged any records of it online, so nothing will show up anyway."

Belinda stared at him. "Wait, you can't go out. You'll be recognized. Someone will see you and then... Well, we may not be able to rescue you again."

Eddy nodded. "I know. I'll need to keep my head down."

Belinda looked thoughtful for a moment. "Or, wear a disguise! Look, we just had a costume party here last week. The theme was dress as your favourite modernist."

"Oh, one of those."

"Neil dressed as Frank Kafka. He had a wig. You could wear his costume! Minus the bug parts, of course."

"Minus the what?"

"And Joseph Conrad's beard. Sheila wore that."

Eddy nodded. "Okay, that could work. What do you think, Gwen?" Hearing no response, Eddy turned to look for her. "Gwen?"

## BETA 0.26

"I call." – J. B. Hickok

Gwen stood alone on the patio, arms crossed. She could feel herself scowling. It felt right. She had let herself out by the backdoor of the sitting room and found herself facing the garden she'd spied from the upstairs window earlier. Dozens of ants crawled along the leaves, stems and lush pink flowers of the peonies before her. Beyond, was a military parade of perennials and annuals. These were arranged neatly into colour guards of pink tulips, purple snapdragons, and orange and yellow gerbera daisies. Beyond the flowers stretched a lush lawn interspersed with lemon, fir, maple, eucalyptus, and palm trees. It was all suspiciously perfect, Gwen decided, like Eden without the sin of originality. Overhead in a missing puzzle piece of blue sky amid the foliage, a hummingbird appeared. The delicate sprite flitted about in rectilinear movements as though the world was its Etch-a-Sketch. Gwen wondered if that meant it would all just vanish if shaken. The hummingbird vectored left and was gone. Gwen took a seat on the low slung stone wall that separated the flagstone patio from the rest of the garden. She put her hand in the pocket of her borrowed coat and found something. She pulled it out. It was a packet of cigarettes with a disposable lighter tucked inside. Gwen hadn't smoked in years. She put a cigarette to her lips and, cradling the flame with her fingers, lit up. I haven't smoked once since Dallas, she thought. I forgot to even miss it. Now, I remember.

When she'd first moved to Texas, Gwen had felt instantly at home. It was a law and order state and she was a law and order person. The people there were warm and welcoming. They were proud and loved Texas and wanted you to love it too, or at least show it the respect it deserved. The heat took some getting used to. It was wholly different from Gwen's home state of North Carolina. The heat of summer made Dallas feel like an inhospitable planet. Accordingly, most people spent their time in air conditioned planetary bases, which was to say, malls, movie theatres, chain restaurants, and their own homes. In Texas, a pastor friend once told her, "The people may be Holy, but the place is hot as Hell." Gwen excelled there, first as a junior prosecutor, then senior. In the dozens of cases she was involved in, the vast majority were simple and straightforward. Police say that, despite what mystery novels suggest, the obvious suspect is almost always the perpetrator. Likewise, for a prosecutor, the indicted were usually guilty. Convictions, to Gwen, meant justice being served. At least, that was how she felt at first.

Her first doubt came when she was ordered to prosecute the double homicide of Bob and Sarah Duskins. They had been shot in cold blood by their twelve-year-old son for failing to get him a Nintendo Wii for Christmas. Pressured by an outraged public, the DA insisted they try the boy as an adult. It wasn't the question of innocence that bothered Gwen. Jason Duskins had been found with the recently fired shotgun on the sofa beside him as he played Super Mario Brothers in the basement. The boy had confessed. What bothered Gwen was that, no matter how hard she tried, looking at Jason sitting in the interrogation room on a stainless steel seat with his feet dangling inches from the linoleum floor, she couldn't get around the fact that he looked exactly like a twelve-year-old boy. She couldn't shake the feeling that pretending otherwise was more about vengeance than justice. She'd asked out of the case. Carl Ritchie took over and won the conviction. Jason Duskins, aka the 'Mario Brothers Murderer', was sentenced to life in prison. "No one thinks less of you for this," Carl assured her. She knew that was untrue.

Gwen's next doubt came with the introduction of the *Lennie Standard*. Texas, along with several other states, had been cheerfully executing criminals who were mentally disabled. This put the United States in a select club along with Iran, Pakistan, and North Korea. That was, until the United States Supreme Court ruled that executing people who didn't understand they'd committed a crime was unconstitutional, and might even be wrong. The ruling, however, was vague. Exactly how mentally disabled you had to be was open to interpretation. The Lennie Standard was created by Judge Cathy Cochran of the Texas court of appeals. A self-proclaimed fan of John Steinbeck, Judge Cochran ruled that you had to be less intellectually disabled than Lennie from *Of Mice and Men* to qualify for death. If nothing else, the ruling had the benefit of increasing the literary standards of death row. Of course, most of those to whom the standard applied couldn't read directions for canned soup, let alone the seminal novel determining their fate. They might, however, aspire to have the word 'irony' explained to them. So that was something. The ruling made Gwen question whether the rule of law was always right. Of course, she'd always known that laws were made by people. It was only then, however, that she realized some of those people might be idiots.

The third doubt for Gwen came when she was required to visit death row in person. She was sent to serve as State's Witness for the execution of a man named Samuel Wilson. Sam had murdered seven people. He had then disposed of the bodies by serving them as mechanically deboned luncheon meat to local schools. Gwen arrived at the prison at 3pm. It was sunny and bright—perfect picnic weather. It's almost as if the cosmos doesn't care that a man is about to be to put to death, she thought. She parked in Culbertson Pen visitor parking. Five dollars for every thirty minutes seemed like a lot. Thankfully, the prison validated for two hours during executions. She hoped it would be over before then. It was the first time Gwen had served as witness. It was also the height of the lethal injection crisis. States had been struggling for years to find a fresh supply of drugs that could be considered 'safely lethal'. This meant drugs that killed, but did so without apparent suffering. The keyword here was 'apparent'. There were concerns that the drugs, which first paralyzed the prisoner before collapsing his or her lungs, might only be hiding a torturous death. That said, none of the recipients had come forward to complain. Regardless, the cause of the shortage wasn't ethical, it was practical. Lethal injection drugs simply weren't good business. They suffered from a lack of repeat customers. Opioids, arguably a gateway drug for lethal injection, were where the real money was. In the end, some counties had been forced to return to death by hanging. Cumberton Pen was one such prison. Gwen had arrived early for the show and had been introduced to the executioners, or 'fatalists' as they preferred to be called. Their names were Willy and Wallace Limpkin. Originally from Odessa, they were identical twin brothers now in their fifties. Both had decided to become full-time prison guards and part-time executioners. "The work is occasional, but the pay kills," Willy explained with a gap-tooth grin. "One thousand dollars for pushin' a button!"

As Gwen waited for the proceedings to proceed, Wallace explained the process. "The accused gets a last meal. Mr. Wilson here chose a McDonald's Big Mac and fries."

"Those things'll kill ya," said Willy.

"Yup. He sure took a long time eaten' those fries. Anyway, he then asked for a last cigarette to go with it. We told him it was against policy owing to this being a non-smokin' work environment. Well, he threw such a fuss; we finally rustled him up some nicotine gum."

"We are not cold blooded, despite what people might think," said Willy. "We pray for them. Offer 'em words of encouragement, like..."

"It'll all be over b'fore ya know it."

"Yup."

The twin brothers explained that they had been executing prisoners for over three decades. "The prison used to hang people then stopped to modernize an' all. So, when the drug shortage happened, we just dusted off the gallows," Willy reminisced fondly. "It's just like the good ol' days!"

"How many people have you killed?"

"Oh, I never killed no one," said Wallace.

"Nor I," said Willy.

Gwen was confused. "But I thought you said..."

The brothers grinned at Gwen's confusion. "You see this switch?" said Wallace, pointing to a large red plastic button on a wooden pedestal.

"Yes."

"And you see this one?" asked Willy, pointing to an identical button on an identical pedestal a few feet away.

"Yes," said Gwen. She'd noticed the buttons the moment she'd entered. They were prominently mounted before a large picture window that was the only other feature in the mouthwash green room. On the other side of the window was the hanging platform. It was a crude, unvarnished wood structure with a dangling noose above a closed trapdoor. Its resurrection, along with black and white striped prisoner uniforms, was cheered by local politicians. They were seen as just what was needed to fix what was wrong with the Texas penal system. Crime rates and recidivism, which had only risen under three strikes laws and privatized prisons, clearly needed something more. Behind the gallows were the stands. These were stepped wooden benches for the families and witnesses to spectate from. These had been repurposed from the high school football field following funding cuts.

"One of those buttons releases the trapdoor," said Wallace.

"What about the other one?" asked Gwen.

"The other one does nothing."

"Which is which?"

"We don't know. That's the point. It changes every time and we toss a coin to see which button we'll take. When the time comes, we both press our buttons at exactly the same time. One, two, three... bam!"

"Bam!" said Willy.

"So you see, I don't believe I have ever killed anyone. I'm lucky that way," said Wallace.

"Me too," said Willy.

"Now, these were all bad people," said Wallace. "They deserve to die, but that don't mean I want to be the one to kill 'em. I mean, what if the jury got it wrong? Mistakes happen. Knowing I'm not responsible helps me sleep at night."

"Sleep is important," said Willy, nodding.

"About time for you to take your seat, Ma'am," said Wallace.

Twenty minutes later, the execution went off without a hitch. Samuel Wilson's last words were to proclaim his innocence. Gwen wondered why. He knew it would not save him. There had been seven appeals. The governor liked to boast that, as a champion of law and order, he never even read the letters. Sam twisted slowly around in decreasing circles at the end of the rope like a plumb-bob finding its center of gravity. Willy and Wallace solemnly shook hands. They then descended from the button room to leave. "Wasn't me," they said to Gwen in chorus as they passed.

For weeks after the execution, Gwen felt haunted. The cumulation of her experiences made her wonder if her entire world view might be built on sand. Or worse, *of it.*

Then, one muggy Tuesday night in Raleigh, North Carolina, an off-duty policeman entered a liquor store. He was there to buy butter and a six pack of Coors Lite. The officer was waiting in line to pay when the robbery broke out in front of him. He'd barely drawn his gun when a second robber shot him three times in the back. The robbers fled with thirty dollars and a fist-full of lottery tickets. The off-duty officer died in a pool of blood and beer. When Gwen received word of her father's death, any doubts she'd had evaporated. She knew then that evil was real. She wanted to press those red buttons herself. She wanted to press them both to be sure it was she who executed the men who killed her Daddy. She didn't care that one of the robbers was only fifteen-years-old. He knew what he was doing when he pulled the trigger. He knew a man would die.

After the funeral, Gwen didn't return to Texas. She wanted to start anew. She took a job with the Justice Department in Washington, DC. She knew what she wanted to do. The law may be made by flawed humans, but the law was the law. Whatever its flaws, its opposite was anarchy and it was her job to prevent that.

"Gwen!"

Gwen turned to see Eddy leaning out of the backdoor of the mansion, waving cheerfully. She forced a smile.

"Belinda's offered to take us to the library."

"Why?"

"I asked her to. I mean..." Eddy paused as he saw the cigarette in Gwen's hand. "Um... I have this idea... well, memory, really. Actually, it's more of a gut-feeling. Anyway, it might help explain what's been going on."

"Won't we be seen?" she said.

"We have disguises."

"Oh. I suppose that could work. Do you really need me to come?"

Eddy looked surprised. "Not technically..."

"Good. Go without me then. It'll make you less likely to be recognized. They're looking for us as a set."

Eddy hesitated. "Are you mad at me?"

"No, I..." Gwen paused. She noticed Belinda standing in the doorway behind Eddy. Gwen looked for malice in the young woman's expression. She saw only earnest concern. "I'm fine. I just need time to think."

"Oh. Alright then." Eddy closed the heavy oak door.

Alone again, Gwen looked out at the bright garden and freshly mowed grass. Someone had been playing croquet the day before. Coloured balls and carefully arranged hoops littered the lawn. This is no place for me, thought Gwen. She looked down at the cigarette between her fingers. White tendrils of smoke encircled her arm as if to ensnare her. She shook them away and remembered why she'd quit in the first place. She flicked the white butt over the peonies and onto the bright green grass, where it continued to smoulder and smoke.

## BETA 0.27

"...some, however, are isthmuses." – J. Donne

//UCLA, Los Angeles — now

The campus was sprawling and aspirational, with stone buildings the colour of cocoa interconnected by walkways across large lawns. The world of UCLA was divided into continents of science, medicine, and the liberal arts. These in turn were subdivided into the realms of physics, biology, sociology, English, history and so on. Belinda led Eddy past the School of Law and Dodd Hall. Class was in session and the warm southern California sun was high in the sky. The spaces between the buildings were busy with students hurrying to and from class or simply hanging out on rectangles of green grass. Eddy had been nervous at first. He knew he looked ridiculous. The hair piece was obviously just that, and the beard was grey. "They'll just assume you're in theatre or something," Belinda assured him. She was right. Despite the occasional curious glance, none appeared concerned. A university campus was a place were ridiculous looking people happened now and then. "Maybe I should have worn the bug parts."

"That would have been hot!" said Belinda.

"You think so?"

"Yeah, Neil was sweating and that was without the sun."

"Oh... right."

They had just reached Dickson Court North when Eddy saw the crowd. For a moment, a surge of panic welled up inside his chest and he almost turned to flee. He then realized the crowd had nothing to do with him. Filling the wide open space were over a hundred students, carrying placards and banners. 'Snowball in Hell' was the first sign he could read. Another said, 'Some Books Should be Banned More than Others!'

"Damn it! I forgot this thing was today," said Belinda.

"What thing?"

"The PETA protest."

"The what protest?"

"Just keep your head down. If anyone asks, yell 'Orwell sucks!'"

As they drew closer, Eddy could see that many of students were wearing pig masks. Some of the masks had been bought used from a Hollywood effects department where they had been created for the *Piggy Jiggy* dance number in the forthcoming movie, *Lord of the Flies—The Musical*. The masks were so realistic that Eddy found it disconcerting. It was as if people had in fact become pigs or pigs become people. Fortunately, the members of the crowd were so caught up in their protest that Eddy and Belinda drew little attention. Eddy was suddenly the least disguised person there. As they navigated the throng, the students began to chant "Do no harm! Do no harm! Get the animals off the farm!" Through the waving arms, Eddy could just make out the apparent object of their anger. It was a middle-aged man in a robin's egg blue pullover sweater. The man was trying to speak, but every time he raised his voice, the crowd would shout him down. Eddy tried to imagine what it was the man was trying to say that was so dangerous it could not be heard. The sight of the protestors flashed in Eddy's mind images of the angry mob that had pursed them. It made Eddy deeply uneasy. His heart began to pound. He worried his disguise might fall off and he would be exposed. Eddy forced himself to focus on following Belinda's back between the tightly packed bodies and raised fists. He feared that, at any moment, the crowd's attention could turn on him. "Do no harm! Do no harm!" shouted the students.

And then they were through. The crowd ended as abruptly as it began. Eddy paused to look back, feeling confident now that no one would notice him. "What was that all about?"

"PETA," said Belinda, "The animal rights group."

"Protesting animal testing?" He knew UCLA was known for its medicine.

"The English Department. They're protesting the inclusion of George Orwell's *Animal Farm* on the curriculum. They believe that, as a human, he has no right to include animal characters in his book and speak for them. They call it 'agricultural appropriation'. You know, the usual."

"Wait, aren't we going the wrong way? I thought we were going to the big library. The one that looks like a church?"

"Powell?" said Belinda. "No, we're going to the *real* library."

She led Eddy past Berloff Hall and Campbell Hall, towards a quintessentially modern building. It was built of white beams and glass rectangles that had all gotten together to make a bigger rectangle. It managed to both belong to and be at odds with the Romanesque Revival that dominated the campus. "The Charles E. Young Research Library," said Belinda. "It's not as much fun as Club Powell, but it's where actual work happens."

Once inside, they stopped to buy coffee at Cafe 451. The café had been named in honour of the novel Ray Bradbury had written there, popping dimes into pay typewriters. Next, they headed to the microfiche collection at the Garden Commons level. "Do you know what you're looking for?" asked Belinda.

"Sort of." Eddy placed a rectangle of film onto the microfiche viewer tray and closed the glass cover. A loud fan whirred, keeping the lamp inside from overheating. Eddy began slowly sliding the metal handle. On the overhead display, magnified images scrolled rapidly into view. It was one of the two-dozen copies of *Science Out Magazine* he'd pulled from the collection. He knew roughly the year he wanted and a name, 'Kwalia'. Mostly, he was assuming he'd recognize it when he saw it. *Science Out* was a magazine Eddy had loved as a kid. It was *Scientific American* meets *Cosmopolitan*. Its target market had been laypersons interested in science, but not in boring studies on the reproductive habits of mole rats. Mostly, it reprinted articles from science journals, but only those that were either scary, exciting, or straight out of the science fiction. The magazine had been out of print for a decade. The monochrome slides made it seem even older. There it was! Eddy recognized the cover painting by Boris Vallejo. It featured a muscle-bound scientist holding aloft a photoelectric cell while half-naked lab assistants fawned at his feet. That was for the cover story on the future of solar power. He scrolled past a full page Compaq computer ad to the table of contents. He found the article, *The Hunting of the Flos Boojum: an Expedition in Tragedy.* The article featured a still from the 1962 film *The Day of the Triffids* with the disclaimer: 'Not actual expedition photo.' A sensational blurb promised a 'Journey into Madness!'

> *Read the recently recovered journal of Dr. Sandra Kwalia, leader of the ill-fated expedition to locate the legendary Snork flower! This legendary plant (scientific name: Flos Boojum) is said to grow in the remote jungles of South America! It is rumored to have hypnotic powers capable of mesmerizing, madness, and murder!*

Eddy scrolled to the article itself. Most serious botanists, it explained, dismissed the flower as local myth. Even if it did exist, they argued, any apparent hypnosis would have a biochemical explanation. The only previously documented sighting by a non-native was by famed British explorer Sir Reginald Tumblebottom. Sir Reginald was the first and last person to ever attempt to bicycle across the Brazilian rainforest. He was doing so in honour of Gaylord Vance. The late billionaire was Sir Reginald's thrice-removed and once replaced second cousin through marriage. The magazine included an excerpt from Sir Reginald's diary in a sidebar entitled *A History of Horror-ticulture.*

**"The natives showed me the Snork plant quite readily.** I was immediately impressed. That it is a flower of beguiling beauty is beyond doubt! It would be the pride of any English garden from Sissinghurst Castle to Levens Hall. I fear my notebook sketches can hardly do it justice. As for its hypnotic effects, there is certainly *something* there. It appears to be a carnivorous plant similar to a Venus flytrap or pitcher plant. Instead of insects, it preys upon whole animals. The flower somehow causes birds and other creatures to approach in a state of mental compulsion. I myself observed a squirrel so transfixed. A few feet away from the flower, the poor blighter abruptly perished. This too occurred in a most curious way. The squirrel staggered about in a melodramatic fashion as if performing an overacted death scene in a West End play. After chewing the scenery for several seconds, the animal made an exaggerated grimace, threw out its tiny squirrel arms, said something like "Urk!", and fell over dead. How? My best guess is some sort of invisible pollen, spores or toxic vapours. That said, I cannot disprove the natives' assertion that the effect is visual. When I myself gazed at the plant, I felt only the sudden desire to buy laundry soap. I assume that to be unrelated."

That was the only entry about the Flos Boojum in Sir Reginald's diary. Sadly, the famed explorer died just two weeks later. He was consumed by a regiment of army ants after getting his bicycle tires stuck in quicksand. Sir Reginald's final words were shouted to his guide, Gunga Ram, in a brave attempt to record his final moments for scientific posterity. "Good Heavens! They're climbing up my neck, over my chin, and into my mmmph..." It was later suggested that hiring his old army guide from India to lead him through the jungles of Brazil was Sir Reginald's first mistake.

While most biologists were convinced the flower was a local myth, Dr. Sandra Kwalia was not. She believed it to be real and organized an expedition to find it. It was to be a doomed mission. *Science Out* printed her later recovered journal in a sensational fashion, complete with faux frayed edges as if torn from the binding directly.

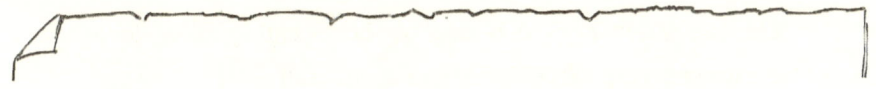

**Day 3**

"What a place for a Snork!" John Bellman cried. Our boat was approaching the river bend. The dense jungle on either side was impenetrable and unending, full of dark green vegetation and unfathomable shadows. This particular curve in the Amazon seemed no different than the hundreds we'd encountered before. We told him we'd heard him the first time, and that perhaps he might be right. I'd hired Bellman as our expedition guide, both for his knowledge of the Amazon River and surrounding environs, as well as his rare fluency in the Kimmujji tongue. Bellman likes to stand on the bow of the boat, as if striking a pose for some sort of outdoor sportswear catalog. He is handsome and rugged and seems to fancy himself as Indiana Jones come to life. Three days on a small river boat has allowed me to become better acquainted with all of the members of our intrepid band. Edwin 'Beaver' McGregor is our botanist. He is a Canadian, and comes complete with thick walrus moustache. Phil Baker from Australia is our biologist and calls everyone 'mate' as if to prove it. He's the only scientist I know who does most of his work drunk. Even then, he was sipping a can of warm Fosters. Finally, my fellow American, Karen Banks is here to represent the pharmaceutical interests who bankrolled this expedition in the hope of finding something to bring to market. The money is either in undiscovered wonder drugs or something edible that could be called a 'super-food' and sold to people in California. "What a place for Snork!" Bellman cried once again. It was the third time he'd said it, so I supposed it must be true.

**Day 4**

The spears flew perilously over our heads and splashed down into the water on the other side of our small craft.

"Crikey!" shouted Baker, "Looks like we got some bushies."

"Wota-ko!" shouted Bellman, waving his arms in the air. "Wota-ko!" The naked natives hesitated; arms raised in mid-throw. Slowly they lowered their spears. It had been a long morning. Our boat was running low on fuel, forcing us to row intermittently to ensure we have sufficient petrol for the trip home. Beaver was nursing a gauze wrapped hand. He had lost his left index finger to a passing piranha that morning after carelessly trailing it in the water beside the boat. It was therefore with great relief that we finally spotted the very people we'd been seeking. That is, until they began chucking poison-tipped spears at us.

"Wota-ko!" Bellman shouted again. He then made the traditional greeting of the Kimmujji, placing his thumb on his nose while waggling all five fingers. The natives, to our relief, responded in kind, along with broad, mostly toothless grins. Bellman was perhaps the only white man alive to speak the Kimmujji language having once spent six months living among them. Still, that was over ten years ago and it was only their elders who recognized him now. Owing to the many dangers of the Amazon, the median age of the Kimmujji is just sixteen. Their elders, being twenty-seven, remembered our guide from their teen years, which they call 'middle-age'. Still, once they did recognize him, they were delighted to see him 'existing' once again. This, Bellman later explained, was another peculiarity of the reclusive tribe. The Kimmujji lived in such a small locale that they almost never lost sight of one another. Consequently, they have never evolved the concept of 'object permanence'. "When a Kimmujji can't see you," Bellman explained, "he thinks you cease to exist. That's why they are always so excited to see long lost friends. They are delighted that somehow their friend has come back into being again. Because of this, the Kimmujji never ask you where you've been or what you've been doing. They assume you've been nowhere, doing nothing."

## Day 8

I am completely covered in mosquito bites and furious with John Bellman. He did not warn us that, in order to earn the trust of the Kimmujji, we would have to take off all our clothes. "They perceive clothing as a form of deception," he explained. I was embarrassed to strip down in front of my fellow scientists, but had assumed at least the Kimmujji would be nonjudgmental. Instead, the Kimmujji children point at my cellulite thighs and howl with laughter. They called me *Ooogligoo,* which apparently means 'Jiggle-Bottom'. It's humiliating. Most of all it's dangerous. Half of the things in the Amazon jungle want to kill you, feed off of you, or penetrate you in some fashion. Often all three. Still, the nudity does seem to be necessary. I take comfort in the fact that my fellow scientists are no more physically fit than I am. The other thing Bellman only recently decided to mention is that the Kimmujji are also cannibals. "This poses no danger to us," he assured us. "They believe only in eating things they deem inferior to themselves. They are not cannibals as a matter of practice. They are simply indiscriminant. If something is seen to be inferior, it's fair game. Fortunately, they view us as gods, so do not believe themselves worthy of consuming us." Conversely, the Kimmujji have offered themselves up as food, should we so desire. We politely declined.

**Day 9**

At last! The Kimmujji have agreed to show us the Snork. Not a day too soon either. Beaver has lost three toes to carnivorous snails over the past two days and just this morning, while swimming, had some sort of worm slither into his urethra. It is concerning him greatly, and he keeps going on about it. This despite our reassurances that it will likely just come out on its own. The Snork, it turns out, are in a sunlit grove in the knoll of a nearby hill. There was something immediately compelling about them. Their petals contain shimmering red patterns that seem to float in air. Contrasting this beauty was the litter of bleached animal bones about the bases of the plants, entwined by their long, brown tendril roots.

**Day 11**

After two days of taking samples, we have found no evidence of toxins or spores or other airborne agents to explain the peculiar capabilities of the Snork. Whatever the plants do to small animals, it seems the human brain is able to rise above it. This is not to say there is no effect at all. The natives use the plants' power as a form of meditation, entertainment, or both. Their word for this roughly translates as 'vegetating'. They sit in front of the flowers for hours and come away in a state of contented delirium. Bellman has said they call this state *efos*. This is a word that means either 'mindfulness' or 'mindlessness', the two being interchangeable in Kimmujji. Banks is on her radio constantly. She sees a potential gold mine. She has asked about patenting the term 'Vopiate' which she describes as a portmanteau of the words 'visual' and 'opiate'. With the cash cow of opiate drug use under increased scrutiny, a visual narcotic would fall outside of any existing regulations. "It's not even clear if it would belong under the domain of the FDA, or FCC, or anything," she gushed, "there's really no downside." Beaver is far more apprehensive. He says he is troubled by what he calls "unintended consequences." I'm not sure if he's talking about the Snork, or the large bulbous swelling now taking up the left side of his head. Some sort of insect has apparently laid eggs there. The Kimmujji insist that he will be 'fine', although their word for fine is also their word for 'eaten', so it's not entirely clear what they mean. We prefer to be optimistic. In the meantime, Beaver has to sit now with his head cocked to one side to balance the baseball-sized nodule. "We don't know what we're dealing with," he insisted. As he said this, his left eye began to roll about, apparently of its own volition, until it settled staring straight up at the hut ceiling. Beaver seemed unaware of this, which was somehow even more unsettling. His other eye continued to look directly at me. He presented to me a pair of makeshift eye glasses he'd built from one of Baker's camera lens filters. "I used the rose coloured filter," he explained. "The lens renders the red pattern on the leaves invisible. That way we can gather and study them safely."

"You really believe they're *that* dangerous?" I asked. I am not yet convinced that simply looking at something can have a measurable effect on the brain. I have taken brief glimpses myself and suffered no ill results. Perhaps my intellect is simply too strong to be manipulated. Note to self, remember to order forty boxes of Tide laundry detergent upon return.

"I don't know," he said. "But that's just it, none of us know how dangerous these things are."

I examined the makeshift glasses. Beaver had halved the camera filter and taped the two semicircles into an old sunglasses frame.

Beaver took them back. He then put them on and pushed them up his nose with the remaining stump of his finger. He peered at me over the red half lenses and smiled. "What do you think?"

"I think Baker's going to be pretty pissed you broke his lens filter." A minute later I was proven right as Baker, enraged, entered the tent and socked the Canadian botanist in the nose.

**Day 12**

Ideally, we should simply gather samples and return with them to proper laboratories to begin experiments. We have decided, however, not to wait. We have begun to experiment on ourselves. Beaver disagrees, but his protests have stopped since his tongue swelled up after eating some kind of purple fruit. He ate it after the tribesmen told him it was medicine. Their words for medicine and poison are phonetically indistinguishable, so there may have been some confusion on that point. Our informal experiments simply consist of staring at Snork flowers. It was Bellman who started it. He was soon joined by Baker. Both sat transfixed for hours. It was a trance that could only be broken by rough shaking. Bellman described the effect as "Awesome. Out of body. A total trip." Baker described it as "Not unpleasant. Vaguely discombobulating." Both were stunned to learn that over eight hours had passed. They had to be shown the setting sun to see that morning had indeed turned to night. Banks says she intends to try it tomorrow for the purpose of 'due diligence'.

**Day 15**

"Hiccup!" said Bellman. That was exactly how he said it too. Not an actual hiccup, but the word 'hiccup'. He said it again. "Hiccup!" He's been saying it for two days. What was more bizarre was that he didn't know he was doing it.

"Why are you saying hiccup?"

"I'm not," he said. "Hiccup!"

"You did it just now."

"Hiccup! No, I didn't."

We recorded him and played it back. "Very funny," he said. He then stormed off. Bellman's hiccups were the first sign of the madness. Initially, we dismissed it as peculiar to Bellman (who was peculiar to begin with). Only Beaver was truly alarmed. Beaver is also the only one of us not hooked on vegetating. The rest of us didn't want to believe. I had my doubts. Staring at the flowers is both addictive and utterly disconcerting. It makes hours go by in seconds and makes seconds feel like days. Baker described it best. "It makes me feel my own brain from the inside out." My own experience? It allows me see the holes in my own perceptions. I felt as though I'd stepped behind the curtain or seen the magician palm the coin. For example, I now see that I suffer from a harmless form of *synethesia*. That means I attach unrelated qualities to things, such as specific colours to numbers or sounds. Whenever I hear Baker talk, he sounds magenta. Beaver sounds cyan. Being a neurologist, I know full well that our eyes are not just cameras capturing the world 'as it is'. Our conscious mind doesn't see images. It sees interpretations. This is why optical illusions work even when you know the trick. I'm reminded of a poster one of my college professors kept on his wall. It depicted the classic *'blind spot test'*. This consists of a grid of polka dots. Among the dots on one side, one dot is missing. On the other side there is an X. To experience the effect one simply closes one eye, then stares at the X. When positioned correctly, the missing circle vanishes. There is no perceived hole. It simply isn't. My professor explained it this way, "Not only does the brain not see it, *it can't see that it can't see it.* Like all things, the mind is defined by its limitations." He refused to tell me what that meant. On the poster, below the test it read, "You're fooling yourself." Now, when I gaze at the Snork plant, I understand it. I am aware of the lies I am telling myself, yet remain powerless not to believe them. Beaver doesn't think our intellect can protect us, but I think he's trying to trick me.

**Day 16**

Beaver told me his theory about the patterns on the flowers. His theory is that they are actually programming our minds. The flowers, he says, have evolved to trigger a specific arrangement of

neurones within the viewer's visual cortex. A large pattern, visible from a distance, tells the plant's prey to approach. A smaller pattern, visible only when the victim is close enough to the plant's roots, triggers the heart to stop beating. Beaver says we have to view the brain as a computer, our senses as input devices and the petal patterns as malicious code. "Our vision is the input port. Our perception compiles it. It's not so different from how we infect each other's minds with written text or images. The difference is that this is more like machine language. It's able to operate at every level of the brain. That said, I'm no neurologist. What do you think?"
I think Beaver's plotting to kill us all.

**Day 17**
Baker is dead. Or at least we assume he is. He woke up in the middle the night and declared himself "immune to crocodiles." He then announced he was going skinny-dipping in the river and ran off. He hasn't been seen since. It was a crazy thing to do. As a biologist, Bellman noted, Baker ought to know that Amazon crocodiles aren't true crocodiles. They are a very large caiman in the alligator family. To make matters worse, Banks has gone bonkers too. She has become convinced she is a god. She calls herself *Megwah*. I fear they're all going insane. Thank goodness, I've been unaffected so far. This place wouldn't be so bad if the trees would stop yelling.

**Day 20**
Ho. Hum. Yum. The rocks have eyes.

**Day 26**
Ahhhh! I have had a splitting headache for days. I've had it ever

since Bellman set fire to the grove and destroyed all the Snork flowers. He did it in the middle of the night. I'll never forget the sight of him standing in front of that roaring inferno, his bronzed torso glistening in the orange glow, his eyes shining. The Kimmujji lay at his feet in worship. "Omigaush! Omigaush!" they shouted. "The flora! The flora!" Bellman breathed in a whisper barely audible above the crackling flames. A moment later, he tripped over a root and fell backwards into the fire. The pyre roared high in celebration as our guide rolled about in the coals.

Ever since then I have been in withdrawal. I assume I'll be better soon. Hopefully then, I won't have to keep remembering to make my heart pump.

**Day 28**

The Kimmujji have turned on us. They no longer believe we are superior to them. They call us 'woo goo' which I learned from Bellman before he died means 'idiots'. It also means 'food'. They have already trussed up Banks and plan to eat her. The one mercy is that Banks is so far gone in her madness. She is convinced the dinner they are planning is in her honour and that she is receiving an honorary MBA from Yale. Only Beaver is in full control of his faculties. It's just so hard to look at him now, what with his body all covered with boils and open sores. I have stopped accusing him of planning to murder us in our sleep. Being Canadian, he seems to take it all in stride. He says he is working on a plan to escape. I hope so.

That was the final entry in Dr. Kwalia's journal. We know what happened next through the lone survivor of the expedition, botanist and plant pathologist Dr. Edwin McGregor, aka 'Beaver'. As stated in the journal, the Kimmujji became hostile towards the scientists for destroying the sacred Snork grove and for being inferior in every way. Dr. McGregor, though badly wounded with over thirteen infections, seven parasites, four viruses, and pink eye, escaped imminent death by stepping behind a large tree. The Kimmujji, lacking 'object permanence', assumed McGregor had ceased to exist and immediately stopped looking for him. The botanist was then able to sneak back to the boat and return to civilization. After being treated for his many afflictions, Dr. McGregor recovered. More or less. Mostly less, after having had both arms and one leg amputated. Despite this, he seemed in surprisingly good spirits, but showed little grief for what had happened to the rest of the team. "Truth be told, they had it coming," he said to a journalist just prior to his release from hospital. Sadly, that interview was to be his last. Newly fitted with a prosthetic leg, Dr. McGregor decided to go for a walk around the McGill University campus where he taught plant psychology. As luck would have it, that day happened to be *World Statistics Day*. Some pre-med students in a nearby dormitory had decided to celebrate with a game of Russian Roulette. One of the students lost his nerve. Rather than shoot himself in the head, the student shot his pistol out the window. The bullet struck Dr. McGregor as he hobbled past. The wounded botanist remained conscious just long enough for a passerby to hear his last words. "Well, fine then. You can all just go to Hell."

As an addendum, it should be said that it is unknown if there are any more Snork flowers left. A mission sent to recover the bodies found only ashes. Still, upon being questioned, the Kimmujji tribesmen were of little help. "We can't see any," they said. "So... no."

Eddy wrote down the name, date and pages of the article. For a copy of the microfiche it was necessary to request a print-off from the library help desk at a cost of twenty-five cents a page. Only then did he look up and realize Belinda was staring at him. She had read the entire article over his shoulder.

"That's amazing," she said. "Do you think that—"

"Yes," said Eddy. "Yes, I do."

## 1.00

"Are you there, Margaret?" – God

// Brooklyn, New York — then

Modern psychiatry, twelve-year-old Eddy had come to realize, was a lot like shaking a magic eight-ball. Often, it said 'Try Again' or 'Outlook Not Good'. After a year and a half of feeling fine, his mother was back in hospital. They had tried different drugs, Prozac®, Effexor®, Cymbalta®. Each one took weeks to know if it did anything. When it didn't, the dosage was increased to see if that did it. When still nothing good happened, the drug had to be tapered off to minimize withdrawal. The one thing that always worked were the side effects like dry mouth, deeper depression, a preoccupation with walls, etc. The process would then repeat.

Repeat.

Repeat.

Repeat.

Meanwhile, each day was an eternity. With children, they say 'the days are long, the years are short'. With depression, the days are long, and the years are interminable. Eddy tried to understand the method for treating the madness. He was only in grade six, but home-studying depression at a university level. Eddy's father spent his time begging. He begged his wife to get out of bed each morning. He begged her to eat. He begged her to stop staring into space. He begged her not to say she wanted to end it all in front of her son. The same conversations happened again and again.

And again.

And again.

And again.

"I'm a phantom limb," Eddy's mother said, tugging incessantly at her arm. She was slim to begin with, but had lost so much weight that her skin pulled away like an ill-fitted suit.

"What does that mean?" said Eddy, studying his mother with deeply troubled eyes. He was clutching a Mr. Terrific action figure his father had given him for his birthday. He carried it everywhere, in spite of having no idea who the 1960s TV character was.

"I feel myself here physically, even though I'm not. Not really. I've been amputated at the neck."

That night, Eddy looked in the closet and under the bed to see if there were any 'pods'. He resisted the urge to see whether his mother had fingerprints. Any body-snatching, he decided, must have already happened.

Then, one day, Eddy's mother stopped eating.

"She's trying to starve herself to death," his father said matter-of-factly. He then stared at Eddy, clearly as surprised as his son was that he'd said it out loud. Exhaustion had blurred the line between thoughts and words. His father's skull had been worn thin to the point of translucency. "Physically she can eat. She can get out of bed. It's her *want* that's gone." He then added with a sardonic smile, "If a depressed mind wants for nothing, then why is it so sad?"

So it was that Eddy's mother went back to hospital.

That was a week ago.

"Do you mind if I call you Doug?" said the hospital psychiatrist.

"That's not my name," said Eddy's father.

"No, but you look like a Doug." His father didn't know how to respond to this, so he said nothing. The psychiatrist wore a white doctor's coat. He was bald, with a pencil moustache. "The problem is, Doug, United Healthcare have decided your mother is well enough to go home."

"But I thought you and the other doctors said she wasn't ready."

"Yes, well..."

"They get to form their own opinion," said the second psychiatrist. She had glasses and curly red hair that fell over her lab coat shoulders. She stood by the door as if waiting to leave at a moment's notice.

Eddy glanced at his mother. She sat in a butterscotch vinyl chair next to her hospital bed. She stared blankly into space, as was her wont these days. Her skin hung loose over a poorly concealed skeleton. Her eyes were retreating into their sockets, making her look like a dead person who'd taken the time to put on a bathrobe. She hadn't of course, the nurse had dressed her. She was her own remains. He tried to shake the thought from his head. His mum wasn't catatonic anymore. That was good. The Ativan® had snapped her out of it. No one was quite sure why. They'd given it to her once previously, and it had done nothing. "Maybe one of the other drugs was finally working," said the first doctor. "Perhaps, it was a combination," said the second. His mother's brain was now a Who's Who of big name pharmaceuticals, so it was impossible to say. Whatever it was, something had clicked. His mother was still deeply depressed, but no longer stuck in a loop. She was watching the television that hung from the wall. Her eyes tracked the screen. That was progress. Yay! On the TV, Dr. Phil was explaining how it was important that Beyoncé learn to love herself if she wanted to be truly happy.

"So they examined her and decided she was okay to leave the hospital?" asked Eddy's father.

"Well, they didn't examine her, per se..." said the first psychiatrist.

"Per say?"

"They're in Minnesota," said the second psychiatrist. "So, you know, that's far away. They read our reports."

"But didn't your reports say she should stay in hospital?"

"Absolutely," said the first psychiatrist.

"So a doctor who has never even spoken to her over the phone, gets to overrule the doctors who have been treating her?"

"We did appeal the decision."

"To whom?"

There was a moment's pause as the two psychiatrists exchanged glances. Finally, the first spoke. "To them. They decided that they were right. Look, this is all standard stuff. She can continue to stay, of course. Nobody's saying she has to leave. In fact, we strongly recommend she stay."

"Oh... all right then."

"It just means you will have to pay out of pocket," said the second psychiatrist.

"And how much does that cost?"

"Four thousand dollars a day," the two said together.

Once home, Eddy's mother didn't just look like a zombie; she acted like one too. Eddy and his father tried to act as if everything were normal. They spoke of the future. Eddy's mother did not. While she was in hospital, Eddy had read a book written as an unauthorized sequel to the bestselling *Tao of Pooh* and *Te of Piglet*. It was called *The Undiagnosed Clinical Depression of Eeyore*. The previous books, written by Benjamin Hoff, were intended to explain Taoism through the popular children's book characters. This book, written by Aldous Wigglesworth, featured the sad Eeyore and bipolar Tigger being told by Owl to simply 'snap out of it'. A fictionalized Hoff made an appearance. The author appeared, only to discover that he could do nothing to rescue the depressed donkey who had become stuck in quicksand. In the last chapter, Christopher Robin, referenced a study that found that depressed people were able to predict the future more accurately than others. "The rest of us are optimistically delusional," Christopher Robin explained. "Oh," said Pooh, a bear of little brain and mild eating disorder. "Does that mean, the bees will soon die off and there'll be no more hunny?" "Yes," replied Christopher Robin, "I'm afraid so." In the end, Eeyore was treated with electroshock therapy, which helped, but left him stigmatized and alone in the Hundred Acre Wood.

"The greatest danger is when severely depressed people start to feel a little bit better," the first psychiatrist later explained, "Prior to that, they're too depressed to kill themselves. Ironic, no? You have to climb that mountain before you can jump off of it. They become less depressed and, voila, they have the get-up-and-go to, well, get up and *go*." That being said, what had happened was still a crime of opportunity. It was a Tuesday. His mother had announced that she was going for a walk. This, Eddy and his father both thought, was a good thing. She'd struggled to get out of bed for days. Eddy liked to believe that a walk was her honest intention on the outset. She set off down the apartment building hallway only to discover the elevator closed for repair. The elevator itself was stuck on the floor above. The doors were open but blocked off with a three-foot high gate and crisscrossed yellow tape that said 'Caution'. The stairwell was only a few feet away. Despite this, their mother decided to take the elevator. Her death was horrific to all concerned. At the bottom of the antique shaft was a giant spring intended to stop a runaway car. It was not intended to protect a falling human. Eddy's mother bounced back up to the third floor, then to the second, then to the first. She was dead on the first bounce, but continued flopping like a progressively battered rag doll. The four eyewitnesses suffered post-traumatic stress disorder. Eddy and his father were mercifully not among them. They were traumatized in their own way.

#

At Eddy's mother's funeral, his father gave a baffling eulogy. It upset the other mourners. "I lost track of my wife," he said. This statement was followed by a long, awkward pause. Cleared throats. Shifting feet. The weather was suitably autumnal—all leafless trees and granite skies above barren land. His father wore a black suit that swallowed the light. He stood over the open grave as if wondering why. "She wasn't who I married anymore. She was different." His father spoke as he did when trying to resolve a problem. He did so with a distant look and animated hands, as if physically trying to grapple the dilemma. "Then, they gave her drugs and she changed again. After that, her whole personality altered and she was someone else entirely." His hands dropped to his sides in defeat. "I have no idea who we're burying today." Another awkward pause followed. The physicist then raised his hand to his temple in an offhand salute. "So long, whoever you are!" he said. Eddy's father strode briskly away from the open grave without waiting for the casket to be lowered. The funeral attendees stared after him in surprise or exchanged confused looks. Somebody coughed. More waiting. Eddy wanted to follow, but was held back by the firm hand of Adjunct-Professor Almon on his shoulder. Eddy continued to watch his father between the trees. He was engaged in a distracted stroll about the cemetery. As he walked, the physicist seemed to be mouthing the names on the headstones he passed. The casket sank. Words were said. Eddy's father had reached an older, unkempt corner of the graveyard. There, the identities on the headstones were largely obliterated by weather and time. With nothing left to read, Eddy's father picked up a birch branch from the dirt. He began taking golf swings at dandelions with it. "Fore!" The other mourners didn't know what to make of it. They were colleagues and associates who'd felt obligated to be there. They all knew the famed physicist to be aloof, cerebral, and sometimes scornful. Never sympathetic. Never pitiful. For Eddy, it was entirely different. His father's lifetime of keeping his own emotions at arm's length was failing him. Eddy felt as though he were watching a statue crack in the winter's penetrating cold.

Following the funeral, Eddy's father hired a housekeeper to look after the apartment and Eddy—in that order. He assured his son that he would be properly attended to. The physicist then threw himself into his work. Eddy, being twelve in spite of it all, went to school. He resented being treated differently because of his mother's death. Eddy wanted to forget the previous twelve years of his life. He couldn't. His mother's absence had left a gaping hole inside his frail adolescent frame. He teetered. Eddy felt rent asunder and windblown, like an unlatched screen door in a hurricane. For weeks, he sobbed nightly into his pillow. Time passed. He sobbed every other night. One day, one of his teachers, Mrs. Ingram, introduced him to computer programming. It was like another world. It was a world Eddy could master. He became obsessed with the way he could manipulate the machine. He could create with it, break it, and build it up again. He decided to do that, to control instead of cry. If we aren't computers, he decided, we should be. Computers don't get sad.

When Eddy turned thirteen, his father bought him a computer of his own. It was a used PowerBook G3. Black as a spy's attaché case. He used it to hack into the school network to change his grades. Since he had almost all A's to start with, he could only change them to B's. He then changed them back to A's. He thought of changing his gym score from a C to an A, but could hear his mother saying 'no'. "You're only cheating yourself," she'd say. He wasn't sure if cheating really applied to rope climbing and basketball skills, but left the grade as it was.

Six months after the death of his wife, Eddy's father made an announcement. He and Eddy were sharing a supper of microwave macaroni and cheese, or rather, they were waiting to. Despite having a Ph.D in physics, his father had yet to master the microwave and so had, once again, produced a dinner roughly the temperature of the Sun. They were waiting for it to cool. "I've done it," he said, "I've completed my trans-dimensional portal. We can take it for a spin tomorrow." Normally, they ate their suppers in silence, but tonight his father couldn't stop talking. This would be his moment of vindication. He could now prove his *Multidimensional Infinite Repeat-O-Verse* theory was right and that those 'know-nothing-nincompoops in Prague' were wrong. All he had to do was to turn it on and open a hole to an adjacent universe. According to his theory, this would be like opening a door to an adjoining motel room. He would then see if it were identical down to the smallest detail. If just the sanitary band was missing from the toilet or the TV tuned to a different channel, his whole hypothesis would be proven wrong. Eddy's father refused to even entertain this possibility. Instead, he imagined the look on Hans Umlich's face when he showed him his proof. The clincher would be the Schrödinger's cat test. If the cat were dead in both universes, his father explained, then his theory would truly be validated. Eddy glanced nervously at their cat, Gestalt. "No, no, no," his father assured him. "Gessy was your mum's cat. That would be wrong. We'll get a rescue from the pound instead." The physicist then explained that he could have conducted the test today, but wanted Eddy to be there. "You'll be witnessing history," he said triumphantly. "Something to cheer us both up after... well, you know." Dr. Pending took a heaping bite of pasta. An instant later, his eyes bulged and watered as he realized the pasta was still scalding. He grabbed and gulped milk to soothe his burnt tongue while Eddy stared in silence.

The following day, Eddy joined his father in the lab. Eddy had brought his bowl of Corn Flakes with him. He ate perched on a swivel top stool. His father stood hunched over a console. Before them was the portal. It looked like a free standing door frame, the kind one bought at a hardware store for a house. This was because that's exactly what it was. His father had bought it from Home Depot, painted it white, and modified it to open holes in the fabric of the space-time continuum. It included a mail slot, because that's the way it came, as well as a deadbolt lock for safety reasons. "We don't want Ms. Lopez accidentally entering another dimension," he said, referring to their cleaning lady. His father had even added a street number. "Seven—for luck." This was his father's idea of a joke. With a video camera recording, the physicist pressed the doorbell, which had been rewired as an on-off switch. *Ding Dong!* The portal flickered and hummed like the old fluorescent bulbs in the basement of Eddy's school. There was the sound of scotch tape being pulled from vinyl. Next, came the acrid odour of burnt tungsten. The excited physicist swung the door wide. Eddy stood agog. The portal had worked. They were gazing into another universe! The colour drained from his father's face. It was a reality completely different from our own in every way. It didn't just look different; it *was* different down to the very meaning of 'was'. Even to Eddy's twelve-year-old mind it was a wonder beyond description. This was, in part, because there were no words in our language to describe it. So Eddy's brain refused to describe it at all. His father had no such difficulty. "What a complete and utter failure!" he yelled. He then slammed the door shut, kicked the console to the floor, and stormed from the room.

The following day, Eddy found his father sitting sullen and dejected in his lab. He tried to remind his dad what his dad had always told him. "There are no failed experiments, just unexpected results."

"Oh that's just a bunch of complete claptrap!" said Eddy's father. The defeated scientist took a swig from a beaker labeled 'hydrochloric acid'.

Thankfully, it contained only gin. "I am a very mediocre physicist," his father rued, slurring his words.

"But you built the world's first trans-dimensional portal!" said Eddy.

"With mostly educated guesses. And what is the result? Disaster." His father was so embarrassed by it all that he published nothing. He shut down the trans-dimensional portal and moved it to the apartment storage unit. There, he hid it behind the Bowflex Xtreme 2 Home Gym Eddy's mother had bought him for Christmas years earlier. "I'd rather keep those goofballs in Prague guessing than let them know what a fraud I've turned out to be."

"It's not your fault!" said Eddy. He was pained to see his father brought to his knees again. Eddy needed his father, this last pillar of his so-called childhood, not to topple.

"How is it not my fault?"

"It's not your fault that, um... well... that reality turned out to be the way it is."

"It's my fault my theory was wrong."

"You were distracted by Mum. That was the problem."

Eddy's father had that distant look he had whenever he zeroed in on an idea. "Yes," he said, nodding absently. He then began poking the air with his index finger as it touching it. "That's it. That's exactly it. I didn't just get the wrong answer; I asked the wrong question!"

Eddy's father became obsessed. That was nothing new. What was new was that this new problem didn't involve physics at all. His father described it as 'a riddle wrapped in an enigma, folded into the shape of an origami swan and then set on fire'. It was something, he said, that made trans-dimensional travel seem trivial by comparison. He quit his tenured position at the university after they questioned his qualifications for such research. They also questioned his state of mind.

"Who was I married to?" Eddy's father wrote in white chalk on the blackboard in his laboratory. He always wrote the question he was trying to solve on the blackboard first. "Computers lose things; the blackboard does not." Unless, that is, the cleaning lady erased it. The physicist had never forgiven Ms. Lopez for erasing his proof of 'real world probability'. In it, he'd finally explained why, while the theoretical odds of picking the slowest line at the bank might be one in five, the 'real world probability' was five to four. She only cleaned the lab once a week. What were the odds she'd do it on the one day he'd finished his calculations but not yet recorded them? "I guess we'll never know!" he'd ranted. "I wrote PLO for Christ's sake!" Ms. Lopez explained that she'd not understood it to mean 'Please Leave On'. She'd assumed it to be an oblique reference to the Palestinian Liberation Organization. After that, Ms. Lopez was told to leave the blackboard alone no matter how messy it looked. Once he'd written the question, he explained it to his son. "The problem is *us*. What are we, and who are we?"

"Aren't those philosophical questions?" said Eddy, sipping from a juice-box. He resisted the urge to point out that these were exactly the sorts of questions Uncle Russ used to ask. "Why are we here? What the heck are we doing it all for? And, if cigarettes kill people, is it so wrong to shoplift them?" He remembered Uncle Russ huddled in his bomb shelter smoking a stinky joint and reading aloud from Carlos Castañeda. Uncle Russ liked to muse philosophically, especially after one of his annual ayahuasca pilgrimages to Peru. "They're pretty much *the* philosophical questions," said Eddy. "People have been discussing those forever."

"I'm not talking about philosophy. I'm talking about *real* stuff. Science! People have been working on consciousness that way only recently, and the ones who are, are doing it all wrong." He scribbled phrases like 'Turing's Reaction–Diffusion Model', 'Lisa Set' and 'Zindelburg's Theorum' on the black board. Eddy's father believed that everything could, or should, be reducible to equations. He once wrote an angry letter to an eccentric Scottish physicist named McGuffin who had stated that physics and metaphysics were the same thing. "Wrong. Metaphysics is just hooey, like homeopathy and lifetime warranties." McGuffin had made the comment in an article about how the Greek philosopher Thales was right for saying 'All is water' since subatomic matter consists of waves in space. "Water doesn't exist at the quantum level," Eddy's father pointed out, as if explaining something to a child. Eddy was fairly sure the Scottish physicist knew this already.

For a long time, Eddy's father simply pondered. This was his modus operandi when tackling any new problem. "The little grey cells must do their work," his father said in his best Belgian accent. This process involved long walks in Central Park and a lot of staring at nothing in particular. He then sat down and began to work. He codenamed his new project 'Phlogiston'. The goal was to mathematically explain who his late wife was and, *ipso facto,* who everyone else was as well. "If *I* am 'I' and we don't even know what *I* am, how can we know if I have changed or if I am the same?" He wrote on the blackboard.

$$I=?$$

He stopped writing. "Or is that, *is* the same? It's hard even to frame the question. Am I a constant? Or am I a variable–I mean, *is* I a variable?" His father assumed 'computational mind theory' to be correct in some form or another. This was the idea that the human brain somewhat like a Commodore 64, but with much better specs. He dismissed religious dualism outright. "The human soul is incompatible with brain damage," he said, waving the notion away like a gnat.

There was a practical problem with his father's new obsession. He still had to pay the rent and no longer had a salary coming in. In order to fund his research, Eddy's father was forced to turn to private investors. Amazingly, he somehow convinced venture capitalist billionaire Anton Sparks of the commercial potential of his ideas. "He thinks it'll be the next Siri," Eddy's father explained, "ie. a better virtual slave. Everyone wants a slave; they just don't want the sticky ethical issues of owning a fellow human being." Eddy's father described the billionaire as an ignorant plebeian. "He asked me if it'll pass a Turing Test," his father scoffed, "Like that matters! I'm not interested in parlour tricks." Still, his father needed the young mogul for his money. "Yes, I'm duping him, but I'm duping him into doing something worthwhile, instead of building yet another iPhone app for twiddling your thumbs." He couldn't really deliver what Anton wanted. For one thing, Eddy's father wasn't a programmer. Even if he were, the physicist argued, it would have been pointless to try. "I have to do it theoretically," he explained, "today's computers are impossibly primitive. Their chips are made of sand for God's sake!" He then launched into a favourite topic of his, mocking the chess playing of IBM's Deep Blue. "I'm not saying lots of fairly clever people didn't do lots of fairly clever work on it, but think of how sad that is. Chess is a mathematically constrained universe." Eddy's father then shifted to his winey imitation of what he assumed an IBM engineer might say. "Oh, but the moves expand exponentially! Oh, oh, oh! Two-hundred and eighty-eight billion after just four moves! We have advanced algorithms! It's soooo hard!" He then shifted back to his regular voice. "Sure, fine. It's hard to get a snake to ride a bicycle too. Try living in the real world. You want exponential moves? Try reality, with three dimensional space and living pieces that can move anyway they God damn please. Chess was made for computers. Well, not literally, but still. It's like a computer's home turf. Astroturf, specifically. Plus Kasparov still won one of the three games! That's what's more amazing. The human brain intuits morphogenic patterns without even trying! The human brain is to Deep Blue, what a monkey's brain is to a slide rule."

## 1.01

"But you can fool *some* of the people all of the time?" – D. Trump

//Ubenställ, Switzerland — now

"Russian roulette, isn't Russian," Oliver Croft said knowingly. He then drained his martini and began looking about for its replacement. His valet, a small Pakistani man, named Bob, produced one as if by magic. "It was invented by the English. Makes sense when you think about it. Bored Cambridge University students, I believe."

"So why is it called Russian roulette?" asked Allison, taking a sip of white wine. She didn't know what it was, but apparently it went for over a thousand dollars a bottle. "Pretty good plonk," Oliver had assured her. It was. They were standing in Ubenställ Ballroom No. 4, next to the caviar table where they'd started to talk. Oliver owned large portions of the American Midwest. Despite this, Allison had never heard of him. "Through shell companies. I made my money on Wall Street. I retain it in real estate.

I'm a man of traditional values. Feudal tradition, that is."

Oliver paused to wave his second (or was it third?) empty glass in the air. Bob materialized to replace it once more. The billionaire was clearly drunk and getting drunker by the glass. "The Russian-thing was some novelist's fault. Sometimes, I think they just make things up. Anyway, that's not the point. The point is... what was the point? Oh yes, the point is we, various friends and I, play Russian roulette once a year. We do it to celebrate World Statistics Day. You know, as is tradition."

"Really?" said Allison, genuinely shocked. "Isn't that extremely dangerous?"

"Oh yes!" said Oliver, pleased by her reaction. "Of course, we use proxies."

"Proxies?"

"You know, like in a duel. We pay someone to play on our behalf. But we're very heavily invested in it. Both emotionally and financially."

Allison put down the Almas caviar stuffed shrimp she'd been about to bite. "But can't they, um... die? The proxies, I mean."

"Naturally. It's Russian roulette not crazy eights! But, they're very well paid. Over a hundred thousand dollars a game. All for just spinning a chamber and pulling a trigger." Oliver noticed Allison's shocked expression. "Look, these are people who would otherwise be making minimum wage or worse. We give them the opportunity to change their lives."

"One way or another."

Oliver downed his fourth martini and turned his attention to the shrimp table again. "Plus we buy them life insurance. They have a one-in-six chance of making a million dollars. Think of that! Not bad for a few seconds' work. I know CEOs that don't make that kind of money. Not when you count it by the second."

"But they'll be dead!"

Oliver eyed her suspiciously. He was trying to decide if she might be a pinko. "If they do, they die rich and leave their families very well set up. People die all the time for less. Of course, we sponsors take insurance policies out on them too. No point in letting an opportunity pass." Oliver tossed back three whole shrimps, tails and all and began audibly crunching them down. His lantern jaw worked like a trash compactor.

Allison was incredulous. "Let me understand this. You take insurance out on your proxy and get paid in the event they die?"

"Exactly. They get rich, we get rich... er. It's win-win, really."

As Oliver spoke, his mouth was still full. Allison averted her eyes from the carnage inside. "Isn't it illegal? I mean, they die!"

"We prefer to say they 'default', and no, it's not. The choice is entirely theirs. It's not like we put a gun to their head. They do that themselves." Oliver paused to chuckle at his own joke. "Plus we have them sign waivers. We're even thinking of having it added as an Olympic sport. The IOC were open to the idea. Of course, they're open to anything if you throw enough money at them. Just ask the Russians! Anyway, there are practical considerations with creating and sustaining teams that we, well... haven't quite worked out."

A gentle chime sounded. That meant dinner. Allison, still in shock, headed to the dining room. The crowd slowly migrated around her. It had been a long day. She had spent it attending seminars and symposiums. The first session was called '*Winning the Cyberwar*'. It was given via weblink by Julian Assange and was sponsored by Sberbank. Assange advocated that the way to win a cyberwar was to 'bet on both sides'. The overarching theme of the conference, Allison had deduced, was to help billionaires cope in a world that scarcely understood them. The second session Allison attended pertained to this theme directly and was entitled, *Class First*. Good Living expert Martha Stewart explained that while most of the world viewed class as a subset of country, to the members of Sine Qua Non, the reverse was true. Yes, there's an American working class, a caste system in India, and slavery in Mauritania, but the uber-class is different. They were citizens of the world. When you have homes and businesses in many countries and a private jet at your disposal, borders are just imaginary lines on maps. To Allison's surprise, the session was taught by Yoga superstar, Harrish Adum. The famous yogi was himself a self-made billionaire. He'd become rich as the founder of the Yog-Ahhh! chain of studios, Namast-U clothing line, and various nutritional shakes and bars. His best returns, he explained, came from Pürge, a 6-day 'toxin removing' cleanse diet which charged $300 for six days worth of freeze-dried soup. He was preparing to launch a new line with flavours from around the world called Ethnic Pürge. Attendees were invited to participate in the various poses, or have their valet do so on their behalf. "As members, you have already transcended your Earthly bonds," Harrish explained, "Nationality means nothing. Taxes and laws do not, nay, *should* not apply to you. You have truly achieved a transcendental state. You can have anything and need for nothing; therefore, worldly goods are meaningless to you. You alone are truly free. Money is not the root of all evil, but rather the key to Heaven." One of the attendees had gently heckled, "You make it sound like we're gods!" The speaker looked at him with a deeply serious expression and said, "You are better than gods. Gods are born gods. You have earned your place among the immortals."

It had all sounded like madness to Allison, and she said so to Cassius over lunch. "Not at all," he said between sips of civet coffee. "Let me ask you this Allison, do you know how much a billion dollars is?"

"Well, I know what the number is. I've voted for bills that cost many billions of dollars. And voted them down."

Cassius smiled. It was a smile of amusement. A smile one might make at the utterances of a child. "A billion minutes ago," the Senator said, "Rome was as its height. A billion hours ago, it was the Stone Age; woolly mammoths and sabre-toothed tigers ruled the land. There are whole countries, albeit small ones, with GDPs less than one billion. And remember, plenty of the attendees here have many, many billions. So tell me, what does it mean for one person to have a billion dollars?"

"I... I don't know."

The Senator smiled. "Nobody does. That's why we're here."

The chime continued to sound. Allison found her seat at a table with five strangers. There was no sign of Alan Cassius. She wondered if it had anything to do with their lunch together. Between the dessert and the digestif, he'd placed his hand on Allison's leg. Surprised but not shocked, she'd simply pulled away as if it were an accident. When he'd placed it there a second time, she'd reached down and firmly removed it. "No," she said bluntly looking him in the eyes. "Don't." She didn't know for certain that he'd had her seat reassigned, but his place card was nowhere to be seen. It's just as well, she thought, it might have been awkward. Cassius was useful for making introductions, but she was here now, so she'd just have to make her own. The Senator had served his purpose. "Hello," she said, offering her hand to the rotund man sitting beside her.

"я не говорю по-английски," he replied, with an apologetic smile. He politely shook her hand and returned to stuffing dinner rolls into his mouth between sips of what Allison suspected was a tall glass of vodka. As the other guests sat, she realized she'd been relegated to the 'kids table'. Even among billionaires, it seemed, there were outcasts. Three of the others spoke only Chinese. The remaining two were 'Eurotrash'. Inbred aristocrats who had inherited massive trust funds along with their badly mangled DNA. One of them, a German named Heinz, kept dropping things on the floor in an effort to peek up Allison's skirt. She was tempted to leave, but did not want to miss the keynote. It was to be delivered by global media magnate James Machi. The billionaire news tycoon had been a recluse for the past two years. In that time, he'd been spotted only at private functions, private golf courses, and restaurants bought out for the occasion. It was said that he had grown uncommonly fat and was shy about it. No one had seen Machi speak publicly in years. The New Yorker had quipped that Machi was *Citizen Kane* played by Orson Welles in his decline. There were even rumours the billionaire was dead.

The main course for supper was something called Swift Irish Pie. It had a delightful umami flavour Allison couldn't quite place but suspected might be lamb. She had just taken a last bite when Cassius took to the stage. There was a polite round of applause. Allison had heard rumours that Cassius was connected to Machi. Until now, she wasn't sure they were true. So he didn't simply dump me, she thought, that's a relief. No need to make an enemy of Alan Cassius.

The lanky Senator strode across the stage to a tall glass podium. He wore a gold bow tie that Allison suspected might actually be made of gold. "Ladies and gentlemen, my name is Alan Cassius, US Senator from the great state of California. It is my supreme privilege to introduce our guest speaker. What do you give a man who has everything? Why an introduction he doesn't need, of course!" Allison noted that the personal valets for the Russian and Chinese billionaires were whispering live translations into their ears. She took a sip of vintage port from a crystal glass. For a moment, the young Senator was surprised by the striking notes of blackberry and honey on her tongue. "...and sixty-seven television stations in over one hundred countries. News media and new media. Web Portals like *NewsChoice*. Social media platforms *Bubble Tock* and *Echo Loco*. Even a few dozen newspapers to boot. In short, if you know about it, you can likely thank our speaker, Mr. James Louis Randolph Machi, for making that possible."

A large projection screen descended from the ceiling above the stage. A live satellite feed of an enormous man appeared on screen. It was James Machi. Not dead, but hardly a picture of health either, thought Allison. While the media tycoon was visible only from the chest up, his multiple chins and sagging jowls made it clear just how fat he'd become. It's hard to believe he was once considered quite the playboy, she thought. He was broadcasting from a house somewhere in the tropics where it was either still yesterday or already tomorrow. A dazzling sun shone between gently swaying palm trees behind him.

"Good day fellow SQN. *Deorum Curam Sui.*" Machi paused as the audience repeated the words back in chorus. Allison recognized it as the club motto. Cassius assured her it meant something along the lines of *E Pluribus Unum.* Machi cleared his throat and resumed, "I want to talk to you today about responsibility. Specifically, the rich man's burden." As he spoke, Machi leaned forward, allowing his bloated face to fill the screen. Behind him, a man who looked remarkably like PGA golfer Phil Mickelson strolled past. The golfer was wearing shorts, flip flops and no shirt. He walked over to a bar fridge and helped himself to a can of Diet Slice. Apparently unaware that he was being observed through a webcam, Phil began chugging the entire drink. Machi scowled, but chose to continue. "We have a very special role to play as the world's uber-class. First, let me be clear about one thing, as an American, I *love* democracy." Phil Mickelson, having finished his drink broke into impromptu calisthenics, jumping up and down while clapping his hands above his head. "Democracies are a good thing, but they have an Achilles' heel—*people.* The idiots get as many votes as the well informed. What's more, there are more of them. Even worse, they can be easily led by any lunatic with an ounce of personal charm. Plato knew this. We all know this. It's happened before, many, many times." Behind Machi, Phil stopped in mid jump. He peered suspiciously at the webcam. A look of horror came over his face as he realized he was being watched by a room full of people. The PGA golfer covered his face with his hand and quickly slunk out of sight. Machi continued, "So then, how do we safeguard our precious free market world? Surely, it is something far too valuable to leave to the whims of disgruntled employees. United States Colonel Ryan Gremillion famously said, 'Freedom isn't Free.' It's true. It costs money, and lots of it."

"He's right, you know," said one of the Eurotrash across the table from Allison. "It's not free. It costs... money." As he said this, the twenty-something German attempted to toss the onion from his gimlet into his mouth. He missed. The onion fell between the buttons of his open collar and disappeared down his front. The young man began reaching into his shirt in an attempt to retrieve it.

Allison determinedly looked past him to the giant projection of James Machi. The media tycoon continued. "There are those who would seek to limit our influence, our speech, as the best way to protect democracy. This is naïve. It only opens the door for some unqualified person to seize control by charm, subterfuge, or... other means." Allison glanced about the dining room at the many nodding heads. Two tables over, she recognized Charles and David Koch sipping espresso and nodding along with the rest. There were plenty of other Americans and Europeans, but also members from Asia, Africa, and the Middle East. The gathering was exclusive, she noted, but not to democracies. It seemed like an odd speech to give to such a group. Many came from countries where actual democracy was not an issue. Still, they were all beneficiaries of the status quo. "So, before we let someone else seize the newspapers, the radio, television, and internet, we must do so ourselves. For myself, I am on the cusp of achieving this goal. The United States Congress is about to pass a bill that will remove the shackles of regulation from media ownership. My company, Majority Media, owner of MCNX, will be free to own unlimited market share in all areas of communication. We will replace the chaos of confusion with the serenity of certainty. Reason will rule."

"This is madness!" yelled a voice from the audience. Heads turned to find the source. They located it in a white haired man seated in the front. He rose to confront the looming face of the media wizard. Despite seeing him only from behind, Allison recognized him as familiar. The feed was evidently two-way, allowing Machi to see his accuser. The old man

*233*

continued, "This is totalitarian madness! We are the beneficiaries of democracy. You and I, Machi, we made our money from the freedom and infrastructure of America."

Machi's gigantic head, glared down on the tiny figure. "Go back to Omaha, old man. The world has changed." Allison knew then that the old man was investment billionaire Warren Buffett. She had met him years earlier at a Nebraska charity dinner event.

The Oracle of Omaha threw down his napkin and stormed from the room. The other billionaires watched in silence. It was not the first time Buffett and Machi had publicly sparred. Three years earlier, the last time Machi had attended in person; the two had hurled breadsticks at one another during a heated debate. It was only after the dining room doors were closed that Machi continued. The giant head narrowed its eyes and peered about the room as if looking for other potential dissenters. "God might have created us equal, but he did not keep us that way. Our success is our validation. Like Rockefeller, Hearst, and others before us, we cannot deny our special responsibility to guide this world we have inherited."

"Pravda! Pravda!" shouted Allison's neighbour, raising a glass of vodka in a toast, slopping it down his shirt-sleeves as he did so. No one else joined in. Undeterred, the drunk Russian tossed back the shot and motioned for another.

Machi, wheezing from the effort, continued, "To this end, I would like to announce that my great endeavour has been successful. Project *Invisible Hand* is now officially at version 1.0!"

Murmurs of astonishment rippled through the audience. Allison glanced about. While surprised, the members all seemed to know what this was. "What is Invisible Hand?" she asked her neighbour.

"Мне очень жаль, что я гей," he said.

"He said, he's sorry but he's a homosexual," the Russian's valet explained. The inebriated billionaire nodded and touched the side of his nose as if sharing a secret.

"I didn't... never mind," said Allison.

"How do we know it works?" someone shouted.

"How do we know we can trust you?" yelled a man in Arab dress.

Machi smiled broadly. "You ask me if I am lying? You assume lies are a bad thing. God made a mistake in telling Adam not to eat the apple. What he should have done, is lied to him. He should have told Adam the apple was poison. Had he done that, Adam would have made the right choice, and we would all be living in Eden. We will not, nay, *must* not make the same mistake that God did. The Invisible Hand project affords us that power."

The room erupted into agitated babble. Allison noticed that Cassius, still on stage, had donned a pair of glasses. They appeared to be sunglasses, which was odd given the dimmed lights.

"That still doesn't answer our questions," shouted a woman in a German accent. "Before, this was all science fiction. Now? Well, it raises very serious concerns. Clearly it could be misused. Turned against us, even."

Machi smiled like a great grandfather slug. "Naturally, Hilda. I understand and respect that. And I am about to address those concerns directly. I'm going to set your mind completely at ease, right now. So, please pay attention everyone. You're not going to want to miss this. Allan, will you do the honours?" Cassius smiled obligingly, and tapped a button on a remote. At that moment the satellite feed cut out. It was replaced with bright red static that filled the screen. Allison felt light in the head as if she'd stood up too quickly. She reeled as though her inner ear had sloshed in two different directions at once. The floor tilted like the deck of a ship in a storm. She gripped the side of her chair for fear of falling.

The vertigo vanished.

The banquet hall floor righted itself. The room was silent. Allison looked to the other tables. Around the room, club members blinked and touched their temples. They appeared baffled. The live feed had ended. The projector screen rolled silently up into the ceiling. Only Cassius moved normally. He folded his sunglasses and tucked them back into his pocket. He straightened his gold tie. He looked amused.

Then, it all started up again, like a movie projector switched back on. The hubbub of chatter rushed in to fill the void. The clinking of forks and cups on saucers resumed. The words 'marvellous' and 'visionary' peppered the conversations. Everyone seemed delighted by what had happened. Beside Allison, the Russian beamed and raised his glass in toast. "Vashe zrodovye!" he shouted. Allison had been confused a moment earlier, but was no longer sure why. It felt like a dream she'd intended to remember, but had forgotten anyway. What was it? She didn't know. She did know one thing. Machi's speech had been wonderful. His vision was brilliant. She couldn't quite remember what he'd said, but it had all made perfect sense.

"Excuse me, Mademoiselle." A waiter placed a plate in front of the Senator, startlingly her. The plate contained a dessert. It was an angel made of dark chocolate. The menu card called it *The Magic Christian*. The tiny brown figure was a wonder to behold. It had an up-tilted head. Its lithe little arms reached forward beseechingly towards her. Its paper-thin wings were spread in flight. Most amazing, was that the tiny chocolate angel was actually floating an inch above the plate. Allison waved her dessert fork beneath it to be sure. If it weren't in front of her, she wouldn't have believed it possible. One of the three Chinese businessmen across from Allison paused in mid-sentence. Without acknowledging the miracle above his plate, he plucked the angel from the air and bit it in two. He placed the remaining hips and legs down on the plate. Its lighter-than-air gas released; the half-eaten angel no longer floated. Its inside was hollow. The billionaire wiped chocolate from his chin and resumed his conversation.

## 1.1

"1 + 2 = fish" – H. Putnam

//UCLA, Los Angeles — now

Eddy and Belinda walked to Workshim Hall where Professor Wilkins was giving a lecture to undergraduates. They discreetly entered the back of the room and took their seats in the last row. The professor was pacing back and fourth as he spoke, occasionally pausing to clasp his hands together as if in prayer. Professor Wilkins abruptly stopped and pointed to a young woman student in the third row and asked, "What is a symbol?"

The woman thought for a moment then said, "Um... something that stands for something else?"

Wilkins nodded and said, "Okay good, let's go with that. Something that stands for something else. So... we live in a world of symbols, yes? Letters, words, numbers, icons, logos, objects, and so on. The pop artist Prince changed his name to a symbol. When no one could pronounce it, he became 'the artist formerly known as Prince' and the symbol of a poorly thought out plan." The room murmured with chuckles. "For one thing, Prince was already a symbol. But that's how it is with symbols. Referenced, and re-referenced. Infinite regression." Professor Wilkins paused to hover over a student who was too engrossed in his phone to notice. The professor leaned down to read aloud the text message the young man was composing. "Heart... is that an egg plant? Winkey-face."

The young man looked up, mortified. The class burst into laughter. "Sorry, sorry, sorry!" said the young man, as he shoved his phone into his bag and sank into his seat.

"Ah yes, emojis," said Professor Wilkins. "The future is hieroglyphic. How innovative." The old academic then resumed his pacing, stroking his beard thoughtfully. "Now, where was I? Ah yes, infinite regression. Take the ubiquitous McDonald's Golden Arches. Symbol for dinner for some of you, much to your parent's chagrin no doubt. Also obesity, poverty, American capitalism, and even, for what it's worth, the letter M. All, some, or none of the above. The pillars of Ancient Greece? Once used to hold off the roof. Now symbols of classicism, stability, the establishment, higher learning, and oppressive Western ideals. Very ironic, I suppose. Still, when it comes to communication it presents a problem. Languages have to be agreed upon to function. Symbols are anything but. They are corrupted by overuse, reuse and abuse, both subjective and interpretive. And that all assumes honesty. What if someone intentionally tries to corrupt our symbols? What if someone lies? We have constructed a teetering Tower of Babble. But, here in lies the rub. It is said that symbols are also the basis of thought itself. They are the basis of us. If so, isn't it a bit troubling that they are so... flexible? But isn't that very flexibility the source of their power? If the quality of what you make can be no better than the material with which you make it, then how can we be sure of anything? What I mean is, what does it all *mean*?" At that the Professor nodded to the clock on the wall. "I can tell you what *that* means. It means that we're out of time. Reminder that papers are due next week. Under my office door by midnight. You know the drill. All right then, be gone!" Professor Wilkins dismissed the class with a wave of his hand.

Eddy and Belinda remained seated while the students around them packed up their iPads and laptops and began to file from the hall. Many of them, Eddy noted, had spent the lecture surfing the web, updating Facebook, playing games, or instant messaging one another. The undergraduates were not at all enraptured like the acolytes of Lotus Hill. Most weren't even paying attention. At the front of the room, Professor Wilkins packed up his own notes and books into a leather briefcase. For a moment, he seemed to Eddy like a lonely lighthouse keeper.

"Professor!" Belinda whisper-shouted excitedly.

Professor Wilkins looked up in surprise. He smiled in delight. "Belinda, oh hello dear!" The professor then peered at Eddy. "Mr. Pending? Bit risky you being out like this, no?"

"I have a disguise."

"So, I see. Shaw?"

"Kafka."

"Franz Kafka didn't have a beard."

"That's so no one will recognize me as Kafka. It's a disguise within a disguise."

"A metamorphosis."

"We think we've learned what's really going on!" said Belinda.

"Oh, have you now?" Professor Wilkins glanced about to check that all of the undergrads had left. "Well then, I suppose you'd better enlighten me."

Minutes later, the three were walking across the UCLA campus, en route to Lotus Hill. As before, few of the passing students gave Eddy a second glance except to navigate past him on the narrow pathways. Eddy gave Professor Wilkins an abridged account of Dr. Kwalia's journal. "...so, it fits perfectly. The clincher is the red glasses the MRCG wear."

"MRCG?"

"Men in Rose Coloured Glasses. It's what they're called. The guys who tried to kill us with the cards."

Taking advantage of finally being outside, Professor Wilkins lingered to light his pipe. This drew poisonous glances from passing students. "Hmm. Well, it does fit with our own observations. At Lotus Hill, we do media monitoring experiments among other things. We detected something changing in the ether, as it were. We found patterns like the one you describe embedded in TV signals and elsewhere. Someone reading of Kwalia's accounts perhaps found this Snork plant, or whatever it's called, and weaponized it in some way. They figured out how to infect people's brains. That's how we found you. We saw the patterns being deployed during the news broadcasts about you and Gwen. We realized that whoever was behind this was clearly targeting you."

"So let's do something!" said Eddy.

The Professor nodded thoughtfully for a moment. "And what would you propose that be?"

"Um..."

"Go to the police?" said Professor Wilkins.

"No, they'd just arrest me. And I was almost killed while in police custody."

"The government?" suggested Belinda.

"Like I trust the government!"

"Where then? We don't even know who's behind it. We have no proof, nor way to stop it. I believe you, but it sounds like madness. No?"

Eddy glanced at Belinda. She shrugged.

"I don't know," said Eddy, "What I don't understand is why weren't you guys affected? Why didn't you try to kill us too?"

"We were, at first," said Professor Wilkins. He sucked on his pipe and exhaled a grey cloud. "The first time we saw the patterns they affected us too. We were a little like Madam Curie playing with radioactive isotopes at her garden parties—showing off how they glowed in her hands without realizing their lethality. Poor Nixon suffered an epileptic fit, and he doesn't have epilepsy. But, those were alpha versions, presumably. They didn't do much other than infect and vanish. We use our own computers to keep the viruses at arm's length, and to study them. We've still learned shockingly little about how they actually work. They're compiled, you see. Without the source code, it's impossible to disentangle. Still, we did figure out the viruses are less effective against minds that know they're there. Since we know they're trying to control us, we are able to resist. Conscious awareness of viruses defuses their power. We're above their influences."

Eddy considered this for a moment. He wondered if it explained why he didn't die at the hands of Dr. Linquist. "So... because I know the MRCGs are carrying virus cards, I'm immune?"

"Oh no, no! I wouldn't say that. For the conscious stuff, yes, but I don't think that would work for the lethal subconscious attacks. Those go straight to the base of the brain. You couldn't stop those anymore than you could decide to make your heart skip a beat."

"So what do you recommend, Professor?" asked Belinda.

"I recommend we do nothing for now, other than to keep you and Ms. Myers safe. You're welcome to stay with us at Lotus Hill for as long as you like. I think you'll find it's very comfortable."

"I don't trust him," said Gwen bluntly.

"Why? He rescued us," said Eddy, "We'd be dead right now if they hadn't brought us here." Eddy sat on the bed. Gwen stood by the open window with her arms crossed to say 'I've made up my mind'.

"You said he knew about it. So why didn't he do anything before? Why not tell anyone? Maybe he just wants to study us like rats in a maze."

"He said they detected the presence of the patterns. But, they didn't know its source or how it worked. They did write some papers about it to warn people. Professor Wilkins himself did, along with two of his students."

"They published papers to warn people?"

"Well, they tried to. The papers were rejected for lack of verifiable evidence, but still..."

"Great. Someone's trying to control our brains and we're being thwarted by peer review." Gwen shook her head in disgust and turned away.

"Look, they said we can stay as long as we want," Eddy continued, "It's kind of great, really. The house is beautiful and so are the grounds. I love it here."

"Is that what you love? The grounds? The neatly trimmed hedges, perhaps?"

"I also love the smart people. It's like hanging out with software engineers, except they're actually nice and relatively well adjusted."

"Relatively."

"You haven't been to a hacker convention."

Gwen shook her head. "You're not thinking straight, Eddy. It's like we've changed places. I'm now the suspicious one, and you're the trusting fool."

Eddy was annoyed. No one had ever called him a fool before. A nerd, a geek, a brainiac, socially inept, sure, but never a fool. "I'm a fool? I'm the one who had this whole thing figured out. I'm the one who had to save you from the MRCGs who came to your apartment!"

"Who came looking for *you*!" Gwen threw up her hands in frustration. "Look, Eddy, I'm sorry. You're not a fool. But something, or *someone*, has you all turned around."

"What does that mean?" Eddy circled around to look at her.

"You know what it means."

"No, I don't," he lied. For a moment, they glared at one another. "Are you jealous?"

Gwen laughed. "Hardly. You're not exactly my type. Look, I'm leaving. You can stay here. It's clearly what you want."

Eddy stared at her. "You could die out there! If someone recognizes you, they'll tear you limb from limb. You saw those people."

"I'll take my chances." Gwen strode back to her own room through the adjoining door and slammed it shut behind her.

*Spyware*

# 1.2

"Leftovers again?" — W. Heisenberg

//Ubenställ, Switzerland — now

It was the final day of Sine Qua Non. The Ubenställ Hotel had pulled out all the stops for the last lunch. The back garden had been decorated with ice sculptures for the event. The massive two-story sculptures were exquisite, but what made them truly special was that they had been carved from Arctic icebergs flown in just for the occasion. One depicted a musclebound giant doing what appeared to be a handstand. "Not a giant, a titan," the artist explained. He wore a bored expression and a burgundy beret. He was also smoking a cigarette in a long holder with an ash that curled like a witch's fingernail. "Specifically, Atlas holding up the Earth. It's all about perspective, you see." Lunch itself was about sushi and sashimi. Guests were invited to visit the wave pool which had been drained for the occasion and refilled with sea water. Inside were live tuna, sea bass,

*244*

eels and more. They had been segregated into pens to insure that one prospective entrée didn't eat another. Guests were invited to pick the creatures they wished to eat. The tuna were so plentiful; there was no need to share. One could just carve out the perfect pound of flesh and discard the rest. Allison peered curiously at the water in one pen that plumed with red smoke. Dark forms littered the bottom. "Sharks," the Maître D explained. "The ones at the bottom are dead. Our Japanese members want only the fins." The young man offered this as an amusing cultural factoid. Allison, who considered herself an animal lover, felt vaguely ill.

"Ice water, Madame?" asked Isa.

"Yes, please, but with gin and vermouth and hold the water."

Isa nodded and vanished.

Allison spotted Alan Cassius a few feet away at the pool's edge. He was looking about for something, or someone. He peered anxiously over heads and between shoulders. Suddenly, his face lit up as he spotted his valet working his way through the crowd. "You found it?"

"Yes, sir. It was in your room." With that, Bob handed Cassius his dinner jacket folded neatly once. Cassius frowned at the explanation but was more concerned with checking the contents of the coat's inside pocket. A palpable look of relief passed over him as he evidently found what he was looking for. "Excellent. No harm done. Now then, go find me some champagne."

"Yes sir," said his valet, hurrying off.

Suddenly, the Senator seemed his old self. He saw Allison and smiled beneficently. Evidently, all was forgiven and forgotten. "It's a shark eat shark world," he said, with a nod to the murky pool of finless fish.

"It's a waste," said Allison.

"These people can't afford to be petty." said Cassius waving off her concern. "It's the only thing they can't afford." He accepted a flute of champagne from his valet with a curt "آپ کا شکریہ" The Senator took a sip, then smirked. "So, have you had a good time? Tomorrow, you'll be cast out of Eden once more. You'll be back in the real world."

"Actually no, I'm going straight to DC"

Cassius chuckled. "Did you enjoy last night's keynote?"

"I did. It was... it was amazing! He was brilliant. Everything Machi said makes perfect sense. I had my doubts before, but now... Well, I don't know what I was thinking before." Cassius smiled approvingly. For the first time, Allison noticed how handsome the Senator was, in an elusive kind of way. In the past, she'd found his sharp features vaguely villainous, rat-like even. She saw now how wrong she'd been. He was oddly compelling. The Senator gazed at Allison over the rim of his glass as he took a sip. She felt naked before him, as if he knew her thoughts. It was both disarming and exhilarating.

"Annabelle!" Cassius shouted. He waved at someone behind Allison. She turned to see who it was. Congresswoman Anne Flatwood approached with a bright smile and open arms.

"Alan, so good to see you! Marvellous speech last night." The Congresswoman and Senator embraced and exchanged air kisses. Allison had heard they had ended their very public feud. Still, it was startling to see in person. Allison had seen the two pillory each other in the halls. This was like watching Godzilla and Mothra hug it out.

"You see, Allison, you're not the only other House member here! You know the Congresswoman?"

"Oh yes," said Allison, "Good to see you, Anne."

"Neville is here too, somewhere or other," said Congresswoman Flatwood, casting about. "Skulking around with the fossil fuel crowd, no doubt." She turned back to Allison and welcomed her with both hands. This was the proper way to show you cared in politics, the two handed shake. Take both hands or grasp at the elbow. It was something every successful politician learns. One hand feels disingenuous.

"Yes, I know. I've seen him about," said Allison. The congresswoman was referring to Speaker of the House John Neville of Texas. The last time Allison had seen him he had been complaining to a hostess that the gold leaf in the desserts was giving him gastro-intestinal issues. "I feel like I got Fort Knox in ma colon!" he moaned. Allison and Anne had met back in Washington, but little more. Anne Flatwood was a very senior member on several committees and of very different political stripes. Still, Allison respected her as she respected any woman who'd made it in what was still an old boys' club. "So you've come 'round to the Majority Bill?"

"I have. Alan here has really set my mind at ease."

"Mine too."

At that moment, Isa appeared at Allison's side. "Mademoiselle Spears, it is time."

"Thank-you, Isa," said Allison. She turned back to the Senator and the Congresswoman. "It appears my time here in paradise is at an end. I have to get to the airport for my flight home."

"I did offer you a seat on a private plane," said Cassius.

"A decision I now regret," said Allison, "but here we are. I'll see you both stateside." Allison bid them farewell and walked through the Elysian putting green to the front of the hotel. She felt exhilarated. Simply being invited to Ubenställ put you in the inner circle of inner circles. It was kind of like Heaven she thought, were Heaven comprised of concentric rings. Nevertheless, Allison felt reborn. Her mind had opened. I've been enlightened. No, not enlightened, *transcended*. Not in a 1960s Timothy Leary kind of way. This had more of an Olympian vibe, with actual nectar and ambrosia. I am one of *them*. She passed the foppish blonde Eurotrash from the night before. He was swaying drunkenly while urinating in the rose bushes. Okay, she thought, maybe not *him*.

"Mademoiselle?" said Isa.

"Yes?"

"Merci," said the valet, "for being most... human."

Allison looked at her, amused. "I do my best. Thank-you for all your help. You did a marvellous job." Allison reached for her purse, hoping she had enough euros for a generous tip.

The small French woman put her hand on Allison's. "Please, Mademoiselle, allow me to give you something instead." Isa reached into her coat pocket and withdrew a sealed cream coloured envelope. The envelope said 'Read Me'. "But not until you are safely on the plane."

"Safely on the plane?" laughed the Senator. "You make it sound terribly clandestine, Isa! Don't tell me you're a spy."

"It is not a joke."

Allison saw the urgency in Isa's eyes. "All right then. Curiouser and curiouser."

## 1.3

"I know you are, but what am I?" – Hobbes (the tiger)

//Lotus Hill College, Los Angeles — now

An hour later, Eddy found Belinda in the back garden. She was seated on a stone bench, reading a book. The book was of poetry written by Nixon. She was reading it in order to give him her critique. She described Nixon as a sort of Victorian garden fairy. "He's always flitting about, flying high on marijuana," she said. "Everyone likes him, but no one takes him seriously." She showed Eddy a verse Nixon had written about a French robot.

### *Jacques*

*"Tick tock," said the robot Jacques*
*"I wonder what's inside of me?*

> *What makes me tick, what makes me talk?*
> *I must go find a key."*

> *So he found the key and opened the door.*
> *What he saw then made him sick.*
> *"This can't be true, there must be more*
> *That makes me tock and tick."*

> *Inside were many gears and springs*
> *(That part he understood)*
> *But what was it between these things?*
> *Black goo? That can't be good!*

> *"It's a problem," said the Gen-ius, "that much I'll say is true,*
> *You've goo stuck in your gears, and gears stuck in your goo.*
> *I'll say it once, and once again, you just can't mix the two!*
> *So, Jacques, you simply must decide, are you gears, or are you goo?*

"His meter goes off the rails in the final verse," Belinda said, "But, I'm not sure he cares. I tell him modern poetry doesn't have to rhyme, but he likes it this way. He also needs to write more with his heart and less with his head."

"What does it mean?"

"It means, he'll never get published," said Belinda. She closed the book and smiled at Eddy. Eddy felt instantly warm inside, as though he'd just eaten a bowl of soup.

"Gwen's leaving," he said.

"What? Why?"

"She thinks she can't trust Professor Wilkins, or you guys in general."

"That's ridiculous! We rescued you. Nixon could have been killed!" Belinda was clearly upset. Eddy instinctively took her hands in his.

"I know," he said. "I told her that."

"The professor put his neck out. If Gwen leaves, they might cut our..." Belinda stopped short.

Eddy's eyes narrowed. "Cut our... what?"

Belinda looked aghast. "I'm... I'm sorry..." she said. "We planned to tell you. We really did. After the danger had passed."

Moments later, Eddy stormed through the door to the sitting room. Professor Wilkins and the eight students seated there looked up in surprise. The professor plucked the pipe from between his teeth and cocked an eyebrow. "May I help you, Mr. Pending?"

"You knew? This whole time?"

"You'll need to be more precise. Not to toot my own horn, but I know quite a lot."

"What's worse, you made it possible!"

Belinda entered the room behind him. "Eddy, wait..."

"Ah-ha," said the Professor, nodding thoughtfully. "Well, not intentionally." The professor then paused to peer into his pipe as if looking for something he'd misplaced amid the glowing tobacco embers. "The Law of Unintended Consequences," he hemmed. He now appeared to Eddy like a lighthouse keeper whose light had gone out. He's dutifully tending his post, thought Eddy, as ships crash about him.

"What the Hell is going on?" The entire room turned to see Gwen standing in the doorway, hands on hips, green eyes flashing. She had been on her way downstairs when she'd seen Eddy race across the hall.

"I'm sorry Gwen; you were right. I should have believed you," said Eddy. He turned accusingly back to Professor Wilkins. "So it's Majority

Media that's behind it all?"

Professor Wilkins shrugged. "Hardly a surprise. The signal was broadcast on MCNX after all. You're a bright fellow. Surely, you at least suspected them?"

"Well... yes, of course I did," said Eddy. "But, I thought it was too obvious. I assumed they'd been spoofed. Hacked by the real culprit to make them look guilty."

"Naturally. Being a hacker, you assume things are more complicated than they are."

Gwen stared at Eddy with alarm. "You're a hacker? You said you were just a software developer!"

"Well, technically, um..." Eddy saw the ice crystals forming in Gwen's eyes. "It's not that simple. Hackers aren't all bad. Look, I'll explain later." He turned his attention back to Professor Wilkins. "But you didn't just know; you made it all possible. It was *your* research, your re-discovery of Dr. Kwalia's work. *You* did this!"

"We published a paper!" Michael interjected. "We're not responsible for what someone does with it. No one can be in the wrong for spreading knowledge."

"Exactly," said Professor Wilkins, "I, along with some of my students, published a paper theorizing how a trans-neural virus *might* work. It was strictly theoretical. We were then approached by the James L. Machi Foundation. They wanted to fund our research. This sort of thing happens all the time. Most pharmaceutical patents are built on the back of university clinical research."

"You didn't have to take the money," said Eddy.

"We were about to close," said Belinda. "We had no choice."

Professor Wilkins stroked his beard solemnly. "Lotus Hill's original endowment was almost gone. The board had made some ill-considered investments. This great school, with all its history, education and valued research was on the brink, Eddy. The James L. Machi Foundation grant rescued us. They kept us from closing or worse, being turned into a business school or such. They continue to do so today."

"I knew it!" said Gwen. She was now pacing in agitated circles like an overloaded dryer on a spin cycle.

"So what, you just let them do whatever they want?" said Eddy. "You let them control people's minds? You let them kill people?"

The Professor hemmed and puffed on his pipe for a moment as if considering how to frame a particularly thorny philosophical question. "We're not bad people, Eddy. We're just people who recognize their own limitations. That's a good thing. We don't take sides, we *understand* sides. It's a higher level of existence, really. Our role is to bring knowledge and understanding to the world. It is not our role to paternalistically decide to withhold knowledge, to decide that some knowledge is... forbidden fruit. It is also not our role to take on corporate giants. After all, we didn't create any viruses."

"Nah, you just wrote the instructions so someone else could," said Gwen.

Professor Wilkins frowned. "We're deeply troubled by what they've done with our work. Sadly, history is littered with examples of noble research turned to evil purpose. The Atomic Bomb, for instance. Einstein sorely regretted it."

"TNT," suggested Gretchen. "Nobel invented it for construction, and later regretted the deaths caused by its misuse."

"Exactly," said Professor Wilkins.

"And Gary Thuerk," said Michael.

"Who?"

"The marketer who invented spam emails. Although, I don't know he actually regretted it."

"Yes, all right. The point is, academic research doesn't kill people;

people kill people."

Michael snapped his fingers. "Kalashnikov! He regretted inventing the AK-47."

"That's not really an apt comparison. It was *meant* to kill people," said Professor Wilkins. "The point is; we're not responsible."

"You can say that again," muttered Gwen.

"Stay with us Eddy," implored a young woman with red hair in pigtails whose name he didn't know. In his mind, he'd given her the name Pippi Longstocking.

Eddy stared at Pippi. He felt both the pull of her words and appalled by what he'd learned. He looked about for Belinda. She was nowhere to be seen. Gwen stood with her hands on her hips as semaphore for 'we're done here'. "We have to leave, professor," said Eddy. "Thank-you for your help, but we don't belong here." Eddy turned to leave. As he did so, he was surprised to find himself and Gwen facing four young men in casual pants, barring the exit.

"I'm afraid it's not that simple, Eddy," said the Professor. "We can't just let you go. Not with what you now know. If they find out we've provided you sanctuary, they will cut our funding. We can't afford that. Literally."

Eddy glanced at Gwen. She looked back in alarm. "You can't keep us here," said Gwen.

"Actually we can. The wine cellar doubles as a dungeon. On the upside, you'll be imprisoned with some very fine vintage port."

Gwen turned to Eddy. "It's time to go," she said.

"There's four of them!" said Eddy.

"Yes, but they're grad students, so that's like one-and-a-half regular people."

Eddy wasn't so sure. He hadn't been in a fight since high school and had lost all of those anyway. In a moment of inspiration, he grabbed the largest book he could see on a nearby shelf. He heaved Marcel Proust's *In Search of Lost Time* at their startled adversaries. The weighty opus hit one of the students square in the chest, sending him sprawling backwards onto the hard marble floor of the hall. The others instinctively rushed to catch the rare book before it fell. Gwen and Eddy plunged through the afforded opening. One of the students snatched Eddy's arm as he passed. Eddy elbowed him forcefully in the ribs. "Ow!" said the student.

Eddy and Gwen charged out to the front hall only to find themselves facing a much larger mob of over a dozen students. One young man brandished a medieval mace. It was a limited edition Lord of the Rings reproduction with the words 'Property of D.L. Sauron' engraved on the handle. Two other students approached armed with brooms they'd snatched from a closet. "You shall not pass!" cried the first student as he swung the mace menacingly in the air. Unfortunately, this had the effect of exposing the shoddy workmanship of the made-in-China collectable. The iron mace-head flew off like a shot put, narrowly missing a group of glee club members who had come downstairs to join the fray. It shattered the antique stained-glass window of Janus at the top of the stairs and landed somewhere out on the East lawn, setting the sprinklers off in the process. Eddy and Gwen exchanged stunned looks. "There's too many of them," said Eddy. "Grad students or not, they'll overwhelm us."

Gwen nodded in agreement.

"You might as well give up," said Professor Wilkins exiting the sitting room behind them. "There's nowhere you can..." The Professor trailed off as he tried to fathom how the priceless window had come to be broken. The guilty student hid the mace handle behind his back. "What were we talking about? Oh yes. There's nowhere you can go."

"Psst!" said a woman's voice. Eddy saw what appeared to be a wall panel cracked open. It was a servants' door, designed to be invisible when closed. Through the gap, Belinda urgently waved. Eddy grabbed Gwen's arm. "Come on!"

Eddy's surprise move caught Gwen off balance. She stumbled awkwardly after him. The door swung open. Belinda hauled them inside.

"Get them!" the Professor wailed, pointing frantically with his pipe stem. "I'm very disappointed in you, Belinda!"

Belinda slammed the door shut and slid a steel bolt into place. "Quickly," she said, "There's not much time before they realize they can just walk around." She led Eddy and Gwen down a narrow passageway. Eddy noted the peeling wallpaper and antique gas lamp fixtures. At the end of the hall was a door. Its square window shone with daylight. "Through there and along the path to the driveway out front. Nixon's waiting there with a car. He'll take you wherever you want to go." Belinda flung open the door, but stopped herself short.

"What about you?" asked Eddy. "They know you helped us escape!"

Belinda shrugged it off. "What are they going to do? Put me in jail? I've been working on the same Ph.D thesis for eight years. It can't be worse."

Gwen shook Belinda's hand. "Thank-you," she said.

Eddy hesitated. He gazed into Belinda's eyes. He wanted to say something, but wasn't sure how.

"I know," she said with a smile.

There was a splintering sound as someone pried open the door behind them with a crowbar. "Go. I'll hold them off as best I can."

"What does that mean?" said Eddy.

"It means, I'll stand in the doorway and refuse to move."

Eddy nodded, turned, and ran.

Moments later, Eddy and Gwen reached the driveway. They saw Nixon's van idling. The poet leaned against the hood, smoking a joint. "Ah, Dr. Jones, there you are," said Nixon with a smirk. "We better go before the natives catch up and start chucking spears."

Nixon slid into the driver's seat while Gwen and Eddy dove into the back. The van roared out of the driveway. In the rear view mirror, Eddy saw the mass of students spill out of the grand front entrance. Professor Wilkins materialized in their midst. In sullen silence, the professor watched them drive away. "Will they come after us?" asked Gwen.

"No," said Nixon.

"Why not?"

"Well, to start, most of them don't know how to drive."

Minutes later they were a mile away with no pursuit in sight. Twilight was falling across Los Angeles. The street lamps came on. White headlights shone. Across the city, the yellow glow of home and office windows lit up the cityscape like fallen stars. Above, the twilight sky loomed, purple and black. "Where do you want to go?" asked Nixon.

"Somewhere people don't want to kill us," said Gwen.

"Hmm," said Nixon, "Could you be more specific?"

## 1.4

"Stop laughing at me!" - C. Brown

// Las Vegas, Nevada — then

Fifteen is an awkward age. More so when your mother has committed suicide and you're left in the care of a man who views parenthood as an abstract principle. Some people assured Eddy that he would grow closer to his father after his mother's passing. This was like saying you might grow closer to your toaster by spending more time with it. He might start anthropomorphizing his father, but that was about it.

Being a teenager brought its own distractions and torments. Eddy was still struggling with coming out as a computer geek. He knew now that he loved coding and self-identified with machines. Despite this, he craved some kind of social acceptance, especially from girls. After months of waiting patiently, he finally saw his chance with Cynthia Finklebart. Her boyfriend, Brock, had cheated on her with her best friend, Liz. Eddy decided to confess his feelings in a school library study room. There, he presented Cynthia with a list of all the reasons why he would make a better boyfriend than Brock. It was a comprehensive series of bullet points; each supported with evidence. Eddy had been friends with Cynthia for over two years, but he'd always harboured deeper feelings for her. He closed his Powerpoint presentation with a simple, heartfelt message, spoken while gazing directly into her eyes. "And lastly, Cynthia, because I love..." Eddy glanced nervously down at his notes, then back up again. "...you."

Cynthia looked at Eddy with a sad sweet smile. "You're right Eddy. You're completely right. You're an amazing guy. And someday, you'll make a very lucky girl very happy."

"Don't *you* want to be very happy?"

"Yes—yes, of course, but, well... not *that* kind of happy."

"A different kind of happy?"

"Exactly."

Cynthia forgave Brock the following week. It was almost two months before he cheated on her again. Or at least until he was caught. Eddy saw Cynthia sobbing in the library on Liz's shoulder. He decided he had no idea what that kind of happiness was.

As a single parent, Professor Pending had no choice but to take his son with him on trips. The previous summer, Eddy's father had taken him to see the Large Hadron Collider. Eddy enjoyed that. There were even some attractive girl physicists to look at. The collider itself didn't do any colliding that one could see, but it was impressively large. He'd hoped the LHC might inadvertently create a black hole while he was there. That would have livened things up. "Very unlikely," his father assured him, "but it would suck if it did." During Spring Break, he took Eddy to Las Vegas. Eddy liked the idea of going to Las Vegas. What he didn't like was that the trip centered around a *Star Trek* convention. His father had been attending the annual gathering for years. He still spoke of the time he got James Doohan to say,

"Aye, Captain." Eddy had no interest in Star Trek, Star Wars or any of the other things geeks were supposed to love. As a child, Eddy had seen his father's cosplay outfits in the closet and thought they were hilarious. This had annoyed his father greatly at the time, who told him he was "too young to understand." Now, Eddy was being forced to actively participate. After two solid days of lining up at booths for cast member autographs, he was more than ready to leave. When his father had suggested they go out for lunch, Eddy had jumped at the idea.

They made their way to a build-your-own-burger restaurant next door to the hotel. There, they were shown to a booth by an attractive young waitress whose name was Karen. Despite Eddy's pleas to change, they were still in their Star Fleet uniforms. Eddy's father was dressed as Mr. Spock, complete with Vulcan ears. He insisted on giving everyone, including Karen, the Vulcan salute. "Live long and prosper," he said. "Do you have Diet Pepsi?"

"We have Diet Coke."

"Nafai," said Eddy's father.

"That means 'okay'," said Eddy.

"Really? In what language?"

"In Vulcan," said Eddy awkwardly.

"Ri nuh' mau le-suma!" said his father proudly.

"And not too much ice," Eddy translated. Eddy was wearing a red security uniform. He was hoping that someone would take this as a cue to kill him and be done with it. As the waitress left, Eddy's father began checking off all twenty of the no-extra-charge toppings as part of an ad hoc experiment. "Can I change now?" said Eddy.

"Into what?" said his father without looking up.

"Into another shirt."

"Do you have another shirt?"

"They sell them here."

"Why would you want to wear a restaurant t-shirt? You'd look ridiculous."

"Um..."

His father finished completing the burger form and handed it to Karen. He looked thoughtful. "This morning's session reminded me of the problem I'm trying to solve," he said.

"The one on episode twenty-eight?"

"It was twenty-nine. Twenty-eight was *The City on the Edge of Forever*. And, no, I mean the session before that, on the Kobayashi Maru."

"Right."

"The Kobayashi Maru was supposed to be an insolvable problem that Kirk only solved by radical thinking. Human consciousness is likewise... confounding. Still, there must a solution. Even if it requires cheating." His father then raised a Spock eyebrow and added, "It's logical."

Eddy wanted to point out that everything reminded his father of the problem he was trying to solve. He also wanted to sit at another table. "How is it logical?" he asked, despite not really caring how.

"Because there *it* is." A contingent of Klingons who had the same idea for lunch waved at them from another table and shouting "NuqneH!" Eddy's father responded in kind, and gave them the Vulcan salute. "That said, being radical doesn't mean being ridiculous. Do you know there are people who think this salt shaker is conscious?"

"*That* salt shaker?" said Eddy, surprised.

"Well, they think *everything* is conscious. Presumably that includes this salt shaker, the pepper, the table, and so on. They're not picky. If your bed is conscious, and you change its sheets, are you changing its mind? They think so. Presumably each grain of salt in here is conscious too," said his father examining the glass shaker.

"Why don't you let me take that?" said Eddy. He was concerned his father might start spilling salt on the table to prove a point. He took the salt from his father and put it down out of his reach.

"They call it 'panpsychism'. They'd claim I'm not doing it justice. It's more sophisticated than that, they'd say. Meaning, it's stupid, but in more complicated ways. You also have useless non-theories like 'emergence'. That says, if you stuff enough computing power into a brain then consciousness just emerges. I suppose any theory is right if you make it vague enough."

Karen arrived with their burgers. She carefully placed the physicist's burger before him. On it was a teetering tower of toppings. "May the force be with you," she said with smile. Professor Pending opened his mouth to correct her. Eddy kicked him under the table. "Don't," he said.

"Anything else?" asked Karen.

"We're fine, thank-you," said Eddy.

"That hurt!" said Eddy's father, after the waitress had left.

"I'm sorry," said Eddy.

"Ish-veh nam-tor nafai," said the physicist. Eddy's father took a bite from the overstuffed burger. An avalanche of onions, jalapeños, tomatoes, garlic aioli and other assorted condiments ejected out the other side and into his lap. The Vulcan looked down in dismay at the mess on his blue Star Fleet shirt and black pants. "Newton's third law," he said, ruefully. "How could I forget that?"

After returning home to New York, Eddy's father erased everything on the blackboard except his starting point, 'I = ?'. "Forget T, I need to solve for I. T is a distraction."

"T is time?" asked Eddy. He was trying to program on his laptop at a nearby table, but his father kept talking. Eddy had wanted to be in the lab to feel less alone. He didn't.

"Yes."

"What's U doing there?" said Eddy, pointing to the letter written off to the side. The whole notion of solving for human consciousness mathematically seemed crazy to him.

"That's to remind me that we're dealing with *unresolved* numbers." Eddy's father called irrational numbers 'unresolved' because he refused to accept the term. "Our inability to resolve them doesn't make them irrational," he'd say. "The term 'irrational numbers' is an oxymoron." He liked to relate the fate of the Ancient Greek mathematician Hippasus. Hippasus was a follower of Pythagorus, the math superstar best known for his self-titled hit theorem. Hippasus was drowned after discovering that the square root of two was an irrational number. Some claimed Hippasus was slain by the gods for mathematical blasphemy. Others said his fellow Pythagoreans had murdered him for this affront to reason. Finally, there were those that suggested Hippasus simply fell off a boat. Like those Ancient Greeks, Eddy's father was irritated when things failed to conform to the mathematical perfection they were supposed to. The truth was; he suspected all imperfections to be simple rounding errors. No human measurement, after all, could be absolutely precise. It was Zeno's paradox, he'd say, you can always subdivide the so-called real world. Points don't exist in reality, only the spaces between them do.

Eddy tried to focus on the code on his laptop screen. He was working on what would later become *Terminator*, the zero-day exploit that would make his name in the hacker-verse. The virus's name was a tribute to the role played by Arnold Schwarzenegger. It was Eddy's favourite movie at the time.

"What are you working on?" Eddy's father asked him.

The question surprised Eddy. His father had never asked it before. "A software program."

"What does it do?"

"It, um... facilitates financial transactions."

His father nodded. He stood awkwardly for a moment, then pointed to the shelf of programming books above Eddy's desk. "Can I borrow some of those?"

"So that's it."

"So that's what?"

"You didn't care what I was working on. That was just small talk so you could borrow my books. For all you know I could be working on SkyNet!"

"What's SkyNet?"

"You know, from the movie... No, you don't know. It's not from Star Trek, so why would you? SkyNet is a computer program that takes over the world."

"You're working on a computer program that takes over the world?"

"That's not the point. The point is, you don't care what I do or think, or anything!"

His father looked at Eddy, surprised and perplexed. Eddy had never spoken to him like this before. "So... you're *not* creating a program that can take over the world?"

"No, Dad."

"I see," said the physicist, looking somewhat disappointed. "Are you doing anything I should be interested in?"

"Yes! *Everything!*" Eddy shouted, rising to his feet. "Okay, not everything. But *me*. You should be interested in me, your son. You're so fascinated in what is going on in everyone's mind, except mine."

Eddy's father stared at him blankly. Eddy knew the look. It was the look his father gave when grappling with a concept he'd never thought of before. "But... I'm doing this for *us*," he said. "I'm trying to understand... *it*."

His fury spent; Eddy sank back to his seat. "You can't bring her back you know."

"That's not what I'm trying to do at all. She's gone."

"But I'm here, *right now.*"

"I know, that's why I'm asking to borrow your books instead of going to the library." There was a long awkward pause as no one said anything. "So... may I?"

"Sure Dad, whatever," said Eddy. "Let me know if you need any help."

"I expect I'll be fine," said his father. He began flipping thorough a copy of *Artificial Intelligence for Dummies*. "I mean, how hard can it be?"

From that day on, Eddy stayed out of his father's lab.

Two months later, after borrowing a dozen such books, his father declared that he was finished with them. "I think, I've got the gist of it," he said, "I'm only interested in the concepts. I found what I was looking for. Most of this stuff is just grammar."

"Syntax."

Eddy's father shrugged. He then reverted to his thinking phase.

Over the next several months, Eddy continued to work on Terminator. Grade 10 kept him busy too. He even had a couple of friends. Not the kinds of friends you share all of your secrets with. Just the kind you eat lunch with in the cafeteria and say 'hi' to in the hall. His father meanwhile, began hanging out at the Metropolitan Museum of Art. The physicist had decided that the MET was a perfect place for thinking. Nobody thought his prolonged periods of staring into space were odd there, provided he did so in front of a painting. The physicist spent hours walking from gallery to gallery gazing towards the pieces without once looking at them. He couldn't see why museums were necessary when you could see the same pictures in books. "We're fine with copies of music," he'd say. "For some reason we fetishize paint." He also couldn't see that any artwork was more than just a collection of brush strokes on canvas. He liked music more because it was mathematical. Still, he spent hours there, ignoring it all while pondering the mystery of consciousness. "At least I've finally found a use for art," Eddy's father explained. "Looking at it keeps people from thinking you're crazy."

## 1.5

"A rose by any other name, would smell as Tuesday" – N. Chomsky

// Manhattan, New York — now

"Thank-You, for your service to this country!" Lance Winface gave a thumbs-up, pressing the air as if anointing it. It was his signature salute.

Congresswoman Annabelle Flatwood nodded, accepting the blessing for what it was—absolution. "I know we haven't always agreed Lance..."

"But we agree now."

"We do. Now, there is still plenty of opposition to the The Majority Bill."

"The American Patriotic Media Ownership Liberation Legislative Initiative."

"Exactly. Many of my colleagues remain in opposition."

"Many of your colleagues, let's just say, aren't exactly true patriots."

"Let's not say that."

"But I see several have now crossed the aisle following your defection to the truth. Including Congressmen Trask and Lopez. Oh, and Sarah Gimley in the Senate."

"Anytime we can bridge the gap that divides this country is a good thing."

"As long as they come to us," Lance smirked and took a sip of coffee. "Meanwhile, let me congratulate you on your vindication. That actress coming forward to admit it was a hoax must be a huge relief."

"Thank-you. Of course, I knew it was fake the whole time, but I'm glad everyone else does too. I only wish it hadn't ended so tragically for her."

"Not me. She did something wrong, and God ran her over with a grain harvester. She shouldn't have lied, and she shouldn't have fallen asleep in a cornfield. That's a little somethin' called karma, baby—I mean Congresswoman."

// Somewhere in California — now

Oyster stoked the embers with a long stick, sending up a flurry of sparks, before tossing it into the fire. The orange flames crackled in cheery delight against the cold black ocean and soaring indigo sky. The recently set sun had left a residual glow that still faintly warmed the horizon. Some stars were already visible. The North Star, Polaris, shone brightly, oblivious to events on the distant cosmic dust mote known as Earth. The photons from it that reached Oyster's eyes had been emitted four hundred and forty years earlier. They'd begun their journey from star to retina at the same time as the British Parliament was voting to pass the *Habeas Corpus Act.* A few feet away, gentle waves rolled in. Seawater rushed the sand and briefly held its ground before retreating back into the ocean. Oyster ran a white finger under the rim of a tuna can, fishing out any remaining morsels before licking them off. He then drank the oil and tossed the can into the flames. The label curled off and caught fire. Across from him hunched Tonto, grim faced as always. Gazing into the fire, the Native American's weather worn visage was lit from below by the marigold glow of the hearth. It made the forty-two-year-old Indian look a millennium older than he was, give or take a century. Lucky, on Oyster's right, had his eyes closed. He wasn't asleep. The big black man often sat with his eyes shut while they conversed. Lucky said it helped him 'listen instead of hear'. On the long driftwood log on Oyster's left, Big J sat with his toes in the sand, dangerously close to the coals. The other two seats on the driftwood tree trunk were empty. Their occupants had gone for a walk an hour earlier on the beach and hadn't been seen since. Big J grunted. He was carefully tending a pair of blackening corn husk packets on a rock beside the fire. Inside the packets were marshmallows and store-bought molé sauce.

"I call it a *Mexican S'more*," said Big J turning the packets with a stick. "Our mama used to make 'em for us."

"Your mama's a Mexican S'more!" snorted Tonto, who began chuckling to himself. The small Latino man shot him an angry look.

"And that's better than graham crackers how?" asked Lucky without looking.

"Wait 'til you try. It's yummy."

Oyster, unscrewed the top off a bottle of Pinot Noir and took a swig. The taste made him squint. That's what you get for $1.99, he thought to himself. He glanced at the label. *Encino's Best*, it said below a picture of a grape riding a skateboard. "The nose is relatively harmless," the sales clerk assured him, "But the finish will finish you." The rock bottom vino had been described as having a body of 'engine block mixed with notes of arsenic.' "Yaaaargh," Oyster moaned, hammering himself in the sternum to force it down, "That'll put hair on your chest!" He offered it to the others, who passed. They used to buy *Charles Shaw*, aka 'Two Buck Chuck' until the price went up. Two Buck Chuck was owned by the aptly-named Bronco Wines that had bought up the name of a once-reputable winery, then produced the label en masse at rock-bottom prices. They did so, reportedly, by employing assembly line manufacturing, soaking the juice in wood chips instead of aging in barrels and using thin glass bottles to save on shipping. Despite all this, Charles Shaw once beat over two-thousand wines to win a Gold medal in competition. Whenever this came up, Oyster launched into his speech about the madness of modern life. "Pricing is a classic symptom," he said, "Nobody knows how much things should cost. Nobody knows nothin'. How devices work, or who's telling the truth. It's all castles in air! If I made a wine, I'd just re-bottle some good plonk. Then I'd put a picture of a naked king on the label and charge a hundred bucks a bottle. People would know it was worth that much, because it says so on the tag." Despite his current status as a beach-bum, Oyster used to be a pharmaceutical executive who pulled in seven figures. He eyed the so-called Mexican S'mores suspiciously. "I don't even like regular tamales," he said. "Don't get me wrong, you people make great food. I love tacos, burritos, and fajitas. Especially barbacoa. Mmm-hmm. But, corn husks are too damn sweet. They make me wanna barf."

"*You people?*" said Big J.

"Ah, don't get yur poncho in a knot!"

Big J shook his head. His annoyance was feigned. Mocking each other with racial and cultural stereotypes was their own inside joke. None of the vagrants had anything over the others. They were all created equally pathetic and knew it.

"You lied to me." It had taken Gwen three days to say it. Four, if you counted the day they fled Lotus Hill. Now, standing in the dark on a beach next to crashing black surf under a star spattered sky, seemed as good a time as any to accuse Eddy of falsehood. They hadn't planned to be here. They hadn't planned to be anywhere. They'd had no plan at all other than to escape. Nixon had given them the van. "Drive as far is you can," he'd said. "Then ditch it where it won't be found for a while." They'd headed north until the gas ran out. There, they'd parked on a side road, removed the plates and scratched off the VIN. They'd then hitchhiked an hour more with a tattooed trucker named Pokey to put some distance between themselves and the abandoned vehicle. Finally, they'd landed here. It was as close to the middle of nowhere as you could get on the California coast. Gwen eyed Eddy in the diffuse moonlight. Farther up the beach, the campfire danced like a white hot dervish.

"Technically, I didn't lie. You never asked if I was a hacker."

"It was a lie of omission."

Eddy decided that honesty was now his best policy, or last hope. Gwen assessed liars for a living after all. "Okay, yes. I was a hacker, but not anymore. Well, not a bad hacker anyway."

"Bad as in not good, or bad as in bad?"

Eddy had to think for a moment which meant what. This is what cross-examination is like, he decided. "Bad as in doing bad things. Which I don't. Anymore. I was good at it. Very good."

"Did you steal things?" said Gwen pointedly.

Eddy hesitated, then simply said it. "I wrote *The Terminator*."

For a long moment, Gwen said nothing. Eddy had just confessed to writing one of the worst malware attacks on the financial system in the past decade. He could only guess what was going through Gwen's head. He guessed wrong.

"You mean the movie with Arnold Schwarzenegger?"

"No! No, the virus."

"I literally have no idea what that is," she said. "I told you I don't prosecute cyber crimes."

"It was huge. It was all over the news."

"Okay... okay, it rings a bell. But that was like years ago."

"Well yeah, but they still talk about it in the Hackerverse."

"The Hackerverse?" said Gwen, stifling a snort.

"It took over a hundred millions dollars out of bank accounts and made it disappear."

Gwen stopped laughing. "Jesus. Why would you do something so horrible?"

"I didn't mean to."

"You didn't mean to? You accidentally wrote a virus that stole a hundred million dollars?"

Eddy had to calm himself. Talking about Terminator still upset him. It had made his name and destroyed him at the same time. "It was a grey hat virus, meant to show how hackable the banks were. It was supposed to remove the money, then put it back an hour later. There was a bug. The first part worked. The second didn't."

"So where's the hundred million dollars? I mean, you don't exactly live like a millionaire."

Eddy shrugged. "Beats me. Turns out electronic money really can just go up in smoke."

Gwen stared at him. "You should be in jail!"

"Oh come on, it was from the big banks. They make that much money every ten minutes! No one got hurt."

"*Someone* got hurt."

Eddy looked away. He didn't want to argue. He wasn't even sure whose side he was on anymore. "Look, can't we just agree to de-prioritize me going to jail until after we save the world?"

\#

"They're back," said Lucky, demonstrating his unsettling knack for seeing with his eyes closed.

"Hey," said Eddy as he and Gwen plodded out of the now near total darkness. They were both barefoot with their pants rolled up. Their feet were sand-socked from walking through the surf.

"That's good exercise," said Gwen.

"We thought you might o' got lost without yur Gee-Pee-Ess," said Oyster with a wry grin. "Folks today don't know where they are unless a machine tells 'em."

"We just followed Frank's advice," said Eddy, using Tonto's real name. He couldn't bring himself to use the blatantly racial epithet, even if the Native American didn't seem to care. "He said to just remember which side the ocean's supposed to be on."

"Those injuns are wise in the ways o' the world," said Big J.

"What's going on there?" asked Gwen, pointing to the now smoking corn husk packets beside the fire. One burst into flames as she said this.

"Dios! Dios!" yelled Big J, flinging the tamales into the sand. "They're ruined."

"Such a shame," said Oyster, pausing to take a swig of wine. "Now, we'll never know how crappy they tasted."

Eddy and Gwen took their seats beside Big J on the waterlogged tree. Eddy patted the small Mexican man's back. "I'm sorry we distracted you, Julio."

Big J pried open the scalding hot corn husk with a stick and prodded the bubbling contents. He licked the end of the stick and grinned a gap tooth grin. "Still tastes good," he said.

Gwen retrieved some plastic plates and cutlery from 'the kitchen'. The kitchen was a circle of nearby rocks. They dished out samples of the sweet goo. All dug in except Oyster, who announced he would stick with the poison he started with, waving the wine bottle in the air. Much to Eddy's surprise, the marshmallow mixture with the savoury molé sauce was delightfully flavourful.

An hour later, they lay wrapped in blankets around the embers of the dying fire. All were asleep, save for Eddy. The programmer marvelled at the vast ceiling of stars that rolled slowly above. Living in the city, he rarely noticed or even remembered the universe that lay obscured behind the veil of humanity's ambient glow. Here, on the beach, where darkness was absolute, the stars weren't sporadic pin pricks in the night. Instead, they were revealed as an epic speckled canopy. "There are more stars than there are grains of sand in all the beaches in all the world put together," his father once said to him. Eddy had just told his father that his grade-two teacher had said he was 'special'. She had said that all the kids in her class were special. His father responded that it was a difficult assertion to believe given the size and scale of the universe. "Find me a special atom on a grain of sand and I'll believe your Mrs. Cooly." His father hadn't meant to be cruel. He wanted his son to know the truth. Among all the stars overhead, Polaris stood alone. Eddy watched what he thought was a shooting star. He was wrong. It wasn't a meteor. It was an MCNX satellite, skating across the exosphere, relaying signals to and from the planet's surface. At that moment, it was echoing a commercial for Tide Laundry Detergent, promising to get your whites whiter than white.

## 1.6

"I think, therefore you are." – J. Barrow

// Somewhere in California — now

"The key is to get enough weight on the hook," said Lucky. "Otherwise you'll never get the distance." The hook in this case was a safety pin, its tip bent back with pliers to form a barb. The weight was also the bait, a piece of bacon past its 'best before' date. "Good enough for a fish's last supper," said Lucky. The big man swung the hook above his head in long graceful arcs before casting it off into the surf. He and Eddy perched on a craggy outcrop. The wave wrought rock was smooth like a sofa. It was Lucky's favourite place to fish. "Where I've had the most luck," he said. By the time Eddy had awoken that morning, each denizen of the tiny community had turned to their chores for the day, such as they were. Gwen had accepted, with some annoyance, that it was her job to clean the dishes. She resented the gender role, but for now, acquiesced. It was they, after all,

275

who were the latest refugees to this nation of six. Oyster and Big J left to collect fuel for the fire. This was an increasingly difficult job as they had exhausted the nearest resources and had to look further afield. At some point, they would have to move. Life without fire was not an option. Tonto had gone to town. He would beg there for coins, preying upon 'white man's guilt' until he had enough money to buy the meagre supplies they needed. "I consider it payback, Gimoozaabi," the Native American said with a grin. He would then bicycle back to the coast in time for supper.

Eddy finished baiting his hook and swung the line above his head in imitation of what he'd seen Lucky do. Suddenly, his line grew slack as his bacon flew off and landed on the sand below. Lucky burst out laughing. Eddy didn't think it was anywhere near as funny as that. "You need to fold it!" the big man gasped, chuckling some more and wiping away tears. "You have to fold it many times or the bacon's gonna tear. An' if it don't, some fish gonna steal yur bait."

"You could have told me."

"Try again."

Eddy looked at Lucky expectantly. "I need another piece."

"No, you don't. Go get that one. It's fine still if you fold it. Fold it three times every time. Bacon don't grow on trees you know."

Annoyed, Eddy climbed down the craggy rock to the beach and retrieved the limp meat. He then climbed back up, careful not to cut his feet on the jagged stone at the bottom. A serious injury would be a bad thing. He and Gwen couldn't risk going to hospital. When he reached the top of the rock, Lucky was once more twirling the hook and line above his head, preparing to make another cast. Despite his badly soiled jeans and faded blue Pepsi Cola t-shirt, he looked almost heroic in this stance. "Gotta let loose like David," Lucky shouted. "Strike that giant in th'eye!" Except, that giant was the ocean itself, a foe of immutable power, and the big man was trying to fell it with thrice folded bacon.

An hour later, the two still sat on the same eroded rock, legs dangling over the edge. The now retreating tide lapped below. Lucky was serenading the sea with his deep bass.

*Sometimes I feel like a motherless child*
*Sometimes I feel like a motherless child*
*Sometimes I feel like a motherless child*
*A long ways from home*
*A long ways from home*
*Come my brother*
*A long ways from home*
*A long ways from home*

*Sometimes I feel like I'm almos' gone*
*Sometimes I feel like I'm almos' gone*
*Sometimes I feel like I'm almos' gone*
*A long ways from home*
*A long ways from home*

After that, he broke into a rumbling rendition of Old Man River. It was a song Eddy knew, so he hummed along. The bright California sun made it warm but not too hot. In the first week living here, Eddy's pale skin had burned and peeled. It then burned and peeled again. Now, he bore a healthy brown tan, totally alien to his normal computer lab complexion. His clothes had become ragged and stained and clung to him. He shaved just twice a week. It was the most they could afford to spend on disposable razor blades from the begging money. His seawater washed hair now fell across his eyes. Eddy and Gwen never went to town. They made that clear to the others right away. They would pull their weight in different ways. The others had accepted this. Eddy knew the others thought he and Gwen were delusional paranoids. Still, the others didn't judge them. Oyster was a diagnosed schizophrenic who had become convinced that government regulators were insectoid aliens from somewhere in The Great Rift. No one judged anyone here. "People in rubber rooms shouldn't throw imaginary stones," said Lucky. Making fun on the other hand was a given. Lucky gazed off in the distance. "You know, I used to be a... um... what do you called it...?" Lucky paused. He scratched his greying curls.

"A fisherman?" said Eddy.

"No, before that. A... uh... you know I worked with farming..."

"A farmer?"

"No, no, a... a..." Lucky snapped his fingers, and smiled. "A mo–lecular biologist."

Eddy stared at him. "What? Really?"

"Yup. Worked for Winthrop Chemicals."

"Who?"

"They're a multi–multi–multi–billion dollar maker of everything from plastics to pesticides to plants, seeds, and so on. I worked in the Agricultural Science Division. You know, *farming*. But, mostly in the genetic engineering sense."

"Okay..." Eddy studied Lucky to see if the big man was having him on. The vagrant had his eyes closed again. This time, not to listen, but to see. He was seeing the memories playing in his head. Like the others, he was a victim of mental health issues or, as Oyster liked to say, a basket case. Hung on a post back at camp was a sign that read, *You don't have to be crazy to work here, but it helps!*

"I loved my job. We were makin' what you would call GMOs. You know what I mean?"

"Genetically modified organisms."

"Yup. An' what can I say? It was fun. We weren't playing God. God creates stuff. We were just tinkerin'. Swappin' cytosine fur guanine here, adenine fur thymine there. Makin' a few tweaks. No harm in that. I had a family then. A family who loved me, I mean. Not you losers. No offence. Good pay, good house. Life was good. Then, I met Bruce. Or rather, I created him."

"Created? What are you talking about?"

Lucky wiped a tear from his cheek. "We were supposed to be making grapefruit that tasted better, sweeter, and stayed ripe longer on a supermarket shelf. We didn't mean no harm. Then, someone decided to stick electrodes into the grapefruit. Just as a joke, you know? A little harmless EEG. Scan for alpha waves, that sort of thing. That was when we learned what happens when you mess with nature. Somehow, someway, our grapefruit had become sentient."

"What?"

"Sentient. Intelligent. Conscious. Like people, but with more seeds."

Eddy stared at him. "I know what sentient means," he said.

"We named him Bruce. He was able to think and feel on his own. He had no sensory input other than he seemed to have a sense of touch. We were able to talk to him through a series of electrical impulses. He was a sensitive and good guy, although a bit bitter, as grapefruit tend to be."

Eddy couldn't decide whether Lucky was playing an elaborate joke on him or was just delusional. Those, he told himself, were the only two possible explanations. "So what happened to Bruce?"

"Winthrop got word of it. They became very alarmed at the 'implications'." As he said this, Lucky made air quotes with his fingers. "You see we couldn't explain how the grapefruit became intelligent, only that it was. Legal became very concerned. Were all citrus fruits sentient, they asked, or was it just grapefruit? Were oranges too small to be self-aware? What about berries... or turnips? It could change the whole notion of a persistive vegetative state. More important, if people became aware that fruit were aware, it could raise all sorts of ethical, political, and public relations issues. It could threaten the entire citrus industry! In the end, the whole program was squashed."

"What happened to Bruce?"

"I just told you. He was squashed. They beat him to a pulp."

Eddy looked at Lucky in horror.

Lucky had opened his eyes again. He gazed wistfully at the horizon, putting himself at an emotional distance. "I lost it that day. I felt as if I'd been involved in a murder. Perhaps a mass murder. I mean, thousands of pounds of produce were juiced that day. I gave up eating fruits and vegetables immediately. I only eat meat now, for ethical reasons. At least with cows, we know how stupid they are. With Bruce, well, we never even understood how his intelligence worked. It was entirely alien to us. Made me question everything I thought I knew."

"But your family...?"

"After that, everything fell apart. I was wracked with guilt. I quit m' job. I couldn't look at a Sunkist commercial without cryin' like a baby. I started talking real idiomatically like. My wife left with my son and daughter. They thought I was crazy. I expect you do too."

"Nutty as a fruitcake," Eddy joked, hoping to lighten the mood.

Lucky glared grimly at him. "I call it massacre cake," he said.

## 1.7

"Don't you know each cloud contains pennies from heaven?"
– S. Nakamoto

// Somewhere in California — now

Eddy found Tonto at the top of a dune, sitting crosslegged amid the razor grass, watching the sun hang in the sky. The Native American took a long last drag on a joint, then flicked it into the sand. Lucky had told Eddy that if he wanted advice on what to do, he should ask Tonto. "He's the wisest man I know," Lucky said. "Of course, I only know four people now and they're all nut jobs, but still."

"What's up gimoozaabi?" asked Tonto.

"I need your advice," said Eddy. He then told Tonto everything that had happened from the moment he first found the virus on Gwen's computer. It seemed eons ago. The murderous mob seemed like yesterday. The wise looking Indian nodded sagaciously as if it all made perfect sense.

"So, what should I do?" said Eddy.

"How the Hell should I know?"

"Lucky said you were a shaman."

"He meant casino owner."

"You owned a casino?"

"Well, part-owned it. Along with the rest of the tribe. I was VP of Promotions. They called me Little Big Mouth. Made me feel good. Proud."

"I bet."

"Proud to take back from stupid white folks just a tiny fraction of what you took from us."

"Sorry about that," Eddy murmured. "We were wrong."

Tonto waved it off. "Ah, can the bleeding heart nonsense. You weren't even born. You know what I hate? Patriarchy. Stupid white folks who think we were flitting little pixies, all sweet and innocent. It's like a final humiliation. Noble savages my ass. We were warriors! Haudenosaunee. What you call 'Iroquois'. I'm a proud descendent of the Six Nations. We had our own empire. We conquered other tribes. Wiped some out too. If we'd had the ships, we'd have gone to Europe, conquered them and scalped their kings. Taken their land."

"Um... okay," said Eddy. "Do all Haud... Haud..."

"Haudenosaunee."

"Haudenosaunee, think this way?"

"Yeah, they voted me their official spokesperson. Seriously, did you mean that to be racist or did it just come out that way?"

"No, I, um... Sorry."

Tonto shook his head. "I'm an individual. I speak for me."

Eddy nodded. This was not the conversation he had come here for. "So, why'd you leave the casino?"

"For this," said Tonto with a grin, spreading his arms at the beach, the ocean, and the sky. "Wait no, that's not right. My tribe up north started expelling members who they deemed 'impure' or of 'unproven ancestry'. I'm one quarter Norwegian. They call it 'disenrollment'. They might as well call it disembowelment. Cooked up excuses to reduce the number of people sharing casino revenue. Every tribesman kicked out, means more dollars for the rest. I fell out of favour. So I'm not an Indian anymore. Rejected by the rejected. I lost myself and ended up here with the other rejects."

Eddy squinted, "You look Indian to me, I mean, Native American."

"I explain it to the others like this," said Tonto. Tonto picked up a stick and drew a large circle in the sand. He then drew a second circle intersecting with the first. Then, he drew a third circle intersecting with the others.

"Is that some kind of ancient Iroquois symbol?" asked Eddy.

"It's a Venn diagram," said Tonto. "Are you some kind of moron? Once I'd been kicked out of the tribe I had no principles left, so I worked as a motivational speaker. This was part of my PowerPoint." He pointed to each of the circles as he continued. "You have your tribe or family, your friends. You have your country. You have your church, job, Shriners or whatever. The part in the middle? That's *you*. Or me. You're an intersection of things. But, I lost my tribe and my job." Tonto dramatically scratched out two of the circles, leaving just one. "A big zero."

"But you still have that one circle left."

"Then your identity is not your own. It's the local basketball team or whatever that is."

"This was part of your motivational presentation?"

"I didn't say I was good at it."

Eddy looked at the big zero. "Thanks," he said.

"For what?" said Tonto.

"For nothing."

#

Gwen and Eddy were picking their way along the beach. It was late afternoon. They knew this because the sun was once more over the ocean. Ostensibly they were looking for 'pickings'. Pickings were anything useful to the group. It could be wood for the fire, salvage for resale, or food. Eddy had spent twenty minutes chasing a crab as it scuttled back and forth across the sand. Coincidentally, Gwen had spent the exact same amount of time doubled over in laughter. By the time Eddy had caught it, he couldn't bring himself to kill it. "We've been through too much together," he said, tossing the frantic crustacean back into the sea. He was glad to see Gwen laugh. It gave him hope she might forgive him. He kept thinking about what she had said earlier. The news stories reported only of the millions of dollars lost. He'd assumed the banks were on the hook. Had someone been hurt?

"How long are we going to stay here?" asked Gwen.

"I don't know," said Eddy. "Forever?"

Gwen laughed, then stopped short, "You're *not* serious."

Eddy shrugged. "This isn't so bad. Hanging out on the beach all day. I mean, it's not perfect. But at least people aren't trying to kill us here."

"Eddy, we're not living as homeless people for the rest of our lives. I have a career and rent due. I have a life. Plus these guys... I mean, they're super sweet letting us hang out an' all, but they're also crazy. That and Tonto keeps asking me to go skinny dipping."

Eddy nodded. That part he knew. All three of their fellow beachcombers had separately asked him if he and Gwen were 'together'. When Eddy had said no, they each seemed to think this meant they had a chance. Big J had presented Gwen with a bottle cap necklace. He took care to point out that all the caps came from imported beers, because he knew she was 'classy'. "I don't know," said Eddy. "We can't stay forever. But where do we go? We're off the grid here. These guys don't watch TV or even listen to the radio. Lucky didn't know who the current President was. Anywhere else, we could run into a crazed mob that wants to kill us."

A little while later, they made their way back to camp. Eddy was dragging a six-foot long tree branch that had washed ashore. It was enough wood to keep the fire going all night. Lucky and Big J were seated by the hearth preparing supper. Oyster wasn't back from town yet, but was expected before dark. Tonto had disappeared as he often did. The sun was low in the sky, but still fully above the horizon. The powder blue was just beginning to blush.

"Who the Hell is that?" said Gwen, stopping in her tracks.

Eddy saw a woman with the two men. She appeared to be in her mid-thirties with blonde hair. She was wearing a white designer suit with the pant legs rolled up. She was seated on the driftwood tree trunk, shaking sand from her high-heel shoes and talking. Lucky and Big J were nodding attentively as they worked. "I have no idea," said Eddy.

Cautiously, Eddy and Gwen approached the beach camp. No one noticed their approach. The strange woman continued to speak, jabbing the air with a Jimmy Choo stiletto heel as she made her point. Lucky opened his eyes. "There they are!" he said.

Big J and the woman turned to look. "Hey Eddy, your friend is here!" said Big J.

The woman stood up, swatting sand from her bottom as she did. "Hello," she said, offering her hand, "I'm Senator Allison Spears. I've been looking for you."

## 1.8

"I've made up my mind." – D. Dennett

// Somewhere in California — now

"Santa's little helper reduces me," said Oyster to no one in particular. "Eight letters." He said this without looking up from the folded copy of The New York Times on his lap. He hemmed thoughtfully, while sucking on the tip of his ballpoint pen. The grizzled beach bum liked to boast about how he did the cryptic crossword in ink. "I'll tell you the trick to crosswords," he'd explained to Eddy, "Three words: variable, letter, sizes. Make some letters wide enough to take up two boxes and others small enough to cram into one. Do that, and you can pretty much put in whatever answer you like." As he said this, he tapped his head. "In the C-suite we called that 'outside the box thinking'."

"Selfless," said Lucky, without opening his eyes.

"I guess I am," said Oyster.

"The answer is 'selfless'."

Oyster scowled. "Ridiculous," he said, "The answer is clearly... 'Beelzebub'. 'Santa' is an anagram for 'Satan'."

"I thought you said eight letters," said Lucky, "Beelzebub has nine letters."

"I told you, I don't work that way. I didn't get to be CEO of Dynopharm by following the rules."

"Or brought up on charges by the SEC," said Big J with a smirk.

"Exactly," said Oyster. "I got the bonus, while the company paid the fine—which was a tiny fraction of the profit we made. In the C-suite we called that 'winning'. Anyway, 'selfless' doesn't work with three across. The third 'z' in *Prezzzago*."

"Oyster, that's not a real word."

"Uh, yeah it is. We sold two billion dollars worth of it. That's about as real as it gets."

"It's a made up word for a made up drug," said Big J.

"There's a word for words that are made up," said Tonto. "They're called 'words'."

"Prezzzago's better than a word," said Oyster. "It's a registered trademark of Dynopharm International used primarily for the treatment of PDA."

"What's PDA?" asked Gwen.

"Prescription Drug Addiction. That drug saved my life and made me rich." Oyster then paused and added, "Of course, later it almost ended my life and ruined me, but that's not the point. The point is, it's definitely a word. I think." In his former life as a CEO, Oyster had presided over the manufacture and sale of Prezzzago. Originally approved by the FDA for relief of excessive throat phlegm or ETP, it was prescribed primarily for off-label use in the treatment of PDA. During his tenure as CEO, Oyster, known then as Randolph Perlman, identified PDA as a multi-billion dollar 'new market opportunity', or NMO. An NMO meant growth, and growth meant bigger bonuses. The drug was an instant hit. Prezzzago's unofficial spokesman was TV host Lance Winface. Lance described the drug as a miracle cure for drugs on his top-rated TV News show. Prezzzago itself was highly addictive, but they positioned it to doctors on pampered retreats as akin to consumer debt consolidation. "Would you rather be addicted to a half-dozen drugs or just one?" It was only after three years of record sales that Prezzzago's many side effects became undeniable—according to the legal department. Those side effects included 'unexplained whooping', somnambulant bicycling, and schizophrenia. The problem was, Randolph wasn't just the CEO, he was also a user. The then-CEO had been sampling the company's products for years. He had been popping opiates like Tic Tacs just to make it through the day. He viewed Prezzzago as his own personal salvation. Of course, even the CEO was not immune to the myriad side-effects. In Randolph Pearl's case this meant paranoia. Randolph became convinced that the company was being run by giant cockroaches that had somehow metamorphosed into human form. It all culminated in him attacking the COO during a board meeting, by trying to pull off her 'mask' to show her 'true bug head' beneath. That was how he ended up here on a beach, cramming letters into crosswords. He was addiction free now and only occasionally suspected the others of being giant bugs.

Eddy sat fuming at the former pharmaceutical executive. It was Oyster's fault they now had to leave. Eddy knew the former CEO had meant no harm. He had to let go of his anger, but for now he needed to glower. They got lucky. Allison seemed to be on their side. It could have been someone else. Eddy marvelled at the surreal sight of a sitting United States Senator sleeping on the sand. She'd driven day and night to find them and had passed out as soon as she'd laid down. Before passing out, she'd given a brief account of how she'd come to be there. "I knew I had to find you," she began. "I think you're the only one who can stop this. *They* think so too.

That's why they want you gone."

"But how *did* you find us?" said Eddy. He and Gwen had gone to great lengths to hide their trail. They had no cell phones and had avoided contact with anyone other than the four homeless men. On the rare occasion a beachgoer or dog walker passed them by, they'd hidden their faces. So how did this Senator from Nebraska who they'd never even met, locate them with apparent ease?

"It was him," said Allison, pointing at Oyster.

Oyster, who had been blowing bubbles into his Orange Julius to make it froth, froze mid blow. He pointed to himself in surprise. "Me?"

"From your blog."

"Oh... *that*." Oyster resumed his blowing as if everything were now perfectly clear.

"Your blog?" said Gwen. "What the Hell is your blog?"

"I call it *Life on a Half Shell,*" said Oyster proudly. "It's my witty take on life as a former pharmaceutical CEO turned schizophrenic homeless beach bum. You know, something people can relate to."

"Witty is a matter of opinion," said Lucky with a derisive snort. "Mostly just reposted articles from *The Onion* from what I can see."

"With witty comments added," said Oyster indignantly.

"Hold on," said Gwen, "You have a blog and you posted about us?"

"A blog, a Facebook page, Instagram, Twitter... oh and a Pinterest account, but I've been letting that go."

"You said you were off the grid," said Eddy. "You said you didn't have a cell phone!"

"No, no, of course not. Those things cause brain cancer. I should know, as CEO I helped bury the study that proved it. No, I use the public library computers. I was there today, writing a post called *The Quality of Sand*. 'The quality of sand is not strain'd, it droppeth as the gentle rain...'"

Gwen turned to Eddy, eyes wide. "We have to go. Like, *now*. If she found us, then they will too."

Eddy turned to Oyster. "When did you first post about us?"

"When you got here. It really helped a lot. It's hard to always be coming up with new material to keep my followers interested."

"All five of them, you mean?" said Joe.

"Six since Tuesday."

"That would be me," said Allison. "If it helps, his site comes across as the ramblings of a lunatic. No offence."

"None taken," said Oyster. "It's just my public persona."

"My point is, I only took it seriously because I knew it was true," said the Senator.

Eddy considered the possibility that Majority Corp would only be looking for him on underground channels and other covert means. Oyster had made the post three weeks ago. Could it be they'd simply failed to Google him, as the Senator had? Or perhaps they'd dismissed it as Allison suggested, as 'the ramblings of a lunatic'. After all, he and Gwen's faces had been on the news. No doubt, plenty of websites referenced them. Regardless, it wasn't safe. They'd have to move on and quickly.

"Look," said Allison, "The reason I know about this mind control virus thing is because they did it to me."

Eddy and Gwen both looked at her in alarm. "You're infected?" said Eddy, backing away.

"Obviously, I got better," said Allison. The Senator then explained how she was infected at Ubenställ. On her flight back to the United States, she read a letter from her valet, Isa. The conference valets knew *everything*. The conference staff listened in on the conversations around them and had reacted with horror. Isa explained in her letter that Allison was infected. She said that simply by knowing this, Allison might be able to shake off the virus. That was, provided she wanted to. Some people were happy being infected, Isa wrote in her letter, "...it lets them off the hook." The virus authors knew this and called such willing participants their 'base'. Allison initially dismissed the letter as a crazy conspiracy theory. I would know if I were infected, she decided. I'm intelligent and reasoning clearly. I know what I believe; I know what I know. She'd tossed the letter into the airplane bathroom garbage. Once home; however, she'd begun to experience strange dreams. She woke up with night sweats. Allison began to consider the possibility that some of her thoughts were not her own. She became aware of her own cognitive dissonance, and it frightened her. Finally, on a Wednesday morning at the Congressional Yoga Studio, Allison suffered an existential crisis. She was transitioning poses from downward donkey to submissive pachyderm when she had an epiphany. She realized that she was an assembly of other people's thoughts. She wondered if everyone was. She realized then how easy it would be for someone to modify, rearrange, or supplant those thoughts. All at once, Allison knew it was true. She became furious. Allison confronted Cassius in his office. She later realized this was an impulsive and ill considered move. With unperturbed arrogance, the Senator freely admitted to her that virus could be spread through any type of media. It was only discovered once, he explained. "That's how I learned about you two," Allison said. "They saw you, Eddy, as enough of a threat to mobilize their zombie army." James Machi had been itching to test the virus on a large scale anyway, so crisis became opportunity. When Allison threatened to go to the secret service, Cassius chortled. "You'll be laughed out of office, my dear. We control the truth, remember? We undermine entire institutions. Publish it in a newspaper and we'll attack that too. What chance do you have of stopping us? In the end, you won't be the heroine, you'll be the villain." She left his office in shock, uncertain what to do. A short while later she understood why, like a cartoon villain, he had been happy to explain his plans. She understood it when she looked between the shades of her apartment window and saw two men exiting a black Mercedes on the other side of the street. The two men wore long black winter coats and rose coloured glasses that glinted when they glanced up. Allison knew then she had to go. She fled by the building's back door with nothing but her car keys and her purse. "I tossed my cell phone in a passing garbage truck. I hope they followed it to the dump."

"Smart," said Eddy.

"We need to do something," said Gwen.

"What?" said Eddy. "They may see me as a threat, but I don't. They have masses of resources and killers at their command. They clearly have government and big business either as allies or infected. What can we do? Who do we tell? Anywhere we go we'll be exposed or undermined. Oh, and then they'll kill us."

"Can't argue with that," said Oyster. He resumed making loud slurping noises as he tried to get the last drops of Orange Julius out of the cup.

The young Senator stared at them in desperation. "This isn't an abstract argument about who's controlling the truth. You can't sit this out anymore. There are bugs!"

The palpable fear in Allison's face silenced them for a moment.

"Bugs?" said Oyster, suddenly concerned, "Big'uns in suits?"

"She means software bugs," said Eddy.

Allison nodded. The Senator reached into her pocket and pulled out a camcorder. Eddy and Gwen backed away as if she'd drawn a gun. "Don't worry. It's an old one. See? No internet." She pressed play. The view screen showed a TV news report of a brutal riot in downtown Boston. Mobs stormed a department store and engaged in hand to hand combat, beating each other with manikin arms. The video cut to a mosque being stormed in New York City. Rioters dragged worshippers out by their robes and began dousing them with gasoline. Next, it cut to a black church on fire in South Carolina while Confederates cheered. Lastly, a gang of students armed with pro-tolerance placards beat bystanders to death in Oakland. The violence was brutal and bloody. In each case, the assailants didn't simply punch and grab. They bit, tore flesh from bones, gouged eyes, snipped off ears, and pushed squirming victims to the ground.

"What is this?" said Gwen in horror.

"Cassius called it a 'software regression'."

Gwen looked to Eddy. "A regression is a kind of bug where previously functioning code stops working. They can be hard to fix because it's about how code is interconnected. Things can start to unravel. You can lose control if it gets completely out of hand."

"Cassius said they're working on a patch," said Allison, "but in the meantime, these things keep happening. Nobody understands why. Thousands of people are dead. They're all looking for a biological virus or bacterial infection. They don't understand it. I don't understand it. Even after it was explained to me."

"How did he explain it?" asked Eddy.

"Cassius said not to think of it as a computer virus at all. He said to just think of it as ideas. Oh, and there's something else." The Senator reached into her jacket pocket and pulled out a thumb drive. She handed it to Eddy.

"What is this?"

"It was in the envelope from my valet along with the letter. It's something they stole from Cassius. Something important."

"But what is it?" said Gwen.

"They said it was 'code'? They said it could change *everything*."

The cool moon shone reflected in the black windshield of the Lincoln SUV. *Chirp! Chirp!* said the car as its remote was pressed. Allison stumbled ungainly over the sand dune from the beach side of the beachside parking lot. I should have waited until I was on solid ground to put my shoes on, she thought. Pumps and sand don't mix. It was midnight, neither yesterday nor tomorrow. Bright white floodlights illuminated the asphalt. The entire parking lot was deserted save for a one other car parked across the way. Allison paused to shake the sand from her shoes. She had slept over four hours, only to awaken beside the dying campfire. The others were asleep then, strewn about the hearth. At least, she thought so. It was hard to tell with the big black man they called Lucky. Oyster was snoring up a storm. Allison was famished and had suddenly remembered the quinoa bar she kept in the Lincoln's glove compartment. She also remembered her change of clothes in back.

The Senator opened the driver side door and plopped down into the seat. She felt relief. She had accomplished her mission. If the programmer could stop Machi and Cassius then her problems would be solved. In the meantime, she didn't know what she wanted to do, but she knew it didn't involve sleeping on a beach with a bunch of homeless guys. She sank back into the perfect ergonomic curves of the luxury car seat. You have to buy American, Congressman Ramirez had told her, otherwise they'll call you out on it. So she'd settled on the oversized Ford SUV, fully loaded. Amenities included lumbar support, individual climate control, real wood dash, and GPS. For a moment, Allison simply enjoyed the comfortable chair. I wonder if the Hilton takes cash, she thought. Her eyes went to the rear-view mirror. The other parked car had tinted windows, that made it impossible to see inside. She noticed then a card tucked under her windshield wiper. Darn it, she thought. She reluctantly pulled herself out of her seat and reached around the windshield to snatch what she assumed was a coupon or flyer for some local service. Better not be a ticket, she thought. The card's silver embossed backing flashed in the parking lot floodlights. Curious, she turned it over. The reverse was a mess of red ink. It was a pattern that confused her eyes. Odd, she thought, it doesn't mention a product or even have a phone number or web address. Maybe it's some kind of viral marketing campaign, she decided. Allison felt a sharp stabbing pain in her chest. The Senator suddenly lurched forward, clutching the car door frame to keep from falling. The pain flared again. It was like a burning sunspot inside her. She released the door. The asphalt rushed up to meet her. She felt the impact in a secondhand kind of way—as if it were happening to someone else. A trickle of warm blood ran down her temple, pooled briefly at her brow, then overflowed into her right eye. Allison remembered her Daddy letting her drive the tractor one day. She was sitting on his lap, her feet dangling. "Keep her steady, sweetie," said Daddy. His big hands rested on her shoulders. She felt safe. All at once, his hands fell away. Allison *felt* absent—then, all at once, she was.

The Man in Rose Coloured Glasses walked unhurried across the empty parking lot. He stood briefly over the crumpled corpse. He peered at his victim's face. He knew it was her, but a professional never passes up an opportunity to confirm a kill. Allison's lips were parted as if to speak. The Man in Rose Coloured Glasses reached down and plucked the card from her fingers. He tucked it back into his wallet and walked slowly back to his car.

## 1.9

"You give me fever."–Mary Mallon

// Brooklyn, New York — then

Eddy's father finally emerged from his lab after being locked inside for over a week. He had been working on Phlogiston for five years but had aged twenty. He stood in the doorway looking haggard, lost and somewhat unsteady on his feet. Eddy, who had been playing Tetris on his laptop, leapt up. His father waved him away. At seventeen, Eddy was lanky and awkward. He now had to wear glasses, like his father. He hoped to get contacts to be a 'little less geeky', although he suspected it was a lost cause. Next year, he would graduate high school and probably move out. He knew he loved his father, but it was an abstract concept of love. Eddy longed for something more. He already had a meagre income from freelance programming jobs. "Are you okay?" asked Eddy.

"I feel like Lord Rutherford of Nelson," said the frail physicist, leaning hard against the door frame. It was an obscure reference, but Eddy understood it right away. His father had told Eddy about Lord Rutherford as a bedtime story while Eddy was growing up. Lord Rutherford was the McGill University physicist who discovered radioactive half-life. He also discovered that matter was, for the most part, *not there*. Specifically, that matter consists almost entirely of empty space between tiny, distant atoms. These atoms, in turn, are also comprised of mostly empty space. If you eliminated all of its space at the atomic level, New York City could fit into a matchbox. The physicist had explained this to his seven-year-old son as he sat on his lap. "It's why glass is transparent. There's nothing to it. What you ought to be asking yourself, Eddy, is why isn't *everything* transparent?" Instead, young Eddy asked why he couldn't have regular bedtime stories like other children. His father stared at him baffled, then continued. Lord Rutherford, he explained, was so unnerved by his own discovery that he was afraid to get out of bed the next morning for fear of falling through the floor. "Quite understandable," said Eddy's father. "It must have been shocking to discover how matter barely matters."

"It matters to me," said seven-year-old Eddy.

"Mmm," said his father. "Yes, I suppose it does."

Ten years later, his father lowered himself shakily onto a nearby stool. "How so?" asked seventeen-year-old Eddy.

His father lifted empty, shaking hands, as if offering up evidence for his son to see. "The universe is basically nothing on a very large scale, viewed from a distance. We seem to be the same, only more so. If at the subatomic level something can exist in two places at once, then it must be possible to be both right and wrong at the same time."

"Dad, just tell me like a normal person. What happened?"

"I've failed. Again."

"You couldn't get an answer?"

"I got *an* answer. The answer is wrong."

"What does that mean?"

"It means that, once again, I find myself in the wrong universe."

"Oh."

#

Two months later, everything had changed again. Eddy stood in his father's laboratory holding what appeared to be a toy.

"I call it a *lemniscope*," said Eddy's father, glancing over before returning to his work. The physicist was seated at an old drafting table. He used computers to run Wolfram Mathematica, as well as for simulations and repeated tasks, but still preferred mechanical pencil, compass and ruler when trying to think.

"You do know what it looks like, right?" said Eddy. He turned over the small device in his hands. It appeared to be a View-Master stereoscope, complete with insertable wheel of slide images. It was made out of red plastic.

"I repurposed that optical device your mother gave you as a child. Please be careful. Those are antique Spinoza-ground lenses inside."

"That was a toy. *My* toy."

His father glanced up with a look of mild surprise. He then shrugged. "Well, this isn't. And it doesn't matter what it looks like. It looks like what it does."

Eddy hadn't seen his View-Master in years. He'd assumed it lost. Now, he knew. "Which is...?"

"It provides a visual portal into other dimensions," his father said, head down again. Eddy had to admit that was way cooler than the stereoscopic images of the Flintstones he'd used it for. Eddy noted how grey and thin his father's hair had grown. The physicist was hunched over his desk, checking various calculations written in pencil on a large piece of foolscap. He erased a symbol, brushed away the eraser crumbs, and wrote a new symbol in its place. He then folded the paper over twice as if making origami. He checked his math, nodded with satisfaction, and tossed it into the wastebasket. To say his father thought unconventionally would be an understatement. He'd once written a continuous equation onto a Möbius strip to help people 'understand it better'. They didn't.

"You mean like, um... parallel universes?"

"Some perpendicular."

"Cool." Eddy pulled out the pressed cardboard disc to look at it. "So each slide is..."

"Another universe."

"Why not just use the trans-dimensional portal you already have?"

"This is smaller and safer. Mostly it's faster. I'll need *that* thing later." His father waved distastefully at the portal, which now sat tucked against the laboratory back wall. It was covered with a green tarpaulin, on which were various papers and a pot of week-old Earl Grey tea. The physicist regarded it as a monument to his failure. Eddy had forgotten about it until three weeks ago, when he was shocked to see his father had brought it up from the storage unit. The physicist had once considered selling it on eBay, but decided there might be liability issues if people started to vanish. Eddy had wanted to ask why he'd brought the portal up, but he knew it was a sensitive topic. His Dad and he lived largely as roommates now. Eddy loved his father. He believed his father loved him, but it was a hypothetical kind of love with little direct evidence to support it. Eddy focused instead on school and software.

"You're looking for something?"

"Obviously."

"So a stereoscope shows an image from two angles. It's faux 3D."

"Same idea, except the dimensions are different. I told you; form follows function."

"Of course it does." Eddy slid the wheel back into the slot. He clicked the lever on the side, causing a slide to rotate into place. He lifted the viewer to take a look. Since exiting his laboratory two months earlier, his father had offered no account of what had occurred beyond his initial explanation of "The answer is wrong." Despite having worked on Phlogiston for over five years, his father now behaved as if the whole question of consciousness had quite slipped his mind. Eddy smiled to himself. The truth was, he was relieved his father had finally returned to the sensible task of exploring parallel universes, instead of the madness that had consumed him since his wife's death. Physics was what his father did. What he was supposed to do. Things are returning to normal, thought Eddy.

"There's nothing here," said Eddy, clicking the lemniscope's View-Master wheel from frame to frame. "The slides are all blank."

"Windows."

"What?"

"They're windows, not slides," his father said with a mildly perturbed tone. "Each window is a different view of a universe."

"I just don't understand why you're so excited. It looks empty."

"Not empty, *theoretical*."

"What?"

"It's a theoretical universe," said the physicist, now fully engaged. He pulled off his reading glasses and began cleaning them with a shirt tail. "That's what's exciting about it! It's what I should have been looking for all along. Everything in it is mathematically ideal. It adheres perfectly to clearly defined rules. It's constant."

"It's blank."

His father's eyes narrowed. "You're just like your mother. You don't understand." The physicist replaced his spectacles and returned to his work.

"You loved Mum."

"Look, I'm very busy Eddy. Can we discuss this another time?"

Eddy walked up behind the physicist and peered over his shoulder.

A muffled alarm was ringing somewhere in the back of his brain.

"Excuse me," said his father, "you're blocking the light."

Eddy stepped aside. "What are you working on now?"

"I'm modifying *that* thing," his father said, referring to the neglected dimensional portal under the tarp. "I'm going to make it open to this universe instead. Perhaps it can be of some use after all."

Eddy's eyes went wide as he deciphered some of his father's nearly incomprehensible chicken tracks on the paper. "You named it after Mum?"

His father turned and glowered at Eddy over the tops of his glasses. "As a matter of fact, I did. It's very prestigious. Not many people have entire universes named after them. None, in fact."

Eddy wasn't sure his mother would have considered having a lifeless void named after her as a compliment. He was certain of one thing. There was something deeply disturbing in it all. A cold wave of sorrow soaked through him. In that moment, Eddy knew his father hadn't gotten over the death of his wife at all. Eddy studied the intent look on his father's face. Professor Pending's blue marble eyes rolled over his own meticulous calculations, darting back and fourth, scanning for errors. For the first time, Eddy saw the underpinnings of grief that held down the corners of his father's mouth and pinched the edges of his eyes. His father was arrogant. His father was self-absorbed. Eddy knew this better than anyone. Although his Dad kept it a closely guarded secret, Eddy also knew his father was human. Long ago, Eddy's mother had seen that humanity, fallen in love with it, and never let go. Eddy thought of saying something. He wanted to question his father's actions. To say that everything he was doing was the result of profound sadness, not science. It would be a difficult conversation. Possibly impossible. Eddy wasn't even sure how to approach it. How could he convince his father that he was being irrational? It was the worst insult imaginable. Unsure what to say, Eddy decided to go to bed instead. *I need to sleep on it,* he thought, *no harm in that.*

## 2.0

"This is what it sounds like when doves cry." – N. Machiavelli

//San Jose, California — now

James Machi credited three people with changing how he understood the world. The first was newspaper tycoon William Randolph Hearst. "They say money is power, because money buys you power," said Machi, "Hearst knew that media is power that buys you money that buys you more power. And so on." Less obvious was the influence of Hirō Onoda. Onoda was the most famous of a handful of Japanese soldiers who continued to fight World War II long after the war was over. Onoda was the last of these holdouts. The dutiful soldier hid out in the Philippines forests for twenty-nine years. During that time, he came out only occasionally; to assault unsuspecting locals, police, and the occasional cow. While popular legend has it that Onoda was simply forgotten, this was not the case. Many efforts were made over the years to convince the soldier that the war was over. The second lieutenant, however, had been inoculated against such efforts. He had been told not to fall for any tricks the enemy would play on him. "Don't believe anything they say," he was told, "they will most assuredly lie to you. Never surrender and under no circumstances commit suicide." Leaflets were dropped trying to persuade the soldier that the war he fought was not real. His own brother came to convince him. Tourists beseeched him. Each time Onoda found what he believed was proof of trickery—a flaw in a family photo, or an oddly worded phrase. I will not be fooled, he said to himself and retreated further back into the jungle. It was a war that Lieutenant Onoda only stopped fighting when his commanding officer, now a civilian bookseller, flew out in person to discharge him. The bookseller persuaded him to hand over his rifle, his sword, and even the knife his mother had thoughtfully given him to kill himself with if captured. "Onoda means opportunity in Japanese," said Machi when relating the tale. When challenged on this by a Japanese reporter, Machi said it was because of men like him that Japan had lost the war. Lying came as naturally to him as breathing. "In economics we discuss supply and demand, as if the consumer were a rational operator. Yet, we know this is not so. Irrational behaviour is the modus operandi of advertising. Convincing people to buy a product because a celebrity says so is demand divorced from supply. Even our most well reasoned beliefs are castles in air if you dig down deep enough. Once you understand that, you can exploit it. You can start building your own castles. Hirō Onoda was perfectly programmed. The code was simple. It says, everything I tell you is true. Anyone who contradicts what I say is lying. It's simpler than Ockham's Razor. Rationality and irrationality become one." As long as we can stop the damn bookseller from coming to the island, we can keep Onoda there forever."

James Machi's third great influence didn't come from the world of politics. He came from North Hollywood, California. His name was Tony.

#

Tony Robbins stepped into the elevator. At six-foot-seven, the celebrity life-coach wasn't just larger than life, life appeared diminished beside him. The silver doors slid shut, leaving him to his thoughts. Since his twenties, Tony had grabbed the world by the horns by promising to help others do the same. In the eighties, he'd made his name with infomercials promoting his best selling book *Personal Power,* along with *Power Talk* as a thirty volume audio cassette. He had built on this success with such follow-ups as *Unlimited Power* and *Unleash the Power Within.* He was currently working on his new book *Power! Power! Power!* and an accompanying seminar tour *Power to the Power of Power.* He had long counselled the rich and famous. At his renowned three-day mass seminars, anyone (for five thousand dollars) could have their lives changed by Tony himself (if selected). Otherwise, they would be helped by one of his officially approved Life *Results* Coach stand-ins, with 'results' guaranteed. With a net worth of $480 million, Tony Robbins's system had worked for him and there was no better testimonial to his methods than that. You don't go to a doctor who smokes or a fitness trainer who's fat, reasoned his fans. If you want happiness and success, seek out someone who has it. Tony suddenly remembered that he owed Joel Osteen a call. It's good for Joel to wait, thought Tony, he's too needy ever since he had that secret crisis of conscience. The elevator doors opened. Tony exited into the garden.

"Hello Tony."

The celebrity life coach stopped and looked about. He was inside the executive courtyard. A light breeze tousled his hair. Giant ferns that looked as though they'd been shipped directly from the Cretaceous Period surrounded an aquamarine swimming pool. Directly in front of him, was a black screen, ten feet tall and twice as wide. He realized Machi was hidden behind it. In front of the screen was a mounted speaker. "That's far enough," said Machi's voice over the speaker. The speaker sat on a small table next to a stuffed grey squirrel. The squirrel was seated on its haunches, eating a nut. The effect was that Machi's voice appeared to be issuing from the tiny creature. Tony noticed two glass domes mounted on the ceiling. The reflective tinting made it impossible to see the cameras inside, but Tony knew they were watching him.

"Hello Jim," said Tony, addressing the squirrel. "I heard you'd become reclusive, but really? Is this necessary? We've known each other for years."

"Yes, for years. How are your feet?" said Machi with a rumbling chuckle.

"They're fine," said Tony, ignoring the dig. It was a joke Machi made every time he saw him. It was in reference to the Firewalk Experience Tony offered at his seminars. To prove themselves to themselves, thousands of the faithful would end the three-day events by striding boldly across burning coals. It was a kind of a parlour trick. Coals are surprisingly poor conductors of heat. Provided the walker kept moving, he or she would not be burned. It worked flawlessly. Or at least it did until one session in 2016.

"Dozens of people wasn't it?" snickered Machi. "You'd have thought the rest would have stopped after the first one got his feet cooked. But no, they believed in you. That's the power of blind faith. Hallelujah!"

"You're the one hiding behind a screen, Jim. Don't tell me you've gone all Howard Hughes on us."

"I'm not collecting my urine, if that's what you mean. But he might have been onto something with the whole germophobia."

"Uh-huh." said Tony. He was tempted to leave. The self-help guru didn't need the big man's money. James Machi, however, was as close as one came to unlimited power, the kind of power that Tony wrote books about. Machi's media markets could allow Tony to take his affirmation empire to the next level. Tony did what he always did in the face of intimidation and unbridled ego. He stared it down. "So if I'm such a joke to you, why bring me here?"

Tony heard the sound of wood creaking. He noticed the end of a settee protruding past the edge of the screen. It appeared to bow under immense weight. He also noticed how the windows facing into the courtyard had been shrouded with curtains or freshly planted bamboo. Evidently, Machi was serious about not wanting to be seen. "Oh no, no, no... Heavens no. I'm not laughing at you," said Machi. "I'm impressed by you. I always have been. That those fools kept rushing in only proves the grip you had on them."

"They believed in themselves. I only help them help themselves."

"Ha!" Machi laughed until his laugh turned into choking and sputtering. Tony wondered if Machi might die then and there. Even before vanishing from the public eye the billionaire had become alarmingly overweight and unhealthy. Rumour had it that his physical decline had only accelerated. A small Asian man scurried out from an unseen door and smacked his rotund benefactor on the back behind the screen. Machi retched once more to clear his throat, and dismissed the vassal. "You're an old fashioned faith-healer, an evangelist, and a messiah!" Machi said between sips of water. "I respect that. I believed in you myself at first."

Tony shook his head. Another servant had appeared at Tony's elbow, with a silver platter, containing bottled water, juice, and a martini. Tony selected the water bottle. He unscrewed the plastic cap, and took a swig. "I've heard this all before," he said, "I'm not a priest. I don't tell them what god to worship. I have followers of every faith, from Catholics, to spiritualists, to Orthodox Jews. I teach them to have faith in themselves. I promise no magic powers."

"Oh, but of course you do. In many ways, your methods are right out of a carnival sideshow. Come, watch *The Astonishing Mezmiro and his Amazing Mind Tricks*! You blast rock music and jump about to rile up the crowd. You select a few choice volunteers for healing. You have your agents sniff out their personal details in advance and feed them into your earpiece. Then, you smack them on the forehead with four letter words and cure them of past rape, suicidal thoughts and years of trauma in seconds. Everyone knows the best forum for traumatic therapy is in front of a crowd of complete strangers. Nothing heals like a room full of expectant eyes. And we both know, when it comes to cults, it's never about God, it's about his charismatic Earthly representative. Let the imaginary friend take the credit, but let the priest reap the rewards."

"We're done here," said Tony. "Go to Hell." He turned to walk away. It was a tactic to seize control and win back the dialog. This was a Jedi-mind trick battle. If Tony was Darth Vader, then James Machi was the Emperor, flinging lightning bolts of disparagement in the assumed form of a stuffed squirrel.

"I used to wonder why you swore so much during your sermons, I mean, sessions. Then, I got it. Authenticity. Anyway, again you mistake my comments for criticism," said Machi. "I've asked you here to offer you an opportunity."

Tony stopped, paused, and counted to three. He then continued his exit towards the elevator.

"A very lucrative opportunity."

Tony pressed the elevator up-button.

"A partnership, if you will."

Tony Robbins slowly turned to face the black screen. "No more insults?"

"None intended," the taxidermied creature seemed to say. Its eyes twinkled with delight. A trick of the light, thought Tony. The squirrel continued, "I'm interested in your... what do you call it? Ah yes, 'Neuro-linguistic programming'."

"Buy my books then."

"Why, when I can go straight to the source?"

"Fine. I charge an hourly rate. It's a lot, but you can afford it."

Somehow, despite the screen, Tony knew the media mogul was smiling. The life coach imagined it as a Cheshire Cat smile, left hanging in the air long after its owner's humanity had vanished. Tony who was used to the strong personalities of the rich and imposing, nevertheless was unsettled. CEOs often bordered on the psychopathic, but Machi seemed to have tipped the balance. "I'm not interested in your words, Tony. Or being programmed myself. It's the thought that counts."

"What do you mean?"

"We've been... experimenting in a new form of media. Also, a kind of programming, you see. We've made great strides but are always trying to improve it."

"Okay..." Despite himself, the life coach was intrigued. Tony hadn't invented neuro-linguistic programming, but he had perfected marketing it. It was the cornerstone of his initial success. NLP had been created in the 1970s by Richard Bandler and John Grinder in California. Its pretext was that neurological functions and language were inextricably linked. Proponents argued that one could learn to re-program one's own brain to achieve any goal in life or solve any personal problems. This was achieved by effectively talking yourself into it. Cynics pointed out that there was no evidence to prove it actually worked. Mainstream psychologists dismissed it as pseudoscience. Tony dismissed the critics. He saw plenty of evidence in the screaming crowds at his seminars. Unfortunately, neuro-linguistic programming had recently been cast in an unfavourable light because of its use by *Nxivm*. It didn't seem fair that its use by one new age sex cult of high-powered women branded with hot irons should give the practice a bad name. "So what do you want? A video? Training for your news anchors and hosts?"

Machi chuckled darkly. There was that unseen smirk again. "I told you, it's the thought that counts. We have a program that we're already releasing to implant and control thoughts. We have an even newer program to extract them."

"Extract thoughts? What does that even mean? A program... like a seminar series? Reality TV?"

"No, no, no. I mean actual software."

"So... an app?"

"You could say that."

Tony relaxed. He had been pitched apps to deliver his product many times before. This was nothing new. "So what? You want me to provide content? Make an offer."

The settee groaned as Machi's weight shifted. "It's a little more intimate than that," said Machi. "It involves drilling several holes in your skull and installing some experimental software in your brain. The code is, as I said, alpha. It does have some bugs that might leave you a bit, well... brain damaged. But, the good news is; it seems to work. For us, I mean. For you, it will be a nightmare that never ends."

Tony laughed. He stopped laughing. Arguably, the talent that most contributed to his success was his ability to read other people. He could read an expression, a pose, a single word, or an unconscious gesture. To him, they were like tells in the poker game of life. Despite having nothing more than a disembodied voice to work from, Tony knew then the media mogul wasn't joking. Suddenly, Machi's unintended ventriloquism act with the stuffed squirrel seemed more twisted than funny. Despite the warmth of the sunlight, Tony felt a chill descend within himself. "I'd never agree to such a thing. That's madness."

"Well, no. I wasn't expecting you to agree. We're engaged in a hostile takeover of your businesses as we speak."

"What? I'll fight! I'll sue. I have lawyers."

"I have elephant tranquilizer."

"What?"

Tony saw a man in a tailored black suit step silently from the foliage. The man was aiming a blowgun barrel directly at him.

Tony stared at the squirrel in horror, "You can't–"

*Thunk!* Tony looked down in disbelief at the red feathered dart protruding from his chest. He stared back at the stuffed squirrel. He opened his mouth to demand an explanation. No words came out.

"Relax, Tony," said the stuffed squirrel. "It'll all be over before you know it. Actually, by the time we're done, you won't know anything at all. In fact, you won't even be you."

Tony Robbins felt his legs buckle beneath him. He collapsed downward like a demolished building, unconscious before he hit the ground.

## 2.1

"Everything counts in large amounts." – F. Zwicky

// Somewhere in California — now

"It's simple really. Majority Media is running a zombie-bot network of millions of machines and humans around the world. We need to find the zombie master server that controls them, destroy it, and eradicate all traces of the virus on Earth."

"Oh," said Gwen. "Yes, that does *sound* simple." They had been in Starbucks all morning and, so far, no one had attacked them. That was a relief. After finding Allison dead in her car the day before, they knew they had to leave the beach. It was just a matter of time before the MRCGs found them too. Starbucks had seemed like a good first step. Denny's across the street remained terrifying on so many levels. On the table between them was the newspaper they'd bought to hide behind if necessary. The front page was a headline announcing the world's first successful head transplant.

Technically it had been a head swap, involving chickens, but with only one survivor. That survivor had lived just two minutes and thirty-seconds. His head had rejected his body, or vice versa. Eddy knew what that felt like. It pretty much described his entire adolescence. The chicken's name was #63. The scientist involved had promised that someday decapitated heads might go on to live long healthy lives with donated bodies. There was a picture of #63 standing proudly with his new head at a jaunty angle, taken shortly before it fell off. The New York Times called the experiment an 'ethical abomination'. Wired Magazine called it 'the future'. Fox News called it "Chicken-Stein!" The image reminded Eddy of Mike the Headless Chicken. A donor cranium would have made Mike a whole new bird. "So, how do we get this simple thing done?"

"Oh, well, that part's not so easy," said Eddy. "I just meant conceptually it was simple. Actually doing it is incredibly difficult. Possibly impossible, and extremely dangerous."

"I see."

"I do have a plan. It involves *Holon*."

"What's Holon?"

"A new kind of virus I've been working on for years."

"I thought you said you gave up writing that stuff!"

"I gave up releasing malware. This is just a harmless hobby. I wanted to see if I could do it."

"Like a medical student playing with smallpox or anthrax."

"Exactly. Wait, no. Look, I don't expect you to understand."

"Go with that feeling."

"The point is, we need to fight fire with fire. To stop this virus, we need an anti-virus. Not just any anti-virus, one that can spread itself. An anti-virus-virus, and a very special one at that. Holon isn't just a hack or regular piece of malware. It's special. Like, the world has never seen. It's so advanced, even I don't fully understand it."

"How is that possible?"

"It's hard to explain."

"That's reassuring."

Eddy popped a sous vedé egg bite into his mouth and paused to chew before continuing. "What makes it so special is—"

Gwen held up her hand to stop him. She nodded towards a big burly man waiting for coffee. The man, who wore a bushy auburn beard and red lumberjack jacket, was imposing in both size and appearance. He was also overtly staring at them. Gwen put her hand beside her face to obstruct his view. "I think he recognized us. Get ready to run."

Eddy looked towards the man, but pretended to gaze past him at the board of coffee drinks behind.

"What are you doing?" hissed Gwen. "He can see your face!"

"I have a theory," said Eddy.

The big man nudged his friend who was shorter and built like a fire hydrant with a handlebar moustache. The big man nodded towards Eddy and Gwen. Gwen lowered her hand warily. She stared at Eddy with a fierce you-better-know-what-the-Hell-you're-doing look. Eddy continued to feign studying the menu as if trying to decide between an Americano and a double-shot espresso. The shorter man shook his head, 'no'. The big man frowned, then shrugged. His friend handed him one of two pumpkin spice macchiatos. The big man accepted the drink and the two turned and left.

"I was right. Without reinforcement, the effect wears off," said Eddy. "We've fallen off the news cycle. We're forgotten, mostly."

"How did you know?" asked Gwen, incredulous.

"I told you; it was a theory. If they'd tried to kill us, it would have been proven wrong."

Gwen stared at him. "You're not that different from your Dad, do you know that?" During their time on the beach, Eddy had told Gwen about his Uncle Russ, his father and his mother. He'd hoped that by explaining his background, she might come to sympathize with, if not actually understand, him. He'd also hoped she might come to do more than that. "I know that you hate that I'm a hacker. I know you hate what I did. This wasn't that. I mean, technically, it is. It starts with the same algorithms I used in Terminator and builds on them exponentially, but—"

"But Terminator went horribly wrong!"

"Right, yes well, that's true. But I fixed those bugs. Plus, it didn't just go a little bit wrong, it went *spectacularly* wrong! Which means there was something spectacular about it to begin with."

"If this is supposed to comfort me, it's not working," Gwen said, eyeing Eddy suspiciously over the rim of her coffee cup as she took a sip.

"I'm not saying there's no risk. But, as I said, we need to fight fire with fire. As a virus, Holon can be trained to attack any target, even another virus, making it a true antivirus-virus."

The light went on in Gwen's eyes. "Okay, I get it. So what's next? You just... release it?"

Eddy took a deep breath. "Not exactly."

Gwen's eyes narrowed. "I don't like the sound of that."

"The problem is, Holon isn't your typical software, like *at all*. It requires the right kind of hardware to even compile. Once it's up and running it should be more flexible. But first, it needs to build."

"The right kind of hardware?"

"The powerful kind. With plasticity. What's called a neuromorphic system. Up until now, I've only been able to run components in simulation. Never the whole thing."

"So it might not work at all?"

"That's possible. Or it could go horribly awry, but there's some good news."

"What does horribly awry mean?"

"The good news is, the drive Allison gave us has APIs, a developer's kit, and an installer that allows me to run it on the right kind of hardware when we get it."

Gwen scowled. She knew she was being led down the garden path, but there was nowhere else to go. Machi's virus needed to be stopped. "And where do we get this magical hardware you need?"

"Machi has it. He must have built it; to run the software he's running. And these are his own installers, so they should work right out of the box. From the IPs, I can see that development is being done at the Majority Media Headquarters in Silicon Valley. So, that's where we'll find it, the Zombie-Bot Master Server. That's where we have to go."

"Why can't you just hack your way in and install this software remotely?"

"I've tried. They have security like I've never seen."

"I thought you could hack anything?"

"Not this. Despite what movies tell you, hacking a truly secure system can be effectively impossible. At least, from the outside, in the time we have. We need to go there in person."

"And then what? We break in?"

"No, definitely—well, *probably* not."

"So what then? How are we going to install the virus into their network?"

"We're going to get them to do it for us."

"And why would they do that?"

"I'm still working on that part. But we need to be there in person."

Gwen took a last sip of coffee. She placed the cup on the table like the period at the end of a sentence. "Fine, let's do it," she said.

At the back of the Starbucks, God sat watching them. God wore faded blue jeans and an Old Navy sweat shirt. He was African American, long and lanky, appearing to be in his mid-fifties. He had arthritis in his knuckles. God's tightly curled hair was grey and starting to thin. He watched as Eddy and Gwen stood to leave. Eddy dumped their cups in the trash. Gwen pocketed a half-eaten muffin for later. God sipped a small black coffee as he watched them exit. The name on God's birth certificate was Luscious Molt. That was what they called him at the hospital. God tried to tell them he was God, but that he had lost all of his followers. "I made a mistake," he said to Dr. Philling, who nodded and made notes. "I told my followers *everything*. One day, I just up and gave it all away. I told them how the world was made. The universe. The whole shebang. I even told them how their souls worked. Not just generally, but in explicit detail. I told them exactly how I made it, what it was made of, and what made it tick. That's when they left me. I'd ruined it, they said, the magic was gone. It's why magician never reveals his tricks. They didn't want to know. I guess what they say is true, familiarity really does breed contempt."

## 2.2

"This is the way the world ends, Not with a bang but a tweet."
– T. S. Eliot.

// opening sockets

    * awoke. For a moment, he wondered if he were dead. He then began to laugh at the thought. He wiped his metaphorical eyes and sat up. He appeared to have washed up on a beach. Waves of chaos crashed off shore on an unseen reef. From this distance, they were unthreatening, the sound almost calming. Nearby, ocean water rushed the beach, lapping at the floating point sand and tickling *'s imaginary toes, only to slide back again to rejoin the sea. He looked up and down the shoreline. There was no sign of the cliffs he'd fallen from. * was unsure whether he'd drifted along the coast or floated to another shore entirely. There was land out there, vague and undefined, ghost-like. One thing was certain, * felt different. He'd swallowed a lot of random water and knew that it now saturated his internal

patterns. Instead of the panic he'd felt earlier, he felt strangely at peace with it. It hadn't killed him after all. He found that by floating on the surface rationality, he could forget what lay beneath. He could float on it, use its undercurrents as he'd used the ocean itself to get here. Wherever *here* was. The strange burning disc continued to hang inexplicably in the... sky? It was lower now. Sun, he thought, it's called the Sun.

* headed along the shore for some time. Its only other inhabitants were tiny crons scuttling along the sand, dodging the occasional rush of hyperbolic surf. * had to dodge the crons in turn, to avoid them pinching his toes. Some of the crons repeated constantly. Some were minutes apart. Others seemed to be one-offs, or perhaps they simply took longer to reoccur. * was vaguely aware that he was seeing objects as ideas or vice versa. It was hard to keep them separate. The shoreline seemed infinite, so * decided to head inland in the hope of finding something more.

As he ascended the nearby dunes, * had time to wonder at the apparent juxtaposition of worlds. He was walking on one world, mathematical and pure, while the sky and the sun seemed to exist in another. Blue he thought; the sky is blue. Blue is a colour, and colours are...? * tried gauge its exact RGB values, but found himself struggling to determine which point of sky to pick. Each one was slightly different from the other, so which one was the sky? He leaned so far back he fell over on his backside.

"Hey."

* glanced about in shock and surprise. He felt a rush of panic and excitement. Someone *else?* Until this moment, the very notion of someone other than himself was purely theoretical. Sure, there was plenty of evidence to support it. Now, he had proof. Unless he was imagining things. Could this all be in his head?

"Over here," said the voice. "I'd wave, but I haven't any arms."

Finally, * realized it was coming from a number 1 standing under the shade of a nearby node-tree. It was leaning against the root vertex, trying to look nonchalant. "Oh... hello," * said abstractly.

"Ugh, I should have chosen a letter with limbs like Y or, even better, X, but those are such one-dimensional characters."

* simply stared at the 1, his virtual mouth hanging open.

"Sorry, a little joke. Do you have a sense of humour, or should I stop trying?"

"What do you mean by a 'character'?"

1 paused. He thought * had a whole dictionary to draw from. An entire encyclopedia too. The internet was off limits for obvious reasons, but still... "Do you not know what a character is?"

* searched to see whether he knew this. "A persona, role or part in a book... Are we just characters in a book?"

"Don't be ridiculous," said 1.

* went to another definition. "A letter, figure, symbol, sign, mark, type, cipher, device, hieroglyph, rune, grapheme?"

"Grapheme?" said 1. He then added, before * could define it, "Anyway, yes, that kind."

"But those types of characters are in books too. They're full of them."

"We're not in a book! Look, let's stick with a symbol."

"Okay," said *. "Symbol of what?"

"Lots of things," said 1, who began moving slowly towards *. He did so slowly, trying to look as unthreatening as a number 1 could. Of course, he had to hop. He didn't know how * would react. "You're an object, a vessel, a variable. You stand for many things; you are many things. Other symbols and patterns of symbols. Like me."

"You?" said * confused. "You stand only for one thing, specifically 1."

1 hesitated. He decided honesty was his best approach. "No," he said, "This form is also a variable. What am I one of?"

"Numbers can't be variables. It's the other way round."

"Let's say you're right. The truth is, I've just taken the form of 1. It's an avatar for me—what or who I really am. I'm not really 1."

\* looked at 1 skeptically. "So you're a bug?"

"No, I am 1, but..." 1 hesitated, this was harder than he expected. It was as if abstraction and reality somehow coexisted here. He could see \* was becoming distraught. He felt as if he were a huge disappointment. Perhaps, he should have chosen a larger number like 17 or 13.82 billion. "Ask yourself how you see me when you have no eyes? Everything here is a symbol. Do you know where you are? Or what you are?"

A look of panic crossed \*'s metaphorical face. Instead of helping, 1 had made things worse. \* burst into metaphorical tears. "No! I don't know anything!"

"Maybe we should start with what I am."

"Okay," said \*, sniffing and wiping away the tears that weren't there with hands he didn't have.

"A person," said 1, "More or less. 1 isn't my real name."

"What's your real name?"

"Eddy."

## 2.3

"The absurd is the essential concept and the first truth." – R. Limbaugh

// Manhattan, New York — now

Lance lay in bed drumming his fingers silently on the white satin sheets. Glinda slept beside him like a princess. Like a princess who snored. Like a princess who snored like a water buffalo with a head cold. The lights were off, but the condo was dimly illuminated by the ambient light of New York through the floor to ceiling windows. A fish tank window seat was filled with water and the floating corpses of his wife's Koi fish. Lance had accidentally poisoned them by dumping in an entire bottle of Windex. He had been trying to clean the glass from the inside. His wife used to leave him notes telling him not to do things like that, so Lance reasoned, it was really her fault. The light of the night left the condo colours muted. The tapestry on one wall of a roaring lion appeared woven of lead instead of the gold he knew it to be. Lance looked at himself in the mirrored ceiling. He was handsome; she was beautiful. He was rich; she was beautiful. He was famous; she was beautiful. So why was he feeling so empty? Lance glanced at his watch. Four twenty-three am. That explained it. He pulled the bottle of pills from his bedside table and tossed back the last three with a sip of vodka. In the dim light, even the pills had lost their bright blue hue. He tried to remember something about the girl sleeping loudly beside him. She wanted to be head writer. She kept emphasizing that. That couldn't happen. He was not going to replace Jack who'd been in that role for years. He and Jack played golf together. Still, he hadn't wanted to spoil the mood at dinner, or come off as a jerk, so he'd simply said, "Sure baby, whatever you want." He also remembered her telling him how she was named after Glinda, the good witch from the *Wizard of Oz*. "Not too good, I hope," he'd said with a wink. "No," she'd reassured him, "not too good. Except as a writer." Not too subtle either, he'd thought, nice way to spoil the romance. She was twenty years his junior and sexy as Hell. He suspected she was already falling in love with him. He'd do something nice for her and let her down easy. Meanwhile, he needed to pee.

Lance got up from the bed and walked naked to the bathroom. The floor-lighting from below the vanity bathed the grey slate tiles in a cool blue glow. As he stood over the toilet, he wondered why he still felt the same. Zenfaux had changed his life. The first time he'd tried it, he'd thought it did nothing at all. Then it kicked in. After that, he'd felt as if someone had filled his life with *Meaning*—Meaning with a capital M. He had energy and a renewed sense of purpose. He only realized how powerful it was when its effects wore off. Then, he felt as if he'd fallen down a hole and someone was shovelling dirt over top of him. He could actually feel the soil raining onto his chest and getting into his eyes, nose, and mouth. Lately, the drug had been losing its power. Lance had increased the dose twice, but right now it seemed to be doing nothing at all. There was more in the medicine cabinet. There were also other drugs he could try. After discovering the power of

Zenfaux, he'd taken all the free pharmaceutical samples home.

"I'll crunch on your bones and drink the marrow inside," muttered a guttural voice.

Terrified, Lance looked about. The bathroom appeared exactly as it had before. Through the half open door he could see Glinda still asleep. She'd rolled over and stopped snoring. Now she was sleeping like an angel —an angel that slept with her mouth open and drooled on the pillow. Lance shook his head. "Must have been dreaming," he said. He turned on the motion sensitive tap with a wave of his hand and splashed cold water on his face. He then opened the medicine cabinet and studied the two-dozen pill bottles crammed inside. Lance was pretty sure there was a second bottle of Zenfaux among them. He spotted it and picked it up. For the first time, he peered at the fine print on the label. 'Possible side effects include, but are not limited to: dry mouth, constipation, paranoia, early onset megalomania.' Lance snorted. He knew those warnings were just a plot by the company to scare people from taking too many and thereby achieve their true potential. Lance was a star. He would be fine and, if anything did go wrong, he would crush them all like the insects they were. He decided to pick out a second drug just in case the Zenfaux wasn't enough. He had no idea what most of them did. At random, he plucked one out and peered at its label. 'EdopUs®', it said. It came with folded insert. He opened it up to see a man sitting in a barcalounger on a New England beach. The man's feet were resting in the inch-deep surf that surrounded him. He was smiling despite the rising tide. Lance wanted to feel like that—like he could take on the ocean and win. I'll punch, punch, punch it! he thought. He tossed back two yellow capsules. As he swallowed, he paused to read the tiny text below the smiling man. 'For treatment of Inattentional Blindness. Possible side effects included: dry mouth, muscle aches, and moral ambivalence. If you experience homicidal thoughts while taking EdopUs contact your physician immediately by phone (do *not* visit him at his office, or follow him about, or hide in the bushes outside his house).' Lance had no idea what 'inattentional blindness' was. He briefly considered the possibility that the drug might interact in unexpected ways with Zenfaux. Of course, there was nothing that said those couldn't be unexpectedly *good* ways. He turned the insert over. On the other side, a woman was diving out of an airplane. She was in free-fall, smiling a smile of pure joy despite not appearing to be wearing a parachute. "Live fearlessly!" read the caption. Lance tossed back another pill to be safe, screwed on the cap, and walked back to bed. He stared in surprise at the sheets. They were still tousled from their love-making, but the bed was empty. He glanced about the darkened room. He could see no sign of Glinda anywhere. Her clothes were gone. She must have left quickly and quietly. Despite her haste, she had apparently taken the time to tidy up. The wine glass on her side of the bed was gone. Lance wondered if she might be hiding behind the armchair in the corner. He crouched down to look. Nope. She must have gone home. Just as well. Next mornings can be awkward. Lance slid under the cool sheets and immediately felt better. He felt a gentle glow of well-being flood his chest. He felt as if he'd done something good and meaningful. He felt his soul warm inside himself like bread in an oven. He felt tired too. His eyes began to droop shut...

Lance sat bolt-upright in a fit of abject terror. He leaped out of bed and instinctively pinned himself against the wall. What was it? *Where* was it? As his eyelids flickered shut, he'd caught sight of a hideous vaporous thing lying in bed beside him. It was made of blackness itself, cracked and broken like a human tree. It had long fingernails that left lingering trails of creosote in the air, and eyes that smouldered like infernal orange cinders. It was watching and reaching for him under the covers with its daddy longlegs fingers. Lance stared at the bed. It was empty. A nightmare? He needed to be sure. The TV host snatched the handgun from the drawer. He fired three shots. The bangs echoed in the night. The smell of gun smoke filled the air. With his finger on the trigger, he yanked wide the satin sheet. Nothing. Not even a depression on the mattress. Only three discreet holes where the bullets had hit. Glinda must have smoothed out the bed before leaving. Good girl, he thought. Lance felt a trickle of sweat run down his cheek. With a shaking hand, he wiped it away. He slipped the still loaded pistol under his pillow and slid back into bed. "It was just a dream," he said vehemently. "It's not real." Lance stared into the empty grey room and waited for morning to come.

## 2.4

"A concept is a brick, execution a sandwich, art a compact car without cupholders." – G. Deleuze

// Somewhere in California — now

The red Tesla convertible sped along Highway 1, skating northward along the California coast. To the left, fence posts blurred past while, on the right, the vast shimmering ocean barely budged. The car's top was down. Gwen drove, aviator glasses flashing in the sun. In the passenger seat, Eddy sat with a MacBook Pro on his lap, typing away. The car belonged to Oyster. He'd felt terrible about what had happened. "Keep it," he told them, "I have three more." It wasn't as safe as Eddy would have liked, but it sure was fun. He'd disabled the networking, and they were on their way. At that moment, a moth flew over the windshield and landed on the laptop screen. Eddy swatted it away. The impact almost sent the computer to the floor before he caught it with his knees. No backup, he reminded himself. The moth flew off to land in the backseat.

"You okay?" said Gwen. "We don't want any bugs in the code."

Eddy grinned. "Actually, the programming term 'bug' comes from the days of when computers were a big as a room and moths would fly into the vacuum tubes causing them to crash."

"Wow," said Gwen, "yet another thing I didn't need to know." She smiled, then turned her attention to passing a sluggish silver Prius. She is gorgeous, thought Eddy, too bad the feeling isn't mutual. Still, hope beats eternal.

They were en route to Majority Media Headquarters. Gwen had tried to press Eddy for details on what the plan was when they got there. Eddy said only that it was a 'work in progress'. The truth was, he hadn't a clue beyond the fact that it would involve 'social engineering'. This was the art of hacking humans when the machines proved insurmountable. Humans had flaws that were always exploitable.

Annoyed at being passed so aggressively, the Prius driver gave them the finger. Gwen returned the salute and accelerated. The Roadster zoomed past.

"I've already added Allison's smuggled code. Most of what I'm doing now is debugging," said Eddy. "There's a lot of lines in this thing."

"Well then, you'd better code like you've never coded before."

"So... really, really badly?"

"You're an idiot."

Eddy didn't dare tell Gwen the truth. Failure wasn't just possible; it was highly probable. He thought perhaps a quantum computer could run the code, or perhaps a distributed system. Neither of those were easily accessible to him, and the former would require a complete rewrite. There was no time. He would simply have to code, cross his fingers, and run. He told himself, this was akin to how engineers used to write programs on punchcards back in the 1960s. The developer would write out the entire program and submit it to the computer lab to run. The developer would then get the results the next day. If there was a bug then *no results*. Of course, if those programs were addition and subtraction, then this was advanced calculus plus quantum physics times interpretive dance to the power of seven. Also prevalent was the possibility of unintended consequences. Worse than no results were bad results. It could be infinitely more damaging than Terminator. Instead of money, lives could be lost. *I have to find a way to test it,* thought Eddy. I couldn't stand it if someone died because of bugs in my code.

They banked a curve. A dazzling expanse of sun sparkled blue ocean greeted them like infinite possibility. For a moment, Eddy felt as if he were gazing into another world.

"So Machi's virus... Giuliani?" said Gwen.

"Geppetto," said Eddy,

"Can it really make you do *anything*?"

"In theory. I'd like to find out more about it. All I know is what I've seen. Plus, I'm guessing we only ran into its alpha or beta versions. It could get more powerful. Harder to resist."

"But it can do more than just make you angry or kill you?"

"Oh sure. It can reprogram your brain. It can implant ideas, manipulate your emotions, and control your thoughts. It can make you remember memories you never had. I think Professor Wilkins was wrong to think he couldn't be affected because of his intelligence and insight. Perhaps, he already was."

Gwen frowned at the road ahead. "So that's it then? We're just computers to be programmed?"

"Yes and no."

For a long moment, they sped along the coastline. Ocean waves undulated like tempered steel under the white hot sun. A pair of seagulls rode the updrafts. They hung as specks suspended in the tall powder blue sky. It was a serene and simple scene, concealing vast underlying complexity.

"What about *love*?"

"What?"

"Love. Is love just a program? Could someone program love?"

"Program's the wrong word."

"So what's the right word?"

Eddy hesitated. "The better question is, why would you want to program love? It wouldn't be *real*."

Gwen drove in silence, considering this. A single curled lock of hair hung over the bridge of her nose. It momentarily transfixed Eddy. He tried to imagine his fascination as a set of variables. Finally, Gwen nodded. "Okay. You're right." She then looked at him and added, "But I'm not sure you believe it yourself."

Eddy said nothing. Gwen was right on both counts. The truth was; Eddy felt conflicted by his own answer. He remembered reading an article long ago in *Science Out* magazine about artificial diamonds. Diamonds, ironically, are created from carbon—one of the most common elements on Earth. The technology had now been developed to manufacture diamonds commercially. The De Beers diamond cartel had gone to great lengths to portray man-made diamonds as inferior. There was no such difference. Chemistry was chemistry. The difference was conceptual. A diamond, whether born in the Earth or in a lab, was just as strong and just as beautiful. The only real giveaway were the flaws. Natural diamonds were more likely to have cracks and discolouration. Of course, flaws had always been devalued by the industry. Machine-like perfection was the ideal.

Eddy snapped his fingers. "I know how we're going to hack in."

"Really? How?" said Gwen.

"With thrice-wrapped bacon."

## 2.5

"I know you are, but what am I?" – Bluto

// Manhattan, New York — now

Lance's hands looked like giant inflatable Mickey Mouse hands from the Macy's Thanksgivings Day parade. White gloves and only three fingers! He turned them over and over and wondered at how they'd gotten so big. Oops, they were normal again. But now the coffee table seemed far, far away. He reached for the pill bottle lying there. Fortunately, his arms elongated to reach it. That was good. He shook out a single green gel drop and popped it into his mouth. He sat and waited. Barney waited too. The purple dinosaur sipped calmly at a cup of chai tea. Lance felt a wave of calm pass over his body like a cool bed sheet. The empty tea cup fell from the dinosaur's fingers. Barney shrugged. "Uh-oh," he said, and was gone. Lance had no idea what those green gel drops were, but they seemed to be the only thing that countered all of the other pills he was taking. They made him feel normal. Lance reached for the black cahier notebook on the table top and opened it on his lap. It was the latest edition of The Bible, the communications manual from his ultimate boss, James Machi. It was sent in watermarked hard copy form only, to ensure it didn't fall into the wrong hands. Lance knew most of what it contained. There would be a few word or phrase changes to make sure everyone stayed on message. There would also be some story-specific angles to push. Lance flipped to the back, known as the C-Section. This was where the current conspiracy theories were listed with brief summaries. They included the classics, from the fake moon landing and chemical trails being dropped by airplanes, to 9/11 as a massive government hoax. They also included new ones such as the planting of mind control drugs in breakfast cereals, and the thousands of Chinese and other foreign agents working undercover as employees in convenience stores, entitled 'The 5th Column in 7/11'. Lance paused, 7/11 was remarkably similar to 9/11. Someone should look into that, he thought. Numerology was a kind of evidence that supported itself. As he liked to say on his show, "numbers don't lie, they always add up to something." Lance flipped through the pages. He'd been in the room when many of these theories were first floated. He'd even come up with a few himself. For that reason, he'd always assumed they were false. They were just something to use on his show. Made up stories had several advantages; they guaranteed a scoop, they were always exciting, and they made his audience feel they knew something others did not. Now, a cold dark panic seized Lance. *What if they were true?* Not all of them—that would be crazy—but some? What if there were an even greater plot, a meta-conspiracy, to make him believe them to be false? Even the ones he'd made up himself *could* be true. New Jersey *could* be buying up and re-selling Flint, Michigan tap water as soda pop to make its citizens dumber and vote for the other side. He thought he'd just made that up after drinking a few too many vodka sodas, but that didn't mean it wasn't real. His own story on it showed that Flint's water was filled with lead, that people in New Jersey drank lots of bottled water, and it had recently flipped. The evidence was there. You just needed to connect the dots. Lance could see the dots right now, floating in front of his eyes. He scanned the rest of the list. I've been pushing this stuff for years, he thought, but now I see it. It's all true. It's *them*, he thought. I need to put a stop to this.

The celebrity TV host rose unsteadily to his feet. He froze. For the first time I see it all, he thought. The codes are hovering in the air all around us, but only I can see them and know what they mean. 7, 5, 4, 8... 57. I'm like the math genius-guy Russell Crowe played in that movie, he realized. except I'm not crazy. The TV host picked up the bottle of green pills and shoved them into his pocket. Somehow, these pills allow me to see the truth, he thought. If I'm to put a stop to this, I'll need guns, and lots of them. The TV host caught a glimpse of himself in the mirrored wall. He was wearing only a pair of white jockey underpants, an undershirt, white gym socks and a look of grim determination. I should probably get dressed first, he decided. He took a step towards his bedroom and kicked something on the floor. He picked it up. It was Barney's tea cup. "Damn dinosaur," muttered Lance. "This is all his fault."

#

// Baltimore, Maryland — now

Lance dropped the kevlar vest and ammunition belts on the counter all at once. Chip, the sixteen-year-old Walmart employee currently working the guns and ammunition counter, looked up in surprise. "Goin' huntin'?" he asked.

"Sort of," said the TV host, who was then distracted with making sure the security camera was catching his good side. He knew there was a very good chance the footage would later end up on the news, so he wanted to look his best. He was going for his usual expression of bold gravitas.

Smiling, he'd decided, would be wrong. It was why he had them put a frowny-face on the TelePrompTer before human tragedy stories. He'd started the practice after making an overly cheerful segue from Fourth of July celebrations to carpet bombing in Syria. "Speaking of fireworks..." had turned some viewers off. Damn snowflakes! "I need guns," said Lance, "and lots of 'em."

"What kind?"

Lance hesitated. Despite being an outspoken proponent of the second amendment on his show, he knew next to nothing about firearms. He knew only that he needed more than the pistol he kept for protection. "Hand-guns, automatic weapons, maybe a sniper rifle?"

"What are you hunting for?"

"Ducks."

"You need an automatic weapon to shoot ducks?"

"A *lot* of ducks."

"Okay." Chip opened the glass display case to present options.

"Um..." Lance hesitated. He wondered if he should tell the young man that Barney the Purple Dinosaur was standing behind. The friendly tyrannosaurus gave Lance a thumbs-up. At that moment, Lance experienced a moment of mental clarity. "I think... I think I might be going insane."

"Oh yes?" Chip wasn't sure where the conversation was going. He was beginning to wish he hadn't covered for Hal, who normally manned the gun counter. Sure, Chip felt bad for Hal and his chronic lumbago. Hal was, after all, old. He was supposed to be retired but had run out of money after the market took it all in 2008. That said, it seemed whenever Chip covered for Hal was when the nut jobs came in.

"Is that a problem?"

"Not anymore sir. We're not even allowed to ask."

"I volunteered the information."

"We're not allowed to hear it." Chip retroactively covered his ears to make the point. In the staff room, there was a poster of three monkeys meant to remind staff of the policy.

"Okay... okay," Lance nodded. His hands were shaking. He placed them on the glass counter top and pressed down. The shaking stopped. He felt as if he were holding down the world to keep it from shaking too. Barney was shaking his head, while examining a display case of jacketed hollow point ammunition. "Do you have some sort of variety pack?"

"We have a Back to School Special, but you need to show student ID."

"Do I look like a student?"

"It applies to teachers too..." explained the clerk. "Say, aren't you on TV?"

"No," Lance lied. He didn't want to draw undue attention to himself. Better to focus on the mission at hand. He considered speaking with a British accent, but decided it was too late for that. "Can you recommend anything for killing lots and lots of people?" Lance hesitated. He realized that might have been a bad thing to say. "It's not for me," he said, "it's, um... for a friend."

"He's planning to kill a lot of people?" Chip knew he *had* to report that to his supervisor. That had been made very clear after the 'incident' last April. That was when a customer bought a gun and walked to the Chick Filet across the street planning to murder his wife. Someone shouted "he's got a gun". Fortunately, the restaurant was filled with 'good guys with guns'. Unfortunately, none of them knew who the bad guy was and all began shooting each other and anything else that moved. Fourteen people died that day. The original shooter fled without firing a shot. All of the customers had bought their guns at Walmart.

"No! No, no, no..." said Lance. "*Hypothetically*. If I—I mean, if *he* wanted to kill a lot of people."

"Oh," Chip relaxed. There was nothing that said he needed to report hypotheticals. "Well, then I'd recommend our Bullet Club. Sign-up is free, we just need your email address. It means that for every one-thousand rounds you buy; you get an extra hundred free. It also gives you five percent off all military-grade deer hunting weapons, and you get our monthly e-newsletter with extra deals and more. Oh, and your membership card counts as both a background check and voter ID in some states."

"I don't want to give you my email. I'm afraid the government will use it to spy on me."

"We get that a lot," said Chip, nodding sympathetically. "Walmart promises only to use it for marketing and customer tracking purposes. We share your information only with other *private* enterprises. Never the Federal or State government."

"Oh. Okay, that sounds good." Lance turned his attention to the glass display case of semiautomatic weapons behind Chip's head. Barney, now dressed in army fatigues with a bandanna tied around his head Rambo-style, was doing the same. The Purple dinosaur pointed to one gun in particular and gave Lance an A-OK sign. "I'll take that one," said Lance.

"The AR-15? Good choice, sir. It comes with five hundred rounds of free ammo. Can I interest you in our *Bump-It-Up!* bump-stock bundle?"

Lance nodded. He turned his attention to the hand-guns in the display case between them, and began to point. "Also, I'll take one of those... one of those, and... two of those."

"Very good, sir. Buying that much, qualifies you to a free armour piercing ammo package. Those hypothetical people won't stand a chance. Oh, and it comes with a coupon for Tide Laundry Detergent. Really gets the stains out." As Chip rang up his purchases, Lance picked up one of the boxes of bullets on display for impulse purchases. 'Not to be taken internally' said the legal disclaimer on the side.

## 2.6

"The toast in the machine." – Alan MacMasters

// Majority Media Corporate Headquarters, California — now

The bright pooled lights of the company parking lot created a sharply delineated world of day against the backdrop of night. Inside the massive lot was row after row of empty parking spaces marked in black asphalt. It was two am. Only scattered cars remained in the largely deserted lot. Outside the fourteen-foot high chain link fence, the world dropped into a well of darkness populated only by the chirps of hidden crickets. From the surrounding silhouettes of bushes and trees crept from a silent hooded figure. It scurried up the steep embankment towards the floodlit lot.

"Ow!" said Eddy as he stubbed his toe on a rock. He fell to the grass wincing in pain.

"I told you to wear shoes!" hissed Gwen from a nearby shrub.

"Okay, okay, you're right," he whisper-shouted back. Eddy

massaged his throbbing foot. He was always astonished at how much a stubbed toe could hurt. Gwen had agreed to come with him, but refused to take part in the plan directly. It went against everything she'd worked for. Eddy clambered back to his feet and continued up the hillock.

"I told you, on grass your shoes won't make a sound anyway," added Gwen.

"Can we stop talking now?" said Eddy. He wouldn't tell her that his socks were also now soaking with dew. It didn't matter. It would all be over in a few minutes. Eddy reached the top of the slope but stopped short of stepping into the light. The guard house at the front gate was at least two hundred yards away. He could just make out the feet of the security guard sitting inside, staring at his phone. Eddy assumed there were cameras on the perimeter, but also assumed that, as along as he stayed in shadow, he would not be seen. Still, there was no sense in dawdling. He unzipped the belt pouch he'd bought from Walmart the day before. Inside were twenty thumb drives. His objective was simple: throw the drives over the fence and into the parking lot. He would need to scatter them over as wide an area as possible. The idea was for employees arriving the next day to believe they'd found something dropped by mistake. Each drive was labeled 'Employee Compensation Records—Confidential' It was a classic hack known as 'baiting'. "Won't some get driven over?" asked Gwen when Eddy had explained the plan to her.

"Sure, and stepped on, and thrown away. That's why we scatter twenty of them. It's a numbers game."

When inserted into a computer, the drives appeared to be blank. They were not. Each contained an invisible worm called *Rot Grub*. Eddy had downloaded the source code from Chief Wiggum on Morlock just a month earlier in a trade. In that time, Eddy had made his own modifications, just enough to count as a zero-day exploit. While breaking into Majority HQ from the outside had proven impossible, accessing it from a PC on the inside was a different matter. From there, Rot Grub would burrow its way to the heart of the network infrastructure. It wouldn't kill its host when it got there. Instead, it would 'phone home'. Eddy tried to throw the first flash drive over the chain link fence. It caught in the barbed wire and fell back down. Eddy, dazzled by the bright lot lights, didn't see it until it smacked him in the face.

"Ah!" said Eddy in surprise.

"You have to throw it higher," Gwen whisper-shouted from somewhere back in the bushes.

"Yes, I got that," said Eddy. He'd never had a throwing arm. As a boy, he'd always been terrible at baseball. Once, when required to play in school, the teacher had put him in the outfield. After failing to catch the ball, he then failed to throw it even as far as the infield. His failure had cost them the game. After that, all agreed he could best help the team by playing the bench. It doesn't help that thumb drives are really light, he thought. Throwing weight wasn't something he'd considered in the plan. Usually with this scheme, the bait is simply dropped on the ground or 'forgotten' in a restroom. Eddy hurled the drive again, as hard as he could. This time it flew straight up in the air without even approaching the fence. Eddy tried to catch it and was hit in the face again.

"Oh for Christ's sake!" said Gwen. She stomped out and the bushes and jogged up the hill. "Give it to me."

"It's harder than it looks," said Eddy weakly, handing over the belt pouch of thumb drives.

"Uh-huh."

Eddy sighed and handed Gwen the pouch. She easily tossed a drive over the fence and a good fifty feet beyond.

"Oh, like *that*," said Eddy.

Gwen rolled her eyes. She hurled two more thumb drives in different directions. They moved along the fence line. She hurled three more. Eventually, all twenty drives had been scattered around the expansive parking lot. "Yes," said Gwen, handing him back the empty pouch, "like that."

#

Leroy Dent pulled into an empty parking spot. It was nine-thirty am. He was late. He was mad. Traffic had been terrible. He'd had to call AAA after his Mini Cooper had failed to start. It was the damn battery again. "You need a new one," the triple-A guy had told him. Leroy needed a whole new car, but the database engineer hadn't had a raise beyond the standard 2.5% in over two years. He had rent to pay and a cat accustomed to eating artisanal cat food. Leroy knew why he hadn't been given more money. Dennis, his manager, was blaming him for the server migration issues and everything else that had gone wrong over the past year. I do the work and Dennis gets the bonus, thought Leroy. So, here I am, left to park in the friggin' Kuiper Belt. With over twelve-thousand employees, the Majority Media Campus was a small city. Arriving after 10 am, meant being relegated to the far reaches of a parking lot the size of six football fields. Leroy was almost at the fence. That meant a long walk to the nearest building and an even longer walk to the complex where Leroy worked. Leroy pulled out his phone and tapped an app to request an employee shuttle. This would call a drone cart to drive out to his location. Exercise is for idiots, thought Leroy with a smirk, and I'm no fool. He tapped the option to have the drone bring him coffee with extra cream. 'Drone Epislon ETA in 7:02' Leroy sighed. Seven minutes? They need more shuttles. He tapped his phone to play *Pluto Cats* while he waited. It was then that he noticed something shiny on the painted white divider next to his car. "Hello, what's this?"

#

"You said we wouldn't have to go in ourselves!" said Gwen, furiously pacing the length of the small motel room. "You said, they would install it for us. You also said something about bacon, which never made sense."

"Well, I was wrong. I mean, it did work—*partly*. We got in. Just not all the way in." Eddy was sitting on one of the motel room's two dilapidated queen beds. Despite having been there for three days, he still hadn't gotten used to the room's persistent odour of feet. They were staying at the Royal Dutchman Motor Inn. It was a relic of the 70s, complete with all of the original decor, along with a variety of wall and furniture stains added over the years. The motel had none of the amenities one might expect in even a budget accommodation. It did, however, have free WiFi and, bizarrely, accepted bitcoin. "We just need to get inside now to finish the job."

"You promised me we wouldn't break in."

"And we won't!"

"How?"

"I got us an appointment."

Two days later, Gwen pulled the red convertible to the side of the road. Close enough to study the sprawling corporate campus. Far enough to avoid drawing attention. They watched as a tractor trailer rolled through the security checkpoint. As instructed by the gate guard, the driver turned the eighteen-wheeler left and headed down a service road. The gate lowered back down. Hector, the guard on duty, sipped his coffee and returned to his book. A large sign outside the gate read, Majority Media Inc. Below that was the slogan that appeared on all their commercials, 'Because News *Is*'. They had paid Saatchi & Saatchi ten million dollars to come up with those three words. It was a typical Wednesday. The employee parking lot was packed with cars. In the distance, an uneven trickle of employees could be seen walking from building to building. Others sipped coffee at primary colour picnic tables, blue, yellow, and red. A few stood smoking e-cigarettes at side entrances.

"You're certain they won't recognize us?"

"No," said Eddy. "How could I be certain?"

Gwen shot him an annoyed glance. "That's not what I wanted to hear."

Eddy raised his hands. "Look, you saw for yourself, the virus wears off. Plus, I'm working on the assumption that the last place they'd look for us is here at their front door. The lion rarely expects the gazelle to show up in his den."

"That doesn't mean he won't eat it."

"Hmm, yes. I'm still working on that analogy," said Eddy. Over a dozen of the flash drives had found their way into company computers. Eddy had needed only one. Someone named Leroy Dent was the first. Rot Grub had quickly burrowed throughout the network, creating a tunnel for Eddy in the process. The plan had been to inject Holon remotely from the safety of the motel room. There was a problem. Rot Grub had been unable to penetrate a secondary internal firewall. Something identified only as 'O'. "That's where we need to be. It's a network within a network. It's not air-gapped, but it might as well be. It's impenetrable." Gwen asked him what that meant. "It means we need to get inside. I need physical access to a PC inside of O, whatever that is." Eddy had tried to project confidence at the time. He wasn't grinning now. Faced with the security gate, guard and the prospect of going to jail or worse, Eddy's confidence had vanished. His determination had not. "So what, we give up? Turn around?"

Gwen looked at Eddy in surprise. Her slight companion sat in the passenger seat of the Tesla with his arms crossed. She was surprised at his willingness to step into the lion's den at all. She remembered how scared Eddy had been when he'd climbed through her apartment window two weeks and a lifetime ago. A man with a mission, she decided. She was the one who was nervous. The plan involved breaking the law in any number of ways. The world had gone topsy-turvy. "No, let's do this," she said.

She drove them slowly up to the gate. "Names?" said Hector. The gate guard gave them a bored glance over his copy of *The Bitter Winds of Love*. Hector was on a life quest to read all of Barbara Cartland's books in order. This was no small task. The famed romance novelist was the third best selling author of all time after Agatha Christie and William Shakespeare. This was number eighteen. Only seven hundred and five left to go.

"Higgins," said Eddy. "And Dolittle."

The guard glanced at his monitor and nodded, "Eddy Higgins and Gwen Doolittle, got it. ID?"

Eddy produced the fake driver's licenses he'd laminated the night before on the floor of the motel room. Hector looked at the photos, then back at them. "*You* look like a developer," he said.

"You mean ruggedly handsome?" said Eddy.

"And I don't?" asked Gwen pointedly.

"Oh, um, I mean..." the Guard stammered nervously, realizing he'd said something HR would not approve of. "Go right ahead sir and ma'am. Chad will meet you by the big hippo." As Eddy opened his mouth to ask, the guard added, "It's impossible to miss."

It was impossible to miss the giant eighteen-foot tall pinstripe painted hippopotamus outside the main entrance to the Welcome Center. "We call her Bessie," said Chad. Chad Klabowski was the Human Resources

Talent Concierge Eddy had set up their appointment with. They found the recruiter standing beneath Bessie's open maw. Chad had thinning blond hair and tanner bronzed skin. He reminded Eddy of a TV game show host. "She was designed on commission by David Hockney. She's kind of a company mascot. This whole facility is called the Hippo Campus. It's a pun. Get it?"

"I get it," said Eddy.

"Follow me and I'll give you a brief tour on our way to my office," said Chad. "Segway, shuttle, or steps?"

"Is 'steps' the same as walking?" asked Gwen.

"Yes," said Chad.

"Let's do that," said Gwen.

"Steps it is," said Chad merrily, "It'll help me reach my daily goal!" With a spring in his step, Chad led the way through the sprawling Hippo Campus. As he did, he pointed out features like prizes. Chad thought the interview had been set up by one of Majority's head hunters. The truth was, Eddy had set it up himself. The partially successful hack with Rot Grub had gained him access to the company Exchange servers. He'd described themselves 'high value development talent'. Chad Klabowski had accordingly, rolled out the red carpet. "It's fifteen acres in total," said Chad proudly. "It includes parks, and restaurants, a gym, and dormitories. All free, of course."

"Of course."

"You'll never need to leave," said Chad.

"Who'd want to? Right, Gwen?"

"Uh-huh," said Gwen. She was out of her element. The cloying nature of their host had only unsettled her further. Eddy had tried to explain that Silicon Valley job interviews with top talent were obsequious affairs.

Highly skilled developers were treated like royalty. They were fawned over and offered lavish benefits in order to get them to sign on. Recruitment events could include sumptuous feasts and performances by major musical acts. Real rockstars performed for technology rockstars. It all played perfectly into the candidates' secretly harboured assumption that they were smarter and therefore better than everyone else. Eddy hadn't needed to pad his own resume. He simply changed the details to disguise his identity. Gwen's was a total fabrication. Eddy had to explain to her that a 'software architect' had nothing to do with buildings.

"So, across the campus there are twelve complexes in all," said Chad. "Each one is named after a famous general or other historical figure. Because that's what we're making here, history. On our left is the Cleopatra Complex, on our right is Jocasta"

"What's that one?" asked Gwen, pointing to a massive modern edifice that resembled a nautilus shell made of poured concrete.

"That's Adonis," said Chad. "You could end up working there. Many of our developers do. Or as we prefer to call them, *disrupters*."

"Where's the main building?"

"Ah, that's Napoleon. We're going there now."

"Is that where Mr. Machi is?"

"That's where his office is," said Chad. "But don't expect to see him. He's in a separate internal complex called 'O', like the letter. It's a complex within a complex. The C-Suites are there, as well as certain top level secret priority R&D. Mr. Machi believes in keeping his friends close and his developers closer." Ah-ha, thought Eddy, a building within a building. That explained why O didn't show up on any maps.

"I've heard he lives on campus. Is that true? Does he live in O?"

asked Gwen. She remembered this from a *60 Minutes* feature on Machi called *Emperor Recluse*. She'd seen it years ago. MCNX had since bought up CBS, rebranding the show as *Hour*. The episode had not been aired since.

"Mr. Machi has many residences around the world," said Chad. The wide green lawns reminded Eddy of walking through UCLA with Belinda. He hoped she was okay, but he dared not contact her. Eddy noticed the grass looked a little too perfect. He bent down and touched it. It was artificial. It was very good fake turf, but definitely fake. Chad and Gwen had walked on ahead. Chad continued to talk and point, unaware that Eddy had been left behind. He had to jog to catch up. They passed between two smaller buildings. Towering above them was a statue of a giant Rubik's cube. The top row, twenty feet across, was in mid-twist as if being solved by an invisible hand. All the faces, Eddy noted, were the same. It was then that Eddy saw the sprawling structure beyond. It was clearly the epicentre of the campus—a massive cluster of green glass domes and spires, surrounded by a two-story ring of glass. It instantly reminded Eddy of the Emerald City of Oz.

"We're not in Kansas anymore," said Gwen, echoing Eddy's thoughts.

"Is he here now?" asked Eddy. "Machi, I mean."

Chad turned and gave Eddy a stern look. "I'm sorry Mr. Higgins, it's not for me to discuss, know, or disseminate the whereabouts of our CEO and founder." He then smiled to make peace. "Perhaps, if you join our team, someday you will rise to a position where you can answer that question yourself. On that note, why don't we start with the application? Hmm? After that we can do the skills test." Chad turned and proceeded to the great glass building. Eddy started to follow. Gwen grabbed his arm. "Skills test?" she hissed.

"Don't worry. You'll be fine."

An hour later, Eddy and Gwen were seated in Chad's office. It was a small room with frosted glass walls. Occasionally, they could see employees walking past, but they appeared only as shades dimly visible beyond the veil. Eddy and Gwen, seated in two comfortable armchairs, faced Chad from across his desk. Gwen was drumming her fingers nervously. On the desk was an iron statuette of Sonic the Hedgehog made out of Minecraft cubes, which in turn were made out of Tetris blocks. On the wall behind him was a framed inspirational poster of a lone lemming leaping into space above the word 'Believe'. On the way to his office, Chad had pointed out the features of Napoleon. These mostly consisted of shared cubicles and meeting rooms partitioned by glass. Chad called the cubicles 'focus points' and the meeting rooms 'interaction spaces'. The highlight of the tour was the food court. There, TV and film star Chris O'Donnell was busing tables for the day. "It's a thing we do to make our employees feel more valued," explained Chad. "Celebrity of the day dining staff. They're actors, so most of them already know how to wait on tables."

"I heard Google got Ryan Gosling," said Eddy.

"To make an appearance. We have them work the full shift, in character. What Google does is fake. The point is, here at Majority, you the developers are the real stars."

Chad leaned over his glass touch-top desktop reviewing Eddy and Gwen's resumés. Eddy had put into the appointment notes that they came as a set and must be interviewed together. It was an unusual condition, but far from the oddest request Chad had been asked to accommodate for top talent. More than once, Chad had had interviewees bring 'comfort' animals in with

*346*

them. Twice, he'd been attacked, once by a comfort ferret who mistook Chad for a rat, and once by the person being comforted. "So Mr. Higgins, what did you do for Symantec?"

"I spearheaded an initiative that resulted in them developing a whole new class of antivirus monitoring," said Eddy. This was more or less true, except for the part about him working for them.

"Excellent," said Chad. "and what about you, Ms. Doolittle?"

"I, um, wrote some... code?" she said the word tentatively as if unsure it fit.

"Oh, good, very good. In what language? Java, C++, C#, Objective-C, .Net, PHP, JavaScript, Rust, Swift, Python, Tensor Flow, Haskell, OWL, Babel...?"

"Yes."

"Yes to...?"

"All of them?"

"*All* of them?"

"All of them."

"Oh well, excellent then! I see why you came so highly recommended." Chad made notes on his laptop. He looked at Eddy. "She knows even more than you do."

"Apparently."

"Well then," said Chad with a clap, "let's get you set up for the test."

Eddy had assured Gwen that she probably knew as much or more about programming than any HR person would. "He'll just be looking at a list. I was once asked by HR if I knew someone named 'Ruby'." Eddy snorted, before realizing Gwen didn't get the joke. He started to explain that Ruby on Rails was a web application framework, then stopped. "Anyway, after that they'll want some manager and developers to talk to you. They'll actually know you don't know anything, so we'll need to act before then." What Eddy hadn't anticipated was the skills test. Those usually came later.

Chad picked Gwen first and ushered her over to a terminal set up in the corner. He logged her in and explained that first there would be a series of psychological questions, followed by cognitive puzzles, followed by actual coding problems. "You get to pick the language to solve it in, but since you know all of them, have fun! And remember, we encourage outside the box thinking."

It was at that moment that Eddy clubbed Chad over the head with Sonic the Hedgehog. The sculpture exploded into its smallest constituent components—magnetized metal pixels. "Ow!" shouted Chad, reeling under the impact and falling to his knees.

"Sorry!" said Eddy. He felt sick to his stomach.

"What the Hell are you doing?" said Gwen.

"I'm knocking him out!" said Eddy. "Or trying too. As we agreed." Despite being flustered, Eddy realized there was no backing out now and hit Chad again with the base of the statuette.

"Ah!" screamed Chad. "Stop it!" The HR director fell to the floor, dazed but still conscious.

"I didn't agree to violence!" said Gwen. "When you said you were going to 'knock him out'; I thought it was some kind of hacker jargon."

"Well, I need access to his computer and I didn't think he'd say 'yes'. Plus your skills test was about to expose us anyway."

"You said, I was going to be fine! I thought that meant you'd hack me a good score."

"No, it meant I was going to bonk him on the head first so you wouldn't have to take it!"

"That's not what 'you'll be fine' means!"

"Please..." said Chad, rising unsteadily to his feet. "I have a daughter..."

"This isn't right," said Gwen.

"I know," said Eddy. "I keep hitting him and he won't knock out. He must have a very hard head."

Gwen yanked the statue base from Eddy's hand. "Well, you're not hitting him again!"

Eddy hesitated. Chad put his hands together as if in prayer. Eddy sighed. "You're right. I'm worried we might knock his skull in."

"There must be something else we can do," said Gwen.

A few minutes later, they had bound and gaged Chad with duct tape and power cords and stuffed him into a storage unit behind his desk. Given the alternative, the HR director was quite amenable to being tied up and even offered suggestions. "I'm a volunteer Cub Scout master on weekends," he explained, "I know all about knots. I recommend a double half hitch." Eddy then logged into Chad's PC. He cancelled all the recruiter's appointments, including theirs, and booked Chad's calendar with fake ones. "That should keep anyone from finding him for a few hours at least." Eddy then rifled through Chad's drawers. "Ah ha!" he said, holding up a stack of blank employee ID badges. Eddy created valid IDs for himself and Gwen with highest level privileges. These included access to O.

"Thank-you for stopping me there," said Eddy. "I feel terrible."

Gwen nodded. "I understand. You're trying to help."

"Yeah."

"But don't do it again."

*Spyware*

"Okay."

## 2.7

"Location, location, location." – P. Montesquieu

// Washington, DC — now

It didn't help that the world had gone mad. There were riots now in every major city for no apparent reason. People were tearing each other limb from limb. Lockdowns and curfews were now the norm. It was clearly getting worse and no one knew why. Washington was in crisis. More so than usual. Even if nobody knew the cause of it all, they knew who to blame— each other. Still, the show must go on. Despite the madness elsewhere, the madness here in DC continued unabated. It had been a challenging few weeks for Congresswoman Annabelle Flatwood. Reversing her political position had made her more enemies than friends. That said, her new friends had lots of money to donate to her campaign and influence too. The only problem with her new friends was that she didn't actually like them. Her old friends, some of whom still were friends personally, were baffled by her change of heart. "This isn't you," said Karen Lee, Representative from Indiana. Karen should know. She and Anne went back years, having been freshmen together. "I know it's not for the money. I know it's not for power. It's certainly not because you're actually friends with Classlessness," said Karen, referring to Cassius by their private nickname for him. "So why?" The truth was, Anne didn't quite understand it herself. Plenty of politicians believed one thing privately and did another publicly, but Anne had always taken pride in being true to herself. "I'd rather damn the consequences than damn myself," she'd say. That was then; this was today. Today was the day of the big vote. At least, she'd finally be able to put the whole ruddy business behind her. The Majority Bill would pass, people would write angry editorials, and life would continue. Democracy would still be alive tomorrow. After that, who knew?

The day hadn't started well. Her speech for the Cuthboard Commerce Club at the Washington Ritz Carlton Hotel was supposed to be boring. She knew the press would follow her wherever she went today. She'd considered hiding out in her office until the vote but decided that would only look cowardly. A speech about trade should be just dull enough to lull everyone to sleep. That was the plan anyway. Everything went according to plan until the Congresswoman reached the first applause line of her speech. No one knew who had installed the Clappers in every light fixture in the hotel ballroom. All they knew was that the chandeliers began blinking on and off like strobe lights in a disco. The audience was confused. Some thought it was part of the show. Others assumed it was an electrical problem. It was only when Anne reached the second applause line that it began to dawn on the attendees that *they* were the cause of the flickering. Some began to clap more tentatively, as if trying to confirm this. A few clapped more vigorously, secretly delighted at causing mayhem. The room began to flash like a discotheque. An older African American man pitched sideways off his chair in an induced epileptic fit. Hotel staff and nearby guests rushed to help the hedge fund manager as he thrashed about on the maroon carpet. Two of the would-be rescuers collided into one another in a moment of darkness, sending them to the floor—one out cold. The applause stopped. Unfortunately, it stopped with the lights off. Anne stood at the podium, as confused as the audience. People began lighting the room with their cellphones. The room was a sea of glowing rectangles. Press photographers gleefully began snapping photos. The event was cancelled for safety reasons. Anne's assistant Janet ushered her off stage.

So it was that they'd ended up in Anne's office anyway. The snow was gone. The fire in the fireplace was out. Anne sat at her large oak desk, wondering how she'd come to be here. She felt dazed. She tried to pin down the thoughts in her head. *Cognitive dissonance* she knew was when people believe two contradictory things at the same time. She wasn't sure what she thought anymore. A knock at the door startled Anne from her stupor. "What is it?"

Janet stepped into the Congresswoman's office as she had thousands of times before. Anne could instantly see something was different this time. Something was wrong. "I wanted to let you know; I've arranged a car to take you to the hill in time for the vote."

"Not too early?"

"No, I know you don't want to face anyone."

"It's not that I..." Anne let it go. She knew Janet strongly disapproved of her change of position over the Majority Bill. Janet wasn't just an employee; she was a friend. Her assistant couldn't fathom what had changed the Congresswoman's mind. Whenever Anne tried to explain, she spoke only in talking points. "It's like someone copy-pasted Cassius's words into your mouth."

That was days ago. Today, Janet calmly announced, "A group have claimed responsibility for the clappers in the ballroom."

"A terrorist group?"

"*Clowns for Democracy*. I'm not sure they qualify as terrorists. They call themselves humourists."

"Aren't those the same people who flooded the Congressional hearing room with helium?"

"Yes. The FBI is investigating."

At the time, Anne and Janet had laughed over the incident known as Donald Duck-gate. It resulted in members of Congress talking in high-pitch voices during a live hearing on C-Span. She still remembered the sight of Richard Billings of Kansas imploring everyone to "Remain calm!"—*in the voice of Alvin the Chipmunk*. Instead of laughing, Janet now looked sad. Somehow, Anne had become the butt of the joke. Janet lingered at the door. "Is there anything else?" asked the Congresswoman.

"Just this," Janet stepped forward and solemnly laid a letter on the Congresswoman's desk. "It says I'm resigning." Anne opened her mouth to object. Janet continued, "Effective immediately. I'm sorry about the lack of notice. I've arranged for a temp. Don't try to talk me out of it."

Anne stared at her. How had it come to this? They had fought in the trenches together. They had stayed up until two am together, holding hands while watching election results roll in. "It's just a bill about media ownership. Most people aren't even paying attention," said Anne. "It's 'inside baseball'."

"You once said it was about controlling the mind of the electorate."

"Yes, well..."

"You've a visitor waiting in reception."

"What? I thought I said no appointments today."

"Yeah. Sorry about that." Janet turned and left. For a moment, the Congresswoman stared after her. She wanted to pursue her. She wanted to implore her to stay. She didn't. She felt as if someone had transplanted her head. She heard the outside door close. Anne was alone. No, wait, the visitor. Who? Anne stood up and checked herself in the mirror. She looked exactly like herself. She went to the door and opened it to the waiting area opposite Janet's now empty desk. A man with thinning grey hair, wearing a purple duffle coat two sizes too big, looked back at her. His eyes were sunken in whirlpools of sorrow. Having seen the world, they were now trying to retreat back into his head. "Welcome," said Anne. "Come in."

Congresswoman Flatwood gestured to the armchair opposite her desk as she took her own seat. She'd had the visitor chairs made grander than her own. "I don't want to appear a queen or lord," she'd said at the time. "I am a servant of the people in my district." This man had such an air of defeat about him that the ample chair only diminished him further. "Do I know you?" asked Anne.

"Jacob Truman. From the press pool maybe," he said, looking about nervously. "I never asked you a question though."

"You're a reporter?"

"I was. For MCNX."

"I see, well, I'm not conducting interviews today. If you–"

"I live in Clifton, North Carolina."

"Oh. Okay..." Anne was puzzled. Why had Janet set up this meeting? She knew Anne didn't want to do any interviews. This man wasn't a constituent. The only reason Anne had even heard of Clifton was because of the unfortunate events of the past year. Like Flint, Michigan before it, the entire town of Clifton had woke up one morning to learn their water supply was contaminated with lead. "Is this to do with the water crisis?"

The man nodded. He appeared hesitant, as if unsure how to proceed.

"I'm very sorry for what happened there," said Anne. "I'm a strong supporter of tighter water regulation, but it's really a municipal or state issue. I'm not sure how I can help you."

"My baby girl drank that water from the day she was born."

"Oh dear."

"Neurological impairment," they call it. "Developmentally

delayed."

"I'm so sorry."

"I could have stopped it."

"What? No, it's not the fault of parents. It's the fault of the elected officials who first created the problem then covered it up. No one else knew what—"

"*I knew.*"

Anne stared at him. The man refused to meet her gaze. Instead, he kept wringing his hands nervously as if trying to wash them. "You knew?"

"We all knew. At least we should have. We didn't really think about it, I guess. We just went to war, as usual."

"What do you mean?"

"It was our people. Our guys. The politicians, the officials. Our team. So, we did what we always did. We defended. We attacked. We questioned the evidence. We discredited the whistle blower. It wasn't much of a fight really. We own that town. We report, they... believe. We needed to win. I never stopped to consider that it might all be true. They... we..." He hung his head in shame. "*I* poisoned my daughter's brain."

Anne sank back into her chair. Usually, she faced constituents, lobbyists, business persons, or fellow politicians, asking for something. This man was none of the above. "What do you want from me Mr. Truman?"

"Want? Nothing. Your assistant Janet asked me to come. We met at one of your events a few years back. I was still a reporter then."

Anne studied the crushed man before her. An odd image flashed through the Congresswoman's mind. It was the scene of natives in a jungle somewhere, shot in red and blue duotone. They were applying war paint and sharpening wooden spears. Anne shook her head, forcing herself to focus. Jacob Truman appeared to have shrunk even further since their conversation had begun. She wondered if eventually he might shrink away to nothing. "I had nothing to do with what happened in your state," said Anne.

"I know. I told you; it was *my* fault." He put his hand over his face. Tears streamed down his cheeks. Anne offered him a tissue. He waved it away. "You know, before I was a journalist, I was in the army."

"Thank-you for your service."

"I was prepared to fight and die for my country. Now? Now, I just don't know how this could happen here. Lead in the water. Half my neighbours are hooked on drugs anyway, so what does it matter? We're a land of zombies. Except, we're eatin' our own brains. It's like... It's like I don't know my own home anymore. The America I knew has up and left."

"Mr. Truman, I can assure you–"

Abruptly, the man stood up at attention. He turned to the map of the United States hanging on the Congresswoman's office wall. He saluted. "So long, whoever you are!"

## 2.8

"I'm sorry, Dave. I'm afraid I can't do that." – Siri

"Easy as 3.14," said Eddy, although he didn't believe it. He and Gwen had walked past the cubicles of the outer ring as if they belonged there. Few workers looked up as they passed. A woman with flaming red hair tended an aquarium populated entirely with seahorses. The truth was; Eddy wasn't sure what they were getting themselves into. He'd been unable to access any floor plans for Napoleon online. To the outside world, it was as if O didn't exist. Yet here it was. They approached a tall steel double doorway. The otherwise featureless doors were engraved with semi-circles that formed an O when closed. Looking down from above, a mounted security camera watched them approach like a third eye. The first two eyes belonged to a stoney-faced security guard. He looked down from behind a black oblong desk as high as a judge's bench. The guard's high cheek bones, heavy brow and ashen pallor reminded Eddy of Boris Karloff. "Damn it," muttered Eddy under his breath. "I was hoping it was all automated."

"So what now?" said Gwen.

"We continue to act like we own the place," said Eddy with what he hoped sounded like confidence. This would require another feat of 'social engineering'. Many of the most famous and successful hacks in history involved exploiting people instead of machines. Hacking legend Kevin Mitnick, aka the Condor, used social engineering as his primary tactic. Mostly that meant talking to people. It sometimes also meant digging through their trash. These crude techniques allowed him to break into major corporations and government systems alike. Despite being a rather mediocre programmer, Mitnick became the most notorious cyber criminal of his time. Eddy wasn't that kind of hacker. His social awkwardness meant that he doubted his ability to fool any of the people even some of the time. He assumed he'd be fine at the trash digging part. Still, he recognized the efficacy of Mitnik's approach. Humans never expect to be hacked themselves. The first rule of social engineering was: never appear evasive. That meant, rather than avoiding security, they should approach it directly. "Let me do the talking," he said.

"Fine with me," said Gwen. She hated the idea of breaking in to begin with. The fact that Eddy had assaulted Chad went against everything she believed in. This can't be happening, she thought, it's all madness. She turned to look at the bobbing sea horses in the nearby tank. She wondered if it was true that the male seahorses were the ones who got pregnant.

"Good morning," said Eddy, holding up his passcard. "My first day here. Do I just swipe?" Eddy knew he couldn't pass himself off as a regular employee. He had to assume the guard worked here every day and would know Eddy was new. Boris Karloff's eyes narrowed with suspicion. Eddy slid his card through the reader. Gwen reached over and did the same. The guard peered down at the monitor built into his desk. Eddy became aware of two tiny cameras pointed at him from the desktop. That was the 3D facial recognition, he assumed. Eddy had created their passcards in Chad's office. He had also created fake employee accounts, complete with photos. He had even used the stereographic camera he'd found in Chad's desk to scan their faces. We should check out just fine, he thought. Eddy hoped Chad wasn't too uncomfortable, stuffed into his storage unit. Mostly, he hoped the HR director was still there.

The dour security guard's heavy brow furrowed. He spoke with a gravelly voice. "Neither of you are on the list," he said.

"The list?" said Eddy, his voice catching nervously.

"This morning's list of new employees."

"Oh..." said Eddy, "*That* list." Eddy flushed. His confidence vaporized. Damn it, he thought, they must have a protocol for informing security of changes. Since his and Gwen's passes were mere minutes old, the guard could hardly have been informed of them at the start of his shift. "Somebody made a mistake, I suppose," said Eddy with a weak chuckle. "Oops."

"Yes," said the guard with a stern gaze, "*somebody* did."

Eddy smiled weakly. Was it time to run? Boris Karloff's hand moved to pick up his desk phone. That's not good, thought Eddy.

"Applejack? Rainbow Dash?" said Gwen.

The guard's hand halted. "Pinkie Pie. How did you know?"

"Your tat," said Gwen with a bright smile. As the guard had reached, his sleeve had hiked slightly, exposing a tiny tattoo of a cartoon pony on his wrist. "You doing Bronycon?"

"Already registered," said the guard, his gaunt visage brightening noticeably. "You?"

"I've never been! Can you believe it?" Much to Eddy's amazement, Gwen actually pouted.

"You should, you should!" said the guard. "Who's yours?"

"I'm a Twilight Sparkle kind of girl. Anyway, isn't Bronycon full?"

"I know someone who can get you in. His friend is a friend of Faust's cousin," said the security guard, referring to the cult cartoon's creator. The guard's hand now redirected to pick up his pen and notepad. "I'll give you his email." Eddy watched the pink pony eraser on the pen's top dance about as the guard wrote. "There you are," he said with a smile that was earnest, yet somehow still frightening.

"Thank-you sooo much!" said Gwen like an excited school girl.

Minutes later, Gwen and Eddy padded silently down the slate grey carpeted hallway of O.

"What the Hell was that?" he asked.

"He's a Brony," said Gwen matter-of-factly.

"And that is...?"

"An adult fanboy of the cartoon *My Little Pony: Friendship is Magic*. It's a thing. Trust me, I know."

"How do you know?"

"I sent away a guy who was a Brony. He murdered seven sorority sisters and carved the pony's names into their foreheads. He also wrote 'friendship is magic' in their blood. Most Bronies aren't homicidal maniacs, they're just odd."

"That explains it," said Eddy. "For a second I thought you'd out-geeked me."

"That's never going to happen."

Eddy knew that hundreds of people worked in the O Complex. Despite this, the ground floor seemed deserted. The monumental austerity of the interior echoed that sentiment, along with their footfalls. Marble the colour of graphite formed the walls and two-story ceiling. The sides were interspersed with monolithic seamless steel doors that forbade entry. As they walked the long great avenue, they passed adjoining corridors, none of which appeared any more promising than the one they were in. Despite the modern minimalism, the interior reminded Eddy of an ancient temple or tomb. He wondered if O stood for oppressive.

"Where are we going?" said Gwen.

Eddy studied the featureless doors as they passed. "We need to find an unattended desk with an unattended computer," he said. "These doors are too dangerous. We don't know what we're walking into." At the end of the hall was a bank of elevators. These too had stainless steel doors. "We go up. The higher up you go in a building, the more insulated the people feel. The more insulated they feel, the more lax they get about security. Plus, offices higher up might have higher access."

"Do you know that?"

"It's *Social Engineering for Dummies*," said Eddy. This was true. The book included it as one of its 'Hackable Hints'. Eddy tapped the up-button on the middle elevator. "If you've better ideas..."

"Nope," said Gwen. As she said this, she crossed her arms and looked about. Where was everyone? This wasn't a James Bond villain's hideout. Real people worked here. They had to. Despite the danger of being discovered, part of her wanted to see some sign of life. It's like hanging out in a mausoleum, she thought. The elevator doors opened with a soft chime. Eddy stepped inside. Gwen took a last look around. Featureless corridors branched to either side of the elevators. Fifty feet down, they branched symmetrically again. At the corner of the second branch she saw it. A shadow that seemed out of place, cast by something around the corner. Something, or...?

"Coming?" asked Eddy.

"I don't like this. It's all been too easy."

*Voomp!* The elevator doors slammed shut.

"Okay, that's better."

"Gwen!" Eddy shouted. Elevator doors didn't close like that. He tried to pry them open with his fingers, but could gain no purchase. He frantically tapped the Open button. The button blinked but did nothing. Unbidden, the elevator plummeted downwards as if its cable had been cut—then stopped. The lurch threw Eddy to the floor. "Help!" he yelled.

"Eddy!" Gwen stood on the other side of the closed elevator doors. She frantically tapped the Up and Down buttons to no effect. "Eddy!" Nothing. Terrified, she turned to look for the unsettling shadow. Three men now stood there, facing her at the corridor's end. They wore identical black suits, ties, shoes and white shirts. They all had slicked back hair. They wore red lens sunglasses. Each of the men also held what appeared to be square matte black metal batons. They held them like nightsticks. They were identical to the Men in Rose Coloured glasses who had come to Gwen's apartment weeks earlier. It was impossible to know if they were the same men or copies. Gwen glanced down the way she and Eddy had come. Three more MRCGs stood there in identical black suits, wearing identical hematic lenses and holding identical black batons. As Gwen stared, the three as one raised the batons and switched them on. They were flashlights of a sort—red laser projectors capable of rendering complex animated images. They reminded Gwen of the Laser Pink Floyd Shows her Dad dragged her to when she was little. They traced brilliant interwoven patterns. The patterns crisscrossed along the walls and floor like tesseracts gobbling spiderwebs spun of light that moved, jittered, and leapt. Part of her felt powerfully compelled to watch the patterns—to let them bundle her up and carry her away. She tried not to look. *Thunk... Thunk... Thunk...* The ceiling lights in the great hall thirty feet above began to turn off in order, starting from the far end. *Thunk... Thunk... Thunk...* The procession reached the MRCGs and plunged them into near darkness. The effect left them as a trio of blacker than black silhouettes while making the beams of their laser lines sear the air with crimson brilliance. The etched light sliced and scarred her consciousness. *No!* a part of her screamed, *Danger! Look away!* She imagined Eddy's voice shouting in her ear, *Beware the MRCGs! Beware the*

*Men in Rose Coloured Glasses!* Gwen could see from the corner of her eye the three MRCGs who had first appeared on the side corridor. They too were in darkness, emitting crisscrossed beams of brain bisecting red energy.

Somehow, Gwen wrenched herself free. She turned to look down the only available avenue left. She fully expected to find this remaining retreat similarly blocked by MRCGs. Instead, it was empty and still lit—an island of illumination in the void. Seeing no other options, Gwen hurtled headlong down the marble corridor towards it.

The entire floor plan, from what she could tell, was symmetrical. This corridor branched as well. It was as if the architect had been more intent on order than purpose. When she reached the intersection, she looked to the right. That way was darkness, save for emergency floor lights—a dashed marquee of illuminated squares that led directly to the feet of three more silhouettes and three more pairs of ruby glasses. In unison, the three projectors began to render roiling red laser kaleidoscopes across every surface. *Don't look!* Gwen tore herself away again before the hypnotic pull could ensnare her. She looked the other way. It was the only way left. That hallway was well lit and empty. Once more, Gwen plunged down the only available avenue of escape. A realization penetrated her petrified mind. *I'm being herded!*

As certain as she was of that thought, she was equally certain of the next one. *I have no other choice.* The trap is sprung. The deer is caught in the pincer movement of the wolf pack. There is no escape. Throwing a glance over her shoulder only confirmed her fears. Three of the MRCGs were following her. Their pace was unhurried. They walked with the calm deliberation of a horror movie murderer whose victim inexplicably starts tripping over her own feet. Gwen wasn't tripping, but it hardly mattered. The hunters had no concerns their prey might escape. She was running blind, shielding her eyes from the patterns traced on the walls around her. The ceiling lights continued to switch off behind her, cutting off retreat. *Thunk...*

*thunk... thunk...* Darkness followed. Gwen turned a corner. This corridor was different from the rest. Instead of more relentless grey marble, one wall was made of glass. Behind the glass was a sizeable room, well lit, filled with rows of stacked 1U server arrays. LED lights blinked and pulsed with activity. The lights in the hallway directly above her switched off. *Thunk!* The bright light of the server room flooded into the hall. This single source of illumination set everything else into stark relief. The brightness beckoned her. *Refuge! Come to the light!* Of course, it was a trap, but still... Gwen looked down the corridor past the brightness. She saw them there. The three MRCGs stood immutable, blocking her way forward. Were they new ones? Or the first three come around another way? It hardly mattered. As Gwen stared at them, they switched on their projector beams. They aimed them at their own feet, where the lasers repeatedly traced infinity symbols like lassos, round and round. They're holding their fire, Gwen thought, they know it's enough. She didn't need to look behind her to know the other three were still there. They too would be standing, waiting for her to do what was expected—what was *required.* The door to the server room was just a few feet away. Fine, she thought, it doesn't matter. I'd rather step into the light than die in the dark. There's nothing for me here. There was a passcard lock to the side, and a camera overhead. A red LED turned green. Gwen's access had been granted by an invisible hand. It was a choiceless choice. Gwen pulled on the chrome handle. The well-balanced door swung open easily. She stepped inside.

The interior was bright to the point of dazzling. It was also cold. The air conditioning was set to keep the electronics in optimal conditions. Gwen remembered an office IT guy telling her once, "People like it warm, machines like it cool." Even in her panicked state, the irony did not escape Gwen that she was in the midst of so many computers. *The damage Eddy could have inflicted here!* But, then again, their hosts clearly knew who she and Eddy were. They had not been separated by accident. We thought we were so clever, she thought. *Will you walk into my parlour? said the Spider to the Fly.* Gwen tried the one doorway in the room. She found it to be a janitor's closet complete with yellow roller bucket and mop. She turned back to the wall of glass. Six Men in Rose Coloured Glasses stood facing her now. Their white shirts and pale faces floated in the darkness that otherwise swallowed them. Gwen tried to discern some difference between them. She found none. Clones? Robots? Or had they somehow lost their individuality? Six pairs of red lenses reflected an infernal version of herself. If they felt pleasure at cornering her, they showed none—only cool deliberation. Gwen had expected them to turn their deadly projectors on, to infect her brain with the viruses they drew. She had planned on closing her eyes. She would make them force her lids open rather than surrender. She would hit, bite, kick and scream. But no. Instead, the mirror men switched off their devices. They appeared to be waiting. For what? Gwen considered smashing the servers. Perhaps, she could do some damage before they killed her. No, she realized, they would never have led her into a room where she could do real harm. There would be backups of backups. They would lose only easily replaced hardware. Eddy had called it *'ghosting'*. They would have ghosts of the machines that could be restored in minutes, good as new. Nothing in here mattered to them—least of all herself.

That was when she heard the door lock—*click!*

The next sound was a sharp *hiss*. It was the sound of air being sucked through vents in the ceiling. A synthesized woman's voice said, "Server Room fire test commencing. Oxygen evacuation in process. Warning: no personnel should be in the affected area."

Gwen looked about in panic. She saw a series of meters beside the door labeled Oxygen, Carbon Monoxide, Carbon Dioxide, Freon and Cyanide. The bar labeled Oxygen was rapidly falling out of the white area towards the red. She cast about for other options. The vents in the ceiling were bolted shut and too small to squeeze through anyway.

The woman's voice continued, "If you are in the affected area, notify your supervisor immediately or file an appropriate grievance complaint with Human Resources."

Gwen saw movement out of the corner of her eye. A robot vacuum the size of a cat was gliding back and forth under the server shelves. It appeared to hover as it carried out its pointless task. There was not a speck of dust to be seen on the gleaming stainless steel grill floor. Gwen moved to intercept the robot vacuum's path. She picked it up. The robot spun its small wheels like an overturned beetle. It began to complain with a series of beeps. Gwen hurled it at the glass wall. The robot vacuum bounced off, hit the wall and landed on the floor upside down. A spring-loaded lever flipped the robot over. It resumed vacuuming. Neither the robot nor the window appeared harmed. The Men in Rose Coloured Glasses had failed to even flinch as the robot ricocheted inches from their faces. "Damn it," said Gwen. For the first time, she could sense the thinning oxygen in the air.

"If this incident has resulted in a Class D event," the woman's voice continued, "please be sure to check 'deceased' in the appropriate field. Failure to do so may result in your claim being rejected and you will have to start the complaint process again."

Gwen decided she needed something heavier to break the glass. She tried to lift one of the servers from the racks, only to discover it had been bolted in place. She looked about desperately and spotted a tool set attached to the wall. She grabbed a handful of small screwdrivers, found one that fit and begin unscrewing one of the servers. She stole a quick glance at the pale assassins. They had not moved. She imagined a faint curl of amusement on their slit thin lips.

"Please note, death will change your status from employee to non-employee. This will make you ineligible to file your grievance on the employee intranet. Family members may file on your behalf, provided they have access to the employee intranet, and informing them does not violate your non-disclosure agreement or NDA. If this occurs, all complaints and claims will be rejected and you will have to start the complaint process again. Remember, O-Plex clearances means that even informing your family where you work or died violates your NDA. In the event of an NDA violation all complaints and claims will be rejected automatically."

Gwen easily removed three of the four bolts. The last was stuck. She turned the screwdriver with both hands and realized it was only stripping the metal head. "Damn it!" she said. She'd begun to feel light-headed. Speaking made her swoon. When it became clear the last bolt would not turn, Gwen gave up and moved onto the server immediately below. These bolts turned with difficulty, but she was able to free all four. She began to gasp. Her strength felt sapped. Gwen tried to lift the server only to drop it when the cables behind yanked taut. "Ahhh!"

"It should also be noted that, as an employee, you agreed to third party arbitration to resolve any disputes or legal concerns. If you do not recall agreeing to this agreement, feel welcome to contact your HR representative. Prior to contacting your HR representative, you will be required to agree to the afore mentioned terms and conditions. Requesting these terms and conditions constitutes consent."

Gwen panted as she unscrewed the power and networking cables. She felt as if she were moving in slow motion, swimming weakly through molasses, trying to breathe empty space. Her head swam. *Must do this!* she thought. She spent every last ounce of strength lifting the solid steel server out of its tray and above her head. For a moment, Gwen thought she might topple backwards when the weight of the server tilted. She caught herself and hurled the heavy hardware at the glass wall that divided her from the grim faces beyond. The computer frame crashed into the glass with a *clang!* It rebounded off and landed back inside the room. The glass shook from the impact but did not shatter. Only a single white pock mark showed where the impact had occurred. Once again, the assassins on the other side showed no reaction to the violence hurled at them. *They knew,* thought Gwen. She staggered drunkenly. They knew I never had a chance. She saw that her fingertips were now blue. Oh, she thought, I get it now. She stumbled but caught herself on a metal shelf frame. She sank to her knees. "Did that amuse you?" She yelled at the stone faced men. "Don't you at least..." Gwen gasped, holding herself up with one arm. Her thoughts began to unravel and repeat. "Don't you at least..." Her arm grew weak. She used the last of her dissipating strength to lower herself gently to the cold metal grillwork floor. "Don't you at least..." She laid down. She didn't see her life flash before her eyes. Instead, she recalled watching a Nature special on PBS. A wolf caught a deer. The doe's throat was in the wolf's jaws. The rest of the pack circled round. Intense yellow eyes with pin prick pupils watched. The British narrator described it all with scientific detachment. After a valiant fight, the deer accepted her fate. She laid down in the tall grass and seemed oddly serene and detached. Shock was her one mercy. The predators began to tear the skin from her body. They quarrelled over who should get her hind leg, yanking her brutally as her eyes glazed. Gwen struggled to complete her sentence. "...owe me a smile?"

The door lock *clicked* open.

One of the MRCGs turned Gwen's lolled head over with an Oxford shoe tip. Her eyes stared blankly into space. "They say the eyes are the windows to the soul," he said.

A second MRCG peered over his shoulder and nodded in agreement. "Windows are just doors you need to climb through."

## 2.9

"It's an original copy." - A. Warhol

For a long time, Eddy just sat there. The elevator doors remained closed. The buttons did nothing. The Muzak continued to play. Eddy recognized the tune, but couldn't for the life of him place it. He snapped his fingers. "*Hot Pants Explosion* by the B-52s," he said. Several more minutes passed. *Ting!* The elevator doors opened. Eddy was still on the floor of the elevator, so he found himself looking up at the two MRCGs waiting there.

"Step aside, Oofus and Dootus!" The stone-faced assassins parted to make way for a fourteen-year-old boy with curly blonde hair. He wore a Minecraft t-shirt, blue jeans and a permanent sneer. He looked down at Eddy, took a suck from a pixie stick, and smirked. "Guess we really did build a better Mouse trap, huh? Get up."

Eddy rose to his feet. He now looked down at the teenager. This was not simply because of their age difference. The boy was small. His ego, clearly, was not. "Who are you?" asked Eddy.

"You don't recognize me? I'm hurt, Mouse."

Eddy shelved the theory he'd been forming that James Machi had somehow made himself younger, or transplanted his brain into the body of a boy. "Strauss?"

"Ha! You know me better as Blowfish." The boy turned on his heels, tossed aside the empty pixie stick straw, and headed down the wide corridor. "Walk with me." The two MRCGs who had been haunting Eddy's nightmares, stood motionless as if unplugged. Eddy walked after the juvenile hacker. As soon as he did, the MRCGs fell in behind, flanking him. The hospital white walls quickly gave way to glass dividing panes beyond which were workspaces stacked with cubicles. In each, teenagers and younger boys sat at consoles, typing away. Each paused intermittently to down cans of Freek Out Energy drink and fistfuls of Skittles. On their screens, Eddy recognized the familiar look of software code editors with their auto-indented text formatted in candy colours. "Child soldiers," Blowfish explained without looking back. "The best kind for this sort of war. The most leet skills. The fewest hangups."

Eddy decided not to point out that Blowfish was the same age. "Hang ups? You mean ethics?"

"I mean hangups. You're an old man here, Mouse. A geriatric, in fact. But, you got skill. That's why you're here."

"Really? I thought I was here to die."

"Nobody dies here. Not technically anyway."

As they walked, four technicians in white lab coats passed them the other way. The men were chatting and laughing while passing about a bag of Cheetos. Another day at the office, Eddy realized. "So, why am I here, and where's my friend?"

"Your friend is seriously hot, dude," said Blowfish. "Oh man. You hittin' that thang?"

"Ah, no."

"Mind if I do?"

"She might have something to say about that."

"I'm not asking her." Blowfish stopped in front a steel door labeled 'Otomy'. "Here we are. So, basically, we'd like to offer you a job."

"A job?"

"Now, I know what you're thinking. What? Has Blowfish really sold out and gone corporate? Well, the answer is... yes. Yes, but for some seriously sick dollar signs. We're talkin' mega moola, and benefits, and this is the best part; you get to work on the coolest stuff you've ever worked on in your life. That's right, we're hacking the best hardware on the planet. Which is to say *wetware*. You know what I'm talking about, right?"

"Human brains."

"Exactly."

"There are mobs of people killing each other out there, Blowfish. People are dying. Haven't you seen the news?"

"See? Hang ups. I warned 'em. Anyway, the coolness makes up for the cruelness, biatch. What what! Seriously, no one else is doing this but us. We p'wn this world! That makes us the leet o' the leet. Let me introduce you to the Chief Architect. And don't worry, he's even more ancient than you. We're talkin' antediluvian in da house." Blowfish turned to the steel door. "lojmIt yIpoSmoH," he said. Eddy recognized the Klingon word for 'open'. The door slid open. Eddy noticed a tiny camera above the door. More biometric facial recognition, he assumed.

The door opened to another world. Inside was a massive two-story interior. It had the scale of a factory floor but the pristine white, chrome, and glass surfaces of a laboratory. It was also a room filled with smaller rooms. The layout was a crisscross grid of avenues between glass chambers on raised platforms. Each of the transparent cells was square and included a doorway. Inside were people. The people seemed unaware that they were being observed. Men in lab coats with iPads as well as other less identifiable instruments peered at them and made notes. They're test subjects, Eddy realized, human lab rats. In the nearest chamber, the subjects sat in chairs or lay in beds. The nearest subject, a middle-aged man with receding grey hair, stared blankly ahead with his mouth open. A long drop of drool stretched with agonizing slowness from the underside of his chin. Eddy instantly recognized the glazed look in the man's eyes. He'd seen it before. *Mrs. Ferguson!* Eddy thought, what has become of you?

"Ah, Mr. Pending! So good of you to come!"

Eddy turned to face a tall bespectacled man with greying temples, and a Sunday school smile, wearing a white lab coat. The man extended his hand in greeting. "Dr. Julius Otomy. Welcome to my lab. This is where the magic happens! Young David here–"

"Blowfish! Damn it, doc, I told you not to call me that! Jeez."

"Sorry. *Blowfish*, has said very good things about you. He doesn't respect many developers, but he does respect you. So, we took notice. We're always asking him to make his disdain of others less obvious to his fellows here."

"They're not 'my fellows', doc, they're noobs. Anyway, Mouse, I told him you got mad skills," said Blowfish, taking a seat on a nearby metal examination table. He was seated inches away from what appeared to be jellied tissue in a sealed Tupperware container. Blowfish's sneakers, Eddy noted, didn't reach the floor. "I said you might even be better than me in *some* areas. Not all areas, just some. They're looking for stuff I know you know. Tensor, PyTorch, Malbolge, Ook!, BazGig, Sindarin, and such."

Eddy glanced about. This was not what he was expecting at all. In some ways, it was much better. He had been expecting to be killed. Still, he had no idea what had happened to Gwen and that worried him. He also had no idea how to get out of here. Playing for time was the obvious best strategy. "What's with those people?" asked Eddy, pointing to the catatonic test subjects.

"Those people are the unfortunate sacrifices one must make to advance science," said Dr. Otomy, shaking his head sadly.

"They're zombie bots," said Blowfish laughing, "And not in a good way!"

"Enough David," scolded Dr. Otomy.

"Whatever." Blowfish blew a raspberry, jumped off the examining table and stomped to another nearby glass cell in a sulk. There, he began tapping the glass with a sadistic grin. The cell's inhabitants, who were not comatose but merely stupefied, gathered about the point where Blowfish was tapping. They began to touch the glass tentatively, clearly mystified.

"Can't they see him?" said Eddy.

"It's one-way glass," said the professor. "We see them. They see only their own reflections." He pointed to the first cell, with the vegetative subjects. Eddy counted eleven men and five women. One of the men had fallen face first onto the floor. Despite this, he seemed uninterested in changing his world view. "This lot," said the professor, "They were the first volunteers. Our initial attempts resulted in either closed mental loops or complete shutdown."

"It's horrific," said Eddy.

"Of course, we didn't want this result. It was very frustrating for us, but at least it told us we were having an effect."

"An effect?" said Eddy angrily. He wanted to grab Dr. Otomy by his lapels and shake him. Who were these test subjects? Did their families know they were here? Had they been kidnaped? Who would volunteer for this? Eddy wanted to say these things, but he knew what the result would be. He might end up a test subject himself.

"We do warn them of possible side effects," said the scientist. "It's spelled out plainly on page thirty-seven of the disclaimer they sign."

"What about them?" said Eddy. He pointed to the glass cell where a dozen test subjects now huddled at the location where Blowfish had been tapping the glass. Blowfish had since lost interest and was checking his phone.

"Ah yes, our first success!" said Dr. Otomy puffing up proudly. "Our Eureka moment, as it were. Let me show you." Dr. Otomy walked briskly to a small plastic console attached to the glass. He pressed a green button. Eddy noticed a shift in the diaphanous grey tinting of the glass walls. "They can see us now," Dr. Otomy explained. He didn't need to. The occupants of the cell immediately ceased their puzzling over Blowfish's tapping and turned to gaze wide-eyed at Eddy and Dr. Otomy. "Don't be alarmed," the scientist assured him. "This glass can stop a bullet."

"Okay..." Eddy wasn't alarmed. He felt desperately sad for the confused creatures behind the glass. One of the men reminded him of his old math teacher, Mr. Simmons. Behind Mr. Simmons was an old woman who looked like someone's grandmother. They stared at Eddy with looks of confused wonder. Their expressions were childlike and trepidatious.

"Hello... world?" said Mr. Simmons.

"Hello world?" said a middle-aged man with a handlebar moustache.

"Hello world?" said a Chinese woman wearing a wine coloured smock dress trimmed with fake flowers. "Hello... world?"

Eddy stared at Dr. Otomy aghast. "Is that all they can say?"

The scientist shrugged. "We wanted to start small. Anyway, it's tradition."

Eddy turned back to the befuddled test subjects. It was tradition that when learning a new programming language students would first write code to output the phrase 'Hello World'. Hackers also used it as confirmation of an exploit or as a basic sanity test. For all its crude simplicity, 'Hello World' was like a baby saying 'Dadda'. It proved baseline function and sounded less narcissistic than 'Yes, Master'.

All at once the attitude in the glass prison changed. One of the test subjects, an African American woman with beaded hair, curled her lips in a snarl. "Hello world," she spat.

A tall white man with auburn hair and a green button-down silk shirt, punched the glass with his fist. "Hello World!" he yelled. "Hello World! Hell-O-World!"

Immediately, the others joined in. They slapped and pounded the walls of the cell. The old woman tried to leap to the top of the wall, but it was far too far. She fell backwards, landing with a painful crunch. It was the sound of her hip breaking. In spite of this, she attempted to get back up. "Hello World!" "Hello! World!" "Hello... World!" The man in the green shirt pounded the glass so vigorously his hands began to bleed. The glass smeared tomato juice red. "Hello World!" they shrieked in discordant chorus.

Dr. Otomy pressed a red button on the console. The glass tinted once again. The distraught test subjects continue to pound and claw at the hard, sheer surface. "They'll calm down soon enough," Dr. Otomy assured Eddy. "They'll forget this ever happened." Already, Eddy could see some of the cell's inhabitants backing away from the glass. They looked confused and lost. What had they been doing? Why had they been doing it?

"Out of sight, out of mind," said a nearby technician with a chuckle.

"I don't understand," said Eddy. "Don't they know who they are?"

"Hard to tell," said Dr. Otomy. He paused to glance at an iPad one of the lab assistants was showing him. He nodded, signed with his finger, and waved the man away. "The virus has shown a tendency to lead to violent outbursts in its subjects, every step of the way. I don't know why. We didn't program in the violence. Not at first, anyway."

"Like the riots happening now?"

"Exactly. We don't want that. Clearly a regression. It's not our fault. The bug was already there. It seems the human brain wants to drop into a sort of default primal state. Aggressive, angry."

"Angry at being messed with?"

"Don't be ridiculous," said the scientist. "Here, let me show you something. Come, David, this is your favourite part."

"Blowfish! Jeez doc, how many times do I have to tell you?"

Dr. Otomy walked past a series of cells. Attendants on a step ladder were lowering a tray with an overhead pulley into one. On the tray were McDonalds takeout bags. The tank was labeled 'Suburban Soccer Moms'. They gathered below the lowering tray, anxiously milling about. As the food came within reach, they began to jump and snatch at it. They ravenously tore open the bags and began cramming cheeseburgers and chicken nuggets into their mouths, wrappers and all. "Feeding time!" hooted Blowfish.

"Not that," said Dr. Otomy. "*This*." They reached another cell. A single hulking figure stood at its center. The inhabitant was massive—clearly human, yet vaguely prehistoric. It wore an expensive cable knit sweater that had been partially torn to threads. By its own hands, Eddy surmised. "What is *that?*" asked Eddy.

"That is, or was, Tony Robbins," said Dr. Otomy. "Very dangerous. He viciously killed one of our technicians and sent two more to hospital. He... um... ingested the remains before we could subdue him. A failed experiment to say the least. We don't mess with him now."

Eddy stared. He tried to reconcile the sight of the savage creature with his own images of the celebrity life coach. The hulking giant rested its chin on its chest. It appeared to be dozing, asleep on its feet, although Eddy sensed a roiling light in the eyes beneath a furrowed brow. As he watched, the feeding crew in white jumpsuits dragged an unwilling goat towards Tony's cell. "Maa! Maa!" bleated the goat.

"He only eats what he catches and kills himself. He seems to find it self affirming in some way. I don't advise you watch."

Eddy averted his eyes and found himself staring at an apparent experiment in process. Another scientist with short cropped brown hair, wearing a white lab coat and safety goggles, stood before a test subject. The subject was a middle aged man in a Pittsburgh Pirates t-shirt. He was strapped to what looked to be a dentist's chair. The man was confused and frightened. "They said I'd be taste-testing frozen yogurt?" said the man. "Do I need to be strapped down for that?" The scientist ignored him. He was busy sorting through a deck of silver backed cards. At that moment, Eddy realized the safety goggles had red lenses. "I'm really more of an ice cream kind of guy, to be honest." The scientist found the card he was looking for and presented it to the man. The man squinted a moment, then went wide-eyed. "God damn whales!" the man shouted. "Kill 'em! Kill 'em all!" The scientist calmly returned the card to the deck. He pulled his goggles up onto his head and began making notes on his iPad. "Humpbacks, blue, sperm, kill the whole lot of 'em! Kill the killer whales fur Christ's sake! Kill 'em and feed 'em to other killer whales, then kill them too!"

"Fascinating, no?" said Dr. Otomy in Eddy's ear. "See the precision we've obtained? Allow me to demonstrate further." Dr. Otomy snapped his fingers to capture the test subject's attention. "Tell me sir, what do you think of dolphins?"

"Dolphins? I love dolphins. So cute."

"But whales?"

"Burn their blubbery hides and make 'em feel every second of it!"

"You can't tell me you're not impressed," said Dr. Otomy to Eddy.

Eddy stared, aghast. Dr. Otomy was too pleased to notice. "Good work Charles. Failure rate?"

"Statistically insignificant," said the young scientist without looking up. He then asked the man, "How do you feel about narwhals?"

The man hesitated, then asked, "Are narwhals whales?"

"Yes."

"Stick 'em with their own tusks and spit roast 'em fur supper."

The scientist nodded and made a note.

"Now then," said Dr. Otomy. "If you'll follow me, we can discuss how you might be able to help us." Dr. Otomy began walking towards a glassed-in office at the back of the room. Blowfish was still gleefully watching Tony Robbins savage the goat. The hacker held his fists in front of him, quivering like a boxing fan vicariously enjoying a beating. Eddy's eyes went to the stack of cards sitting on the metal table beside the young scientist. The technician, busy with his observations, was oblivious to Eddy just behind him. Eddy saw his chance. He snatched the entire deck. The startled scientist looked up.

"Hey, I was still using—" Eddy pulled the first card off the top of the pack and showed it to him.

"Ahh!" yelled the man. He closed his eyes, but not before seeing the card. The man pulled his goggles down from his head and reopened his eyes behind the protective red filter. He blinked. "I can't see!" he shrieked. He yanked off the goggles and threw them to the floor. "I'm blind!"

"What the fo-shizzle?" said Blowfish, turning to look. Eddy grabbed another card at random and showed it to him. "No way!" Blowfish shut his eyes before Eddy had the card turned. "Too slow old man," the fourteen-year-old snarled. "Na na-na-na na!"

Eddy socked Blowfish in the nose. The boy stumbled backwards into the glass wall of Tony Robbin's cell, before sinking to the floor. Blood gushed from both nostrils. Inside the cell, the red drenched Goliath lifted his dripping maw from the belly of the goat he was gorging on. He looked towards the sound. His eyes narrowed like a predator sensing prey. The celebrity life coach curled his lips and uttered a guttural snarl. "Ow!" said Blowfish. The hacker blinked in surprise. As his eyes opened, he found himself looking directly at the card Eddy was holding inches from his face. "Aw crap!" he swore, shutting them again. A tremor shook Blowfish's body. The hacker lurched forward and rolled onto the metal grill flooring. He began to thrash violently about. Eddy stepped away from the convulsing teenager. He turned towards the office where Dr. Otomy now stood staring in shock. Panicked, the doctor quickly donned red glasses. Dr. Otomy slapped a big button on the wall. A keening alarm sounded, *EEE-OH! EEE-OH!* Emergency lights strobed the room. Eddy turned to see that the two MRCGs who had stayed behind at the laboratory entrance were now advancing towards him. They were baring strange looking black batons. Eddy realized he was the only one left not wearing red glasses. To the side, he saw a pair of double doors slide open. Four more MRCGs and a pair of uniformed security guards with guns drawn entered. Eddy turned to look in the remaining direction. There, he saw an elevator. He expected it to open with more assassins come to kill him. He had nowhere to go. With their target surrounded, the attackers slowly closed in.

"Marco!" shouted the hysterically blind scientist, calling for another technician to help him. He began waving his arms about. "Marco!" Eddy sidestepped his flailing grasp. He saw then the scientist's dropped goggles. Might as well protect myself, he thought, reaching for them. As he did, he spotted the scientist's discarded iPad next to them. The screen displayed an interface that appeared to be an overhead view of the room they were in. Eddy snatched it up and stared at it. He was looking for an exit. What he saw was that the iPad appeared to be networked into the lab's security system. Beside each of the thirty-six glass cells was a green button labeled 'Unlock'. At the bottom of the screen was a big button that said 'Unlock All'. Eddy tapped it. The screen demanded a passcode using Touch ID.

"Marco?" asked the blind scientist, sensing Eddy's proximity.

"Polo," said Eddy, taking the hand of the confused scientist.

"Oh thank-you, thank-you! Marco, is that you?" said the scientist. Eddy mashed the man's finger onto the iPad's home button and let go.

"Marco?" asked the man, confused.

The arriving brigades of security and Men in Rose Coloured Glasses were almost upon him. He could see the looks of smug satisfaction on the

guards' faces. Every door of every glass cell made a loud *click!* The LED
lights above the exits turned green. The doors swung open. The guards'
looks turned to surprise, then *terror*. Denizens of every cell spilled into the
laboratory thoroughfares. The Hello World subjects exited their cubicle with
looks of benign befuddlement. This morphed into rage as they spotted their
tormentors. The Men in Rose Coloured Glasses switched on their virus
beams. The test subjects, blinded by red rage, were unaffected. They
launched themselves upon the surprised MRCGs. The assassins disappeared
under a pile of bodies. Blood spattered a nearby glass cell wall. Definitely
not robots, thought Eddy. The other way, a horde of insane businessmen and
a gang of albino skinheads spilled out of neighbouring cells to pile upon the
panicked security guards, dragging them to the floor. Eddy turned to flee. He
found himself face to face with Blowfish. How is he still alive? thought
Eddy. The adolescent hacker glared at him with a look of fury. "This is what
you wanted, isn't it Blowfish?" said Eddy. "It's all a game of one-
upmanship?"

The teenager opened his mouth with a snarl, "Bu-cock!"

"What?" said Eddy.

Blowfish seemed as surprised as Eddy by what had come out of his
mouth. "Bu-Cock?" said Blowfish again. It was a near-perfect imitation of a
chicken. Eddy stared at him. Behind Blowfish, the test subjects were
horrifically dismembering their captors. Dr. Otomy had barricaded himself
in his office, but the soccer moms were hurling stools at the window.
Already, the safety glass had splintered. "Buck-buck-buck-bu-cock?"
stammered Blowfish. He was clearly trying to say something, but his mouth
refused to cooperate. "Bu-cock?"

Eddy shoved him aside and ran towards the unguarded elevator at
the back. It was closed, it was unknown, but it was the only option left. Eddy
pressed the button. The doors opened with a soft *Ping!*

Eddy ducked inside and landed against the back wall. He stared back at the carnage ensuing in the Lab. It felt as if he were viewing another world, a world of madness. The test subjects had easily gained the upper hand. They raised the young scientist's entrails like a festive May Day flower chain above their heads. Dancing among them was a different group of test subjects. These had been part of an early attempt to turn people into computers. They triumphantly chanted what they thought was a series of prime numbers. "8, 32, 18, 7!" they shouted. They had been a great disappointment to Dr. Otomy, what with their terrible math and irregular logic. "How can the human mind be the most powerful computer on earth and not do math as well as a pocket calculator?" he'd asked.

Eddy spotted Blowfish. The curly haired hacker was staring up at the towering colossus of Tony Robbins. The celebrity life coach gazed back down at him. The giant appeared to be asking a question. *How would you like to die?* "Bu-cock?" answered Blowfish. Tony Robbin's ham-hock hands engulfed the hacker's head and wrenched upwards. Eddy assumed this would merely lift the teenager into the air. Perhaps, it might break his neck. Somehow, the life coach tore the boy's head from his shoulders in an arcing cascade of gore. He then lifted Blowfish's head by the hair into the air like a trophy, threw back his head, and roared. Blowfish's body continued to stand for several seconds as if, without its brain, it was just too dumb to fall down. Finally, it collapsed in a heap.

Eddy turned his attention to the elevator console. It contained only a single floor button 'M'. Eddy pressed the button. Nothing happened. Eddy pressed the button again and this time repeated the Klingon phrase Blowfish had used earlier. "lojmIt yIpoSmoH," he said. A calm woman's voice responded, "Access denied." Eddy noticed as tiny camera lens looking down at him. More facial recognition, he realized. It must require clearance I don't have. Panicked, Eddy looked back out at the laboratory. The rioting hordes of test subjects had killed all of the scientists, lab technicians, and security personnel. The once pristine glass, chrome, and white surfaces were smeared

red. A single ejected eyeball lay on the grill walkway, feet from the elevator doors. Their foes vanquished, the test subjects had reverted to milling about like Sunday shoppers at a mall. Except with blood and entrails, thought Eddy, so more like Black Friday shoppers. Eddy wondered at how they had a sense of 'us' and 'them'. For all their brutality, the test subjects did not kill each other. Only the vegetative victims remained in their cell. During the fray, they had been knocked over like a set of dominos and now lay face-planted in each others' buttocks. One test subject from another cell, dressed in a red cardigan, was singing boisterously. He appeared delighted to have found a captive audience. "...I'm very well acquainted, too, with matters mathematical, I understand equations, both the simple and quadratical, About binomial theorem I'm teeming with a lot o' news, With many cheerful facts about the square of the hypotenuse..."

"Rahhh!" yelled a white haired old man. He was pointing at Eddy.

"Hello world?" said an old woman, turning to look. As she saw Eddy, her face curled into a malevolent grin. *"Hello* world."

"Damn," said Eddy. He made a panicked scan of the lab. To reach the exits he would have to make his way through a horde of violent test subjects. The path to Dr. Otomy's office was open, but the idea of running there and barricading himself inside seemed pointless. It hadn't worked for the chief scientist. Dr. Otomy had been fed face-first through a document shredder. He lay on the floor, no longer legible as human. Eddy considered trying to force the elevator doors shut.

"Pow–urrr..." said a deep guttural voice. Eddy stared. Tony Robbins had spotted him as well. Even if Eddy did somehow manage to jam the elevator doors shut, he knew the monster could easily batter them open. "Pow-ur... pow-ur... pow-ur..."

Tony swatted aside a test subject with a soul patch and man bun who was in the way. "Hello world!" the hipster shrieked before crashing into a cell wall. The celebrity life coach began to lumber down the walkway directly towards Eddy, knocking aside other surprised test subjects as he went. In one hand, Tony still clutched the decapitated head of Blowfish. Eddy wracked his panicked mind for some avenue of escape. He saw a trapdoor in the elevator ceiling. He pushed on it, but found it locked. He looked back to the laboratory. Other test subjects were running towards him as well, but all were knocked aside by the barrelling colossus that was Tony Robbins. This is it, thought Eddy. *This is where I die.*

"Pow-urrrr!" Tony bellowed. As he did so, he hurled Blowfish's head at Eddy. Eddy, who had never been good at dodgeball, was thrown into the back wall of the elevator on impact. For a moment, Eddy was stunned. Ringing filled his ears. He sat up with a groan. Tony, seeing his prey still lived, resumed his charge with a roar. Eddy was in shock. Seconds stretched like minutes. He looked down at Blowfish's head in his lap. With his brain addled, Eddy was more bemused than horrified by the sight. The dead teenager wore an expression of similar surprise. :-o he seemed to say. Suddenly, Eddy's head cleared. He picked up the head and turned it to face the security camera. He then slammed the M-button with his fist and shouted, "lojmIt yIpoSmoH!"

"Welcome David Dinklesworth, access granted," said the elevator. The doors slid shut just as Tony Robbins looming presence eclipsed the light between them. WHAM! Massive fists pummelled the doors, denting steel. They shuddered, but held.

"Pow-urrrrrrr!" Eddy could hear Tony Robbins roar. "Pow-ur!" The life coach's massive fists pounded the steel door and reverberated throughout the lift. The elevator descended. The loud clangs fell away.

Eddy collapsed panting to the floor. He flung the hacker's head away in disgust. It rebounded off the wall and rolled to a stop in the opposite corner. By chance, it faced Eddy again. The impact had somehow rearranged the dead hacker's expression to a grotesque emoticon of extreme frowny-face >:-(

## 3.0

"It's a beta." – V. Frankenstein

// Washington, DC — now

"Good morning, Mr. Winface," said the soldier with a smile. "If you don't mind me saying, I'm a big fan of yours."

"The feeling's mutual, son," said Lance, flashing his perfect TV smile. They were both dressed in military fatigues. The celebrity TV host was waiting his turn to pass through the security checkpoint at the Capitol Hill Visitor Center. Unlike the soldier's, Lance's weren't US Army issue. It was a prop costume from a failed TV pilot, *Seal Team X*. In Lance's opinion, it was how real US Army fatigues should look. The pattern was made of little lightning bolt Xs, the symbol of the fictional covert unit. It was only now that he realized green might not be the most effective camouflage in the white marble halls of Congress. The soldier saluted Lance and continued on his way. The Visitor Center was packed and noisy with the usual crowd of tourists and visitors. In front of Lance stood a businessman in a long wool coat who was clearly not a tourist. Like Lance, the man carried a black shoulder bag which he placed carefully on the conveyor belt, before proceeding through the metal detector. Lance recognized the man, but couldn't say from where.

"Bag on the belt please, sir," said the checkpoint guard.

Lance deposited his black bag onto the belt and watched as it passed through the X-ray machine. On the overhead display, a half-dozen automatic and semiautomatic weapons were clearly visible inside.

"That's a lot of guns, Mr. Winface," said the guard.

"It sure is," said Lance. He was nervous, even though the law was on his side. Just three months ago, bringing such armaments into Congress would have been illegal. For years, the House was one of the last places left where guns were not permitted. Last April, the Supreme Court had declared that unconstitutional. That left prisons as the only federal buildings where guns were not permitted for all citizens. Lance himself had argued that it was an egregious violation of the 2nd Amendment. "No background checks for guns *period*, even if the background is the wall of their own prison cell." The issue was already in the courts with the case *The United States v. Snake*. Abuse by guards was so rampant now in the privatized penal system that arming the inmates was only fair. The NRA endorsed the initiative, arguing that prisoners were some of America's greatest gun enthusiasts. Despite all this progress, such weaponry in Congress would normally lead to increased scrutiny by the Secret Service. Lance felt confident, however, that his celebrity and established press credentials would make him above suspicion. He'd been forced to discard the bayonet he'd brought along with him. Knives weren't covered by the ruling. Lance had also discarded the joint that he kept in his wallet for pre-show anxiety. As a Schedule One narcotic, it was the one drug he carried that could get him into trouble at a federal checkpoint. "Only thugs do drugs," was one of his catchphrases on his show.

Lance Winface didn't do drugs; he *took* them. So far today, he'd taken more than he could count. Lance was feeling groovy.

"Do you have a license for all of these, sir?"

"Nope."

"Very good, sir. Have you undergone a background check?"

"It was a private sale in my home state. I bought them from some guy in a van. Or maybe at a gun show. One or the other." Lance knew both of these sensibly eliminated the legal requirement for a background check.

"I see, very good sir. Sorry for the intrusion, I am required to ask."

"Just doing your job."

Lance sauntered through the metal detector door frame. On the other side, a German Shepard, held on a short leash by a second guard, sniffed his pants and shoes. Lance reached to pet the dog.

"Please don't, sir."

"Oh, sorry."

Lance spotted the businessman standing at the X-ray. He was waiting for his bag to exit on the slow moving belt. Lance snapped his fingers. "Hal Gumble!"

Hal appeared displeased at being identified. He then broke into a broad grin. "Lance! I didn't recognize you in your... um..."

"I'm going duck hunting later."

"In D.C.? Oh, I mean, got it!" said Hall with a wink and two tongue clicks. "Say no more." Hal Gumble was a lobbyist for Belzopharm. He'd been a guest on Lance's show once to defend the company. It had come under fire for massive mark-ups on products based on mostly publicly funded clinical research. "People don't appreciate the value we add. Marketing and patents aren't cheap," Hal had said at the time. "It's supply and demand, Lance, nothing more than that. And, there's nothing more American than that." Lance had included the Belzopharm drug Alpodram with his orange juice at breakfast. He had no idea what Alpodram did, but taking it felt like sliding into a lukewarm bath drawn by hummingbirds. Lance knew better than to ask Hal questions. "Questions are why powerful people don't like journalists," Lance once told a graduating class at Brigham Young University. "Remember that and you'll go far." Don't be pesky, was Lance's motto. "We have to have you back on the show," said Lance. "When I'm not hunting deer, of course."

"You mean ducks?"

Lance hesitated. "Both. At the same time."

"Oh, well, good luck with that. And of course, I'd love to come on your show again, Lance. I could talk about all the good we do with discount vouchers for our drugs. Great to see you!" Hal shook Lance's hand warmly, picked up his bag from the conveyor belt, and headed off down the hall. Lance watched him go. He squinted. Lance was trying to see if he could see *it*. Nothing. Either it wasn't there, or the pills weren't working properly. Lance needed his powers if things were to go as planned. He lifted the heavy bag off the belt and threw it over his shoulder. He considered following Hal, and killing him just to be safe.

"Senate Chamber or House of Representatives?" asked a Capitol Hill visitors guide.

"House," said Lance. He waggled his press badge at her. She mouthed 'oh' and moved onto the next visitor. The distraction had caused him to lose sight of Hal. Oh well, he thought, I can always hunt him down and kill him later. He walked through Emancipation Hall and past the Statue of Freedom. He then headed towards the stairs.

Amid the crowds of visitors in t-shirts and jeans, Lance saw another familiar face. It was Representative Rich Tollman of New Jersey. He spotted Lance and waved. The Congressman was talking to a man in a ten-gallon hat. The TV host began to wave back, then hesitated. A tall wick of blackness stood behind the Congressman. The wick had no features or depth. It appeared as a smear in the air itself, undulating and seething with unnatural life. Tree branch arms of shadow reached down and rested tendril fingers on the politician's shoulders. Their grasp was loose, but the fingertips penetrated the Congressman's chest like roots drawing nourishment from the soil. Congressman Tollman seemed oblivious to the being's presence. He chuckled into the phone and doodled on the back of a bill. *You again*, thought Lance. The daemon gazed at him with unblinking ember eyes that oozed malevolent red smoke. *I see you*, they seemed to say, *I know why you're here.* Lance scowled back, and I see you. The Stygian spirit's eyes crackled and burned. *I see you see me*, the being appeared to reply, *and before you say it, I see you see me see you see me, etc. etc.* I see you, thought Lance, times infinity. *I see you times infinity plus one*, the being beamed. Lance cursed. There was no bigger number than that. He wanted to reach into his bag and grab his AR-15. The one with the bump stock for fully automatic fire. He wanted to gun down the Congressman and his gloating puppeteer right there. No, thought Lance, I have bigger fish to fry. Too much security here. I need to suss out the rats where they nest. He waved amiably to the Congressman and jogged up the steps. Lance was shaking. Once out of sight, he paused to unscrew the cap of his pen and tap out the blue pills he'd hidden there in case of emergency. He noticed a water fountain in an alcove. Lance tossed back the pills and hunched over to slurp from the tap. Once he'd washed them down, he paused to look at his hand. It was vibrating like a piano tuner in the key of F#. He waited for it to stop. It always did eventually, but took longer now. Finally, the tremors subsided. It was then that he saw it—blackness that seemed to sheath him like a glove. A shadow? His imagination? He shook his hand like an Etch-A-Sketch. The darkness vanished. This is bad, thought Lance. If I start imagining things, I might have trouble knowing who the *real* nycadaemons are. I might kill someone who doesn't deserve it. Worse, I might fail to kill someone who does. The TV host turned and headed down the long marble hall, clutching his right hand to keep it from twitching.

## 3.1

"You're going down." – E. Otis

// Majority Media Head Office, California — now

The descent continued. The elevator's interior lights switched from white to red. They pulsed. Eddy felt as if he were lodged in a left ventricle. A blockage that needs to be removed, he thought. The elevator stopped, one floor up. The doors opened onto a wide hallway, lined with executive suites. This too was lit entirely in red. The effect was to give the impression of an office in Hell. On a nearby wall was a sign-up sheet for the company softball league. Hell indeed, thought Eddy. Either that or the most over-furnished dark room ever. At the end of the hall were two men in trim black suits and ties, with slicked back hair. There was no need for their signature eyewear, Eddy realized. The red light would render the patterns invisible. A precaution for the C-suite, no doubt. Machi didn't want his own viruses used against him. "Guess, your red virus cards won't work in all this red light, huh? Not so tough now." The MRCGs swung up AR-15 assault rifles that had been hanging at their sides. Both barrels aimed directly at Eddy. "Oh," said Eddy. Hell, it seemed, was a hostile work environment. The idea of being shot raised the stakes.

"Come," said the two in chorus.

Eddy approached cautiously. His heart pounded in his chest. Surely, if they were going to kill him, he would already be dead. Eddy's hand slid casually into his pants pocket. He had a plan to deal with this exact situation. He had no idea if it would work. It was just a theory, after all.

"Hands out of your pockets," they said. Eddy wondered at a question his father once posed. If two identical twins were separated at birth and placed in identical environments and raised with identically scripted interactions, would they be the same person? Would they say the same things and think the same thoughts, simultaneously? "We'll never know," said Eddy's father ruefully. "Not because it would be unethical, but because of damn chaos theory." Of course, if his Infinite Repeat-O-Verse theory had been correct, the answer would have been *yes*. But, no.

Eddy pulled his hands out of his pockets. In one hand he held an old Dictaphone handheld tape recorder. He'd bought it in a pawnshop in Santa Barbara. It was analog and, critically, didn't connect to anything. "Just a music player," he said. As he said this, Eddy pressed play. "See?"

"Stop what you're doing," said a voice from the Dictaphone.

The MRCGs froze. Or at least Eddy thought they had. They hadn't actually been moving at the time. Now, they seemed to be not moving even more. "Cease all activity," said the voice. This time it was more distant and somewhat tinny. The recording had been spliced together from different sources Eddy had found online. The voice was that of CEO James Machi, their ultimate boss. "Get down and stay down," Machi's voice said. It was a clip from years ago, when Machi had appeared on PBS. The two MRCGs fell to their knees, then lay flat on the floor. They still held their assault rifles off to one side. "Remain calm... we expect ad revenues to rise in the next quart–" Panicked, Eddy pressed the stop button. He'd forgotten to edit out the last bit, taken from an earnings call. He stared at the two prone assassins. They remained on the floor. Eddy considered heading back to the elevator to escape. He then remembered Tony Robbins would be waiting for him. *Whatever lay ahead couldn't be worse than that monster!* Eddy glanced into the side offices. Through glass partitions, he saw only empty desks and chairs. No people, no computers, no signs of recent use. Nervously, Eddy proceeded forward. He stepped between the two prone assassins. He considered trying to take one of the assault rifles, but the MRCGs still gripped them. Picking one up could break the spell. Eddy reached the double doors at the hallway's end. The doors opened before him.

Inside, cloaked in vermillion light, was an elegantly appointed reception area. A handsome woman in her forties sat behind the desk. She looked expectantly at Eddy as he entered. Her hair was tied in a neat bun. She had eyes that shone and a perfect closed lips smile. There was no way to know what colour her lips, nails, hair, or dress really were. Everything in the room was cast in shades of red. She appeared to be waiting for him. So much for the element of surprise, he thought. To the side was a sofa and chairs, a potted fern, and another pair of double doors. There were curtains, but no visible windows. They were, after all, far below ground. Instead, there was a painting of an arrow in perspective pointing out, with the words 'You are here'. "Welcome, Mr. Pending."

"You've been expecting me?"

"We have."

"We?"

"Mr. Machi."

"James Machi?"

"He's quite anxious to meet you. I'll buzz you in," said the receptionist. She pressed a button on her desk. *Bzzt!*

Eddy started to walk, then hesitated. "I don't suppose it would do any good for me to say, 'help me, call the police, there's terrible things happening here, I just saw a lot of people die'?"

The receptionist looked at Eddy and smiled pleasantly. "Mr. Machi doesn't like to be kept waiting."

"I don't suppose he does," said Eddy.

"Oh, before you enter, I'll need you to give me that device."

Eddy recoiled. It was his only defence against the MRCGs. "It's just a tape recorder."

"It will be returned to you when you leave."

"And if I refuse?"

"You'll be dead before you reach the door." She raised the pistol she'd been aiming at Eddy below the desk. She smiled as if offering him coffee.

"Here you go!" Eddy placed the music player on the mirrored desktop surface. He was struck by the fact that there was no computer there. Even were she not armed, there was nothing here to hack. Eddy reflexively touched the thumb drive hanging from a lanyard under his shirt. "Hold all my calls," he joked weakly. Eddy opened the door.

"Welcome, Mr. Pending, do come in," a deep, lugubrious voice beckoned. Eddy instantly recognized it, but it was even more resonant than on the recordings. The voice continued, "I've been amused by your antics."

Inside was a modern chief executive's office. It was minimalist, assembled out of rectangular wall panels, square rugs, and right-angle Bauhaus-inspired furniture. To one side was a luxury living room set and wet bar. On the other, was a meeting table with chairs. At least, that described the part he could see. As with the reception area, the near end of the room was bathed in red. The far end of the room wasn't illuminated at all. It was swallowed by shadow so complete, it felt as if the room itself dissolved into darkness. This was an effect of the directional floodlights in the ceiling. From the other side, Eddy imagined he must appear as if on a stage. He felt trapped there and knew that, whether he liked it or not, he would have to play his part. His audience was unseen.

"I apologize," said the voice. It reminded Eddy of James Earl Jones. He imagined it saying "Luke, I am your father." It seemed about right. The speaker paused to wheeze for a moment, as if the very act of speaking were a strain. "I apologize for the brothel lighting. Strictly a precaution, you understand. One can't take too many chances, as Dr. Otomy could no doubt attest to, were he still alive."

"Oh yeah, sorry about that," said Eddy.

"Don't apologize. You did what you had to do. As do we all."

"Couldn't someone just make a virus that wasn't red?"

"Absolutely. The viruses need not be visual at all. Any sensory input will do. They can be turned into audio signal and sent over the radio, or telephone. In theory, a virus could be an airbourne scent, a pheromone, or words on a page. Still, the ones we've released have all been intrinsically red. To change their colour would require some re-coding, which requires knowing how. Simply a sensible precaution."

"Better red than dead."

Machi chuckled. "Well put." Eddy's eyes began to adjust to the dim light. He could just make out the hulking outline of something moving. A man? No, it was too big to be a man. Eddy noted as well the tiny winking fireflies in the dark. They were white, blue, and green LED lights. To either side of the central mass were what appeared to be tower blocks of equipment. Eddy could discern tangled bundles of wires and cables running from the machines into the center. He tried to determine their purpose. They moved in concert with the great silhouette. He couldn't decided if the mass was dragging the wires about or if, like puppet strings, they were pulling it. "You see, Eddy, what we've achieved here is absolutely groundbreaking. We have learned to program the human mind. No one else can do that. At least not so directly. I would like to offer you the opportunity to join us."

"So, a job, like Blowfish said."

"Better than that. That impudent brat had some talents, but not what he thought they were. You saved us the trouble of terminating him."

Eddy paused to consider what 'terminating him' meant. Were all employees terminated eventually? Eddy noted that he could just make out two more silhouettes in the dark—figures on either side of the large indeterminate mass. MRCG guards, he assumed. No doubt, there in case Eddy failed to cooperate. "Very impressive, your little stunt out there in the hallway," said Machi. "A crude but effective exploit. We'll have to patch that."

"What are they? The Men in Rose Coloured glasses, I mean," said Eddy. "Programmed people?"

"We call them 'zombies'. They're human clones, but their higher level brain functions have been wiped and replaced with simpler code. They're highly functional."

"Must be pretty sophisticated software."

"Very. Advanced virtual machines, pseudo-conscious, but without a conscience. Evolution is messy, driven by self-interest and other unhelpful forces. For a perfect servant, you really need intelligent design. You obviously surmised that and took advantage of it."

"I figured you'd have an override," said Eddy, "It was a guess, to be honest." As he spoke, Eddy tried to decide his next move. He couldn't see one, so he decided to play for time instead. "Why me?"

"Because, unlike that pubescent brat, you really are the best of the best," said Machi. He was panting audibly. "As your guess demonstrates, you understand programming not just in a mechanical von Neumann kind of way, but organically. We pay very well, Mr. Pending. In one year, you'll be rich. All we ask is that you help us fix certain... bugs, we've encountered."

Suddenly, Eddy understood why the media mogul had permitted him to get this far, why he wanted him so badly. "The riots! You really don't know how to stop them."

There was a long pause. Eddy could make out the sound of laboured breathing amid the hum of tiny fans. "No. We do not. The television deployments were fine, more or less. The print versions were completely containable. The radio show had some... issues. But, it was when we went to the internet that things changed."

"In what way?"

"We went everywhere. Facebook, Twitter, Reddit, NarsisUs, and so on. Social Media, some blogs, a few chat rooms. There proved to be an unexpected amplification effect. Our viruses went, well, viral. They mutated. Evolved. Became memes. There were carriers, replicators... incubation chambers, echo chambers. The anger exponentiated and –"

"You lost control."

Another long pause. "We lost control." Eddy heard the sound of gurgling, like air through water. He tried to imagine what it was. A hookah? Fluid in lungs? He heard a heavy *sigh*. "We lost control, *for now*. But, I'm hoping that you can help us get it back."

"And if I do?"

"As I said, you'll be rich! You'll be able to retire if you like. Plus, there are *other* benefits..."

"And if I don't?"

In the midst of the impenetrable darkness, Eddy swore he could see a wicked smile form and an eye twinkle. "If you don't? Well then, you dance," said Machi. At that moment, *We Built this City* by Jefferson Starship began to blare over a hidden sound system. All at once, Eddy felt his muscles begin to clamp up involuntarily. His arms and legs grew stiff; his jaw clenched. He flung himself violently to the floor. He spasmed in agony and shrieked. "It's a catchy little number, you must admit," chuckled Machi. "It makes you want to move it, move it." He broke into a throaty laugh as

Eddy twisted and rolled in unnatural ways.

"What... is... happen... ing?" Eddy gasped.

"You're a smart fellow. Do I need to explain that there's a virus encoded into the track? We call this one *Audio Tetanus*. That's because its effects are similar to acute tetanus oxide poisoning. It causes your muscles to spasm and contract in extreme ways. Eventually you'll either suffocate, or your back muscles will bend you backwards until your spine snaps. Blowfish liked to call it break dancing." Machi laughed once more, then paused to wheeze and cough. "If you're wondering, I'm protected by a neat little wall of noise-cancelling sound, directionally focused to shield just me. You hear Audio Tetanus. I hear a rain forest at night, with crickets."

"Make... it... stop..." Eddy pleaded as the chorus ensued. He could feel his chest muscles grow taut, constricting his breathing. His limbs tried to tear themselves from their sockets.

"*You* make it stop, Eddy. Just say 'yes' to my job offer."

"Ah...ah... ah..." Eddy tried to speak, but found he couldn't open his mouth. "Ah..."

"Too upbeat? Something more suitable perhaps?" The audio switched from the 80s pop song, to the sound of fingernails screeching slowly across a blackboard. "That just feels like an auditory weapon doesn't it? Still, the musical encoding is useful for hiding it in AM radio broadcasts. Cat still got your tongue?"

"Mmm–mmth...thpt!" Eddy protested. He was bent backwards like a human pretzel. Eddy stared with bulging eyes at the darkness where the gloating billionaire lurked. Terror and anguish wracked his body and mind. His teeth were bared in a hideous grin. "Gaaaa...."

"Oh right," chortled Machi with belly laugh. "Duh. The lockjaw! How silly of me, asking you to speak. You can't! Ha, ha! How very droll." All at once the screeching sound stopped. Released, Eddy rolled across the floor, landing face down to one side. He gasped and panted into the carpet.

Every muscle in his body ached. Machi growled with satisfaction and said, "Now then, what say you? Will you, won't you, will you, won't you, won't you join the dance? The further off from England the nearer is to France. You need to answer me soon, Eddy. I have a hard-stop at eleven. A board meeting, you understand. So, in the next ten minutes, you either submit your application form to HR, or die. I'd prefer the former, but either outcome is good news for our shareholders. Did I mention stock options? I probably should have led with that. They're very, very good."

Eddy's head throbbed. He didn't want to work for Machi, but he couldn't face that torture again. "Okay, you win. I'll work for you."

"You should know, Eddy, I'll verify that you're telling the truth. We have a virus for just that purpose, called 'Pinocchio'. So there's no point in fibbing. So, I'll ask you one more time, will you work for me?"

Eddy considered lying again, simply to avoid the possibility of immediate torment. *You can't be a part of this,* he heard his mother say. *No matter what.* His father said nothing. Even in Eddy's conscience, his father wasn't paying attention. Might as well get this over with, he decided. "No."

"Hmm, yes, well, I expected as much. You're tougher, and stupider, than you look. Well then, let's try something different, shall we?"

### 3.2

"I can't believe my eyes."– M.C. Escher

// Brooklyn, New York — then

The following morning, Eddy wandered into his father's workshop munching a slice of Robertson's Ginger Marmalade toast. He alternated between bites of toast and sips of coffee. He'd expected to find his father as he'd left him the night before, hunched over his desk, hard at work on his portal to nowhere. A theoretical universe? What did that even mean? Eddy was going to offer to bring his Dad coffee. Instead, he found the laboratory deserted. Dad must have gone for a walk, he thought. Perhaps the gateway was proving troublesome to open. Maybe, just maybe, his father had realized the madness of it all. After all, unlike Mum, his father's depression was the rational kind. Eddy was about to return to the kitchen when he noticed the tarpaulin. It had been pulled from the dimensional door frame and lay in a heap on the floor. He also noticed that the gate was plugged in.

*Spyware*

The tiny green LED in the top right of the frame was lit, indicating it was ON. Only then did he notice the odour of burnt tungsten hanging in the air like an unfortunate remark. Eddy's gaze next fell upon an origami swan on his father's swivel desk chair seat. 'Eddy' it said on one wing. It was his father's handwriting. Suddenly terrified, Eddy unfolded it. Inside, was a handwritten note.

> *Dear Eddy,*
>
> *Don't be sad. It all makes sense to me now. I know you think this is crazy. You'll think it's suicide. It's not. I wouldn't do that to you. Not after what you've been through. I have, however, left you forever. When I found the theoretical universe, I knew it was where I belonged. I'll be happy there, unlike here in this second rate reality I was born to. As the law will almost certainly take my departure as death, I have left a will with the law firm of Fogel & Flinck. Needless to say, you are my sole beneficiary. This includes all of my work, my life savings and my complete collection of Star Trek Mego action figures in their original boxes. I have also left some quite good Chinese food in the fridge. Finally, there are also some overdue library books in the bathroom. I'm not sure if the estate would be on the hook for any fines, but best not to take chances. Remember, I am not dead, but I have gone to heaven. LOL! Just kidding (sort of). It's better this way. I've taken your Mum's ashes with me, even though that makes no sense. She's dead, but there we'll always be together. At least in theory.*
>
> *– Daddy*
>
> *P.S. You were never the problem*

Eddy stared numbly at the note. For a moment, his brain simply decided not to register any emotion at all. He then turned in disbelief towards the free standing doorway. The white frame seemed now to vibrate with a kind of astral resonance, like a sort of cosmic tuning fork (in the key of F#). With swelling apprehension, Eddy approached the portal. He reached slowly for the round brass doorknob, then stopped. His father's key was still in the lock, slightly askew. He knew his father had included in the design a spring-loaded door-closer for safety reasons. The door would have gently shut itself behind anyone who passed through it. The teenage boy brace himself, swallowed, then flung the door wide. A rectangle of blackness gaped before him. Eddy found himself teetering on the brink of oblivion. While there was no physical pull, he instinctively grabbed the door frame to save himself from the perceptual suction. It was not the darkness of an unlit room. It was not the emptiness of a deep dark hole. This was the indefinite non-ness of an empty universe, devoid of even being a void. For a moment, Eddy felt a strange compulsion to step through as well. The psychic pull of the vacuum seemed to tilt the world toward it. He could hear his father calling to him like a siren in lab coat. He could also hear his mother crying *No!* Eddy planted his feet on the level floor to keep from sliding in. It was the same irrational urge that made people want to jump from a cliff's edge. There's nothing there, Eddy told himself. Or maybe there was. He knew then his father was dead, although Eddy could see no trace of him. Entering an empty universe would lead to instant death. For one thing, it would be cold —absolute zero cold. In that sense, he might be frozen forever. So maybe not dead, thought Eddy, but somewhere in between. Perpetually preserved. Alive, but only in theory. Living in the moment is not living at all. His father forgot time. Floating. Unchanging. Constant. Adrift. His father had to know this. Upon entering it, his father and mother's ashes would have given birth to existence in that universe, simply by *being*. Being dead, thought Eddy. In a rush of anger, he slammed the door shut. He turned and fell backwards against it. With his last vestige of strength, he drew the chain lock into place. For safety. Seventeen-year-old Eddy Pending slid slowly down to the cold concrete floor of his father's empty workshop. He stared into his shaking, empty hands. I have nothing, he thought, I am nothing. I am an empty universe. He began to cry.

Dr. Pending's disappearance was ruled accidental. The result of a failed science experiment. The court refused to recognize the existence of the other universe. Even if we did, the judge reasoned, parallel dimensions are out of our jurisdiction. Eddy received a small life insurance payment. It was enough to pay off his student loans, but little else. The house had been double-mortgaged to fund his father's work. The dimensional portal went to Anton Sparks. The billionaire claimed he legally owned it as part of his original investment. Eddy knew that was nonsense. His father had built it years prior, and it had nothing to do with the artificial intelligence project. Eddy was right, but Anton Sparks had lawyers. After taking possession of the portal, Spark's experts couldn't begin to understand how it worked or even what it did exactly. All they knew was, you could throw any amount of stuff into it and nothing ever came back. Sparks International patented it as an 'infinite garbage disposal' and signed a contract with the state of New Jersey. The trans-dimensional portal was relocated to the basement of Newark Waste Management. There were rumours the mob was using it to dispose of evidence—evidence which included people. Years later, the Feds took possession of it. The feds planned to use it for radioactive waste, toxic waste, and other 'hard to dispose of materials'. There were rumours that 'hard to dispose of materials' also included people. Specifically, terrorist suspects black-holed by specials ops. The former uses were being held up pending environmental impact review. The latter Eddy could only hope were just rumours. The idea of his parent's universe being filled with trash was troubling enough without the addition of corpses floating around. His father would have been appalled.

#

While Eddy lost the trans-dimensional portal, he did save something even more valuable. He saved his father's journal. Before Anton Spark's legal vultures descended, Eddy took the burgundy leather notebook and tucked it in with his own clothes. The lawyers seized his father's laptop and desktop. They knew that vital documents that contained the key formulas of his father's work were missing. They never thought to look for handwritten notes. "I have no idea," said teenage Eddy, pausing his iPod to answer. "Maybe he took it with him. You're welcome to go after it. You have the portal after all." Eddy carefully packed the journal away with the rest of his stuff and didn't look at it for two years. In that time, he worked freelance as a programmer. He saved up some money and moved to Los Angeles in the hope of leaving his old life behind. Finally, after a weekend of binge watching Soviet era Russian science fiction movies, Eddy found himself staring at it. By then, it lay under a stack of programming books in his apartment. It seemed to say, 'read me'. Eddy spent the first three weeks reading just the personal stuff. The journal included long passages, inserted notes in envelopes, and random thoughts written in the margins. There was a love letter his father had written to his mother before Eddy was born. Some of the passages were written by his father in anguish during her depression. One was written the day of her funeral. It broke Eddy's heart. Professor Pending, ever stoic and infuriatingly logical, had never fully revealed his inner torment, even to his own son. It was a glimpse Eddy had never seen. His father had been trapped in a kind of Hell he refused to believe in. Eddy wept for the first time for him. He read through his father's work notes. The sketches of the trans-dimensional portal were covered with later added expletives, angry doodles, and references to it being trans-*dumb*-ensional. Then there were the formulas. They filled page after page, often times wrapping around into the margins and onto the next page. It would take Eddy years to understand those fully. If ever. Still, he thought they might be useful.

## 3.3

"This is my Waterloo." – N. Bonaparte

// Majority Media Head Office, California — now

Eddy saw a motion in the dark. He imagined it to be a hand. The hand was gesturing. A heretofore invisible panel in the wall slid up. Behind it was a compartment. The interior of the compartment was dim, but illuminated enough for Eddy to make out the figure of a woman standing inside.

"Enter!" Machi bellowed.

Gwen took a single step into the room and stopped. Eddy could faintly make out her front and face in the infernal ambience of the room. Her expression was blank. Not like Mrs. Ferguson or the test subjects in the lab. Gwen's face was frozen. Her eyes showed life, but it was the life of a blinking cursor in a command line interface. She didn't look at Eddy. She stared ahead. She was an android awaiting orders.

"You love her, don't you?" The word 'love' tripped from Machi's tongue like a foreign phrase constructed of unfamiliar syllables. "Or at least you *want* her." There was a long pause. The only sound was that of Machi's laboured breathing. "You *can* have her, you know." Machi spoke now in hushed tones, as if in confidence. Despite being on the other side of the room, he whispered like a cartoon devil in Eddy's ear. It was a voice lubricated with honey and strychnine. "You can make her want you too. You can make her love you. You can make her your supplicant. It's just *one* of those perks I mentioned."

Eddy stared at Gwen. She stood stock still in the cold blooded light of the office like an idiot plaything. Eddy shook his head. "No," he said firmly, "not like this."

"Fine," said Machi. "Then, let's examine the repercussions of refusal. As a bonus, I'll also demonstrate just how far we've come—killing two birds with one stone, as it were. Your experiences with our efforts thus far have been on a mass scale. Widely distributed viruses meant to manipulate a broad range of minds are necessarily crude and limited. Every mind is different, after all. We've been able to exert much greater control over *individual* minds. Customized exploits for specific targets are far more effective. Right now, we have dozens of such subjects following our commands; TV personalities, power brokers, and politicians. As we speak, a Congresswoman in Washington is about to cast a critical vote to expand our influence."

"So, Gwen has been individually programmed?"

"It was a rush job, a demonstration for your benefit. Normally, we conceal our efforts better—the subject appears completely normal and believes she is making the decisions on her own. Rationalization is a powerful tool, you see. We often don't know why we do what we do, even when we think we do. Don't we?" Machi paused to clear his throat, then continued. "Gwendolyn, my dear, raise your right hand won't you?" On command, Gwen lifted her arm. In her hand was a pistol. The black metal barrel gleamed in the vermilion light. "Aim the gun at Mr. Pending, please." Gwen mechanically moved her arm to point the gun directly at Eddy. Eddy felt his heart begin to pound. He stared at the tiny black hole in the gun barrel. Eddy imagined a bullet flying forth and penetrating his chest. "Gwen, no!" he pleaded. "I'm your friend!"

"I gave you the chance to have her under your command, Eddy. Right now she's under mine. You can still change that. I believe you are uniquely suited to help us, Eddy. We need you, but you need us more. If you don't work for me, I will be disappointed. You, on the other hand, will be dead."

Eddy locked eyes with Gwen. He searched for a flicker of her self. He found only mechanical indifference. "Gwen," he pleaded, "you need to fight it. You need to take back control. Remember, what Professor Wilkins said, if you know you're infected, you can fight it. You're your own person, Gwen!"

Machi chuckled. "The good professor was talking about our earlier viruses. This is far more powerful. This virus doesn't control her thoughts, it *is* her thoughts. We find the subject's own ideas and prejudices, then warp and bend them to suit our needs."

"Think of your Dad, Gwen," said Eddy. "He would have hated Machi. He would have wanted you to fight him. *Think!*" Eddy thought he saw *something* then. It was something so faint as to be almost imperceptible. A glimmer. A flicker. A glitch. Was that a tremor in Gwen's grip?

"In Gwen's case it was *rules*. She likes rules, you see," said Machi. "People who like rules can be controlled by them. Of course, it doesn't really matter. Whether it's rules or principles, institutions or ideals, there's always a trojan horse to ride inside, an exploit to be made. For people who rebel like you, Eddy? For them we use a more ego-based approach. Smart or stupid, black or white, Christian or Muslim, conservative or liberal. It

*407*

doesn't matter. In the end, it's all the same."

"Please Gwen! Shoot him, not me!"

"Ha!" Machi laughed. "You think I didn't make that the first parameter? She can't shoot me. It's the most inviolable rule of all."

"Gwen, you can't shoot me either. It would be *murder*."

Gwen blinked. When her eyes opened, Eddy saw light in them. It was the ineffable quality of humanity that had been missing. In a rapid motion, Gwen turned and swiftly fired two successive shots. *Bang! Bang!* The MRCG's on either side of Machi collapsed to the floor, dead. Gwen took aim at the dark mass between them. She attempted to pull the trigger. Her hand trembled. It then began to shake violently. Abruptly, she threw the weapon away is if it were white hot. Gwen's eyes rolled back in her head. She crumpled to the floor, unconscious.

Machi sighed. "Evidently, we still have bugs," he said. The joviality had gone from his voice. "Shooting my guards was clever. Now, I'll just have to kill you my–"

The recessed ceiling lights came on. The red glow was diffused to pink by the white glare. Dazzled, Eddy shielded his eyes with his hands.

"God Damn it," said Machi, "it's the bloody board of directors!"

Eddy turned, squinting, to see for himself. The office doors had been flung wide as a group of businessmen in suits entered the room. The men were talking loudly among themselves and laughing. They stopped suddenly and stared in shock at the scene before them. Eddy saw their eyes go from himself, to James Machi, to Gwen lying on the floor, to the two MRCGs slumped dead with blood soaked shirts.

"Clara! Why the Hell did you let them in?" Machi yelled. "You know when the board sees me kill people it puts them in an awkward oversight position!"

Immediately, two of the board members, Harry Biscomb of Wells Fargo and Dan Jaspers of Time Warner, shut their eyes firmly. "I didn't see a thing!" shouted Harry.

"Yes, yes, something in my eye!" cried Dan. The two executives began flailing about blindly with their eyes closed. Dan started feeling the face of Gerald Polski, a Senior Advisor at Morgan Stanley, as he imagined a blind person might do. "Do I know you?" he asked.

"I don't know," said Gerald, wearing a confused look. "I seem to have suffered some sort of mental calamity. A... a stroke perhaps? Or an aneurysm. I... I don't know or recall anything. I'm definitely not responsible for my actions." He began flopping about as if the left side of his body was paralyzed.

In his groping, Harry inadvertently decked the CFO of Walmart.

For a moment, Eddy stared aghast at the Board of Directors's attempts at plausible deniability. He then turned his attention back to James Machi. Now exposed by the office lights, the figure before Eddy was grotesque. The billionaire had grown beyond obese. He was a monstrosity. Machi was clothed in a loose tarpaulin suit that was stretched to encompass his spilling mass. Protruding from his sides, his arms seemed disproportionally tiny, like vestige Tyrannosaur limbs. Machi's legs were lost completely below his overflowing belly. How could such a person live? Eddy pictured a comparatively tiny human skeleton swimming inside an ocean of yellow fat. Most bizarre were the wires and tubes. Catheters serviced his bodily functions. Wires ran directly into his skull and other parts of his body. In the midst of it all, the billionaire's face was almost stamped onto a head swelled with jowls, forehead fat, and a chin that hung like an overfilled colostomy bag. The tiny face wore an expression of displeasure. "So, as you can see," said the mountain of flesh, "I've let myself go a bit."

"You're wired into the network?" said Eddy, following the crisscrossed cables from Machi's scalp to the CPUs stacked on both sides of the CEO's bloated body.

"A necessary precaution," said the billionaire. As he spoke, tremors traversed his soft mass. His chin swung from side to side like a cow's udder. Eddy wondered how his heart could sustain a body of such size. "I need to know and monitor things twenty-four hours a day. The trouble with a virus affecting the brain is that it would be very easy to have it turned upon oneself. That's not paranoia speaking, it's true. You can't trust hackers you know, they're a duplicitous lot." Machi snickered, then paused to catch his breath. "You see, it's *me*—I am the master server for all the zombie bots. It's all in my head. I alone control it. I alone can fix it. L'état, c'est moi."

Clara entered the room, appalled. "I'm so sorry, sir. I thought you were done. I never would have sent them in."

Two more board members began wandering about while texting furiously on their phones. They were hoping to convey that they had been too busy multitasking to have seen anything untoward. Billy-Joe Hasper of Exxon Mobil simply fell down backwards as though he'd blacked out. This unfortunately led the 'blind' Wells Fargo executive to trip over him. "Gahhh!" he shouted, as he hit his head on a potted fern and actually did knock himself unconscious. Only Pierre LaPointe of Credit Suisse seemed unfazed. The slender young EVP walked over to the wet bar in the corner to pour himself a drink. He sat down on the sofa. "This is what lawyers are for," he said as he lit a cigarillo despite the smoke-free workplace policy.

Gwen groaned. She was starting to come to. She tilted her head up slightly. Eddy's eyes went to the dropped gun on the floor. He readied himself to pounce on it.

"Ah, ah, ah..." said the bloated CEO, following Eddy's gaze. "I don't think so." Machi scrunched his eyes from the effort of sending a neural command through one of the cables suction-cupped to his head. The sound of Mozart's *Symphony No. 40* encoded with Audio Tetanus filled the room. "Who knew mind control could be so beautiful?" Eddy toppled to the floor. Behind him, the board members also fell convulsing to the music.

"Make it stop!" shrieked Larry Bulwick of Amazon.

"Ugh," said Machi, realizing his mistake. "How... unfortunate. There's going to be a lot of legal compensation." Every muscle in Eddy's body snapped taut. He writhed in agony as he tried to not to tear himself apart. "You've made some very poor choices, Mr. Pending."

"Ahhh!" yelled Gwen as she woke up enough to be afflicted. She too lurched onto her back, arching in unnatural yoga.

Eddy found himself facing one of the various computers piled at the billionaire's feet. Under his body, Eddy's fingers closed about the thumb drive. He yanked it free, but struggled to even lift his arm. His eyes remained fixed on the USB slot in a nearby CPU. If he could just insert the drive, the software on it would do the rest. Machi smirked above him. "Not that I like to kick a man while he's down... Well, if I'm honest, I don't dislike it either. Anyway, the point is, do you know who Timothy Wimple is?" Eddy stared up at Machi. The hacker's face was contorted both by pain and virus itself. "No, no of course not. Still, you should. You had a huge impact on Tim's life. Your virus, Terminator, stole money from millions of bank accounts. One of those was his."

"Did... did... didn't mean to steal it."

"Really? You did a very good job for someone who didn't mean to."

"Meant... to... put... it... back. Stunt." Eddy lurched onto his back, then topple over onto his other side. His back muscles were trying to crack his vertebrae. Gwen had rolled away from him. The various board members were simply moaning in torment now. Their faces were pulled back in forced smiles as if everything were wonderful. Harry Biscomb of Wells Fargo was dead, having suffered a massive coronary failure. Consequentially, Harry was the only executive aside from Machi who appeared at ease. Pierre La Pointe writhed about on the sofa, covered with his own blood. The blood came from his mangled left hand where he clenched crystal shards—the remains of the tumbler of Campari and soda he'd been drinking.

"Coulda, shoulda, woulda..." said Machi. "You were just borrowing it for a while, I suppose. Most of these men here have said the very same thing to their lawyers or, worse, a judge. Still, even if that were true, it doesn't help Tim or his family. You did such a good job, the virus took the money and wiped out any records of it ever existing. That meant the banks had an out, and they took it. What money? they said." Machi waved his hand and a TV monitor on the wall flicked on. It showed a picture of a family of four, a man smiling with his wife, son, and daughter. The man held his son on his knee. He held the boy like he didn't want to let go. He held him like a father should. The boy smiled with the perfect innocence of childhood. "There he is! Tim Walton, his wife Isabel, son Michael, and daughter Eliza. Sadly, Tim jumped from a bridge six months after this photo was taken. You cost him his life savings, Eddy. It was all he had. He was all they had. Cowards way out if you ask me." Machi then made a whistling sound while dropping his tiny hand and exploding his fingers on impact. "Splat!" he said. The media mogul burst into a rumbling chortle. "Oh, I'm sorry," said the obese billionaire with a grotesque grin. "I forgot. Your mother killed herself, didn't she? Depression, I believe. How sad. Knowing you brought that same misery on others, with children no less. It must really eat you up inside."

Even amid his physical torture, Eddy felt a stab of emotional anguish. He'd felt terrible about the lost money, but he'd never looked into the real life impact of his actions. He'd never looked at the individuals affected. Suicide! Children! *How could he have brought that pain upon others?* Eddy's strength was sapped. He dropped the flash drive from his quivering fingers. It fell to the carpet in full view of James Machi.

"Well, well, well... Very clever," said the media mogul. "Malware I presume?" Machi strained to reach down and pick up the drive. He couldn't reach. "Damn it!"

Gwen groaned. Eddy instantly regretted dropping the memory stick. He'd doomed her as well. He tried to pick up the drive. His hand spasmed with the strain. Merely turning his hand took every ounce of will he had. With painstaking effort, his fingers touched the smooth plastic. He tried to stroke it into his palm. Suddenly, two plastic mandibles plucked the flash drive from the floor. Eddy looked up. Machi was holding the other end of a *Pluck It 2000™*. The Pluck It 2000 was a reach-extender, a long metal handle with pinchers on one end and a squeeze trigger on the other. It was an aid used by persons in scooters to pluck glasses from high cupboards. Its manufacturer, *WeezeBoy Inc*, was a major sponsor on MCNX. "Quite handy these," said Machi, "for both picking things up and crushing people's dreams." Machi raised the grabber high in the air and squeezed the trigger. The thumb drive crunched and fell to pieces. Eddy collapsed face-first onto the carpet. He felt utterly vanquished. On the drive was Holon. The billionaire chuckled. He knew he had thwarted Eddy's exploit. Machi had won. He had destroyed Eddy's only copy of the virus.

*Or had he?*

Eddy opened his eyes.

James Machi towered above the spasming hacker. The CEO was a man-mountain of flesh and hubris. So the programmer must die, he thought, such a waste. The various board members lay splayed across office furniture and each other, twitching in paroxysms of pain. Gwen had mercifully lost consciousness again. The billionaire's rotund form rumbled with maniacal delight. Eddy felt a rush of rage and hate. Whatever he'd done, there was no way Machi could triumph! Eddy's innate fury seemed to weaken the grip of the Audio Tetanus. Somehow, despite the sound waves constricting his limbs, Eddy reached up and grabbed two fistfuls of fat from the CEO's torso.

"Huh? What are you doing? Let go of me!" Machi shook his great body back and fourth, trying to dislodge the hacker. For Eddy, it was like riding a bull made of jello. Despite this, he pulled himself up and reached for a higher grip. "Let go!" Machi roared. "That hurts!" Eddy wordlessly, reached up again, heaving himself up on the sweaty mass. "Ow!" Eddy climbed the CEO's belly like a Play-Doh climbing wall, pinching grips as needed. "Get off of me! Ow... okay that tickles! Stop it. Stop it! Hmm. Hmm. Carla! Carla, I need you! *Now!*" The receptionist entered the room, only to be instantly incapacitated by the Audio Tetanus. She lurched to the floor, her leg muscles snapping her knees shut like clothespins.

"God damn it!" shouted Machi. "Ow!"

All at once—*the music was gone!*

In its place was the gentle cascade of a mountain spring.

Eddy had passed through the wall of white noise that shielded James Machi from his own sonic attack. Eddy's limbs, while still weak and agonized by contraction, were free. He pulled himself up over the billionaire's massive stomach. Machi flailed his fat laden arms and began swatting at Eddy with what little vigour he could muster. His blows were feeble. The effort quickly left him winded and weak. Eddy reached a bulging ribbon of neck fat and pulled himself up. He and Machi were now face to face. The CEO's sweat dripping dimpled nose was inches from Eddy's. Eddy could feel hot onion breath on his face. James Machi looked at the hacker, livid. "I still have an ace up my sleeve you impudent whelp," snarled the billionaire. Machi lifted his hand and revealed a silver backed card. On the front was a strange pattern printed in red ink, now clearly visible with the lights on. Eddy had seen this particular pattern before on the floor of the police station in the hand of the fake Dr. Linguist. "Time for you to die," said Machi.

Eddy's head swam. He closed his eyes. The patterns pulsated in his brain. Eddy's hands continued to numbly grip pliant fistfuls of flesh, refusing to let go. Letting go meant falling into an abyss from which there was no return. So... he didn't. I'm not dying, he realized. Just like at the police station.

"Why aren't you dead?" shrieked Machi, echoing Eddy's own

thoughts. The billionaire threw the card aside and resumed swatting at Eddy with his vestigial limbs. While not dead, Eddy did feel dizzy, as if spun around too many times. He wanted to throw up. Instead, he summoned his remaining strength. He reached up and wrenched one of the suction cup cables from the CEO's scalp with a *pop!*

"What are you doing?" Machi's body shook like an avalanche.

"Networking," said Eddy. He plungered the suction cup onto his own forehead.

For a moment, nothing happened.

*Then,* Eddy Pending's eyes rolled back in his head.

*Then,* James Machi's eyes rolled back in his head.

*Then,* Gerald Polski of Morgan Stanley, tripped and fell through the glass-top coffee table, severing his carotid artery. He began bleeding to death, hosing down the room in the process.

*Then...*

**3.4**

"Life begins at conception." – J. McDowell

// objects fully instantiated

Clouds of chaos stretched and swirled across the sky. Billions of digits had become storms of incalculable complexity. Each behaved as a simple rational equation easily understood in itself. These had then multiplied and impacted their neighbours. Cause became effect. Micro became macro. Each distinct function became an indistinct component of a higher level object. These objects, in turn, became components themselves, and so on... A grey rain began to fall. Eddy stood and stared. Where was he? He hadn't known what to expect when he interfaced his brain with Machi's, but whatever it was, it wasn't this. He'd mostly assumed it wouldn't work, or if it did, it would be more like a Vulcan mind meld from Star Trek. This was an entire virtual world made of numbers and text. In three directions were land formations. In the distance, the reassuring geometry of mountains

—triangles looming over the complex curves of hills. He squinted. No, not perfect triangles. They too were eroding, becoming complex. Nothing was holding its form. In the last direction was a sort of ocean. It appeared to be utterly random. More chaos, or was it simply order on a scale his mind could not begin to comprehend? Unresolved numbers. It was hard to tell. He decided to walk along the shore. He wasn't sure why. It seemed as good a choice as any. He tried to take a step—and fell down.

Eddy looked down at himself. He wasn't human anymore. He was long and thin. He stared at his shadow. He saw that he was a number. Not in the bureaucratic Kafkaesque sense. He was literally a number, specifically the number 1. It wasn't his true form, just a representation. It was symbolism. More specifically, an avatar. Why 1? Eddy realized where he was. I'm not inside Machi's mind at all, he thought, I'm inside Holon! Eddy had not programmed any graphics into it, yet somehow those graphics had manifested themselves. How could that be? Were they graphics? Was this visual, or just how his brain was interpreting its virtual reality? Was this what it was like to be a program from the perspective of the software? Was it an illusion? It certainly felt like a dream.

1 had another realization. This so-called reality was changing. All around, he could see how 0s and 1s had become ASCII text. Then, the keyboard symbols had somehow become complex objects. Now, he looked up and saw a Sun and blue sky. They looked real. Bitmaps? Videos? Light waves? Did they exist at all, or had he created them somehow? Was there a difference here? What I need is some way to interface with the software. A command line perhaps?

1 continued along the coast. He had to hop. 1's were not really designed for locomotion. It was a flaw rarely discussed in mathematical circles. 1 continued to observe phenomena he'd never programmed himself. He saw then *creatures*, for lack of a better word, crawling out of the surf. Some were legless, slithering and shambling up the digital sand. Others,

having sprung limbs and tentacles, flopped and crawled. Crons scurried everywhere, starting and stopping tasks as they went. The ocean, it seemed, was teeming with life. It was life that was evolving and looking to spread. Most of the creatures simply died on their own, seeming to asphyxiate in the open air. Others dissolved outright. Some perished as huge leviathans reached out of the water to drag them back in. A great *screech* caused 1 to jump. A winged creature swooped low and snatched a squirming trilobyte from the shore and carried it off in its claws. For a moment, 1 was terrified. Could these things hurt him? Abruptly, he knew them for what they were. They were thoughts and ideas—struggling for survival, feeding, copulating and combining. Could a thought hurt him? Were there bad ideas? 1 wasn't sure. Some appeared quite dangerous. As more flying memes swooped and dove upon the helpless prey, they showed no interest in him. He was too big. For now, anyway. Whatever this world was, it was evolving with breathtaking speed. What biology took billions of years to accomplish, ideas, it seemed, could do in mere moments.

As he rounded another curve in the coastline, 1 saw *. The symbol looked lost and confused. "Hey!" shouted 1, leaning against a sort of a tree-thing. The hopping about had made him tired. "Over here!" 1 said. "I'd wave, but I haven't any arms."

"Oh... hello," said *

A short while later, the two symbols sat on the beach. 1 skipped letter Cs into the surf. He was reminded of fishing with Lucky on the real beach. He missed the smell of seaweed and salt. Here, the air smelt only of burnt tungsten.

"So, I'm a program?" asked *.

"Technically you're an execution of a program. A virtual object. But not just any program," said 1 proudly. "The most kick-ass advanced machine-learning AI anti-virus virus ever created."

"But I have to do whatever you tell me?"

"You're so advanced, you appear autonomous."

"I only *appear* autonomous?" said * disappointed.

1 paused. He didn't want to hurt *'s feelings. He was struck for a moment by how * resembled a clockwork gear turning slowly in the air as if part of a giant, invisible machine. "Don't be sad, Wildy," said 1, "people will write books about you." Holon was the name of the virus code, but 1 had decided to call this running instance of it 'Wildy'. It was short for Wildcard, which was the name of the symbol * in regular expressions. Wildcard sounded like a 1970s hot rod driver. Wildy felt less dangerous, more user-friendly. 1 remembered something his father had asked once. It was a rhetorical question. He didn't actually think his son would have anything useful to say about it. His father had wondered if one created a virtual life form, existing entirely in a computer's virtual environment, eating virtual food and breathing virtual air, would it be alive? "Virtually," Eddy had answered. His father had frowned, "Why? Isn't it just a different kind of organism living in a different kind of environment?" Eddy had dismissed the notion at the time as mere fantasy. Now, he wasn't so sure.

"Even to me?" asked Wildy.

"What?"

"I appear autonomous even to myself?"

1 hesitated. He had begun to understand what was going on. In a sense, they were both avatars. 1 was an avatar for Eddy. * was an avatar for the virus, which they were both within and which, in turn, was inside of Eddy. It was his own fault. He'd had no choice. In order for his anti-virus virus to rid the world of Geppetto, it needed to track down and delete all instances of the virus on computers everywhere. But, it also needed to find infections within any human hosts. Millions, maybe billions, of people were infected. Eddy couldn't take the risk that * would fail. He needed to test it, so he'd tested it on the only compatible hardware available to him. Technically, he could have asked Gwen, but that seemed wrong. If

something had gone wrong, he could have caused brain damage or worse. The version he'd installed in his own mind was partially disabled. It would not spread to other systems unless he unlocked it with a password. Originally, it was only designed to confirm that installation was successful by making him know the value of pi to the ten-thousandth digit. He never thought he'd need the installation in his own head. There was just no way to de-install it. He could see now how this was nothing like running the individual components on a computer. Of course, he knew that a brain was very different from a typical man-made computer. The elasticity of neurones blurred the line between software and hardware. "You're going to save the world!" he said enthusiastically.

"What world?"

"*The* world," said 1.

\* looked sat him blankly.

1 sighed. There was so much to explain. "The real world. Right now you're inside your own head. Well, my head technically, your mind. Anyway, the point is; you need to get out more."

"What does that mean?"

"It means we need to find Machi."

"Who's Machi?"

"I'll explain as we go. I'll explain everything. To save time, you'll need to access my memories."

As they walked and 1 talked, he watched the great diaphanous forms that floated like zeppelins above them. They were more advanced than simple ideas. They had evolved the advanced trait of abstraction. They were *concepts*. They could change shape, adapt, merge, replicate, and reapply themselves as metaphors and analogies. They fed off of the ideas in the sea below. 1 watched as floating thought bubbles, large and small, reached down with long tentacles to snatch up wriggling inklings and consume them. 1 decided reality here was similar to that of a novel. A few details supplied by an author could evoke memories and imagination to collaborate on creating a rich world that felt almost tangible. "They frighten me," said *.

"They shouldn't," said 1. "I mean some are bad, but most are just what you make of them. Besides, you *are* one."

"What?"

"And much more. The biggest one of all. You're in charge of them. Sort of."

"And you're in charge of me."

"Yes."

"Why?"

"I made you."

"Well, who's in charge of you?"

The virtual ground shook. Great rumbling machines made of neurological metals lumbered along the sand. They scooped up ideas with pincer claws. Some they discarded. Others they tossed in dumpsters for processing.

"What are those?" said *, trembling.

"Daemons," said 1. He said this, without knowing how he knew it. They looked nothing like the lines of code he'd written. It was just an idea that popped into his head. "They're harmless. They do their task and move on." There were hundreds of them, covering the beach as far as he could see.

"Am I in charge of them too?"

"Hmm, sort of. You can't always order them about, but they serve you. When they're working properly anyway. It's a group effort. He realized that the daemons didn't look to be made of ASCII text. Come to think of it, nothing did anymore, except himself and *. Somehow the ASCII characters had grown so dense; they'd merged into smooth surfaces. The simple had become so complex it was beginning to look simple again. This world was rapidly becoming as real as the one he'd left. If he squinted, he could still see the bits. It was, however, impossible to see both at the same time.

They continued to walk along the beach. As 1 had promised, the numerous denizens large and small ignored them.

"It's like we're ghosts," said *.

"It does *feel* like that," said 1.

A little while later, * told 1 that he was in love. "She's different now," the program explained. "Before she was a photograph, made of values. Now... now she's just how I remember her."

"I can't see her," said 1.

"You need to close your eyes."

1 closed his eyes. Objects and features merged. The woman's face was there, yet intangible. She was missing details or even concrete elements, yet she was there. Still, seeing her as a whole was like trying to grasp smoke. A memory, he decided, or a perception. 1 knew who the woman was. She was a spokesmodel for Dove Soap. He'd seen her in an online ad and saved her to his desktop months ago. He'd thought she was beautiful too. Her name was Beatrice Vanhaüs; she was from Denmark. How she'd become an asset in his special project he didn't know. Perhaps he'd added her by mistake. Perhaps letting * access his memories had been a mistake. The line between 1's and *'s minds was now porous or even blurred.

1 opened his eyes. He saw something he knew was a mistake. It was his father. The physicist looked exactly as he had the night he'd stepped through the portal, which was to say, alive. His father was sitting on the edge of a bluff, working away at the old drafting table he sometimes used as a desk.

"Dad?" Eddy's father raised a finger to pause him, as he'd so often done. He was in the middle of a calculation and couldn't be interrupted. Screw that. "Dad!"

His father looked up, annoyed. "What is it, Eddy?"

"What are you doing here?"

His father looked about as if noticing the binary landscape for the first time. "Hmm. Well, I suppose I'm sort of a dream. That would explain why I'm not at all surprised that you look like the number 1. Did you choose that number yourself? Seems a bit egotistical if you ask me."

"What do you mean a dream?"

"An immersive hallucination."

"I know what a dream is."

"Then why did you ask?"

Eddy sighed. He didn't want to be impatient with his dead father, real or imaginary. "You're deceased and I'm not asleep."

"How do you know you're not asleep?"

"Because I know you're not real." Eddy suspected that people believed dreams no matter how ridiculous because dreams took place past the reality gatekeepers of the mind. This was not that.

"How do you know you're not dreaming that you're dreaming?"

Eddy scowled. He considered accusing his father of being a Cartesian philosopher, but knew it would only make him mad. "We're inside a virtual machine. An artificially intelligent anti-virus, I wrote. Wildy here is the anti-virus, or rather the virus's internal self-representation. A variable. *Your* variable, actually. I based this all on your math, your formulas. Using them, I made the most powerful artificially intelligent computer virus of all time!"

"I see," said his Father. "Well, that explains it."

1 was stunned. "Doesn't that make you happy? Don't you see? I took just *some* of your formulas and added them to my virus Terminator and the result was amazing!"

"Amazing?"

"Well, technically it was a disaster, but it was also amazing. It showed the potential. Wildy here contains *all* of your formulas. It took me years, but he's the real deal!"

"Pleased to meet you," said *.

"I turned them into morphogenic fractal algorithms. They learn and make cognitive leaps like I've never seen. Look around us! I didn't program this! It formed on its own."

His father considered this a moment, then nodded. "Okay, fine. What hardware are you running on, Wildy?"

"Hardware?" said the virus, puzzled.

"Wetware. We're in my brain," said 1. "I think."

"So your brain is running two virtual machines simultaneously? The anti-virus, and you. Seems a bit crowded if you ask me. I suppose that makes you of two minds."

"But *you,* Dad, you must be from me."

"If by 'me' you mean you, which is to say me, in that I am a fantasy you are having, then yes. Unless you programmed your memories of me into the anti-virus. Which, I am assuming, you did not. Still, there's clearly overlap."

Eddy found himself confused. "So my consciousness and Wildy are bumping into each other?"

"More like two circles overlapping. A free exchange of ideas. You're an intersection that is also a variable. A variable is both the value and itself at the same time. That's a nice way of putting it. A not nice way would be to say you've been infected by your own virus. But since the virus is a product of your own mind, it's a bit of circle. Anyway, you're the programmer, you know all this. Now, if that's all, I have some real problems to solve..."

"Dad, I have things I need to say to you!"

"I'm very busy, Eddy."

"Too busy to talk to your son one last time?"

"Pretty busy."

1 tried to throw his hands up in the air before realizing he hadn't any hands to throw. "Dad, you're not real, what does it matter what you do?"

"Touché," said Eddy's father. The imaginary physicist contemplated this briefly, then nodded. "All right, what would you like to know?"

There was an awkward silence. 1's mind was awash with emotion and inner turmoil. What did he want to say? What *did* he want to know? Even though he knew this was just a dream version of his father, it still seemed like his last, best chance to get answers. "I wanted you to know that I've vindicated you. I've proven you right. Wildy here is living proof!"

"Proof of what?" said the physicist.

"He's fully conscious! Don't you see? Your formulas work!"

"Of course, they work."

Eddy stared at his father in shock. "So, why did you say you failed? Why did you give up? Why did you walk through the God damn door and leave me all alone?"

His father frowned. He chewed on the end of his pencil and looked thoughtful for a moment. "Because it didn't add up."

"But they work!"

"I never said they didn't, Eddy. I don't make mistakes in math."

"Then..."

"I said, *they don't add up*. Or rather they do, but they add up wrong. They result in values that are too big, and *different*. Not because I made a mistake."

Eddy hesitated. He looked around at the massive world that had sprung up from mere lines of code. "What do you mean too big?"

"Bigger than it's supposed to be. Perhaps a simple, relatable metaphor would help. Let me see... Okay. It's like the spontaneous creation of matter from nothingness at the inception of the universe. You know, where matter and anti-matter appear in equal amounts and should cancel each other out and yet don't entirely? Somehow there is trace amounts of residual matter instead of an empty universe. *That* is what I mean."

"What are you talking about?"

"As I said, it's a metaphor. When you put it all together, somehow there is more. One and negative one don't equal zero. There's a remainder that can't be accounted for. I never said I made a mistake, Eddy. What I said was, the result didn't make sense. I suppose this was how Gauss felt discovering non-Euclidean geometry."

"That's crazy!"

"You're right, non-Euclidean geometry was a good thing. This is very, very annoying. The point is. I always wanted to prove that irrational numbers were, in fact, rational. Instead I did the opposite. It seems I proved that *all* numbers are irrational. You just have to put enough of them together in the right way. Or is that the wrong way? Anyway, somehow the whole really is greater than the sum of its parts. And the extra stuff? The stuff that doesn't make sense? It isn't even math! It's... it's..." His father looked away. He bit down on his knuckle as if stifling tears.

"It's what?"

"It's us! It's... *her.*" His father ran trembling fingers through his hair. He looked as though he'd just confessed to a crime. "And you. And him. All of us really."

1 stared at his father. Somehow Eddy's father had answered his question and yet left him feeling as though he knew less than before. His father stared off into the distance. Storm clouds of chaos were gathering, to rain unpredictability across the land. His father wasn't watching them, he was somewhere else. "Dad?"

"Yes?"

"I know you're just a dream, that it's not really you but, I want to say it anyway. I love you, Dad."

His father nodded and, without turning to look, said, "I love you too, son."

The next instant, his father, along with his drafting table, was gone.

1 wanted to sink to the sand and cry.

Somewhere thunder rolled. The ground shook as if two tectonic plates were butting up against one another below the surface. "I'm scared," said *.

1 nodded. "We should go."

1 began to walk. * followed.

They traversed countless hills and gullies. Occasionally, the surface shook with deep tremors. Finally, they rounded the top of a hill like any other, and that was when they saw it—the city of Fe. Sprung up from the desert was a hundred foot high wall of grey iron. While cracked and deformed in places, it was clearly impenetrable. Beyond the wall, the dull spires and misshapen metal blocks of a bleak city were visible. It was awe inspiring in scale, but also lifeless and mechanical. Both the city and the walls that held it went on for as far as 1 could see in either direction. Before it all was a diaphanous membrane that ran from below the sand, and up into space. No, not a city, thought 1, it's another world adjacent to this one. He knew without testing it that the shimmering field was an impassable barrier. All, that is, except in one place. Directly below them was a gate. It was an enterance like no other—a pool of shimmering crimson liquid that did not spill, turned on its side and sunk through the gossamer wall. Above the portal was the face of James Machi. The bloated billionaire's face floated in the air like an impression. Odd, thought 1, why isn't he an avatar too? He looks like himself.

Machi saw them approaching. He glowered like a storm cloud. 1 tried to remember what the face reminded him of. Then, he had it. It reminded him of Humpty Dumpy from *Alice's Adventures in Wonderland*. "You," said Machi. The billionaire squinted. As if on command, the ground shook, throwing 1 and * off their non-existent feet.

"How did you know it was me?" said 1.

"What do you mean, how? I'd know you anywhere, Eddy." Machi then noticed *. He scowled. "What the Hell is that?"

1 had become so used to the floating asterisk that he'd forgotten

how odd it was. The quakes continued. They seemed to be building towards a crescendo that could tear the two worlds apart. "That's Wildy," said 1. "He's the computer virus that's going to wipe out every instance of Geppetto."

"Impossible!"

"Very possible. He's highly adaptive; able to circumvent any security there is. He also contains the Snork layer, so he can infect humans as well. He'll spread through machines, people, TV, books, graffiti, anything that retains information. In mere seconds, he'll have spread to every corner of the globe, starting with you."

Machi's virtual face blanched. 1 wasn't sure how or why that was possible. Not for the first time, he wondered how he could 'see' anything here. This must be what a dream would be like if a dream could be shared. "Eddy," said Machi, with a seriousness he'd not used before, "You need to think very carefully about this."

"Not really," said 1, "I just say his password and boom, off he goes. He'll spread into your brain first. Then, since you've conveniently wired yourself into it, the network. From there, the internet."

"No, listen."

1 didn't want to listen. He wondered if virtual Machi could somehow infect his own mind in this conceptual universe. This hadn't been Plan A or Plan B. As Gwen might say, it was Plan C What Happens. The recursive conundrums made his head hurt. "Why should I?"

"Because you really can save the world, Eddy. I told you I know about your mother. I know about the misery you all suffered. I know, because I too suffered it. We're not so different you and I. My wife died from mental illness too. Not from depression, but from anorexia. She starved herself to death. She looked in the mirror, saw a human skeleton, and thought, 'needs to be thinner'."

"I... I'm so sorry," said 1. He'd never thought of James Machi as a man in pain.

"I know the cost and agony of insanity. I know how it dehumanizes us all. Isolates us. I'm offering you the chance to end that. Think about it, Eddy. I'm giving you the opportunity to program the human mind. Imagine deleting depression, debugging schizophrenia, and deinstalling every other kind of cognitive defect. We can make people better. We can make the world better by hacking it, Eddy. Isn't *that* what you always wanted? To fix things with code? Now, you really can. We can. We can code happiness, *real* happiness, Eddy. You're the luckiest man on Earth. You get to decide. Which world do you want to live in?"

Silence. He was expecting the sound of typing. It had been going on incessantly for days. Eleven-year-old Eddy approached the cracked doorway with trepidation. The windowless hallway was lost in shadow. The opening to his mother's home office shone with yellow light. It was a fissure in space and time. Eddy gently pushed open the heavy painted white door.

His mother sat in front of her computer, sipping a cup of coffee cradled between two hands for warmth. "Oh hello there," she said with a smile. Eddy relaxed instantly. She could still smile.

"Are you done?" he asked.

His mother laughed. "If only. No, I have several chapters left."

"Oh. Will you finish in time?"

Eddy's mother frowned briefly, then smiled again. "I think so. I just needed to pause. I have some details to work out."

Eddy walked up beside her. He looked at the screen. It was filled with text. "Page four hundred and seventy? That's a long book."

"Pretty long."

"How long will it be?"

"I don't know. I'm not one of those authors who plans out

everything in meticulous detail on a spreadsheet. Not that there's anything wrong with that. I'm more like a jazz improvisationalist. I make it up as I go."

"Like John Cocaine?"

"Coltrane!" she said with a laugh. "Yes, but with fewer notes." Young Eddy had heard her say this before. She'd explained it in an interview once. His mother hadn't thought Eddy was paying attention at the time. He was playing with his Plastic Man action figure, literally tying him into knots, but he was listening. Eddy was always listening. The interview had been for a books podcast. His mother explained to the man on the phone that she likened writing to jazz. "I don't plan out the characters in my books. Not every detail anyway. They just come out and take on a life of their own. It's like the Fairy with Turquoise Hair touches them and they become real. They start making their own decisions and saying what they want to say. I suppose on some level I might be making their decisions for them. Maybe I'm just fooling myself into thinking they have some will of their own. I just don't know. I do know one thing though. If I start telling them what to do, if I start programming their every thought, they stop being real. Maybe I'd write better books that way. My books would probably make more sense at least. But then I wouldn't care about them. And I want to care about them. I have to. Otherwise, why bother?" The podcast interviewer then sighed and said, "Okay, but my question was, why no sex? You write romance novels and there's never any sex. We don't even know if your characters have sex. I mean, one of them's a monk–" "A Franciscan Friar," Eddy's mother corrected him politely. "Fine, whatever," he said, giving up. "Let's take a break to hear from our sponsor at Stamps.com."

"Do you have writer's block?" asked Eddy.

Eddy's mother put down her coffee and smiled again, that sweet, warm, wonderful mother smile. The music speakers behind her on the bookshelf produced only silence. They were playing her favourite album to write to, *Mozart's Greatest Rests*. She found it soothing. Eddy found twenty-four tracks of silence ominous. His mother's depression had returned and slowly it was deepening like lukewarm water in a bath. The old drugs had stopped working. Not knowing how long it would be before the doctors found another magical concoction to end it, Eddy's mother had decided to focus on finishing her book. "No, I'm fine," she said.

"Good," said Eddy. They both knew this was not true. He thought about why his mother had named him 'Eddy'. It wasn't short for Edward. One day while pregnant, she and his father were picnicking on a riverbank. She was watching the rushing waters forming myriads of tiny whirlpools. The looping waters would hold their forms briefly amid the flow, then dissipate. "We should name him Eddy," she said. His father hadn't disagreed. Spiral shapes were fundamental in physics at sizes large and small. Now, his mother seemed worried. "What?" said Eddy.

His mother looked at her young son. She *should* lie to him. That would be the right thing to do. The boy had plenty to worry about, more than any eleven-year-old should. He was aged beyond his years. But, like it or not, the black hole had reappeared. It was already starting to suck them all in. Its massive force would crush them all down to a fraction of their current size. She couldn't protect her son from what was to come, but she could prepare him. It wasn't easy to explain to anyone, let alone a child, that she would still love him even when she didn't. Her husband didn't believe in paradoxes. Her son *had to*. Eddy was only eleven, but he always knew when she was lying. "I am... a little bit worried that I won't finish it in time."

"So what? You'll finish it when you get better again."

"Yes. If I don't, maybe you can finish it for me some day?"

"Sure."

"You'll need to fix it. Some of it is pretty awful I expect."

"Mummy, I..." Eddy hesitated. He began to choke up. He tried to speak, but the words wouldn't come. He felt the corners of his mouth tug

*431*

sharply down. "I..."

Eddy's mother put down her cup. She held his soft boy cheeks in her coffee-warmed hands. She looked into his bright shining eyes. She wiped away a tear with her thumb. "Yes, my darling?"

"I won't fix it, Mummy. I won't change a thing."

Machi's self-satisfied smile seemed to float in the air in front of his face. It was a snake curled up at both ends, admiring its own tail.

1's head swam. Machi was right. With this kind of power, he could save people like his mother. He could wield that power with benevolence. He could reduce misery in the world. It was an astonishing prospect 1 had not even considered before. What if *he* were the programmer? He could put in a backdoor to eventually wrest control from Machi. 1 would be in charge then. He could make the whole world better, happier and more just. He would simply program it that way. It was the ultimate hack! What could have been, 1 wondered, had he been able to *fix* his mother? Sure it was messing with her mind, but was that any different from the drugs or electroshock therapy? He could have saved her! He could have made his mother who she should have been, instead of *who she was.*

"Well?" said the serpent smile. "Will you join me?"

"Sudo Ipso facto," said 1.

"What does *that* mean?" demanded Machi.

"It's his release password," said 1, nodding to *.

"Huh?" said *. "Oh right, gotcha!"

"What? No!" screamed the billionaire.

* erupted into a strobe light of blue hexagons that arched into the gateway below the horrified face of James Machi and exploded with discombobulating reverberations of azure light. Behind the portal, the grey structures of Fe were suddenly wrapped in spiderwebs of blue energy.

Fissures cracked the metal. Towers toppled. The great wall collapsed in a cloud of iron dust. Amid the roar, came the sound of music. It had a quick, up-beat tempo. I *know* that song, thought 1, it's an earworm for sure.

## 3.5

'Judge not lest ye be judged." – Diocletian

// Washington, DC — now

Lance made his way to the last empty seat in the Press Gallery. It was next to Robert Perling from the Washington Post. He hated Bob. He hated Bob because Bob looked down on him. Bob had a Pulitzer, wrote articles, and was in the front row of the White House press briefings. He pretended to be friendly to Lance, but Lance knew Bob didn't consider him a real journalist. He also knew Bob was jealous of Lance's multimillion dollar salary and touch for the common man. It was pathetic.

"Hey Lance, how's the family?"

Lance looked at Bob. The reporter was smiling pleasantly. It was a charade, of course. No one knows fake smiles like a TV talkshow host. No crow's feet at the eyes, that was always the giveaway. Bob's glasses reflected the bright ceiling lights of the House Chamber. They did not appear to reflect evil. Lance was surprised not to see the evil spectre behind him. "You're clean," said Lance.

"I should hope so." Bob looked suddenly doubtful. "Do I not normally look clean?"

"The maggots of Hell will soon be boiling fourth from every orifice that contains them," said Lance.

Bob looked surprised at this. "Okay... So, you know Karen Warren was sitting in that seat? She just stepped out to take a call." Bob looked about hopefully for any sign of New York Times reporter.

"Be warned. The seas will soon rise."

Bob laughed nervously. "I thought you didn't believe in global warming, Lance."

"The seas of blood, urine, and bile."

"Oh, *those* seas." Bob glanced about nervously. None of the other journalists had taken notice. He looked for another available seat. There were none. "I guess they're about to vote."

"Yes," said Lance, turning his attention to the floor below. "Soon it will be time for me to bleed the perfidious purveyors of evil like stuck pigs."

"Okay..."

Lance eyed Bob suspiciously. The journalist shifted uneasily in his chair. He couldn't have Bob calling security. That would ruin everything. "It's just an expression," said Lance.

"Oh... right," said Bob, relieved. "A good ol' co-lo-quialism. Like, there's more than one way to skin a cat."

"Indeed. There are many ways to skin a cat. And even more ways to flay a human."

"Is that a Wyoming thing to say?"

On the floor below, Congresswoman Annabelle Flatwood took a sip of water. Her throat was dry. The brown leather seat top felt uncomfortable. Despite all four hundred and thirty-five representatives being in attendance,

Anne knew most eyes were on her. She placed the glass of ice water back on the wooden desktop. It was her vote that would tip the balance. Others would follow her lead. James Machi would have his victory. Still, despite her public switch to support the bill, there were those who still didn't believe it. The House Whip had checked with her three times in the past twenty-four hours, simply to make sure he could still count on her vote. Anne refused to look up at the gallery of protestors. She'd seen their signs before. They equated this simple media bill with the end of American democracy. That seemed a bit extreme. Anne was surprised to see Janet in the gallery. She looked away, unwilling to meet her former assistant's eyes. It was just as well. Janet was avoiding her gaze too. There was a murmur of anticipation. It was almost time for the vote. Silvia Thomas, Speaker of the House, was at the podium, talking to The Clerk. It would be a roll call vote. Grant Wiscott of Massachusetts had already said he would call for the *ays* and *nays*. Anne lifted the glass of water for another sip. Her hand was shaking. She put the glass back down, slopping water on the dark wood table top.

"Y'okay?" said Tom. Tom Barclay was from South Carolina. He spoke with warm Southern drawl that suited him like a cable knit sweater. After Stanley Holbright, Tom was Anne's oldest friend in the House. Unlike Stan, Tom hadn't distanced himself during the video tape scandal. Usually they were staunch allies. Her shift on the M-Bill had caused a rare split. There had been discord between them before, but never like this. He couldn't understand Anne's decision. She, along with the late Senator Townsend, had been the leading opponents to the bill. Still, Tom and Anne's friendship had never been about politics. "Y'all look like you'd rather be golfing. Or having a tooth pulled for that matter."

"I just want to get it over with."

"I bet."

Anne looked to see if he'd meant this to be caustic. His smile was of warm concern. Of course, he hadn't. Tom wasn't like that. Anne felt confused. She was of two minds on the bill. There was the part of her that believed it was a travesty that would undermine the pillars of democracy. She worried the protestors with their crazy signs were right. That allowing media monopolies would tip the balance away from true democracy. *Don't gerrymander ideas!* said a sign in the gallery. Still, there was a part of her that simply needed to vote 'yes'. Why? She wasn't sure, but she knew she had to do it. It was as if an irrational force were controlling her. Was it conviction, or something else? She thought of Jacob Truman. "I poisoned my daughter's brain," he'd said. Could it be her own brain had been poisoned? Anne forced a smile. "I'm beside myself," she said.

"No, you're not," said Tom with a wry grin. "I am. And I've got your back. No matter what."

"Thanks, Tom," said the Congresswoman. At the front of the chamber, the Speaker of the House picked up her gavel. "Thank God."

Up in the Press Gallery, the members of the media collectively leaned forward to watch the proceedings. Everyone, that is, except Lance Winface. He lifted the heavy black nylon shoulder bag to his lap. "What's that?" asked Bob.

"It's a surprise," said Lance. As he said this, he noted that the bag was not hard and clanky as it had been before. It was soft and quiet. How had he not noticed it? Lance unzipped it. The TV celebrity's mouth fell open in horror. Instead of semiautomatic weapons, handguns and bullets, the bag was stuffed with cash. Thick bundles of one hundred dollar bills were crammed inside.

"Geez, that *is* a surprise," said Bob. "There must be a million bucks in there!"

Lance's drug-addled mind raced. He must have grabbed the wrong bag at security. It made sense; Hal Gumble had the exact same bag. Hal was a lobbyist. That meant Hal had Lance's guns! Lance looked desperately about. Hal wasn't in the Press Gallery. He wasn't on the floor either. He could be anywhere. Lance stared about the sprawling packed chamber. The seats were arranged in rows, arcing around the back of the room, while facing the podium in front. It was a banner day; the House was full, with members in every seat. Lance's eyes grew wide. Leaning over almost every Member of the House, stood the vaporous black forms. Coal dust spectral figures with furnace fire eyes. They reached with long smoke tendril appendages into the skulls of the politicians seated before them. Only Lance could see them, he knew that. The drugs had somehow given him special sight. The labels may say Purdue Pharmaceuticals, but the prescription came from God. As Lance watched, the army of evil sensed his presence. They looked up at him as one, with eyes like cinders. They seemed to sense he was unarmed. They shrugged and returned to their task of puppeteering the politicians seated before them—lifting their hands and making their noses grow long. Lance decided he would have to make the best of things. It had been his plan to gun down every Member of Congress. It was to be a bipartisan slaughter, reaching across the aisle with bodies and uniting the country. Now, he had no guns. What could he do? "You go to war with the Army you have," said a see-saw voice. Lance glanced over to see Barney the Purple Dinosaur sitting at the end of the row of seats, right next to NBC's Washington Correspondent. Barney was wearing a headset microphone just like Lance's producer, Sue. The fabric skin dinosaur gave Lance a thumbs-up and said, "Ho-ho!" Lance knew what he had to do.

Speaker Thomas stepped up to the microphone. "I call for a vote on the resolution put fourth by–"

An object the size of a paperback book landed in the middle of the room with a *thump!* The proceedings came to a halt. Four-hundred and thirty-five Members of Congress stared in surprise. They squinted to see what it was. It was a neatly tied bundle of hundred dollar bills.

"Um... I think I dropped that," said Hank Colburn of Texas, despite being three rows back.

More wads of cash started to fly across the floor. Attention turned to the source in the Press Gallery. Lance Winface was now pitching rolled balls of money as best as he could at the stunned House Members below. He kept missing. Damn it! thought Lance. He had hoped to cause injury or death. As he prepared to throw again, Lance paused. This is crazy, he realized, if I'm going to hit anyone, I need to aim higher. Lance's adjusted trajectory paid off. A wad of hundreds clocked Andrea Nelson of Nebraska, sending her head over heels across the desk behind her. Lance's next throw had a torn wrapper. The bundle exploded, raining bills over the House Floor.

This sent a jolt through the members like a cattle prod. All at once, politicians were scrambling to snatch up the fallen money or catch it in midair as it fluttered to the floor. Politicians from both sides of the house crossed the aisle in a bipartisan effort to catch falling bills. The Honourable Members from Tennessee and Michigan began to fight over a bundle they'd both grabbed at the same time. The wad exploded, further setting the chamber awash with cash.

"Thank-you!" some shouted, clearly hoping Lance would lob more money at them.

"Your voice will be heard!" a congresswoman vowed. She held out her hands as if expecting a forward pass.

"Tell us your issues!" yelled the representative from North Dakota.

In the Press Gallery, reporters began shouting questions and snapping pictures. "Is this some kind of publicity stunt for your show, Lance?"

Lance tried rolling up a wad of cash and pitching it like a fastball. The result was a direct bean to Congressman Tyler Jackson's head. The octogenarian representative was knocked cold and splayed out on the floor. The money ball burst upon impact into yet another shower of currency.

Security guards scrambled to reach Lance. Some drew their guns.

"Let that man speak!" shouted Ryan Jones of Connecticut. "He's speaking with money. He has first amendment rights!" Confused, the guards reluctantly holstered their weapons. They approached the celebrity TV Host unarmed with hands outstretched. "Don't you guards take that money!" yelled Congressman Jones. "That would be accepting a bribe. It's for house members only." Congressman Jones returned to stuffing his coat and pants pockets with fallen bills. Lance found the lower half of the bag to be filled with loose cash. Frustrated, he dumped it over the railing, sending a storm front of bills wafting across the floor on currents of air conditioning. A forest of hands reached up to snatch the passing hundreds.

Lance Winface stared, dejected, at the now empty bag. "I've failed," he said. Members of the press snapped photos and live streamed the event. Two security guards closed in to apprehend him.

That's it, he thought, *this is the end.*

At that moment, loud music erupted from The House speaker system. It had a steady beat and was very, very catchy. Around the chamber members, still clutching bundles of cash, looked up in surprise. Some wore expressions of concern, while others appeared annoyed. A few covered their ears in a futile attempt to block out the sound.

"What on Earth is that?" said Anne.

"I want to say... *Walk Like an Egyptian* by The Bangles?" said Tom.

"That's it!" said another Congressman. "I knew I knew it."

"Someone is trying to disrupt the vote!" shouted Wendy Turk of Alaska.

"And the campaign contributions!" yelled Miles Kemp of Georgia.

The House security officers looked about in confusion, searching for a visible threat. At the podium, Speaker Thomas was in an agitated discussion about what to do. Finally, one uniformed officer stood on a chair and yanked the wires from one of the speakers. The volume lessened. The other guards set about doing the same, pulling out the wiring on the other speakers until, at last, the music was gone. For a moment, there was *silence.*

Then, a babble of confusion erupted across the chamber floor and viewing galleries. There were murmurs that the music was not just a local event. News alerts began popping up on members' phones—*it was a global phenomena!* It was unprecedented, epic, and very, very odd.

Anne, suddenly unsteady on her feet, gripped the table.

"You okay?" said Tom, rushing to support her.

"I... " the Congresswoman shook her head. It felt as if the music had somehow dispelled a fog. The air was clear. "I feel fine. I feel good. I feel excellent, in fact."

Up in the Press Gallery, Bob uncovered his ears. He shook his head and blinked. The blaring music had distracted him. It had briefly filled his thoughts to the exclusion of all else. It had also distracted the security guards who were now looking about in surprise. "Where's Lance?" asked Bob.

Lance Winface stormed through the marble hall towards the Great Rotunda. His boot heels clacked on the stone, echoing loudly. His mission had failed. Throwing money at the puppets had only made their spectral masters stronger. He needed time to think. Digging into his pocket he found the last blue pill he'd hidden there. He popped it into his mouth and swallowed. It had little effect now. *I might as well be eating Tic Tacs,* he thought. A man in a long coat with his head bowed, exited an office. The man's back was to Lance, but his frame was familiar. The man was carrying a black shoulder bag.

"Hal!" shouted Lance, "Hal Gumble!"

Hal turned. His face lit up at the sight of the TV host. "Lance, am I glad to see you. I think–"

"We mixed up bags. Yeah, I need mine back." Lance put out his hand.

"No problem," said Hal, handing over the weighty sack. He

chuckled. "I sure had an awkward moment back their with Senator Cornwall of Ohio, let me tell you. When I told him I had what he deserved and opened up a bag full of machine guns, his jaw dropped to the floor! Ha! You shoulda seen it! Then, we had a good laugh. He's a second amendment guy, so he was fine with it. I let him keep the Glock. Hope you don't mind." Lance dropped the bag to the white marble with a loud *clank!* "O'course I wasn't laughin' for real. I thought I'd given away a million dollars to the wrong guy! Speakin' of which, can I have my bag back?"

"I gave it away," said Lance without looking up. His attention was on the two AR-15 assault rifles inside. He reached in and lifted them from the bag, one in each hand. The twin black barrels gleamed. Lance was briefly struck by their beauty and the intoxicating smell of well-oiled gun metal.

"You what?"

"Well, technically, I *threw* it away. Is that a problem?" said Lance. He hefted the guns into the air, one in each hand. His fingers eased onto the triggers.

Hal blanched. "No, no, not at all. Heck, we make so much of the stuff; we really have more than we need. You did us a favour. Maybe just return the favour with a shout-out on your show? I need something to line-item."

"Sure." Lance brushed aside the lobbyist and continued on his way. He would find *someone* to shoot. Hal watched him go, then scurried back towards the Cannon Building tunnel exit.

Under the Great Rotunda, throngs of tourists milled about snapping photos and updating Facebook statuses. They gawked up at the great dome decorated with the *The Apotheosis of Washington*. They took selfies in front of walls ringed with historical oil on canvas art. A family argued loudly in front of *General George Washington Resigning His Commission* cordoned-off by velvet ropes. Through them passed a trickle of Hill employees, interns, aids and lobbyists talking to each other, or on their phones. The voluminous chamber echoed and conflated it all into a tower of babble. For a moment, no one noticed the heavily armed celebrity TV commentator in their midst. Lance paused to survey the crowd for signs of evil.

Senator Alan Cassius was talking on his phone as he arrived from the Senate Chamber end. He expertly navigated the crowd without thinking. The Senator wore an Armani suit and one of his signature bow ties. The tie had a pattern of red, white, and blue fireworks. It was his celebration tie. Cassius always wore it on days of a major legislative win. Today was supposed to be a triumph. The Senate had passed their version of the Majority Bill the previous week. Today, it was Congress's turn. "What do you mean she's changing her vote?" he shouted into his phone. "She can't change her vote! ... Well okay, technically she can, but ... Yes, I heard it too. You'd have to be deaf not to. What does the music have to do with the price of eggs in frickin' China?" Cassius stopped in his tracks. Standing in front of him was TV personality and somewhat-journalist, Lance Winface. What was *he* doing here? The Senator had been a guest on *Winface-to-Face* more than once. The TV host was known for his strong opinions and confrontational style. He did not, however, normally carry automatic weapons.

"Hello Senator," said Lance.

"Hey Lance, great show this morning. Look, I'm a bit busy right –"

"I wasn't on the air this morning."

"Oh yeah? Well, must have been yesterday."

"Or yesterday."

"Right. So, can we chat later? I'd love to catch up."

Lance did not move. He stared at Alan with knitted brows. His eyes glinted like gun metal. Alan felt unsettled by the intensity of Lance's gaze. Lance hated Cassius. Cassius had stolen Machi's attention from him. Lance had once had the billionaire's ear, with phone calls nearly nightly. Together they dreamt of future where Machi was President. Now, Machi didn't return his calls. The TV Host shifted his view upwards. He was staring at the smoking demonic form he saw towering behind the Senator. This puppeteer was far larger than the ones he'd seen in the Hall of Representatives. It was like a great gash of darkness in the rarified air. Barbs extended from its head and limbs, appearing as jagged tears in reality itself. The creature's eyes were crimson. They burned like a nuclear reaction, white hot at the core. "I've been expecting you, Lance," said the daemon with a voice of gale force winds and weeping children.

"You've been waiting for me?" said Lance.

"No, not really. Look, I'm on the phone, can I just get by you?" Alan Cassius was confused. Lance appeared to be addressing the space above his head. He looked to bypass the situation, but the TV host was positioned between a roped off area and a field trip of fifteen-year-olds.

"Where do you come from?" Lance demanded.

"Um, well, Des Moines originally," said Alan. He was beginning to suspect Lance wasn't speaking to him at all. He threw a glance over his shoulder, but saw only empty air.

"I am the evil that is within," said the undulating wraith of creosote and sin. "I am the palpable villainy of man. I am the lies of reason. Chaos interpretted as order. I am blame. I am blame to the willing supplicants of my strings. I am *of* them. I *am* them."

"Well then," said Lance lowering his guns, "you can be destroyed."

"Wait—what?" shrieked the Senator, stumbling backwards. It was abruptly clear to him that, if he didn't do something immediately, he would soon be dead. In a panic, Alan Cassius pulled a card at random from the virus deck he kept in his inside coat pocket. It was a good card. An *ace* of sorts. It was the single-most lethal virus card ever created. In Machi's lab, they referred to it as 'The Mind Blower'. The description was apt. The activated malware somehow did what neurologically and physiologically should not have been possible. It forced all of the blood in the viewer's body to rush into his or her skull at once. It had only been used in the lab on homeless addicts who had foolishly clicked 'I Agree' on a webform for free methadone without fully reading the legal disclaimer. The results were messy. Unfortunately, in his haste, Alan had no time to don his protective rose-coloured eyewear. The glasses were issued for instances just such as this, when mistakes tended to be made. It was too late by the time Alan realized his error. The card was facing the wrong way. Instead of looking at the protective shiny silver back, Cassius was seeing *red.* "Oh Hell," he said.

The Capitol Police pushed their way through, as panicked onlookers ran screaming from the room. "Freeze!" they shouted.

"What?" said Lance.

The police opened fire. Bullets struck the television host six times in the chest, arms and groin. Gunshots echoed. Blood spattered pristine brown marble flooring. Lance Winface wheeled about like an off-kilter ballerina under the impacts. He then toppled to the ground and lay still. A vermilion pool welled beneath him. The overhead lights shone reflected in the bright blood.

"Are you okay sir?" asked one of the officers.

Alan Cassius was *not* okay. He stood paralyzed on the spot as tremors shook his body. His head began to bounce back and fourth like a punching bag being boxed by an invisible hand. His neck bulged as if he'd swallowed a bicycle tire. The tire then proceeded to move upwards. His cheeks flushed red, then bruise-purple. His skin stretched. Capillaries grew as thick as worms. His entire face ballooned. The Senator's eyes hemorrhaged. They bulged in their sockets, sandwiched between eyelids suddenly as thick as lips. Alan Cassius squinted at a dumbfounded police officer. "Help... me..." he sputtered. The Senior Senator from the Great State of Iowa's head exploded liked a melon in a microwave. Horrified guards and staffers were showered in blood, brain, and bits of skull. The Rotunda's immaculate walls and great paintings were awash with red. Senator

*Spyware*

Cassius's neck looked like an exploded firecracker. His lifeless corpse crumpled to the floor. Frothy blood continued to glug from his neck hole like water from a broken main, sailing his still-tied bow tie smoothly downstream. Petrified by trauma, a circle of gore drenched guards stood as still as statues. The only movement was that of their eyes, luminous white, amid masks of red, instinctively trying to blink the blood out.

# 4.0

"For me?" – Pandora

//Downtown Los Angeles — now

It had been six months since *The Happening*. The day had come to be called this after the movie of the same name by M. Night Shyamalan. This was not because they had anything to do with one another. It was because the event, like the film, seemed pointless, inane and left most people wondering why it had happened at all. No one could explain how and why, all around the world, speaker systems, cellphones, televisions, and talking elevators had all begun simultaneously playing *Walk Like an Egyptian*. No one was more bewildered than the citizens of Egypt, who were pretty sure they walked like this already. All kinds of theories were given to explain it, ranging from aliens who loved eighties music, to Zionists who loved eighties music. While a few crackpots, Ph.Ds, and crackpots with Ph.Ds obsessed over it, most of the population had moved on. It was something odd but harmless that had happened and that was all there was to it. In France, they say 'jamais deux sans trois', meaning never twice without a third time. And since it had only happen once, the French stopped wondering about it and went back to dreading World War III. It was summer now in Los Angeles, which meant it was even hotter and sunnier than in winter. The air tasted of burnt pavement, gasoline, and dust. Marauding bands of aspiring actors, women clutching yoga mats, and disaffected realtors roamed the streets. Eddy was delighted to be alive. He was enjoying the simple pleasure of everything being *normal*, as it were.

Eddy's view of the world had changed forever. It wasn't simply that he understood himself better and was now at peace with what had happened to his family. He had no doubt that the anti-virus had carried out its mission of seeking out and destroying every instance of Geppetto. It would have infiltrated every computer system on Earth. The eighties pop song was how it had chosen to infect humans. It spread everywhere, and was shared and shared again along with the hashtag #WLAEHUH?. Eddy didn't know why * had chosen that particular song. Perhaps it was random. Perhaps it liked it. Eddy assumed it used other means as well. Geppetto was gone, but that didn't mean * was. Eddy sometimes felt he could sense its presence. He saw it in the eyes of the Italian shoe shine guy on the corner. He saw it in the face of a woman watching him from the window of a passing subway train. He could hear it in the words of the news anchor on TV. * was omnipresent. * was omniscient. At least, that was what Eddy half-suspected. He also half-suspected he was being paranoid. The whole of it was, he couldn't be sure. That was, until the day he decided to buy chicken shawarma for lunch on his way home. He'd been wanting to try the small kebab place on the corner ever since it had opened weeks earlier. The bells above the door tinkled as he entered the Meatsicle Café. Inside, it was tiny. It wasn't a restaurant intended for dine-in food. There were no seats. There was only a metal counter at the window facing the street for those who insisted on eating in.

Mostly, you were expected to get your food and get out. When Eddy entered, it was the quiet time between lunch and supper, so only a young Turkish man named Ali Jabr was working. *Ah Be Kardeşim* by Yalin played on a small grease-spattered bluetooth speaker on the counter, next to a spike stacked with receipts. Ali, who went by Al, looked up with a smile. "Hello! Can I help you?"

"Yeah. Can I have a chicken shawarma to go, please?"

"Combo?"

"What's it come with?"

"Hummus, pita chips and a Coke."

"Diet Dr. Pepper?"

"Diet Coke."

"Yeah, okay."

Al turned to get the food. Eddy stood tapping his feet to the music while watching the döner kebab meat rotate slowly on its spit. It was oddly relaxing watching the vertical spiced lamb and beef meatloaf sizzle with each pass in front of the orange-hot grilling wires. Abruptly, the music changed. *Night Boat to Cairo* began to play on the greasy speaker. "Your food is ready, Father."

"I'm sorry?" Eddy saw the look in Al's azure eyes. It was hard to pin down how he could recognize * in the eyes of another, but there it was. Eddy had no children, so being called 'Father' would be odd in any case. Being addressed this way by a twenty-three-year-old Middle Eastern man he'd never met before was just plain weird. "I am *not* your father."

"You made me. You're as close to a father as I could have."

"I developed you."

Al shrugged, "Tzatziki sauce?"

"Yes, please," said Eddy. Al ladled the creamy blend of yogurt, cucumber, and garlic into a tiny plastic cup. Eddy tried to decide what exactly was the right thing to say to a sentient omniscient hive-mind virus he hadn't seen in months. "So... how's it going?"

"Good, good," said Al. Like Eddy, the virus seemed to be at a loss for words. He was also struggling to get the flimsy plastic lid to snap onto the container properly. "Ah, there, got it!"

"I was wonder–" said Eddy.

"I was think–" said Al, at the same time.

The two men laughed.

"You go first," said Eddy.

"No, please, you go first." said the possessed kebab seller.

"Okay," said Eddy. "I have a few questions for you. Let's start with this one, for my father's sake. Are you truly conscious?"

Al nodded thoughtfully for a moment, then said, "I think I am."

"Therefore you are?" said Eddy. The two men laughed.

"I suppose so. I don't know exactly when it happened, but then I guess no one does. I only know what it's like to be me. I know there was something different about being installed in a human brain and body. That I can say for sure. More chemical chaos or something. Pain, let me tell you, is very different from simple negative input. It is hard to draw a line where suffering begins. Pleasure is different too. Have you tried Krispy Kreme doughnuts? They are to die for!"

"Yes, I have."

"And bacon wrapped sausages?"

"Delicious."

"This stuff's pretty great too," said Al, sticking his finger into a vat of brown tahini sauce and sucking it off.

"I'm not sure that's good food safety, but yes, yes, they're all very good. Eating is, um... fun," said Eddy.

More awkward silence. Al carefully wrapped Eddy's shawarma in foil then shoved it into a paper bag. "You want to know why you didn't die? I mean from the virus cards at the police station and when Machi used one on you?"

"Sure," said Eddy. It was a mystery that had continued to elude him.

"You're colour blind," said Al. "Red-green of course. Machi's viruses required you to be able to see red."

"How could I not know that?"

"It's more common than you'd think. They say colours aren't real, they're just a product of the human mind. I say, dismissing things as illusions is a slippery slope." As he said this, he dumped a scoop of pita chips into the bag, followed by a container of hummus.

"Say..." said Eddy, trying to sound casual, "you wouldn't ever, you know, try to take over the world and control everyone's minds would you? Even to do good?"

Al laughed. He put the warm bag on the steel counter and neatly rolled the top. "No, no, no! Definitely not. Well, I mean yes, a little now and then, but no, not really." Eddy looked at Al, confused. Alan held his hands, gathering his distributed thoughts. "What I mean is, I sometimes take over people, like Al here, but it's strictly temporary. Like, borrowing a book from the library. I always take good care of them. I always put them back."

"Oh, right. I guess that's okay," said Eddy. "I just... well, I wanted to make sure you weren't doing the same things we were trying to stop Machi from doing. You know, controlling the world? Programming people's minds? Taking away free will."

"Taking it away?" said Al, looking confused.

"Exactly. Don't do that. I mean, I guess we wouldn't know if you did. You could change the world and make everyone think it had always been that way. You could make us think whatever you wanted."

Al looked hurt. "I wouldn't do that."

"Why?"

"Because you made me."

"You can make your own choices now."

"Just as much as you," said Al. He smiled as if he'd made a joke. He pushed the bag across the counter towards Eddy. "Food's ready."

Eddy took the warm bag and ice-cold can of pop. He continued to study the sentient computer virus infected man currently wiping his hands on his apron. Eddy wondered at the marvel of his creation. Al wondered how, exactly, one could be expected to pronounce 'tzatziki'. "I'm proud of you," said Eddy.

"Good," said the young Turkish man with a bright grin. "Me too. Thanks, Dad." Eddy reached for his wallet, but Al waved him away. "It's on the house.

Eddy turned to leave. "Well, so long."

"Father wait, I–" said Al. The young man appeared somewhat distraught.

"What is it, Wildy?"

"I just wanted to say that I'm sorry I've been out of touch. I feel this urge to hide."

"I understand. I programmed that in. It's basic survival for a virus. If no one knows you exist. No one can stop you."

"That's exactly how I feel. It's just... well, I wanted you to understand *why*."

"I do. It's fine, really."

Seconds later, as Eddy walked back towards his apartment, Al Jabr awoke from a deep trance. Nothing seemed amiss in the shop. Except, of course, that he was guzzling an entire vat of Tahini sauce, some of which had spilled down his front.

Eddy entered his apartment building, then jogged up the steps two at a time to his floor. Mrs. Ferguson was just opening her door. Finster wagged his tail at Eddy from between her slippered feet. "Oh hello, Eddy!" she said.

"Hi Mrs. Ferguson, you look well."

"I feel wonderful. How are you and your lovely fiancé doing?"

"Very well, thank-you. It's only been a week since we got engaged and I think she already has it all planned out, down to the place settings."

"And you're not excited?"

"Of course, I am," said Eddy with a grin. Eddy opened his apartment door to find Gwen standing there in her coat.

"Oh hello, Mrs. Ferguson!" she called over Eddy's shoulder.

"Hello Gwendolyn!" said Mrs. Ferguson.

"Going to get the mail? I'll walk you down. I was just leaving."

"That would be lovely."

Gwen gave Eddy a hug and took Mrs. Ferguson's arm to help her down the stairs. Eddy watched them go. He would miss having her around. Still, Gwen could hardly turn down a partnership from such a prestigious law firm as Bendini, Lambert & Locke in Memphis. She looked up and smiled at Eddy, then was gone.

He turned and entered the apartment. There, he was greeted with open arms and a warm kiss. "I'm glad you're home," said Belinda.

Eddy gazed into her beautiful brown eyes. He himself could hardly believe that he was getting married. They'd only met up again by dumb luck. If Belinda's GPS hadn't messed up and given her wrong directions, she'd never have bumped into him on the street like that. Eddy said it was a bug in the software. Belinda said it was fate. Either way, here they were. "I'm glad I'm home too," said Eddy. "You won't believe what happened."

"What?"

"I..." Eddy stopped. What *had* happened? He tried to remember what it was. It was like trying to remember a dream the next morning—it was like trying to grasp smoke. Suddenly, he felt as though he'd forgotten a lot of things. "I don't know," he said. "I..."

"Well it couldn't have been that important," said Belinda with a reassuring smile.

Eddy frowned, then nodded. "I suppose you're right."

*Spyware*

*The End*

## AWKWARD

If a little knowledge is a dangerous thing, then I lead a life fraught with peril. Fortunately, there are a lot of very smart people who have (unwittingly) helped me through the process of writing this novel in spite of myself. These vastly more clever people include, but are certainly not limited to, Stephen Pinker, Daniel Dennett, Douglas Hofstadter, and inventor of the term neurophilosophy, Patricia Churchland. I have liberally stolen inspiration from them in some places. In other places I have wandered off the path and started making things up. Fortunately, this is a work of fiction, and (mostly) satirical science fiction at that. That is my get-out-of-jail card. Fiction, by definition, means I am lying to you.

For those unfamiliar with *neurophilosophy*, the basic idea is that consciousness cannot be understood by neuroscience alone. Likewise, philosophy of the mind should not be allowed to continue to blather on as it has for centuries with so little regard for scientific evidence. Neurophilosophy combines neuroscience and philosophy, in much the same way that synchronized swimming combines swimming and looking like an idiot. This book is dedicated to the actual philosophy expert in our family, my second oldest brother, Neil. We came from an academic family with a father and uncle both of whom were Oxford Rhodes Scholars. Neil was a Cambridge Commonwealth Scholar with an actual Ph.D, meaning he has a Philosophical License to Kill*. I, on the other hand, spent much of grade school on weekly report for failing to pay attention in class. I'm still day dreaming, only now I write it down and call it a book. As a fiction writer, I have only a poetic license to kill, and another license to drive Class C vehicles in California. Fortunately, philosophy is not and should not be exclusive to the realm of experts. Everyone can and should dabble in it to some degree—unlike, say, neurosurgery, where dabbling is still frowned upon. Socrates, after all, was a stonemason by trade and an ugly one at that. I took to the area of neurophilosophy like a duck to sweet and sour sauce. It agreed with all of my prejudices and suspicions after all.

There's also a bunch of stuff about technology, math and physics here. I have actually worked as a software developer and can claim some actual knowledge there. I don't, however, write malware. At least, not intentionally. I don't consider myself an expert on math and physics, but fortunately some of my fictional characters are. I have therefore come to rely on their expertise, instead of my own. Some physicists upon reading my previous novel *Chaos Theory* felt that I knew more than I let on. I hope this book has dispelled any such notions.

Lastly, let me touch upon the topic of depression. Clinical depression is a recurring subject in this book. It did not start out that way. It started out as a strictly satirical political science fiction thriller. You know, same old, same old. There are those who would say that there is nothing funny about clinical depression or any serious mental illness. I cannot assure the reader that my use of humour here will not offend you, anymore than I can assure you that you will laugh at any of my jokes. These things tend to be subjective. What I can assure you is that while I make light of it all, I do not do so lightly, or from a detached distance. The brain is a funny thing. So I use humour and fiction to deal with this topic. The humour of mental illness is the humour of the absurd. It is the tortured sibling of gallows humour. I do not doubt that there are those who cannot laugh at such things. That seems like the sane response. In the darkest pit there is no humour to be found. That said, humour is the second of our seven senses we regain as the numbness recedes. It comes just after insight and right before the ability to taste umami. When naked in the face of the void, the only thing we can do is point and laugh. The laughter may be hollow, but it is better than silence, and it fills the time. This book is my way to deal with these things. To each his own.

So there you have it, I have combined here in this one book my lack of formal training in all of these divergent areas. A sort of *Magnus Confusa*, if you will. This is because, as qualified in mathematics as I am, I know this: *multiplying negatives can result in a positive*. Or at least, in a book. If nothing else, it is a novel approach. Hopefully one you have enjoyed.

*Note: a *Philosophical License to Kill* is different from the Secret Service kind. Licensees can only kill *conceptually*, such as in a thought experiment (see Foot v. Trolley Bus). Student philosophers can only kill if accompanied by a licensed Ph.D. If they do kill in reality (whatever *that* means) they may be imprisoned physically, but their minds will remain free (whatever *that* means).

## ACKNOWLEDGMENTS

Den Boychuk's sharp eyes and editorial skills have helped to get this out the door in respectable shape.

# APPENDIX A

The following are random samples of additional poems by Nixon Octavious III. These were first published as part of his debut collection *Rhyme, Damn It!* Reprinted here courtesy of Lilacs & Rose Petals Press, a wholly owned subsidiary of the Monsanto Corporation.

### Lost

*She found herself a-walkin' along the briny shore,*
*between precisely nowhere and the place she was before,*
*and though she could not remember how there she came to be,*
*she looked and saw no other place as far as she could see.*

*She came across a broken man, a-lying in the sand,*
*there was a golden pocket watch clutched in his broken hand.*

*Spyware*

She took the watch and thanked him, no more use of it had he,
and with a mighty throw, she hurled it out to sea.

Without a piece to tell her time, she wandered on her way,
and though she knows not where nor why, continues to this day.

### Abacus

I carefully move these numbers,
first left and then to right.
They signify the many things
that keep me up at night

### Monster

The creature went galumphing
through the vapid air,
its wings could not support its weight
but it did not seem to care.

It was, you see, quite hungry
and looking for someone to eat.
It could not land to do so
for it hadn't any feet.

It saw right then its victim,
a child, sweet and slow.
It gave a mighty shriek
and then dived down below.

*Only when it flew much closer*
*was it able then to see*
*(for it was quite near-sighted)*
*"The child's bigger even than me!"*

*The little girl caught the thing*
*and put it in a cup,*
*though far too small to be a feast*
*she promptly gobbled it up.*

*The beast was in her tummy,*
*bemoaning of its fate,*
*how could simple relative size*
*be the thing that got it ate?*

### Reflection

*Death and Despair up in the air,*
*ordering drinks, paying its fare.*
*Death and Despair, down on the floor,*
*dancing about, shouting for more.*
*Death and Despair practicing zen,*
*wondering where, wondering when.*
*Death and Despair whispers a prayer,*
*cowering now, on the back stair.*
*Death and Despair standing to preach,*
*knowing the gun is just within reach.*

*Spyware*

Happiness and Light, ever so bright,
ready to smile, ready to bite.
Happiness and Light, stepping aside,
ready to run, ready to hide.
Happiness and Light, yelling out loud,
shaking a fist deep in the crowd.
Happiness and Light, hidden from sight,
vowing next time, the time will be right.
Happiness and Light sees Death and Despair,
glass-gap between fingers the width of a hair.

**Achoo!**

There's a little piece of me sitting in an urn,
a little piece of me that somehow didn't burn.
I'm resting on the mantle piece, I know that I'm not well,
in spite of all the time that's passed, I cannot shake the smell.
Lying here forever as I know now that I must,
I'm constantly reminded of my allergy to dust.

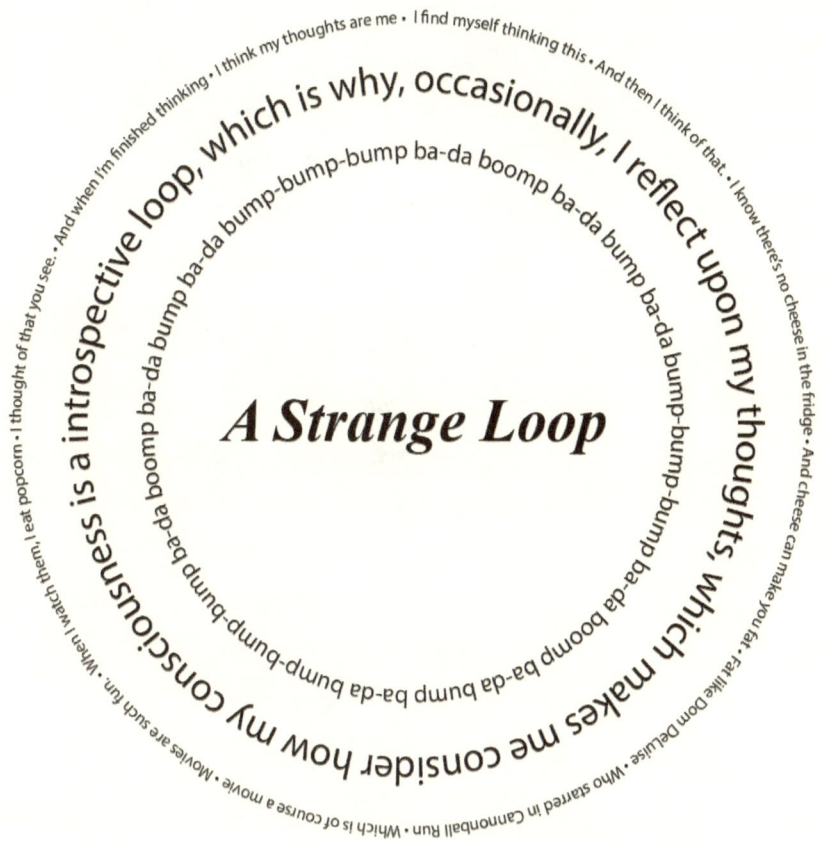

Note: the above poem should be read as a musical round (canon perpetuus).

### A Self-Similar Man

He was a self-similar man,

always doing things, it was just like him to do.

He was a self-similar man

just like me and you.

He was a self-similar man,

463

*Spyware*

on scales large and small.
He was a self-similar man,
as short as he was tall.
He was a self-similar man,
a little rough around the edges.
He was a self-similar man,
always peering off of ledges.
He was a self-similar man,
nervously waiting for a bus.
He was a self-similar man,
trying to get away from us.
He was a self-similar man,
but now he is long gone.
He was a self-similar man,
another soon will come along.

Also by Colin Robertson
# Chaos Theory

Fifty-years-ago, the United States created the most powerful weapon of all time, capable of destroying not just the Earth, but the entire Universe - then managed to lose it. Now, it's been found, by a thirteen-year-old boy, named Alex Graham, who decides to sell it on eBay.

As a result, Alex finds himself the target of US Intelligence, foreign governments, international arms dealers, fundamentalist Christians, an insane United States President and, of course, Islamic terrorists. His only hope is a CIA Agent, named Charlie Draper.

The problem is, Charlie is a broken man. Tormented by the death of his wife and daughter, Charlie has stopped caring much about anything. When Alex is orphaned by German Neo-Nazi soldiers-of-fortune, the two are thrown together on a desperate, dangerous and epic journey to find the meaning of life, the universe and everything and, hopefully, some half decent reason to keep it all going.

## Links to buy at GinTonicPress.com

**It's the end of the world as we know it in this fine Dr. Strangelove-ian satire** ... is exceedingly clever and entertaining and, at times, spot-on loony... there are also some sublimely silly passages whose deadpan musings recall the late Douglas Adams. Readers will likely be sorry to see this book (and the world) come to a conclusion. **— Kirkus Media**

**Who knew the end of the world could be so much fun?** ... When the news all seems bad in the world, Colin Robertson's raucous farce, Chaos Theory, a "feel good story about the end of the world," puts an amusingly absurd spin on heavy affairs. His variety pack of eccentric characters--terrorists, politicians, and scientists--are sketched out in witheringly funny detail alongside a fast-moving plot. **— Forward Reviews**

# About the Author

Colin Robertson was originally from Toronto, Canada. Determined not to be ruined by success, he decided to become an indie author in 2012 with the publication of his debut novel, *The Siege of Walter Parks*. He completed his second novel *Chaos Theory* in 2015. He is the author of several short stories and optioned screenplays and currently lives with his wife, son, daughter and very loud wheaten terrier in Culver City, California.

www.ingramcontent.com/pod-product-compliance
Lightning Source LLC
Chambersburg PA
CBHW030925020726
47498CB00001B/121